A Far Piece to Canaan

A Far Piece to Canaan

Sam Halpern

HARPER PERENNIAL

NEW YORK • LONDON • TORONTO • SYDNEY • NEW DELHI • AUCKLAND

HARPER ● PERENNIAL

A FAR PIECE TO CANAAN. Copyright © 2013 by Sam Halpern. All rights reserved. Printed in the United States of America. No part of this book may be used or reproduced in any manner whatsoever without written permission except in the case of brief quotations embodied in critical articles and reviews. For information address HarperCollins Publishers, 10 East 53rd Street, New York, NY 10022.

HarperCollins books may be purchased for educational, business, or sales promotional use. For information please e-mail the Special Markets Department at SPsales@harpercollins.com.

FIRST EDITION

Library of Congress Cataloging-in-Publication Data has been applied for.

ISBN 978-0-06-223316-5

13 14 15 16 17 OV/RRD 10 9 8 7 6 5 4 3 2 1

To Joni,
the love of my life

Fifteen miles south of Lexington, Kentucky, on a road that dwindles from superhighway to brush-hidden, black-patched, gravel-strewn pike, stands a fractured, unhinged gate. The mud-washed lane behind the gate leads to a tumbledown farmhouse, which, devoid of human life, has knee-deep weeds for a lawn. On a sunny windowsill, head on forepaws, rests a cat with the mange, while a cowsucker snake, the only other inhabitant, glides slowly under the remains of a screened-in porch. There is silence and everything seems small.

1

I was exhausted, and the monotonous sound of the commuter plane's engines irritated my already frayed nerves. My subconscious had been tracking the time and I knew I was nearing my destination. I shut my eyes and drifted into sleep. This afforded me relief from boredom until my brain conjured up giant horses, leaping flames, and wailing voices.

I gasped awake. With sleep, I had traded boredom for terror. I turned in my window seat and looked outside the aircraft. Clouds and window-blurring rain obscured everything beyond the engines. Thoughts of my childhood friend Fred wandered through my mind. A feeling of foreboding crept through me. The captain's voice was a welcome intrusion.

"Ladies and gentlemen, we're about fifteen minutes from touchdown. This weather's pretty deep, so please fasten your seat belts. Flights are stacked up because of the storm so we'll be in a holding pattern. If you're in a window seat, get ready for an aerial tour of the heart of the bluegrass."

My anxiety returned as we dropped bumpily lower. I saw wisps of ground through thin gray cloud, then, suddenly, the earth became a brilliant kaleidoscope of color. The plane banked and the view was spectacular—Kentucky in early summer. The Lexington of my memories had grown larger but still spread like a patchwork quilt into horse farms, deep green fields of corn, tobacco, and alfalfa set among bluegrass pastures that caressed slowly flowing creeks.

We began losing altitude rapidly, mushing through the air. Suddenly, the engines surged and we flew in a circle. The Kentucky River appeared, twisting and turning like a shiny blue-gray ribbon as it meandered through intense green vegetation. My breathing picked up instantly and my mouth became dry. Then there they were, the river's two great curves, first the Little Bend, then, as the plane continued its turn, the Big Bend. I fought for control of my emotions as I searched for landmarks. To my amazement, much of the land between the two serpentine flexures remained undeveloped; indeed, it looked nearly as wild as it had sixty years past. It was mystical to me now . . . something foreboding . . . known, yet unknown. I wiped my wet palms on my pants. My heartbeats became more powerful, slamming against my chest wall. "This is ridiculous," I whispered, and angrily yanked my seat belt tighter.

The plane slowed, we moved onto glide path, and a short while later the screech of tires formally announced to my quivering psyche that I had arrived in the land of my birth.

I picked up my bags and the rental car, drove to my hotel in downtown Lexington, checked in, and nearly collapsed on the bed. *I'm back*, *Nora*, I thought. *I kept my promise.*

2

Agood night's sleep vanquished much of my fear, and the next morning I drove into a glorious new day. The road from Lexington to my destination reminded me in some ways of my life. Both had changed so much that I hardly recognized them. The interstate highway I was driving was a number now, wide, smooth, and impersonal. Gone was the intimacy of the old Dixie Highway that had allowed a close-up view of white-railed fields of the bluegrass country and sleek, grazing racehorses. The rental car was silent, no complaining engine, rattle, or squeak of brakes. I felt nostalgia for our green '36 Ford sedan with its broken rear window and the oil leak that killed the grass whenever Dad parked the car near the front yard.

"Dad, why do you want to make this trip?" my daughter Candy had asked as she saw me off at Boston's Logan Airport. "I could understand if it was Indiana; Grandpa's farm was there. But Kentucky? Penny and I are worried about you. It's hot in the South and you could get sick. What's there for you in Kentucky anyway, after all these years? Every time either of us asks what you did as a kid in Kentucky, you give a stock answer: 'The same thing the other sharecropper kids did; I worked in the fields.'"

I laughed at Candy's baritone imitation of my voice. How do you tell your daughter you are on a quest for something unknown at the behest of her dead mother? "Not to worry," I said, "I'll be fine."

An exit sign on the interstate said Harper's Village. That sounded suspiciously like the tiny village of Harper's Corner I had known as a child, so I took the off ramp. Nothing looked familiar. I drove past a mall and motored slowly down a picturesque country road. The tobacco fields I knew as a boy had been separated from the blacktop and its easement by barbwire. The barbwire had given way to white rail fences that guarded elegant pastures and homes. The horses in the fields were fine saddle horses, not workhorses. I checked the names on the mailboxes. None was familiar.

A few minutes later, I rounded a curve and saw a wooden arrow pointing toward a dirt road that cut through the easement. I stopped to read the words on the arrow: "Old Cuyper Creek Pike." My road! I carefully maneuvered the car over the weedy, rut-filled turnoff, which was actually a tractor path that allowed farmers access onto the ancient blacktop.

The old road was in relatively good repair and drove easily. A few miles later, I passed an unmarked lane I thought I recognized, then decided I didn't and continued down a long curvy hill. Then I saw the sweet apple tree. Some of the branches and a part of the trunk were torn away, but what remained was dutifully producing fruit. The apple tree meant the entrance to the farm was only a short distance ahead. I felt an urge to eat one of the apples so I pulled close to the tree and parked.

Climbing the sweet apple tree hadn't been easy for me as a kid, and it was going to be harder at seventy-two. In my mind I could hear the banter between Fred and me.

"Y' know, Samuel, if'n you can take a little longer, I'll be done pickin'."

"I'm climbing quick as I can, Fred Cody! I just ain't fast at climbin's all!"

It now took me twenty minutes to build a ramp of rocks to get into the branches. I picked three apples, then lay back on a big limb, exhausted but exhilarated. Sixty years had passed since I had last been up in this tree. What would they say, my colleagues, if they could see me up in the sweet apple tree? My peers in the world of comparative English literature? What would they think if they knew the history I had shared with this tree? A joyful, chaotic, wonder-filled, terrifying time that had been a secret prelude to my becoming their grudging choice for the Johnson-Goldsmith Prize, comparative English literature's highest award.

> *For exceptional scholarship that sheds new light on the*
> *nonlinear structures of late Cornish literature*

So said the award plaque. Sounds awful, but that's academia, and it hasn't changed since Plato invented the concept under his own tree in Athens. I was amazed that I had received the award, having spent the majority of my career out of sync with so many people in the field.

Nora was sure my problems with academic polemics were because I had lived my formative years in what she referred to as "wacko-world." By that she meant among the hill people of Kentucky. Nora was always sure. My little Brooklyn belle, wife of fifty years who had sometimes referred to me as the Jewish Rhett Butler she saved from that bitch Scarlett O'Hara. Rhett Butler, I am not. Samuel Zelinsky, I am—an emeritus academic doted on in recent times by his students, his peers, and his elite New England liberal arts college that periodically detested his presence.

I bit into one of the apples and a gush of saliva and juice filled my mouth. The apple was still green but so good. Just the way I remembered. Sometimes I felt there were only memories in my life now, the clear and solid drifting from substance into a mysterious fog that rolled and shifted and entwined the past, the living and the dead, into a swirling labyrinth in which everything seemed equally distant and ethereal. My parents and siblings were gone, my Nora to cancer, my daughters married to husbands and careers, my students off to the real world, my college in search of a greater trust fund, and me to my dotage as Professor Emeritus of Comparative English Literature, which somehow rang more hollow with each passing day. I looked around at the rugged countryside. What did I want from these over-farmed hills after sixty years? I had no idea, but only days before her death, Nora had made the request that I return. I felt honor-bound to make the journey.

I arranged the remaining two apples on my belly, then threw away the core of the one I had just eaten. I listened as it fell through leaves, ricocheted off limbs, and hit the ground. Swish, bop, bop, thump! Music! The day was hot and I was tired. I closed my eyes and let my muscles sag into the old tree's limb. I missed Fred. This was my first time up in the sweet apple tree without Fred on a limb near me. My memory of the day we moved onto Berman's was so clear . . .

It was cold, boy. You could blow your breath and see wisps of smoke come rolling out of your mouth just before the icy wind blew it away. I was doing okay, though, in my mackinaw, except for the spot near my left armpit where the seams was giving way and a little trickle of cold snuck in if I raised my elbow, which I didn't. Mr. Berman, the landlord we were renting from, took us to see the new house. We had come a long way from Moneybags' place where we had been renting, going down one road after another before coming to a big white gate. From there, it was a quarter mile back to the house. Mr. Berman kept telling Dad and Mom what a great road it was. I liked it too, especially the chuck holes in the gravel that caused the tailpipe of the big Buick to scrape. I was sitting in the backseat right behind Mr. Berman's head. He really had a fat head and neck. He didn't look anything like me or Dad. I kept thinking how odd that was because I heard Dad say that this was the first Jew we ever rented from and he didn't look like us at all and we were Jews too. Dad's head looked lean and hard and tanned. Mr. Berman's looked squishy. Matter of fact, I wanted to push my finger into it to see if it would dent, but I didn't. Off in the distance, patches of melting snow surrounded bare, black ground. Things looked dead, but there was a smell in the air. Spring! It was coming up spring in Kentucky.

"What are the people around here like, Nate?" Dad asked, looking past Mom, who was sitting between him and Mr. Berman.

"Like the goyim you knew in Bourbon County, maybe a little more meshuga," Mr. Berman answered, meaning they were Christian and a little crazy.

"Meshuga?" said Mom, straightening up, and I knew her eyes were wide in her round, chubby face. "What do you mean, meshuga?"

"Nothing bad," said Mr. Berman, laughing. "It's just that they're full of superstitions. Like when I was buying this place in January; the first time I came to look at it, there were maybe twenty people in the yard. A tall goy with a wild look in his eyes was shouting at the others about evil and floating Bibles in the river."

"Floating Bibles? Why?" Mom asked, a little scared.

Mr. Berman laughed again. "I don't know. The meeting broke up with some shouting. Since I was a stranger I didn't ask questions. It's a *bobbeh meisseh*." Grandmother's tale.

That scared me. I could see that my sister Naomi, who was sitting beside me, was worried too. Mom turned toward Dad, who was laughing.

"Morris, what do you think it means?"

"Nothing," said Dad, turning toward her. "There were nutty people around Moneybags' place too." Then he looked at Mr. Berman. "Nate, what shape's that tobacco barn in?"

"Good shape," said Mr. Berman. "Throw on a few shingles, it's good as new."

As the barns got closer you could see the roof of the tobacco barn was about gone.

"Few shingles, huh?" Dad muttered, and Mr. Berman just kept driving quiet.

Mom didn't say anything either, but I could see her face in the rearview mirror.

Her lips were pursed and she had pulled her arms together under her big chest. She was acting like she hadn't gotten over that stuff about evil and floating Bibles. Even though Dad didn't think much of it, it bothered me that Mom seemed worried.

We come around a curve in the lane and there stood a white

frame house with a big yard that had a thick kind of wire fence around it that folks in our parts called road wire. The gravel lane kept curving until it ended in a muddy stock barn lot. Mr. Berman veered off before he got to the barnyard gate and parked just outside the road wire fence.

The yard was full of trees that didn't have leaves yet but you could tell they were going to shade everything soon as they come out. There was a rock path that led to a big screened-in porch which had about half its screen rusted out. Next to the yard was an orchard and I knew one of the trees was a cherry. I loved cherries.

There were lots of buildings you could see from the front yard. From where Mr. Berman parked, the field sloped down to a deep hollow with a creek at the bottom. On top of the other slope of the hollow, three, four hundred foot from us, was a tobacco barn. A corncrib and sheep barn were strung out after it like the navy ships I saw in picture shows, the buildings all creosoted black with shingle roofs. On down the hollow from the sheep barn, maybe another quarter mile, was a hired hand's house. I knew it was empty because no smoke was coming out of the chimney. It was pretty though, nestled below a big hill that was shaped like a volcano with the creek in the hollow running maybe fifty foot from the front porch.

The house we were renting had electric lights and a telephone. We'd never had those before. The kitchen was just like what we had at Moneybags', with a peeling linoleum floor, a place for a cooking stove, and a big pantry. Behind the kitchen stove was a wood bin we could use for coal. We always burned coal even though most folks around us burned wood. I figured Jews had to burn coal to set them apart from the goyim. Out back was a yard with a chicken house. It had a flat rock path to it that went on past the chicken house and ended at an outhouse.

I was with Mom and Naomi in the kitchen when I noticed Dad and Mr. Berman talking in the kitchen yard. I went out through the kitchen's screened-in porch to get close so I could hear, figuring they were talking about renting and that I'd be doing it someday and had better learn how. Dad was leaning against the fence that separated the kitchen yard from the barnyard. Next to Mr. Berman, Dad looked big, all muscled up in his Levi's with his red flannel coat unbuttoned and light blue work shirt open at the neck. Mr. Berman was wearing a brown suit and looked like a pear with legs.

"Nobody rents money rent these days, Morris," Mr. Berman was saying. "It's share or nothing," and he looked away from Dad toward the stock barn.

Dad nodded. "What kind of deal you offering?"

"Same as you had on Coachman's."

"Fifty-fifty on the tobacco?"

"Yes."

Dad's lips squenched together. "What about the fertilizer and labor and all?"

Mr. Berman's face went hard. "You paid it at Coachman's, didn't you?"

"Yeah. Moneybags wasn't fair either. You got fourteen acres of burley, Nate. I can't do all that myself. Payin' help will take a lot of my share. Why don't we split fifty-fifty on that?"

Mr. Berman's face stayed hard. "Because that's not what people do here, Morris."

Dad's mouth squenched harder. "What about the livestock?"

"You can have every third lamb."

"Every other."

"No."

"What about the cattle?"

"You can pasture your livestock, raise hogs, and chickens, but everything else is shares."

Dad looked toward Mom and Naomi, who were walking across the yard toward another part of the fence. The last tenant had made a garden there. I could see beehives too.

"What about the garden and honey?" Dad asked.

"Shares. Everything but what we've agreed on is shares."

Dad turned back to face Mr. Berman. "You got a hired hand can help me?"

"Yeah, there's some white trash named Mulligan on the other side of the place. You can hire him when he isn't working for me. The other tenant house is empty."

They stood there for a while, Mr. Berman looking at the barn and Dad looking at him. Then Mr. Berman turned. He was the shorter, but, somehow, he kind of looked down at Dad.

"That's the deal, Morris. You won't find a better one."

"I don't know about that," said Dad, giving a little short laugh.

"Well, that's the deal. It's getting late for renting. I got to know tomorrow."

"Yeah, well, I'll talk it over with Liz and let you know," Dad grumbled.

Mr. Berman walked back to his car taking care not to get his fancy shoes and suit dirty, and sat listening to the radio about how the Allies were capturing some town. Mom and Dad talked in whispers in the yard and I was close enough to hear them.

The wind blew strands of Mom's red-gray hair across her face and she pulled the top of her blue coat tighter around her neck. "Well, what did he say?"

I could see Dad's jaw muscles work. "Says he'll give me what he would any goy."

"Morris, we have to have a place, but I'm worried about the people around here."

Dad kind of snorted. "I'm less worried about the neighbors than the rotten deal Berman is offering. The tobacco base is big though, and with a little luck, we can make some money."

"Morris, I don't like this place. We've never lived among hill people."

"M'dom, twenty-five years ago when we first started farming, you'd never been out of New York City. You were worried about everyone around us, remember? Over the years, they became our best friends."

"I know, but they were nice country people, not a bunch of superstitious hillbillies."

"That's not what you thought then."

Mom looked up into Dad's face. "You're not worried then?"

"About the Bible stuff?" Dad said with a laugh. "M'dom, they're just like the greenhorns from the old country. They're ignorant and superstitious, but they're not bad."

Mom looked away, then back into Dad's face. "Morris, I don't like religious fanatics around the children. They're always looking for evil. And I don't know what they think about Jews. Samuel is just at an age where they can scare him into thinking all sorts of things."

Dad shook his head. "I don't think we should turn it down for that kind of reason."

Mom stood quiet for a minute, then sighed. "I guess you're right. The house has electricity and a telephone, and it can be made nice. Maybe we should try it for a year."

Dad nodded and gazed around. "There's so much work here. There's fourteen acres of burley, and every boy old enough to work's been drafted. We'll have to swap work where we can. It's gonna be tough, M'dom. It would be tough for people of thirty, much less fifty."

Mom squeezed Dad's arm and smiled up at him. "When did work ever scare you?"

I looked around at everything then, because when I heard Mom say that, I knew this was going to be home.

3

It was several days before we got the house cleaned up. I got out to the stock barn once, working my way through its muddy barnyard. To the right of the barn was a big gate which opened into a hog lot. The cobs from the corn they were fed had kept the lot dry.

The barn was creosote black and had two tall red doors that met in the middle. They were supposed to slide, but were part off the track and I had to wriggle through. It was a pretty nice barn. It had a big hayloft and a feed room that was also used for horse gear. I passed half a dozen pens until I got to the back doors. They were off their slides too, but I shoved one out until I could squeeze through and get a look.

What I saw was a long, narrow field with a little pond at the bottom. The ground run up from the pond onto the big hill that looked like a volcano. I was about to push on through when I heard a noise and looked that way. A boy was sitting on top of one of the two wooden gates that opened into other fields. We just kind of stared at each other.

"Hidey," he said.

" 'Lo," I answered.

"What's your name?"

"Samuel Zelinsky."

I waited for him to say his name but he didn't, so I stayed put, moving the buttons of my mackinaw back and forth against the barn door. He was skinny like me and about my size, but looked a year or two older, with a long face, a regular nose, and straight black hair. It was cold but he wudn't wearing a coat, making do with three or four raggedy shirts. A Bull Durham sack with a yellow purse string stuck out of one shirt pocket. Socks and toes peeked through where his soles come loose from the tops of his shoes and wudn't any heels at all. He reared up on the gate, hitched his Levi's, then pulled out the Durham sack.

"Smoke?"

"Okay," I answered. I had never smoked but I was afraid saying no might hurt his feelings.

"This is just th' makin's," he said, swinging the sack back and forth by its yellow string. "Got some brown paper sack at your place?"

"We just moved in," I answered. "Ain't any yet."

Figuring it was time to come out of the barn, I did, and climbed up on the gate with him. "Can I see your makin's?"

"Shore." And he opened the drawstring pouch. "Picked hit m'self."

Inside the sack was a wad of white cotton junk looked like it come from a belly button. "That ain't tobacco!" I said pretty loud.

"Life Everlastin'," he said, closing the bag by pulling one of the strings with his teeth. "Some folks calls hit rabbit tobacco but hit's really Life Everlastin'."

"Uh . . . that grow in a tobacco patch?"

"Huh-uh, you can get lots out in that field yonder," and he nodded toward the big pasture behind him. "You never smoked Life Everlastin'?"

"Naw, just tobacco," I lied.

"Well, hun'ney, Life Everlastin's good for you. Keep your bronical tubes open, Pa says."

"You ever smoked a tailor-made?" I asked, moving a little to keep the gate slats from cutting into my tailbone.

"Had a butt off'n a Raleigh once. You smoke tailor-mades?"

"Roll my own."

"Your pa know you smoke?"

"Lordy, no. He'd skin me alive. What's your name?"

"Fred Cody Mulligan."

I remembered then that Mr. Berman had called the hired hand Mulligan. He also called him white trash. I wondered if Fred was kin to him. Fred didn't look like trash. "Where's your house?"

"West side of Cummings Hill."

Just then I heard Mom's voice. "Samuueel!"

Fred grinned. "That your ma?"

"Yeah."

"Mine yells like that too."

"Reckon she wants me for supper."

"Yeah, hit's gettin' late."

"Samuueel."

"Got t' go," I said, and jumped down. "Will we be goin' to th' same school?"

Fred looked out in the pasture, which was bleak and dead, and scuffed his no-heel on one of the slats. "Yeah, I s'pose."

Then we just stayed for a few seconds. "Well, see you at school."

"Yeah. Here's a purty for you," and he pulled the prettiest buckeye you ever saw from his pocket and handed it to me, then jumped down on the other side of the gate.

"Thanks, Fred," I said, walking away. "I'll give you somethin' sometime too."

"Samuueel . . ." come from the direction of the house.

"Yeah, Mom, I'm comin'!" I yelled, squeezing through the barn doors. I raced to the hole in the fence that was just four, five foot to the side of the garden gate that separated the barn lot from the kitchen yard.

Mom eyed my buckeye when I came puffing up. "Where have you been? You haven't gotten the coal, and supper's ready. What have you got there?"

"A buckeye."

"Where'd you get a buckeye?"

"Out behind th' barn."

"What were you doing out there?"

"Foolin'."

Mom took a deep breath and sighed. Her eyes looked tired and she seemed shorter and fatter than usual in her sweaters and old brown coat. She and Dad had been working day and night, trying to get the house fixed up before spring work. "Get the coal and wash your hands."

The first day of school, Naomi and me didn't know what time the bus came, so we left the house at seven o'clock and walked to the end of our lane. About halfway there I could see someone waiting and took off to meet them. I climbed the gate and when I got to the top, I saw this girl and almost fell off. She was the most beautiful girl in the world, with kind of blondish hair and blue eyes. When she smiled and said hi, I tried to speak but couldn't. Pretty soon Naomi got there and she and the girl got to talking. Her name was Rosemary Shackelford, and she lived just up the road. She and Naomi were both sophomores.

"Is he your brother?" Rosemary asked Naomi, glancing toward me.

"Yes," Naomi said. "Didn't he say hello?"

"No," she giggled. "He hasn't said a word."

"Well, Samuel?" said Naomi, frowning at me. "Don't you say hi to neighbors?"

I tried, but I still couldn't talk. Most I could do was nod.

About that time, tires squalled, and this rickety old yellow bus come roaring down the hill and passed us, then picked us up on its way back about ten minutes later. We went near a mile, then turned down a blacktop lane called the Dry Branch Road. It stopped at the west side of a big hill which I figured was Cummings Hill because Fred and his two sisters got on. From there, we belted on around the bottom rim of Cummings Hill, over the wet spot in the road where the culvert was too small to carry the load of the Dry Branch Creek that was flooding from melted snow and rains, then screeched through more curves to where the blacktop run out. A gravel lane went on from there, but we turned around. A bunch of kids got on. One boy nodded to Fred, who said, "Hi, LD." Then the boy sat down next to another boy called Lonnie who had got on wherever the bus had gone when it passed our gate.

About this time I began to get over meeting Rosemary and moved next to Fred. Nobody said much to me, which I understood being new, but nobody said anything to Fred either. He just looked out the window and chewed his thumbnail, every now and then spitting out a chunk. I didn't know where it come from because his nails was already eat back to the meat.

At one stop, four redheaded kids got on. One of them spotted Fred and grinned. "Hey, feed sack!" he yelled.

Fred's eyes blazed, and he whirled. "Who you callin' a feed sack, John Flickum?"

"You, that's who. Mulligan's a feed sack, Mulligan's a feed sack, Mulligan's a . . ." Then all the Flickums took it up.

It wudn't true. The clothes the Mulligan girls had on were made of Purina feed sacks with big yellow flowers, but Fred had on denim pants and a blue denim shirt.

"Mulligan's a feed sack, Mulligan's a feed sack . . ."

"You leave him alone," screamed Fred's big sister, Annie Lee. "He ain't no feed sack. You all sonamabitches, alla you," and she swung a book at one and grabbed the hair of another, fighting like a she-devil alongside Fred. I figured I was going to have to fight today anyways, so I picked out the skinniest Flickum and socked him in the mouth.

"Hey, you kids, set down back there!" the driver yelled, but the fight kept going. "*I said set down back there! Now set down!*"

We all set down. Fred was so mad, he was crying and yelled toward the driver, "He called me a feed sack. I ain't no feed sack! I'm a-wearin' as good a stuff as—"

"*And shut up!*" yelled the driver.

Fred quit crying and looked out the window, then his whole body got tight and squeezed like a shriveled lemon. "Ain't comin' back here n'more," he said, under his breath. "Told 'em I wouldn't . . . hate th' sonamabitches . . . alla them!" and tears poured down his face. LD and Lonnie had kept out of it, but you could tell they didn't like what had happened. I took time to study the bunch that was riding Fred. It was some of these I'd have to fight. I hated fighting, but wudn't nothing else to do when kids rode me about Jew.

School was pretty much the same as the one I came from except it only went to the sixth grade. Naomi had to go on to Middletown High, which left me by myself for the first time. I was lonesome and a little scared. Fred and me wudn't in the same class. I was in the third and he was in the second so we didn't see much of each other at school.

Outside was still cold and wudn't nothing to do at recess but run around the big open-field schoolyard. I kept waiting for the skinniest Flickum to show. I must've got in a good lick because he didn't. Nobody else bothered me so I didn't have to fight that day, but I did the next.

It happened with Lonnie. At the start, I thought I might win because Lonnie was no bigger than me and just as skinny. Neither of us wanted to fight, but some of the older boys egged us on until there wudn't nothing else we could do. It didn't take long to find out why they wanted to see us fight. Lonnie's fists went so fast you couldn't see them. I fought back and got in a couple punches but it didn't make any difference.

Lonnie's last name was Miller, and he lived on the Little Bend bottoms. We didn't say nothing to each other for a few days, even though we rode the same bus. One afternoon the teacher picked us to dust erasers. I kept wondering how he'd act alone, and was hoping we could make friends because he seemed quiet and nice. When we came to the rock fence that surrounded the schoolyard, I nodded for him to dust first.

"Naw, you go ahead," he said, shaking his head so hard his shaggy black hair moved about. "I dusted first last time I was out."

"You sure can fight," I said, beating the eraser against the rocks until the chalk dust went up in a cloud. "Bet you don't lose many."

"Ain't never lost," he said. "Not even with them big ones. I don't like fightin'. Wish we hadn't of fought . . . wudn't no reason."

It was real honest the way he said it. "I don't like fightin' neither," I said.

Lonnie kind of raised his chin. "We won't do hit n'more. You fight purty good, Samuel. We'll just tell them old boys from now on they want some fightin' they can try us together!" Then his blue eyes lit up. "You like fishin'?"

"Yeah!" I answered, which somehow I knew even though I'd never done it.

"Let's go fishin' this summer at your place. You can catch newlights a foot long out of your pond down by Fred's."

"Well, sure, come on down. That's a far distance from th' Little Bend, ain't it?"

"By the road, yeah, but I cut across and hit's only about three mile. One day I caught thirty-nine brim and five big newlights at your place. Hit made a good mess for th' seven of us."

"Well, we'll sure go this summer," I said, and I knew I had another friend.

I saw Fred maybe three times a week on the school bus, which was about all any of the Mulligans went except for Annie Lee, who was the oldest. We got together on Saturdays and Sundays when he'd wander over with his dad, Alfred. It was real nice living on Berman's. The folks in the hills were the first people I'd ever been around that didn't ride me about Jew. One boy did, and I won that fight. It turned out to be a good one to win because nobody liked him since his folks wudn't croppers. Nobody held losing to Lonnie against me either. Everybody lost to Lonnie.

4

March and early April crept by in their wet, cool, blustery, miserable way, and real spring come on with its bee-buzzing sounds and warm-wind feeling. The brown hills turned dark green and the apple trees busted out in pink-white. The creek in the hollow below the tobacco barn settled back inside its banks and it was a great feeling to belly down beside it and listen to its sounds and let the sun beat down on my back and smell the grass and warm, black, soft, moist ground.

Fred come over almost every evening to help me with chores so our dads could work late in the fields. There was a lot to do and he showed me how a lot of the tools worked. I'd never used a corn sheller before and he could really make ours fly. It made getting corn for both families' chickens quick and easy. One day when we finished feeding the chickens and collecting the eggs, he said why didn't we go down by the creek and make some plans. I could see our cows heading toward the barn and wanted to get one milked before Dad come in, but I figured we had a few minutes to spend making plans.

"It's gonna be a great summer, idn't it, Fred?" I said as we sat on the bank.

"Aw, yeah, hun'ney. First thing we got to do is get a real good old inner tube."

I kind of looked at him, not knowing what he was driving at. "Why?"

"Can't make slingshots without one. What'd you think we was gonna use?"

"I didn't even know we were gonna make slingshots."

"Aw, yeah. Hit ain't summer without a new slingshot. Broke my old one t'other day. Makin' one's about as much fun's shootin' one. Problem is, with th' war on all th' inner tubes is bein' sent t' th' army."

I thought about it, then said, "Bet I can get one. Dad's got a friend who runs a junkyard. He's got lots of inner tubes. I'll ask Dad t' get one from him."

"Hot dog!" Fred yelled. "When you gonna ask?"

"Tonight," I said. "What else we gonna do?"

"Gonna fish our eyes loose and maybe tempt that old ghost down't th' Blue Hole."

Everything sounded good except the ghost part. "What's th' Blue Hole?"

"Hit's a water hole by th' river down't th' Little Bend bottoms," Fred said, and then he leaned toward me and his voice got low. "Hit's about seventy, eighty foot across and fed by this underground river, see, and no matter how little hit rains, hit's always full and blue. Nobody's ever found th' bottom, and them what swims in hit dies somethin' awful."

"How so?"

"Ghost gets 'em. This big old skeleton hand comes up and gets your leg and pulls you down and you don't never come up."

That scared me. "We ain't swimmin' in it, are we?"

"Lordy no! We just gonna tease th' ghost. You know, stand back where th' hand can't get us and throw rocks. I done hit couple times. Didn't see no hand, but Johnny Flickum said he seen it. Course, you can't never believe a Flickum."

That was true. Nobody in those parts ever believed a Flickum. A Flickum could come in the house and say the barn was on fire and wouldn't nobody move.

We swished our feet in the creek awhile more, then I said I had to get going. We climbed the hill toward the stock barn and on the way, Fred kept talking. He said he might get a bicycle on account of things going so well for his pa.

"Th' acre of strawberries we put out ought t' bring us in some money and Pa says we're gonna buy a bunch of shoats. We got us a good show this year."

When we got to the barn, Fred climbed the hog lot gate, then put his hands on the top slats and grinned. "Samuel, hit's gonna be great this summer. We just gonna have a big time."

"Yeah," I said, grinning back. "S'long, Fred."

"S'long, old buddy," and he walked off whistling and dragging his no-heels in the dust.

It took us three weeks to set the tobacco. We had fourteen acres and swapped work with the MacWerters, who had twelve acres across the Cuyper Creek Pike from us on Mr. Charlie Cornwall's place. Mr. MacWerter's name was George, but folks called him Mr. Mac. He had a boy named Edwin who he called Babe. Edwin didn't like being called Babe since he was about thirty-five, but wudn't much he could do about it. I learned how to set tobacco on the setter with my sister Debby while she was home on leave from the Army Nurse Corps. We finished the last part of May and I was free, which meant having fun with Fred.

It was really a fine morning to learn fishing the day I did. Clear blue sky, warm sun, a little dew, and a honeysuckle smell in the air. Fred come over early so we could walk together, this being my first time across country to his place, it being a lot quicker than taking the roads. I was excited as we climbed the rickety, half-slung gate where I first met him, waded the creek at the bottom of the slope, then skipped along a dusty path through the big field that rose gentle toward a hickory and locust thicket. The thicket was dark green with lots of bluegrass and ended at a gap that was made of three strands of barbwire tied to a pole. It was saggy unless it was hooked up right, which we did by putting the bottom and top of the pole into loops of smooth wire that were lashed to a line post. It looked flimsy, but it kept the cattle in and if you ever fooled with barbwire, you know why.

On the other side of the gap was another big field that stretched to a wooden farm gate everybody called the hog lot gate because it was next to the Mulligan's hog lot. About thirty foot on the other side was their house.

The house was small and covered with black tar paper and had a porch in front and back. It didn't have a yard, just kind of set in an acre space made by fences. The front of the house was maybe fifty foot from the Dry Branch Road. The backyard had a chicken house and a privy. Tin cans lay everywhere and a few Dominicker hens wandered around clucking.

We climbed the hog lot gate and walked to the kitchen window where a shovel was stuck in the ground. Fred picked it up and started digging. Pretty soon, Fred's sister Thelma Jean, who was eleven, come out and helped us by smacking clods against the side of the house and collecting worms to put in our can. We were all set to go fishing when Mamie, who was Fred's mama, come strolling to the window and leaned her skinny chest and elbows on it. Her eyes shined in her thin, brown, hill-woman face, and her mud-colored hair hung straight down.

"You Mr. Simpsky's boy?" she asked, shooing the flies away from her face.

"Yes, ma'am," I answered, figuring it wudn't going to do any good telling her my last name was Zelinsky because she'd never say it that way. Hill people never could.

"What's your Christian name?"

"Samuel," I answered, and she thought for a minute.

"Hit's a good name." She nodded finally. "Had 'nother boy, I'd of named him Jacob." She straightened up and looked at Fred. "Fred Cody, reckon you think you're a-goin' fishin'."

"Yes, ma'am."

"Well, I got news for you, young man, you ain't a-goin' nowhere 'til you get some fresh water from Pers' spring, then you can go fishin'."

We got the bucket and started down the hill to the branch. "Hit'll only take a minute. You'll get to see Pers' spring. Hit's hainted. My uncle Charlie seen th' ghost."

"He sure it was a ghost?"

"Hun'ney, hit couldn't of been nothin' else. My uncle Charlie can tell a ghost a hunnert yards off and if'n he said hit was a ghost, hit was a ghost!"

"Ain't you kind of scared going down there now?"

Fred seemed a little put off by my question and we walked a distance without sayin' anything. Then he said, "You don't know much about haints, do you?"

"I know lots about haints," I said, gettin' my dander up. "We lived with one for three years. Reckon I ought to know about them."

"Didn't he haint you?"

"Every now and then he'd make a little noise, but mostly he just stayed in that old attic. He left us alone, and we left him alone."

"That's a good kind," said Fred. "Ain't like a haint's been murdered. Th' one at Pers' spring must of been, 'cause he come out at Uncle Charlie madder'n a hornet."

To get to Pers' spring, we had to go down the Dry Branch Road to the culvert, then cut across the creek. About a hundred yards or so past Pers' cabin was a spring that come out from under a big tree and trickled down to the branch.

After we drank and filled the bucket, we went wading in the branch. It was harder for me than Fred since he'd been going barefoot since late April and had thick calluses. It sure felt good, though, and I decided to carry my shoes and go barefoot. We must've waded longer than we thought because Mamie started calling.

"Fred Codeee!"

"Yo!" yelled Fred, then he turned to me. "We better get on up there, hun'ney. I don't want none of her hidin's today! Come on!"

We ran up the Dry Branch Road as hard as we could, Fred on one side of the bucket and me on the other with water slopping all over the place.

"Where you been, Fred Cody?" Mamie asked when we got to the house.

"Down't th' spring," said Fred.

"Hit don't take no forty minutes t' get t' th' spring and back. You been wadin' in that branch, ain't you?"

"No'm," he said, and Mamie looked us up and down. Our Levi's was rolled up over our knees, and the edges was wet. A half-sick grin spread over Fred's face.

"Go get me a dipper 'n' quit lyin'," she said, and he took off like a shot.

It was after ten by the time we got to the pond. Since I didn't have a pole or line, we had to make up my gear from scratch. That's when I found out how Fred did things. He wouldn't use nothing but elm, and the limb had to be perfect. We checked every elm tree around until I was about to go crazy. It was almost an hour before he settled on one, but then he whittled it into shape in no time. All we had left to do after that was tie on my line, attach a hook and a little whiskey-cork bobber that Fred got from his uncle Charlie, and we were fishing.

I kept watching Fred, trying not to seem dumb. "Reckon that's enough worm?" I asked, holding up a six-incher.

"Hit'll choke 'em t' death if nothin' else. Use about a inch off his hind end," and he pinched off the butt of a big fat worm. "You give a brim more'n that, he'll just steal hit."

We started, and I was learning about fishing undercuts and sunken tree limbs, and how much bobber to let a brim take before you jerked him, when Fred took a pain.

"Got t' go, hun'ney. I'll be back in a minute," he said, and took off.

Fish were biting like crazy. Suddenly there was a thrashing in some blackberry briars. I whirled around and there stood a man looked like a hundred with hair down to his shoulders, long scraggly beard, and rags. His clothes kind of hung on him because he wudn't more than skin covering bones. His eyes were strange, and he come straight for me.

"Bob warr'll cut ye," he said, coming to maybe three foot of me, holding a hickory stick he used for walking.

"Ye . . . yeah," I said, and backed up a step. His eyes didn't have lashes and were sunk so far back in his head I figured he couldn't see from the sides. One of the eyes was cockeyed too. When his mouth opened, there was only a couple teeth that looked like they were in the way.

"I said bob warr'll cut ye. S'matter th'you boy, ain't ye got no ears?" And he moved a little closer, shaking the hickory stick in his skinny old hand and kind of jiggling.

"Hidey, Uncle Lex," come Fred's voice.

The old man doddered in a backward circle until he was half facing Fred, then stood there swaying from side to side. "Uh . . . hidey . . . hidey. Hu . . . you Alfred's boy, Fred Cody?"

"Shore am, Uncle Lex. You seen me just last night, remember?"

"Hu . . . shore I do . . . Uh . . . that there your uncle Charlie?"

"Naw, Uncle Lex, that's Mr. Zilski's boy, Samuel. Him and me's fishin' today. Whyn't you go up th' house and get some cool water?"

"Huu . . . don't know no Zilsy. Where's he live?"

"In th' big white house on th' other side of th' place. Where Berman goes."

"Berman? Huu . . . that th' Jew owns th' place?" and he staggered around more.

"Yeah, hit's him."

"How do he Jew? Ain't never seen one do it."

"He gets along okay, Uncle Lex. Say 'lo t' Samuel."

"Huu . . . you Zilsy's boy?" he said, looking sideways at me.

"Ye . . . yeah," I answered. "And howdy, Uncle Lex."

"Hidey, hidey," he said. "You know bob warr'll cut ye?" And he pulled up the sleeve of his long underwear and showed me some scars on his skinny arm I figured was from barbwire.

"Yeah, it sure will," I said quick.

Fred moved next to me and said, "You go on up and get some fresh spring water, Uncle Lex. Samuel and me just brought up a cold bucketful out of Pers' spring."

"Hu . . . yeah," he muttered, and began staggering toward the Mulligan house.

"Uncle Lex won't hurt you," Fred said, after Uncle Lex was gone.

"Does he live around here?"

"Lordy, yes, hun'ney. He's a Cummings."

"He live on Cummings Hill?"

"Naw," Fred answered as he threw in. "Uncle Lex lives back on th' Big Bend cliffs."

"What's wrong with him?"

"He's crazy. All Cummings is crazy. Always have been."

"What makes them crazy?"

"Folks say th' Lord done it. Cummings have always been crazy far as anybody knows and lived back on th' cliffs. They used t' own all this land."

"Are there any more of 'em?"

"Aw, yeah. Uncle Lex has a woman . . . Aunt Belle . . . she's crazy too."

It seemed odd, both of them being crazy. "She go crazy when she married Uncle Lex?"

Fred laughed. "Naw, she was already crazy. She was a Cummings. A Cummings won't marry nobody but a Cummings. Say, Samuel, when you gonna get that inner tube?"

"Real soon," I answered, reaching for my pole as the cork went under. "Dad told Mom just th' other day that he was goin' t' see his friend Ike right after th' corn was in and he ought t' finish plantin' by Friday."

"Lordy, a whole tube," Fred whispered. "Ain't never had a whole tube before. I'm gonna make us some daddy slingshots. Man, are we gonna go froggin'!" and he put his arm out like he had a slingshot in it and drawed back with the other. "Bam! Got one a foot long!"

We fished until six and talked about everything, the ghost at Moneybags' place, Fred's uncle Charlie, and all sorts of people who lived around us. By the time we quit fishing, I felt like I was born on Berman's.

5

I was relaxing in the tree when I felt ants crawling up my legs. I stuffed the two remaining apples into my pockets and quickly climbed down. When I reached the ground I de-anted myself, then drove to the farm's gate. I was here! Even though I hadn't wanted to return, I felt a rush of excitement. It had been over sixty years since our family had followed a truck out of the lane en route to our own farm in Indiana. Indiana had never felt like home to me; now, eerily, this place did. I checked the mailboxes, but the names were unfamiliar.

I decided to park and walk. The entrance gate was dilapidated. Most of the gravel had washed out of the lane and at times I couldn't tell if I was still following it because the weeds were so tall. Someone was farming the land though, because off to my right, on the other side of a fence, was a tobacco patch. The plants were knee-high and deep green. The creek was still in the hollow, but there was no tobacco barn, corncrib, or sheep barn.

Ahead of me was a grove of huge maples and oaks, so dense that everything beneath was lost in their shadows. I began walking faster and entered the grove. The yard fences were gone but the house remained, or rather, what was left of it. The walls were tilted inward and the roof had collapsed. I could still see parts of the screened-in porch and the window of my room. A mangy cat was sunning himself on the windowsill, oblivious to me, but a cowsucker snake did take notice and slithered under the porch. I moved closer to see inside my old room, waking the cat, who skedaddled. The interior was a mess, the walls collapsing and floor rotted away.

I glanced over my shoulder toward where the orchard had been. Only the cherry tree remained. It was loaded, so I picked a handful of cherries, then continued to reconnoiter.

The weeds were lower in the kitchen yard. There were also three new trees, two maples and an oak, undoubtedly the progeny of my old friends in front. The kitchen and its screened-in porch were almost totally collapsed. I walked toward the kitchen door and stubbed my toe on a crumbling concrete slab. The top of the cistern! I started searching and found the housing for the chain that had brought up the little cups of water and dumped it into a bucket. It was rusted out, but the dent I had put in its side with a baseball was unmistakable. I turned toward where the stock barn had been. Now there were just interconnecting fences, one of which guarded the growing tobacco. The fences were new. There was nothing where the barn had stood. Then I noticed a huge line post. Hinged to it was a new wooden gate. Was that my line post, the one that held the gate Fred had been sitting on when we first met? I ran to it. Yep, still had the gouge the wagon bed had made when our horses swung too close and hit it.

After patting the line post, I put my arms on top of the gate and looked across the field. It had been pasture land when we lived on Berman's, but now it was covered with twenty acres of alfalfa. The little creek still ran through it, creasing the field. In the distance I could see the hickory and locust grove. I had walked this way to the Mulligans' so many times. In my mind I could still see Fred, sitting on top of the old gate in his Levi's, multiple shirts, and no-heel shoes. Fred had been the portal to a great adventure—part beauty, part terror, all wonder.

It was getting toward noon. The heat and humidity were making my clothes sticky, and the sound of insects filled the air with a hum. I scanned the vista. Open meadows, dark groves of trees, and green hills covered with patches of wildflowers. Below the hills were valleys with slightly different carpets, but just as remarkable in their glory. I could almost hear the hills speak to my soul. *Embrace us, embrace us, our prodigal son. You've been long away, but we still love you. Come, mingle, lie among us and become the soil of life.*

I inhaled deeply and the air filled my body to my socks. Had I returned to Canaan?

Fred leaped back into my mind. He was a year older than I, so he would be seventy-three. I wished he were here beside me. Then again, would he stand beside me? Would any of them? What would I say when I met them? The summer of that first year on Berman's was the best summer of my life and through it all, Fred had been my mentor. All that summer I had been barefoot, naked to the waist, deep-tanned, and wore the same pair of Levi's every day until Mom wrested them away from me for a wash. I remember . . .

. . . we fished pretty nigh every day. Sometimes, Lonnie and LD come over, but mostly it was just Fred and me. Pretty soon, I could hit those brim fast as they nibbled my hook, and sometimes I made one worm last two, three fish. Fred said he never saw nothing like it, how I caught on and all, and that I was on my way to being a fishing daddy and would be just as soon as I done some river fishing and pulled in a few big channel cats and a buffalo or two.

"When you wanta go?" I asked as we walked away from the pond one night.

"Tell y' what," he said, "tomorra evenin's meetin' time and LD and Lonnie's gonna be there for sure 'cause Brother Fletcher is holdin' th' meetin' and their moms like listenin' t' him. When things are over, I'll see when th' best day is for them. We can fish down't th' Little Bend bottoms and that way we can go to th' Blue Hole. I'll let you know tomorrow and you can get an okay from your folks."

"Great. See you tomorrow," I yelled, and waved as we split up.

The next evening, Fred come by just as I was settling down to milk the last cow. I was doing the milking in the barnyard now because it was hot in the barn. It was getting deep dusk and Fred

looked fuzzy from where I was milking, him up on the swing post
of the hog lot gate, his bare feet pressed into the slats and kind
of whistling soft-like while the milk squirts sprayed against the
bottom of the bucket. Pretty soon, I was milking away to Fred's
tune and giggling, trying hard not to laugh because I didn't want to
scare my cow. When I finished, Fred climbed down and followed
me to the tall milk can where I poured in.

"You 'bout ready for some river fishin'?"

"When we goin'?" I said, leaning up against the barn, opening
and closing my hands, which were cramped from squeezin' tits.

"How's tomorra suit you?"

"Dandy, if I can get Mom and Dad t' let me go. Lonnie and LD
both goin'?"

"LD, anyways. Lonnie's ma said he could go, but hit'll depend
on his pa. Can't never tell about Lonnie's pa. If he ain't in a good
mood, don't nobody in th' fambly do nothin'."

I'd heard about Lonnie's pa and he sounded scary. "He's mean,
ain't he?"

Fred brought a foot up and scratched its bottom. "Pa says no,
less'n he's drunk. Then he's mean. You just got t' know when t' stay
away from him."

"How'll we know if Lonnie's goin' or not, then?"

Fred laughed and took a swipe at a lightning bug. "Hun'ney,
ain't nobody knows those parts down there like Lonnie. He'll just
show up if he's comin'."

"What you figure we'll start doin'?"

"Lordy, I don't know. Maybe fish first, then we'll throw some
rocks at th' Blue Hole. Y' know, if we had some slingshots we could
stand back and shoot at th' Blue Hole."

"Yeah, I know," I said. "We'll get that inner tube, Fred. A whole
one and it won't be patched or rotted. You'll see."

Fred nodded. Pretty soon he sighed and said he'd better be getting home; then he climbed the hog lot gate and was gone.

6

The next morning, I woke up just as dawn was breaking and went out the door of my room and onto the screened-in porch. It wudn't even 5:30 but you could already see and really smell, especially the hay Dad had mowed a couple days before. Everything was still, and the hollow was full of fog and dew, which was glistening on the tops of the tobacco and sheep barns that stuck out of the fog like mountaintops. It was great to watch and listen to the day come on. I knew it was gonna get hot and muggy though, it being July.

I'd been thinking how to ask Mom and Dad about going to the river ever since Fred mentioned it, but I still hadn't come up with a good idea. I decided to act like it was nothing special and hope for the best. When I heard Dad come in from milking, I went to the kitchen where Mom and Naomi were fixing breakfast and he was washing up.

"What do you say, Samuel," Dad mumbled into a towel as he wiped his face. "Up kind of early for a man of leisure, aren't you?"

"Fred and me and LD and Lonnie are goin' fishin'," I said.

"What else is new?" he said with a chuckle.

I pulled my chair up to the table and folded my arms on the red checkered oilcloth. "Yep, fishin' th' Little Bend today. Get some cats and a buffalo or two."

"The Little Bend!" Mom said, looking up from her cooking. "You mean the river?"

The way she said it was what I was afraid of. "Uh-huh," I said like it wudn't nothing.

Mom's eyes were large. "Down on those cliffs? With those wild boys?"

"They aren't wild boys, Mom," I said. "They're buddies of mine."

Mom looked at Dad as she put the hash brown potatoes, eggs, and grits on his plate. "Morris, are you going to let him go down on that river with those boys?"

Dad wrapped his hand around his coffee mug and sprawled out. "Don't see why not," he answered after a gulp. "Those kids know that area well."

"There are cliffs down there, Morris, and the river is deep. I don't like it."

"M'dom, he's a boy. You can't lock up boys." He turned in his chair and looked at me. "You got sense enough not t' step off a cliff or get in th' river don't you, Samuel?"

"Sure," I answered.

Mom's lips pursed and she moved around the kitchen quick like she always did when she was upset. "I see him running around with those wild boys and starting to be just like them. Is that what you want for your son . . . to grow up to be a tobacco yap moonshiner?"

Dad sighed. "M'dom, there's nothing wrong with those boys. They're good kids and they treat him like one of their own. They don't hold it against him that he's a Jew. They don't look up to him or down at him, just across, and that's what I want for Samuel."

Mom didn't say anything for a minute but the way she kept scurrying I knew was trouble. "Morris, I want Samuel to grow up like us. I want him to know we're different from these people. I want him to know who he is."

Dad smiled at Mom like I had seen him do so often when they talked. "I do too, Liz," he said soft. "Let's let him grow. He'll be a fine man."

Mom took the biscuits out of the oven of the old white cooking stove, shook the baking tin into a little towel-bottom basket, then carried the biscuits to the table and sat down. She looked at Dad, shook her head, and they both laughed. Then she turned toward me.

"Promise you won't get in the river and you'll be back before dark," she said, looking so deep in my eyes it was like she was seeing the back of my head.

"I promise."

"What are you going to do for lunch?"

I eyed the biscuits in the basket. "Take some biscuits."

"Just biscuits?"

"Sure."

"No wonder you're so skinny. I'll put some butter and jelly on them."

"They'll get my pocket sticky, Mom."

"What! You'll have a bag."

"Aw, Mom . . ."

Mom stopped moving and her little fist went on her hip. "In a bag or you don't go! And remember something: you get into trouble with these meshuga friends of yours, and that's it. No more bony or loony, or kids with just letters for names. Understand?"

I knew she meant it so I just said, "Yes, ma'am," and shut up.

Along about eight, Fred and LD showed up. It was a long way to the Little Bend, shortcut and all. When we come to the path along the cliff, we set down under a big oak tree for a rest.

"You guys want some biscuits 'n' jelly?" I asked, and opened the bag and poked it toward them. LD's hand went inside so quick I almost dropped the bag. They took a couple each, which left two that I ate in a hurry, figuring if Lonnie showed up, I was going hungry.

When we finished the biscuits, Fred picked up his pole and the worm can and started down the cliff. The path was about two foot wide, mostly dirt and rock. Brush and roots covered part of it and it didn't take anybody to know if you tripped, you were going to fall a hunnert feet. About halfway down, the path widened and curled back on itself. As I made the turn, I could see a hole in the upper part of the cliff maybe ten foot wide and about that high.

"Hey, Fred, what's that?" I asked, and pointed toward it with my fishing pole.

"Old cave. Lots of 'em down here, hun'ney."

"Ever been in it?"

"Naw, but I been in others. Dozens of 'em between here and th' sandbar."

I looked downstream and could see a strip of sand in the far distance that kind of made a beach. Then I looked back toward the cave. "Can we go in it?"

"Reckon. Let's wait'll Lonnie shows up and see if he's been inside. Might narra down in just a few feet. No reason t' make a climb for nothin'."

I said okay and we went on down to the bottoms.

"Where we goin', Fred?" LD asked, as Fred started leading us through the river brush. "They's a great fishin' spot about a hunnert yards from here where I caught a mess of buffaloes with Daddy one time. Figured we'd start there."

It was a great spot. The bank was clear of brush for about thirty foot. We were catching some little cats, then LD's cork shot under and when he jerked, his elm pole bent double.

"Whooee," he yelled. "Got me a big 'un!"

The fish took off and LD's line cut through the water. Any way it ran, LD followed, pulling hard until finally the fish's big body flashed.

"Hit's a buffalo," Fred yelled. "Don't lose him, LD!"

Me and Fred were jumping up and down. In a few minutes its silver side showed again, but the fish was moving slower. Little later, we had him out on the bank.

"Whooee!" LD yelled. "He'll go four pound for sure. Now, that's a buffalo!"

"Yeah," I said, "that's a real buffalo!" even though I never seen one before.

As soon as we put him on the stringer, we all put our lines back in the water. I was tingling all over. Wudn't but a couple minutes until my pole was almost jerked out of my hands.

Fred and LD kept yelling, "Hold him! You got him! You got him!" But the fish kept swinging back and forth, making deep swirls. Just as I drug him up on the bank, the hook straightened and he flopped back onto the water's edge. Fred come out of nowhere and landed on top of him, but the fish squirted out of his arms, and LD and I dove for it at the same time. Mud and water was splashing everywhere as we tried to throw it up on the bank. Somehow, we did. He was a beauty, and must've weighed five, six pound. We were sopping wet, laughing and talking, when all of a sudden there was crashing in the brush. It was Lonnie.

Nobody said anything, then Fred pulled up the stringer of fish and Lonnie yelped and started unwinding his pole. We fished for about two more hours and caught four more buffalo, two big carps, some channel cats, and then they quit biting.

We'd been sitting there watching our bobbers for quite a while when Fred stretched and stood up. "Guess that's hit for today," he said. "What y'all say we take off? With this much fish we got a lot of fish cleanin' t' do and them carps and buffaloes ain't easy t' clean."

"Okay by me," I said, then everybody agreed.

We pulled up our stringer of fish, which was heavy, and started walking. We hadn't gone too far when LD got a funny look on his face. "Fred, why we goin' downstream? Path up the cliff's over yonder," and he pointed with his pole.

"Blue Hole's a ways from here and I figured we'd take a look at hit since Samuel's never been there before," Fred answered.

LD stopped and his eyes got wide. "I ain't supposed t' go there. Pa says hit's evil!"

"Ain't goin' close," said Fred, soft. "We'll just throw in a few rocks and leave."

"Fred said it's hainted," I said to LD. "Where do you figure its haint comes from?"

"That's where they found th' Collins family," LD answered. "Th' river flooded long time ago, come up fast and caught 'em in their shack. Somehow, they tied themselves t'gether with a rope and tried t' swim out and they all drowned and got warshed up in th' Blue Hole. That's where they found th' woman and two little girls, anyways. Mr. Collins wudn't there, but th' loop that went 'round his waist was. Blue Hole's been evil ever since. Other people's drowned there too. They use to find dead animals around hit, but not n'more."

"Ain't no wild animal'll go near th' Blue Hole," said Lonnie. "Some folks claim they've seen tracks of a man around hit though."

"Yeah," said LD. "Old man Hackett trapped mink down here. He told everybody he seen a wild man. Said he just barely got away from him by goin' up th' cliff, wild man right behind callin' in th' name of th' Lord."

I thought about that for a little, then said to LD, "If Mr. Hackett was so old, how come he got away from th' wild man?"

"Dad-burn nigh didn't," said LD. "Old Hackett claimed he was almost grabbed when th' wild man slipped and fell back down th' cliff."

"You figure it's th' wild man makes th' tracks and does all that stuff?" I asked.

"Nobody knows," LD said. "Most folks thinks hit's the ghost of Mr. Collins. Pa thinks hit's th' Devil and we ought have a prayer meetin' at the hole and float a Bible on it. Won't nobody do hit so I reckon he'll just stay there."

It came to me then what Mr. Berman said the day we were renting, about the people that were in the yard yelling when he bought the farm. It was a tall man that was wanting to float a Bible. "LD, is your pa a tall man?"

"Yeah," said LD, stopping to untangle his pole from a bush. "Why you askin'?"

I didn't want to say what Mr. Berman had said, so I told him I just figured his pa was because he was so tall himself. LD had a good three inches on me even though we were about the same age. He was big all over too, big round face, big nose, coal black hair and dark brown eyes. He was always nervous though, but since he treated me okay, it didn't matter.

We started walking again but nobody talked. Then the dry sandy bottom started getting moist under our bare feet. You could see our tracks plain, but there hadn't been any animal signs for a while. Something stunk awful.

LD pulled up. "Somethin' smells dead."

"Probably a dead bird," said Fred, and kept walking.

Lonnie shook his head. "Hit ain't a bird smell. That's a animal smell."

Finally, Fred stopped and held up his hand. "Blue Hole's about two hunnert foot from here," he whispered. "If we circle behind hit, they's a knoll we can see hit from and be far enough away so's we're safe from th' skeleton hand. Lots of rocks t' throw too. Come on."

Fred and Lonnie and me started, but LD didn't. "Lordy, we oughtn' be doin' this," he said. "My daddy knowed, he'd skin me alive," and his voice quivered.

Fred looked at LD and kind of sneered. "Scaredy cat."

"I ain't a scaredy cat," said LD, "but you ain't never seen my pa when he starts with his razor strop. He almost don't stop. If he knows I've been here I don't know what he'll do t' me."

"Stay here, then," said Fred, and the three of us went on. Pretty soon, I could hear LD coming up behind. Fred looked at me out of the corner of his eye and grinned.

The circling was hard going because the brush was taller and thicker than what we had just come through, but we finally made it to the top of the knoll. I could see this big pool of water down below, just as blue as the sky and looking cool and peaceful. We stood a time, then Fred reached down and picked up a rock and gave a big heave, not quite making the water. I was next and fell short too, but Lonnie hit the edge and LD plunked it right in the middle. After that, Fred hit it and I finally got it on a bounce and said that was good enough for me.

"I've had 'nough too," Fred said, and picked up his fishing pole.

"Let's get out of here then," said LD, and we started walking toward the cliff path we come down. We hadn't gone very far when Fred stopped dead.

"Wha . . . what's wrong?" LD croaked. Fred just pointed, then he took the tip of his pole and pushed back some brush. There, in a little sandy clearing, was this black dog with his head all bashed in dead and swole up with flies and maggots all over him.

"Footprints," said Fred, pointing.

There sure was, boy. Big and barefoot all around the dog, tearing up the sand.

"Baby Jesus, help us all," LD jabbered. "Hit's th' Devil! Let's git!" and he started running and we took off after him, leaping over logs and brush, jumping and twisting and stumbling on and on and tangling our poles until we broke through onto a bare spot and stopped, gasping for air. Fred and Lonnie and me were shaking, but LD looked like a bowl of jelly.

"Ain't ever goin' near that thing again," LD puffed. "Hit was th' Devil killed that dog!"

"Th' Devil," said Fred, his eyes wide. "Why you think hit's th' Devil?"

"Didn't you see?" LD said, flailing his arms. "Th' right foot was turned in and cloved?"

"All I seen was footprints," said Fred. "I was so scared I didn't see nothin' else."

I was scared too, but I recollected something. "Fred, I think LD's right about th' footprints. Wha'd you see, Lonnie?"

Lonnie's eyes were wide and he looked scared. I had never seen him scared before and that really bothered me. "I seen th' same thing as LD," he said. "Th' right foot was turned in and cloved halfway't th' heel. Left foot looked okay, though."

LD dropped his fishing pole and both of his hands went to his head. "Hit's Lucifer! Pa said hit was all th' time. He's gonna come for us; I just know it. Lordy, I don't know what t' do."

Fred started looking around. "I don't know what t'do neither, but we can't stay here on th' low bottoms 'cause if hit was a man, he'll find us. We got t' git someplace that's safe."

Lonnie looked up at the cliff. "They's a big old cave right up above us. I been in hit. Hit's a easy climb. Whyn't we leave the fish down't th' bottom, then climb up and figure what t' do?"

Fred looked up. "That was the one Samuel wanted t' go in. Hit's a good idea. Let's go."

7

The cliff was a lot easier to climb than I thought it would be because it had kind of a path up it. We were inside the cave in just a couple minutes. It was big, going back fifty, sixty foot before the roof and floor come together. The place stunk something awful and everywhere you looked there was feathers and fur and bones that Lonnie said come from quail and groundhog.

"Shooee. Wonder what kind of critter's been livin' here?" said Fred.

Lonnie squatted down and looked at the bones. "Hard t' say. Some new stuff since I was here before. Prob'ly brought by a bobcat from th' looks a all these bones."

"Yeah . . . be a good place for a bobcat," said Fred. "Hit's a easy climb from the bottom. If hit was a she, she could get a litter here and they'd stay dry and safe unless hit rained real hard."

While everybody was talking, I was looking further back in the cave. It was hard to see because the cave faced east and the sun was already in the west. The going was easy though because the floor was smooth rock. I went as far as possible and stepped on a wet spot with my bare feet. It was so cold I yelled. "Hey, there's water back here!"

"All of 'em has a creek in hit," said Lonnie. "Lots of times in th' spring, after a hard rain, water shoots out these old caves like a waterfall."

I moved my foot around. "This one ain't runnin', it's just wet."

"Hit'll run though, if we get lots of rain," Lonnie said, coming back toward me.

While Lonnie and I were trying to see what was in the back of the cave, LD was fooling around one of the walls. "Look at this," he said. "There's a big old stick in here."

"Maybe it warshed in," I said.

"Ain't likely," said Lonnie. "Cracks th' water runs out of are too small for a big stick."

It got quiet, then LD spoke. "Lordy, I wonder if this here's Satan's cave."

"Naw." Fred laughed. "Must've been somebody up here before and left hit. Hit's a easy climb. Bring it over t' th' light, LD."

LD started for the front of the cave and we all got there together. "Blood!" croaked LD. "Blood 'n' black dog hair! Let's git!"

We did, boy, scrambling down the cliff as hard as we could go. At the bottom, Fred grabbed the fish and we took off for the path up.

"Hit's Lucifer!" LD screamed and pointed at some tracks coming toward where the cave was, "Hit's Lucifer! Hit's Lucifer! Hit's Lucifer!" and we run harder, shooting up the cliff path we come down. When we got to the top we kept running until we couldn't go anymore.

We must've lay on the ground ten minutes sucking air. I sat up. LD, Lonnie, and Fred were on their backs, and the fish were draped across Fred's belly with one big buffalo gone.

"Lost a buffalo, Fred," I said.

Fred pulled the stringer up straight with both hands until he could see them all. "Must of ripped out hits gill," he mumbled.

"Wanta go back and look for it?" I said, and we all laughed.

"Hun'ney, ain't no wild horse gonna pull me back there," said Fred.

"Gonna do my river fishin' down below th' sandbar from now on," said Lonnie. "Man, I ain't ever been that scared."

"Me neither," said LD, and he was still shaking. "You see them footprints? They was twisted and cloved! I tell you we dealin' with Lucifer here," and he shook even harder.

That scared me silly. We never talked about the Devil at home, but I had heard a lot about him at school. Fred and Lonnie didn't seem too scared though, so I calmed down.

Fred rolled over on his side, pulled a blade of grass, stuck it in his teeth, then glanced at Lonnie. I could tell Fred was thinking. Pretty soon, he pulled some more grass and looked at Lonnie again. "You gonna tell your pa, Lonnie?"

Lonnie set up. "Hadn't thought about it."

Little time went by and Fred pulled some more grass. "Whatcha figure he'd do?"

"Don't know," said Lonnie, and he made kind of a choking sound.

"We talk about th' cave and th' Devil 'n' all, I'll get a hidin'," said LD. "My pa will figure I been around th' Blue Hole, and he'll ask. He knows if I lie. I promised not t' go nowhere 'round that thing. He'll beat th' tar out of me for breakin' my word."

Fred picked a little more grass. "Yeah, hit's th' same with me, only hit'll be my ma what does th' lickin' so hit won't be too bad. She'll never let me go river fishin' again, though."

Then I remembered what Mom said about getting into something. She wouldn't let me do anything with my buddies again and it shaping up to be such a great summer.

Lonnie swallowed. "Reckon you guys can say what y' have to," he said, and there was that choking sound again.

By this time Fred had dug a little hole where he was pulling out grass. "Ain't no fish."

"Huh?" said Lonnie.

I could see right off what Fred was driving at. If our folks saw these big fish they were going to want to know where we caught them and we would have to lie and say we were downstream of where we were because LD, Fred, and Lonnie weren't supposed to be anywhere around the Blue Hole. Maybe some grown-up would come upriver if they wudn't catching anything below the sandbar and see our kid tracks. They might follow the tracks to the Blue Hole. Not much was going to happen to me and Fred if our folks found out, but it was going to be bad for LD and really awful for Lonnie. That had to be the reason Lonnie choked up when he talked about it. He was brave, but he was scared. Fred was right; we had to get rid of the fish.

"We don't take nothin' home," said Fred. "We don't have fish. We can say we was just foolin'. Ma never asks me what I was doin' if I say foolin'."

"Mine don't neither," said Lonnie, and LD said neither did his, and I said mine did, but that I could wriggle out of it.

"We bury 'em then," said Fred, getting up. "They's some big rocks on a pile close t' Bess Clark's place we can roll over on th' bunch after we bury 'em. That way they won't smell as much and th' rocks will keep the varmints from digging 'em up. Then we warsh our Levi's in Cuyper Creek t' get rid of th' river smell." Fred lifted the stringer again and shook his head. "Best mess I ever helped catch and I got to throw them away."

"Hit's a real shame," said LD.

"Nothin' else we can do," said Fred with a sigh. "Let's go, boys."

"I'm gonna cut across toward home if you guys don't need me for fish buryin'," said Lonnie, and he nodded in a different direction than we were going.

"Go ahead," said Fred, and Lonnie drifted off toward some brush and was gone almost before I could wave goodbye. That was the way it was with Lonnie. He'd come out of nowhere and disappear the same way.

We buried the fish under the rock pile, warshed our Levi's, wrung them out and let them dry some, then the three of us went to Fred's house so everybody could see we were together.

From the gap we could see Alfred out by their hog lot gate, talking to Pers Shanks. They looked funny together. Alfred was short with thick shoulders and his waist and hind end were about the same size, while Pers was tall and skinny. The thing everybody noticed about Alfred, though, was his head was kind of square and covered with thin hair, and he always had a black stubble beard. As we got closer, we could see their mouths moving, but being out of earshot, we couldn't hear. It looked funny when Pers talked because his Adam's apple jerked up and down.

"Hidey boys," said Pers as we come up. "What you three been up to?"

"Just foolin'," said Fred, and I could feel my belly churn.

"Foolin'," said Alfred. "Thought y'all were gonna get a mess of buffaloes t'day!"

"Nope," said Fred, "Don't have a one."

"Well, I swan," said Pers. "Hear tell you three can catch fish in a rock pile," and Alfred and Pers laughed. Me and Fred and LD nigh puked.

The three of us hung around the hog lot gate with Pers and Alfred, listening to Alfred talk about breeding the sows he had and feeding the pigs out with the corn Mr. Berman was going to let him raise, and how much money he was going to make from putting out the strawberries and how he was going to buy a team of mules. He figured with a little luck, the next year he'd get farm equipment and maybe get to rent Red Bill Rogers' place because Red Bill was stove-up. We threw around a baseball until finally I said it was starting to get late and I had promised Mom I'd get home before dark.

I climbed the hog lot gate and started down the path toward home. While I walked, I thought about what had happened. It didn't make any sense that the ghost of Mr. Collins would have all those bones in his cave since ghosts didn't eat. By the time I come to the gap I was pretty sure it wudn't a ghost at the Blue Hole. Supposing it was the Devil like LD said, though. He could come right in the house at night. Wouldn't even have to open the door. LD and Lonnie and Fred would be okay if it was the Devil because they all had crosses at their house, like in the movies where they hold up a cross and keep Dracula out. We didn't have a cross at our place. A preacher had tried to give us one, but Mom told him we didn't need it because we were Jews. Now when I needed one, I didn't have it! I was going to have to make a cross real quick.

About that time, I come to where the hickory and locust thicket ended. In the distance was our barn and house and not another tree until the yard. Lucky for me, the biggest hickory in the grove was right on the edge of the thicket and had a low dead limb. The limb was dry, but it was still tough to break. I wudn't sure a hickory cross would work, but I decided it wouldn't make any difference so long as the pieces got hooked up right. My biggest problem was I didn't have any twine to do the tying with. I figured there had to be vines somewhere, and began running from tree to tree looking. Nothing! The more I run, the more scared I got. There was still about half a mile to go and it was getting twilight and I knew Dracula always comes out when it gets dark and don't go back in until morning and maybe th' Devil too. I grabbed the sticks and held them together but they kept slipping because my hands was shaking so I whipped off my belt and started lashing the pieces together but they wouldn't stay like a cross and kept slipping like an X and I took off running as hard as I could go, my legs feeling like rocks was tied to my feet and I knew it was th' Devil because I could hear night birds and rain crows calling with low sounds and swallows flitting through the air and I was starting to cry when something big came out of the side toward my eye looking like Daisy or Gabe, our horses, but could've been, probably was, the Devil in a horse shape, until he got on me and whinnied and electric shot my body and legs and I screamed and dropped the cross and went flying over the ground, belly-rolled the gates, banged through the barn door, and almost had it made until this big Devil shaped like a cow let out a bawl and I cleared the backyard fence and busted through the screen door into the house and run behind the kitchen stove.

8

Next couple days we were real scared. Didn't make it any better for me that Mom wudn't buying my story about just fooling and kept asking why my Levi's were damp and why I wouldn't say just what kind of fooling we were doing and why I was acting so strange, which I didn't think I was until maybe I started acting strange because she thought I was acting strange. I still had nightmares about the Devil. I asked LD if a cross would help and he said it didn't matter what it was, a cross was gonna help and that he'd been sleeping with his.

I talked about it with Fred too. He didn't figure it was the Devil at all but was the ghost of old Collins. He said he thought about it being a person but they'd have to be crazy and mean, and that there were only two crazy men around and one of them was Uncle Lex, and he was so old and blind he couldn't do all the stuff had been done, and besides he wudn't mean. The other was Red Bill Rogers, who was crazy and mean but had a stove-up leg and couldn't climb the cliffs. The more I thought about it, the more I figured Fred was probably right. It bothered me though that there were tracks, because I had never heard of ghost tracks.

To be on the safe side, I decided to ask LD how you made a cross. He gave me the measurements and told me to make it out of pine 'cause that's what the wood was in theirs. I said it made more sense to make it out of oak because it would last a lot longer but

he said it ought to be pine because all the crosses he'd ever seen
was pine.

I got on it that same day. The closest pine thicket was on Mr.
Mac's place and I traipsed over carrying Mom's sewing machine
tape, a handsaw, a hammer, nails, and a butcher knife for barking.
Pretty soon, I had two sticks and it wudn't nothing to nail them
together. It was a good cross, boy. Trouble was it was sticky, being
fresh-cut pine. No matter how much dust I rubbed it with to cut
the stickiness, it was sticky again in no time. Sticky like that, I
couldn't put it in bed with me. I couldn't put it under the bed
either because Mom might see it, so I put it between the springs. I
had some trouble with the pine smell because Mom couldn't figure
where it was coming from. I told her I'd been fooling around with
pine and that was probably it. The cross worked great and in a few
days I felt safe.

It was a fine summer. Fred and me fished a lot and every now
and then Lonnie and LD come down. Everything would've been
perfect except Fred and me didn't have slingshots. Something
always come up that kept Dad from going to see his friend Ike.
Lonnie and LD had their slingshots from the year before, and Fred
was getting down in the dumps because we didn't have anything to
shoot. Finally, one Sunday, Dad said he had to go to see Ike about
a heifer and promised to ask about an inner tube. What he brought
home was a beauty.

I had told Fred that Dad was going to see Ike the day before and
when I got to the barbwire gap to tell him about the tube, he saw
me and we started running toward each other, me yelling, "I got it!
I got it! Whole inner tube. Grade A shapes."

"Hot dog! Whooee!" he yelled, and it was like light shot out
over his face.

"You got all th' other stuff?" I asked.

Fred started pulling pieces of rawhide and yellow Bull Durham
twine out of every pocket. "Got it all 'ceptin' th' handles and we'll
cut some elm for them."

"Where'd you get that much twine?" I asked.

"Pa and Uncle Charlie was a-savin' hit for me 'bout six months now. That's a purty good lot of smokin', six months."

"How come we got to use that? We got lots of white string at th' house."

Fred shook his head. "Hun'ney, white string ain't no good. Always use Bull Durham twine for slingshot bindin'. You make five, six wraps with Bull Durham twine and hit'll stay 'til th' cows come home." He cocked his hands like he was holding a slingshot and said, "Bam, got that big old frog right between th' eyes," then he jumped up in the air and flopped down flat on his back with his head to the side and tongue hanging out. I flopped down too, and we laughed like fools and rolled around on the grass. In a few minutes, we stopped and set up.

"Well?" I said, waiting for him to make the next move.

He didn't though. He just kind of grinned. Then he jumped up. "Well? Well's a hole in th' ground. Hun'ney, let's git t' work!" And we struck out for an elm thicket.

On the way to the thicket we went around a low rim of the volcano hill. It was too steep to plow and was used mostly as a sheep pasture, and like any sheep pasture it was full of little paths about a foot wide. Sheep paths are all alike. Nothing grows on them, not even Bermuda and it'll grow out of rock. This part of the trip was nice since the path was covered with fine dust that we could drag our bare feet in. Fred was feeling great, and come on singing.

Get out th' way, ole Dan Tucker.
Hit's too late for t' get your supper.
Get out th' way, ole Dan Tucker.
Hit's too late for t' get your supper.

Now, ole Dan Tucker was a nice ole man.
Warshed his face in a fryin' pan.
Combed his head with a wagon wheel.
And died with a toothache in his heel.

When we got to the thicket, Fred started checking trees for handles. He wouldn't use just any forked limb, it had to be a perfect Y and that ain't easy to find. It took us forever to get just what he wanted and I thought I'd go buggy. Then we had to bark them. Elm bark don't come off easy and you cut a little too deep you're back hunting forks, so it took a couple more hours just to skin them and cut the grooves around the top. Once we had that done we cut rubber strips about a half-inch wide from the inner tube and tied them over the grooves in the handles with the Bull Durham twine. We made the loaders out of some soft rawhide. Boy, they were pretty. Fred loaded up a rock and took aim at a fence post. Bam! He hit it, leaving a dent in the split locust log. I didn't do so hot, but managed to hit the post third time around.

"Bet you never been a-froggin', have you, hun'ney?" Fred said, grinning at me.

"Not with slingshots," I said.

Fred cocked his head. "Well, that's just what we're gonna do. I been watchin' around th' pond and hit's got th' best crop of bullfrogs in years. Let's go!

"You ever eat frog legs?" Fred asked as we walked.

"No."

"Well, hun'ney, they're good, but you got to keep a tight lid on when you fry 'em."

"How come?" I asked, stopping to pick a nettle out of my heel.

" 'Cause they'll jump right outta th' skillet's why."

"Aw."

"Yeah, I ain't a-lyin'. When your ma fixes them she better put a lid on or they'll come right out on th' floor."

It sounded like a tall story, but Fred had never lied to me. "They taste good?"

"Oh, little like chicken. We ain't had a good mess of frog legs this year 'cause I didn't have a slingshot. Pa's been a-workin' so hard. I'd like to bring him home a mess."

"You can have mine today," I said, wondering if frog legs was kosher. I felt sorry for our dads because they had been working so hard. When Alfred did find a day off, he'd have his old radio on, listening to the Cincinnati Reds. Most of the time, though, he just worked terrible hard.

It was almost three before we got to the pond because we had to pick up rocks for ammunition and get a gunnysack. The rocks had to be perfect to suit Fred, of course. When we finally got started, Fred said he'd lead and that I could get the second frog.

"Keep low," Fred whispered, hunching down. "There's a big one usually sets right in that little nick in th' bank just on th' other side of that willa."

We hunched down more at the edge of the tree, getting lower and lower until we were on all fours and going so slow and quiet you could hear all sorts of sounds around us. At the spot, Fred put in a load and slowly started getting up like he was afraid his backbone would pop and make noise. Finally, he was standing straight as an arrow. You couldn't even see him breathe. Then he raised the slingshot and pulled back until the rubber got tight, then back some more.

Yurrkkk ker-splot, splot, splot, splot and I almost jumped out of my skin as the frog shot out over the water making four or five leaps on top before he sank.

"He's a big one," said Fred. "Half a foot long if he's anything. I'm gonna get him before this day's over," and he didn't seem put out at all about not getting the frog.

"You figured he'll be waitin' next time around?" I asked.

"They always come back. That's one thing about a frog, he'll always come back to th' same spot, and we'll get him if . . . Hey, looky there," he said, changing to a whisper.

"I don't see nothin'," I whispered back.

"Right next t' that clump of brush," and he pointed to a dead limb that stuck out in the water and there next to a twig was the head of a frog. Fred took dead aim and let go. The frog let out a *yurrkkk* and flopped over on his back. He was a big one. Fred picked him up by the hind legs and walked over to a fence post and bam, bam, bam, he bashed its head against the wood until its tongue popped out and it quit wiggling, then dropped him in our gunnysack.

"Hit's your turn, hun'ney," Fred said, and grinned.

I felt a little scared because frogging idn't like fishing. Fishing's easy once you learn it because all you got to do is get a worm on a hook and wait, but if you're frogging you got one shot and you got to hit or you got nothing. Two hours before, I missed a fence post two times out of three and now I had to hit something about four inches long and three inches wide and I figured wudn't any chance. "You sure you want me to try now? I ain't had any practice."

"You ain't ever gonna get good if'n you don't try. Hit don't make no difference you miss, we got lots of time."

"All right, I'll try, but I ain't makin' any promises," I grumbled, and took off in front.

Yurrkkk, ker-splot, splot, splot and a big old frog jumped before I moved five feet.

"Hun'ney, you got t' slow down. You ain't a-drivin' sheep."

"I was goin' slow," I said, kind of mad. "He heard me, is all."

"Well, keep low and sneak up."

"Why don't you get another one and I'll watch," I said, straightening up.

"You ain't ever gonna learn watchin'. You got to get one or I don't shoot another frog."

I knew he meant it, so I slumped low and started creeping along. We'd gone about ten feet and my back got a crick. I straightened up a little and something brown-green caught my eye about a foot away. It was a frog that made Fred's look like a midget, just sitting on the mud, looking at a beetle crawling his way. I knew I had to shoot, but my arms felt weak, my heart pounded, and sweat broke out in my palms. Slowly, I raised the slingshot and pulled back on the rubber until my hand was quivering, then WHAM. The frog didn't even *yurrkkk*. He just flattened and lay there, his whole head bashed in.

"You got him, hun'ney!" Fred yelled.

He was a whopper. Must've been king frog in the pond. I felt great, and rolled it up and down my arm feeling the cold, puffy belly, while Fred was telling me how I ought be ashamed of myself saying I couldn't do something when I got the biggest frog in the pond.

That evening, when we headed up the path around the foot of Cummings Hill we had enough frogs to feed the whole Mulligan family, even though I missed more than I hit. When Alfred saw them, he let out a yell. "Mamie, come here and look!" Wudn't half a minute before all the Mulligans was pushed in around us. We laughed and talked for a while, then I took off home feeling great. I'd just started frogging and come up with the biggest frog in the pond. I couldn't wait to tell Dad and Mom. Berman's was really fun.

9

I pushed away from the gate and headed back to the car thinking about the joys of my youth, walking again through the area where the stock barn had been. The grass was ankle high and I stumbled over something and fell. When I got up I saw a round knob sticking out of the ground. It was green and worn, but there was no mistaking its identity to a 1940s farm boy. This was part of a workhorse's hames. I grabbed the knob, pulled, and brought up a rotten, curved piece of wood attached to rusted metal. I wondered if I had geared Daisy or Gabe with this relic.

I took a deep breath and tried to imagine the smell of the feed room where we kept the harnesses. A delicious odor, harness oil and cattle feed. Perhaps Fred and I had eaten sweet apples on this very spot, lying on feed sacks and dipping the apples in coarse cattle salt. My childhood friends were reborn nostalgically in my mind. Funny, Mom always worried I'd become like them. In retrospect, I had adopted many of their ways of thinking, especially their strait-laced view of what was expected of a man.

Nora's question about one of my colleagues came to mind when she urged me to make more friends. "What's wrong with Jason Tilden as a friend, Samuel? He's bright and humorous. His wife, Regina, is fun."

I didn't answer that Jason's lectures were canned, that his creative work peeled back at least three atoms of depth, and that while

Regina Tilden was fun and nice, I had accidentally walked in on Jason servicing a coed.

No, what I did was change the subject and use any excuse to bring back the bubbly Nora I loved so much. Why the hell hadn't I told her that I couldn't respect a guy who didn't challenge his work and wasn't faithful to his wife? I wondered if I would rat out Jason Tilden if I could call back those years. I doubted that Fred would have done it, or Lonnie. What Tilden did was unacceptable to them. A man did his best at work and was faithful to his friends and his woman or he wasn't a man.

Thoughts of Fred had ricocheted through my mind for several days following Nora's comment. I wondered where he was, and how he was doing. He had wanted to see me again and I hadn't responded. Had he needed me? I didn't know, but I had found excuses why I couldn't make the time. I had lived most of my adult existence by the creed of these hill people, but I sure as hell hadn't followed it that time. Now I had to face them, face Fred, and it bothered me.

I pitched the hames into the grass and walked to the car thinking about the first time the old barn had made a difference in my life. It was 1945 and . . .

. . . I was having a great summer. It turned out to be an even better summer than I thought it would because the war ended. The day it was over, I was standing by the chicken house and heard Dad yell, "Liz! Liz! It's over, Liz! It's over!" and I went running up to the house and busted through the screen door. There was Mom, crying and clapping her hands and Dad just staring off in the distance with his eyes wet and Lowell Thomas talking on the radio. The war was over and my brother Bob would be coming home safe, and that meant more than anything in the world to Mom and Dad. Me too!

We got a call from Bob a few weeks later, and he said his ship had just got into San Francisco, but he didn't know when he would be getting home. We didn't hear from him for quite a while, then one Sunday morning he come walking up the lane, just walking through the ruts in his sailor suit, carrying his duffel bag over his shoulder with a cigarette hanging out of his mouth. I was in the yard, gave a yell, run and flung my arms and legs around his middle, yelling and yelling and him laughing and trying to hold me and the duffel bag at the same time. Soon everybody was there, crying and laughing and having a great time.

Just a couple hours after Bob got home it seemed everybody in the hills knew about us having a boy home from the war and neighbors started dropping in. First the MacWerters; then Rags Wallace; Bess Clark and his wife with Buster their boy; Pers Shanks and his wife, Bea; Mr. Lamb and their boy who had been in the navy; Mr. and Mrs. Shackelford, who was Rosemary's mom and dad; a man and woman who didn't even live around us, who lost their son at a place called Tulage and put their arms around Bob and cried and nobody said nothing for a while; a woman from Middletown and her boy who lost his legs at Normandy; Mr. and Mrs. Langley who lived where the bus turned around on the Dry Branch Road; Mr. Carl Budkins who was also from Middletown and was the best banjo player in the parts and had been on the radio once; Mr. Dillard and his boy JR who had got shot two, three times in France; and lots of others.

Everyone was milling around in the yard, talking and laughing and telling Bob how great it was he was home and what a great thing he had done for his country. Bob just kind of acted sheepish. A couple minutes after Bess Clark got there, he went out to his pickup and brought back a quart mason jar filled with white mule and all the men took some drinks and kept passing it around and suddenly Mr. Mac yelled, "We gonna have us a hoedown, by God," and everybody yelled, "Yeah!" and Dad said all right, he'd clean out the center of the stock barn, throw down some straw, set some planks on sawhorses to put stuff to eat on, and we'd sure as hell have one and for everybody to come back about seven o'clock and tell everybody around they were invited. The women said they'd bring food and get other neighbor women to do the same. Bess Clark, who was short but had a big pair of shoulders, kind of laughed and said he thought he'd just bring something to drink.

Several people said they'd bring their music, including Mr. Budkins, so we knew we were gonna have great music because Mr. Mac was a fiddling fool hisself and most everybody played something in our parts.

Later that day, I saw Fred and asked him about inviting Lonnie and his pa because there was going to be drinking. Fred said we shouldn't invite Lonnie and that he'd understand. As far as LD was concerned, his pa wouldn't let him go because there was going to be music and dancing and drinking and LD's pa didn't believe in doing that because God didn't like it.

You should've seen the barn. Everything was spiffed up. Pretty soon folks started coming in. All the men were dressed in new Levi's and their best colored shirts, and the women wore bright dresses that swung out when they turned around. Bob and JR and the other boys who had been in the war were wearing their uniforms, and everybody was helping get set up for the hoedown. Man, there was a lot to eat. Ham, roast beef, fried chicken, candied yams, Sunday potatoes, peas, corn, beans, squash, four, five different kinds of salads, eight, ten pies and cakes and biscuits with honey, and coffee and iced tea and beer and, of course, white mule.

While people were eating, Mr. Mac began tuning his fiddle and sipped on some of Bess Clark's stuff. It was funny watching him because he was kind of tall and old and skinny and his face was wrinkled and brown but he was rawboned and when he held the fiddle by the neck, about half of it was covered. Pretty soon all the musicians were tuning up while they were gnawing on chicken bones and plunking on guitars and banjos and every now and then tightening the little screws at the tops. It was starting to get dark and people fired up coal oil lanterns and hung them from the rafters or on pegs that stuck out from the big beams between the sheds. They really made a pretty light. Then Mr. Mac and the other players put down bales of straw kind of stacked like and started playing. They could really play, boy, beginning with "Old Joe Clark," and a lot of people were clapping hands and stamping feet and one of them was Rosemary, who was there with her folks and dancing with JR and Bob, but mostly with Bob. I could tell she really liked him and that he liked her and my heart jumped up in my throat. He was my brother and this was his dance and wudn't anything I could say. I kept trying to get up enough nerve to go over and ask her to dance when it hit me I didn't know how to dance. Jeanette Dillard, who was my age, did, so I asked her to teach me and before I knew it I was out there with the rest of them. So was Fred and old Alfred and pretty soon everybody was on the floor dancing, Mom and Dad too, and Naomi with JR Dillard, and the music was playing louder and faster, then Bert Raney and his family come in and Bert yelled, "Yehoo!" and danced around and shook hands with all the soldiers and sailors. While he was dancing he picked up a jug and had a long pull and passed it along and people was yelling "Yehoo!" and dancing like fools and old Alfred was just stomping like mad and Fred was dancing part with Jenny Raney and part with Jeanette until I was laughing fit to be tied, and then Jake West come in with his family, one of which was Joy with her long black hair so pretty and I was dancing with her in a second and she looked like she loved it, but Jeanette didn't so I'd dance with first one and then the other, and pretty soon Bob and the other boys was doing the Virginia reel and I run in and got to dance one reel with Rosemary. When our hands touched, I almost busted. Joy was really pretty with her long black hair but I loved Rosemary. She was a lot older than me, but if she would just wait! I wanted to tell her that so bad but somehow I just couldn't. I come close though, because right after she finished dancing with Bob once and was near the barn door getting air I walked up and started to say something when she looked at me and said, "Hi Samuel. You havin' a nice time?" My throat closed up and nothing come out. Most I could do was just nod, and she laughed and mussed my hair with her fingers and went back to dance.

That was some barn dance. It lasted late and by midnight all the people making music were drunk and laughing. Matter of fact all the men were drunk and the women were trying to get them to come on home while they could still drive. I looked around for Bob but he was gone. I walked around the barn through the hog lot and there he was with JR Dillard, leaning up against the line post where the gate I met Fred on was hung. I could just make them out against the sky. Both of them were really drunk. I stayed low and got up close where I could hear. They were so liquored it was hard to tell sometime what they were saying.

"Ever . . . ever think you'd make it back, JR?"

JR's head shook kind of slow. "Naw," he said. "Shit . . . they don't know, Bob," and he staggered and caught himself and motioned toward the barn. "They don't know . . . if they knowed how scared I been past two years they'd run me right outta here . . . almost shit my pants at Normandy . . . when . . . when we went over th' cliff at Omaha . . . scared all th' way t' th' Rhine . . ."

"Shit, man," said Bob, "you don't have t' apologize. We took a kamikaze on th' flight deck. I was handlin' a quad 40 . . . had th' firing mechanism down and was so scared I couldn't let up . . . almost melted th' barrel. Talk about scared . . . shit . . . I . . . shit . . . once when a torpedo was runnin' at us I don't remember what I done . . . couple minutes my life I don't even remember. We done our jobs, though, buddy. We done our fuckin' jobs."

"Yeah . . . we done them . . . and we got back. Different now . . . don't wanta crop like Dad. Gonna use th' G.I. Bill 'n' get me an education. Not gonna bust that fuckin' sod out there rest of my fuckin' life."

"Me neither. Not th' same now. Somehow, everything has cha . . . changed . . . uhh, I'm gonna be sick JR . . ." and he puked and JR put his arm around him and held his shoulders until finally he quit puking and the smell of whiskey come my way. Bob wiped his mouth and spit a few times. "Thanks," he said.

"That's okay." JR laughed. "Hey man, you better sober up some. That little honey you been dancin' with has th' hots for you."

"Rosemary?" said Bob, and I almost screamed. "Naw, buddy." Bob laughed. "That's San Quentin quail. She's sixteen. Don't need any shotgun weddin's," and they both laughed and I calmed down and went back inside before they could see me.

In the barn, things were petering out and people were either leaving or standing and talking. Alfred was telling Dad about how much he appreciated the show he was getting and how nobody else ever done that for him and how he wouldn't ever forget it.

Fred was standing next to Alfred. When he saw me he yelled, "Hey, where you been?"

"Just went outside for a minute," I answered.

Fred grinned at me. "I seen Joy West watchin' you. She's sweet on you."

"She is not, Fred Cody," I shot back, and Fred run off laughing like a fool and me chasing after him.

10

It was great having Bob home, especially when he and Alfred decided to run a trot line down on the Big Bend bottoms and include Fred and me in. We got started in October. It would've been perfect except I had to be in school. You're supposed to run your lines twice a day, but since I couldn't help on school days Bob just put them out on Wednesdays during the week, then Saturdays and Sundays. He had gotten the use of a skiff from Ben Begley, who lent it to him because Bob was a veteran. That was something because Mr. Begley never had much to do with anybody, and people were a little scared of him. I'd never even seen him.

Our first time trot lining was a Saturday. It was Indian summer and the leaves on the trees were yellow and green and red with a fall smell in the air. We picked up Fred and Alfred in Dad's old Ford, then drove to the edge of Mr. Begley's melon and pumpkin patch and parked. From there, we circled his cabin, not wanting to get close to his dogs. Everybody talked about how mean the dogs were and they come out at us like wolves, snarling and barking and rattling their chains. There was no other sign of life, and if the dogs hadn't been there you'd have sworn the place was empty.

The river was low and hardly moving. It looked like glass until the leaves setting on it would jiggle. A couple hundred foot below Begley's cabin we found the skiff tied to a young sycamore that hung out over the stream. It was a good-sized boat, and held the four of us easy. Fred already knew how to use it, but I had to learn from the start, and it ain't as simple as it looks. To make it worse, the oars was heavy, and everybody could see I wudn't too strong. I got it going, though, and later on I could do a tolerable job of rowing.

We strung the line from the sycamore about a hundred foot across the stream to a willow trunk. Every five foot or so, we lashed on a jingle line and baited its hook with chicken guts or worms. We caught fish, boy. I mean like you never seen! What the four of us caught that time above the Blue Hole wudn't nothing to what we were catching now. There was this one old channel cat I couldn't believe. We were just starting the run and Alfred was handling the boat when the line started swinging about. Bob was taking off fish and rebaiting the hooks.

"Hold her steady, Alfred," Bob said. "I can't bait if th' line's movin' this much."

"We ain't movin'," Alfred said. "Drop th' line 'fore you get hooked, Bob. We're on t' somethin' big! Drop hit quick!"

Bob did, and you could see the main line moving fast back and forth under the water. There was a swirl a couple of minutes later and the biggest catfish I ever saw rolled.

"Hit's a monster cat," Fred screamed, and almost jumped over the side.

"Sit down, Fred. You'll turn us over!" Alfred shouted.

Meantime, Bob picked up a sculling oar and yelled, "Bring her around, Alfred, so I can get a lick at him if he comes up again."

Alfred pulled like mad with Fred and me trying to stay out of his way. The cat rolled again and WHACK! Bob almost cut it in half. It weighed forty-two pound.

In the next few weeks, we ate so much fish I thought I'd turn into one. Wudn't a family in ten mile that didn't get one mess from us and sometimes two or three.

It was a warm fall and everything went fine until near Thanksgiving when it started raining. It kept raining and we knew the river was going to rise and tear up our line. Bob said, wet or dry, we were going to run the line the next day, which was a Saturday.

It was 8:30 when I woke up. We generally got started earlier, so I jumped into my clothes and run to wake Bob. He wudn't there! His bed had been slept in but he was gone. Dad's car was gone too. Bob left me! They run the line without me!

I was screaming mad and took off for the river at a run, down past the Mulligans' to where the Dry Branch Creek was roaring across the road making me cross at Cummings Hill narrows by crawling over it on a tree limb, on past where the Langleys and LD caught the bus, running and crying until I was wore out and had to walk in a cold rain down the lane toward Ben Begley's.

By the time I got to the bottoms, I was wet through my hide. I fell going through the melon patch and got mud all over me. Then here come the dogs. I was so mad I wudn't thinking about them. They scared me and I took off running like a fool toward the river and downstream. I must've really been moving because when I looked up it was nigh a quarter mile back to the sycamore. The dogs were barking their heads off, their big yellow bodies almost being yanked onto their backs by the chains as they leaped up in the air toward me.

The river was something to see, roaring and rolling with big trees coming down it and the water about as brown as the mud in the melon patch. I walked along the edge toward the sycamore. The sound was so loud I could hardly hear the dogs anymore. I could see the skiff now, bobbing up and down and swinging about. All of a sudden, the ground gave out from under my feet and just before I went over the bank into the river I managed to grab hold of a sapling. I was trying to pull myself back up on the bank when I felt the sapling start to give. I looked down and there wudn't nothing under me but water and it was cutting deeper into the bank. Just as the sapling pulled out of the ground a big hand grabbed my wrist and yanked me in the air, then two giant arms wrapped around me and we moved back from the river. I started bawling like a baby and wrapped my arms around whoever it was and hung on.

"It's okay, you're safe. You're safe, son. Calm down. You're okay. Ain't nothin' to be scared of," a man's voice said soft and nice.

Just then rain started coming down in sheets. My face was against the man's neck. I kind of leaned back, and there, through the driving rain, was a wild-haired, red-bearded giant with shoulders wide as an ax handle I knew had to be Ben Begley. I was scared to death but his arms felt warm and good, so I didn't yell. He turned me around then and started toward the cabin carrying me belly down, his big, hairy arm around my waist and hip pressed against my side. When we got past the dogs and into the cabin he put me down, then took off his boots and closed the door. He didn't throw the bolt though.

"Don't worry about nothin'," he said. "Ain't nobody gonna hurt you. You decide you wanta get gone though, ask me first 'cause Cain and Abel'll tear you apart. Understand?"

I did. I was cold and stood there shivering, my teeth chattering so loud you could hear them in the next county. Begley pulled a quilt off the end of his bed and put it on a chair along with a clean towel, then started stoking the fire in the fireplace. "Get out of them wet things," he said with his back to me. "Dry off and wrap that spread around you."

I was more than happy to do that, but being all mud-splattered, I didn't want to get the quilt dirty. "I'm gonna get your covers muddy."

"There's a basin and water in th' corner," he said without turning around.

I cleaned up, then rolled the blanket around me. In a few minutes, the fire was roaring, and I began getting warm. I was hungry, and when he saw me look toward his pantry he got out some biscuits and bacon and a jar of honey, set them on the table, then hung the coffeepot on the fire. His stuff was good, boy, even though I knew the bacon was *traif*. While I ate, Begley sat in his easy chair, lit a pipe, and studied me. Neither of us said anything for a long while.

The cabin was a lot different inside than out. It was pretty and clean as a pin. All the furniture was handmade. There was a red cloth on the table, and a bright yellow cushion on the table chair. Next to the fireplace was an easy chair all cushioned up and covered with mink and rabbit, and a big rug in front of the fireplace made out of the same stuff. The bed was covered that way too. Things carved out of wood was everywhere. Ducks, geese, quail, foxes, bobcats, and groundhogs. And they were all doing something, like this one old groundhog was reared up on his hind legs showing his teeth, and a fox was coming at him snarling. Some carvings were on shelves and little stands, while others were placed real neat on the floor.

"You Bob's brother?" he asked finally.

The sound of his voice caused me to jump even though it was soft.

"Yes, sir," I answered.

"I'm Ben Begley," he said, and we nodded to each other. "Your brother and them other folks didn't run th' line this morning. They come, but th' river already got it."

We sat for another thirty, forty minutes not saying nothing, just listening to the rain beat on the roof and flood down the one little window. Then he got up and went over to a trunk and got out some clothes. There was a shirt, Levi's, and even underwear.

"Put these on," he said after warming them.

They fit almost perfect. I wondered how he come by the clothes but I didn't ask since it wudn't any of my business. He kept looking at me, and it made me feel funny. I wudn't scared, which was odd, because everybody around was a little scared of Ben Begley even though he had never hurt anyone. But here I was, in his house, wearing his clothes, eating his food, and sitting by his fire with his dogs outside that could rip me apart and I wudn't scared.

"You spend a lot of time on th' river?" he asked.

"Some," I answered.

"Ever go to th' Little Bend bottoms?"

"Once."

He sat for a time, sucking on his pipe, which had gone out. Then he fired it up again. Big puffs of smoke rolled away from his red beard. "Don't go there n'more."

"Why?" I asked, and started getting scared.

"Just don't," he answered.

Somehow, I said, "Wh . . . why?" and a lump come up in my throat.

Begley smoked for a time, then said, "There's evil in th' Little Bend bottoms."

"You mean a devil?"

He took another puff on his pipe and nodded. "Kinda. Lives in hits own little hell, I reckon," and smoke rolled away from his mouth and curled up around his head.

So there really was a devil in the Little Bend bottoms. LD'd been right. How did Begley know, though? I kept trying to figure out some way to ask so he wouldn't think I was doubting his word but the more I thought, the harder it got until I just went ahead and asked.

"How do you know there's a devil in th' Little Bend bottoms?"

"I just know, son," he said. "And you stay outta there, okay?"

Along about noon, the rain let up.

"Well, I reckon you can make hit home now," he said. "Roll up your pant legs and go 'round by th' oak grove and you'll stay pretty dry. There's a bag over there for your wet stuff."

When I was ready, he started toward the door, but I didn't. I was thinking about the dogs.

"They won't hurt you while we're together," he said, figuring what I was thinking.

We walked past where the dogs' chains come and stopped and he smiled for the first time. When he did, his whole face changed. He was an awful big man, and even with what everybody said about him, being strange and all I mean, his face seemed kind. He was plenty old enough to be my dad, and his curly red hair had some gray in it, especially around his ears and at his forehead, which was deep-grooved and sunburned. His eyes were blue with little wrinkles at the edges, and his nose looked like a crag. His white teeth almost sparkled when he smiled. The rest of his face, except for his upper lip, was covered with a red sailor beard.

"I'd appreciate if you didn't tell about meetin' me or about th' cabin or th' clothes. And don't worry about bringing them back."

We stood for a few seconds. Then he said, "What's your name?" That's when it hit me I hadn't told him. "Samuel Zelinsky."

"Take care, Samuel," he said, as I started to walk off.

"You too, and thanks," I called. "And don't worry. I won't tell."

By the time I got home I was soaked, and boy did Mom raise hell. Bob and Dad had been out looking for me, and it was tough explaining where I had been and where the clothes come from because I couldn't tell them Ben Begley's. Just as well I couldn't because then I'd've been in real trouble. Finally, I lied about the clothes and said I got soaked on the way to the river and some people down there lent me the clothes but I didn't know their names. Nobody believed a word of it and for the next while I hardly got to go anywhere.

11

It was very hot and I was beginning to get tired. More time had slipped by than I had budgeted for the first day. I decided to go back to the hotel, have a swim in the pool, eat dinner, then read until bedtime. I walked back to the lane and just as I got to the gate, a car turned into what had been the entrance to the MacWerters' driveway. I hailed the driver, who stopped. I came to his open window. "Excuse me, sir, do you live on this farm now?"

The man was about forty-five, well-dressed, and looked me up and down. "Are you Mr. Higgins?"

"No, my name is Zelinsky. I'm just visiting. Why did you think I was Mr. Higgins?"

The man tilted his head toward my old gate. "That farm belongs to a Mr. Joshua Higgins. I've lived here two years and I've never met him. I'm told he's old, difficult, and bought the farm just to spite his wife. Apparently he's owned it for a long time. It's a huge place. He has someone who raises his tobacco and a little alfalfa. Other than that, no one farms the land."

"Are you a farmer?"

The man laughed. "I'm an executive with IBM. I work in Lexington. Someone else works my land. I just enjoy it."

"Do you know the name MacWerter?"

"I came here from Albany, New York. I wouldn't know anyone you're looking for."

That was disappointing, but not unexpected. I got in the car and drove to my hotel.

Three hours later I had finished my swim, eaten dinner, purchased a bottle of my favorite Kentucky bourbon, filled my bucket with crushed ice, and relaxed with a book and bourbon on the rocks. About ten o'clock I wearied of reading and decided to retire early. But when the lights went out, my brain refused to take the hint. I was so lonesome. "Nora, I used to believe in ghosts. I wish you would show up. I'll speak hillbilly to you if you will. That's a promise, Nora."

Her spoken name brought memories. We met in my second year of graduate school at NYU. I was living on a stipend that kept me poverty-stricken. Then, a windfall! My parents, who had always struggled financially, were now doing well and had sent me a one-hundred-dollar birthday gift. To celebrate, I went to a bar in Greenwich Village. After the bartender poured my drink, I discovered I had forgotten to add the money to my wallet. I was a dollar short and trying to placate a screaming barkeep. Suddenly an arm materialized from behind me, slammed a dollar on the bar, and a woman's voice said to the bartender, "There's your dollar, jerk. Now shut the hell up!"

That was my introduction to Nora Epstein. For the rest of the evening we wandered Greenwich Village and talked. Nora was twenty-two, a senior at NYU, about five-foot-five with a pretty face, black hair, large dark eyes, and a breathtaking figure. She was also fun, the only joy I had encountered in New York. I hated the city. I considered it dirty, vulgar, loud, violent, overpriced, and inhospitable. Yet Nora was a New Yorker, and she was joy.

We had been seeing each other for about a month when she offered to make us dinner. My kitchen was a disaster. The refrigerator leaked and only one burner operated on the grungy gas stove. My cooking utensils were an iron skillet, two pots with loose handles, and a pasta strainer. In the "silverware drawer" were two knives, two forks, and one spoon. But I had four plates, four bowls, three regular glasses, and, for some reason, a champagne glass.

Into this stark culinary landscape came Nora, bearing groceries. Steaks, potatoes, dinner rolls, the makings for a salad, and the crowning touch—a bottle of red wine. I can still remember her initial reaction when she saw the kitchen.

"Oy vey!"

We feasted, laughing and talking across from one another, our meal teetering at times on the peeling vinyl top of my unstable card table. When we were together, cold, hard, New York City warmed and softened.

After dinner we drank the rest of the wine as we danced to music from the radio. Somewhere during "Stars Fell on Alabama," we kissed. Then we kissed some more. And then we slowly danced into the bedroom where we gently disrobed each other, slipped between the sheets, and made tender, passionate love. A half hour after we finished, we made love again. This time even more passionate, and with a bit more abandon. Then we talked and stroked each other. My God, her body was beautiful. Eventually we fell asleep in each other's arms.

A siren outside the hotel brought me back to the present. I got up, poured myself another shot of bourbon, then went back to bed. Soon I returned to my reverie. I thought about waking up that Sunday morning after a perfect night. I was in love and desperate to whisper it to Nora, but I was terrified. We had known each other such a short time and I wasn't sure how deep her feelings went for me.

I worried that if I got serious too soon, I might lose her. How could she know how she felt in one month? But then, what did I know about Nora? We had talked at length about literature, politics, philosophy, Judaism, and a little about me. We hardly ever talked about Nora. When I told her I was born in Kentucky, she retorted that no Jew was ever born in Kentucky! I was either the second coming of Christ or lying. I stared at her sweet face. God, I loved her! While I was getting back into bed, she woke up. She smiled and stretched like a beautiful cat. "Good morning, sweet prince."

"G . . . good morning," I stammered. "Want some breakfast . . . or are you too tired?"

Nora laughed as I realized the double entendre. I could feel my face turn scarlet.

She giggled. "I am tired, but it's the sweetest tired I've ever been. Come here."

I was happy to enter her arms, and even happier to hear at our climactic moment, "I love you, Samuel . . . I love you, Samuel," partly smothered by kissing lips and gasps for breath and my own voice, which shouted, "I love you too . . . I love you, Nora!"

I was engaged! Sort of.

A few days later, I met Mr. and Mrs. Epstein. Both were teachers in the New York City public school system, both children of immigrants from Eastern Europe, both political liberals, and neither had ever been to Indiana, the state where we bought our farm after leaving Kentucky. Dinner brought many questions about how a Jewish boy wound up on farms in Kentucky and Indiana, all of which I answered clumsily. I left their home that night feeling they would have been more comfortable if their daughter were seeing a New Yorker, but the fact that I was in graduate school and Jewish gave me a leg up, even if I was a barbarian.

In mid-June of the year Nora and I met, I bought an ancient Chevy and drove my fiancée from Brooklyn, the city of homes and churches, to Crawfordsville, Indiana. It was during that trip that I was to learn that living with Nora would never be dull.

We were traveling through the heartland when she saw a bumper sticker that read:

IMPEACH EARL WARREN

She screamed. I almost wrecked the Chevy. She could not believe Republicans actually existed and that she was now "surrounded."

Nora knew nothing about a farm and her reactions to agrarian life were fun to watch. One night, she came upon Dad decapitating the main course for our dinner. Her later description of the event, including the chickens flopping around with blood flying from their headless necks, would have made Kafka faint. She did not eat the chicken.

She learned where veal comes from and I, a lover of veal scaloppini, could never again order it in her presence.

When one of our cows went into heat she asked my always practical father if he would put the cow and bull in the barn so they could have privacy. My parents talked about that every time we visited.

In the end, however, my entire family loved the bubbly, happy, ever curious, and always enthusiastic Nora. She was everything my parents wanted for their son, more than I ever dreamed would fall in love with me, and she sent a buzz through my high school classmates that the Kentucky hick had a gorgeous New York girlfriend. Jennifer Walding, one of our school's cheerleaders and the sexual fantasy of every Harlan Jeffords High male, actually crossed the street to speak to me! And to meet Nora, of course, who I suddenly realized was more beautiful than the now widening belle of HJH.

A year later Nora and I were married in a reform shul two blocks from the Epsteins' Brooklyn home and "only one subway change" from where my own mother had been raised. The barefoot boy from the Kentucky hills, naked except for his Levi's, now met the man he had become, tuxedoed and yarmulke-clad, standing in front of a Brooklyn rabbi.

It took me four more years to get my doctorate. Nora made our living doing social work for the city and I added a little money as a teaching assistant. Then I had a bit of luck. Leland-May College, a venerated little Ivy League clone set in an idyllic New Hampshire town, was looking for a junior faculty member with a background in Victorian literature. They were offering a year as an instructor, following which they would decide whether to offer a tenure-track position. A year later I joined the Leland-May faculty with a mediocre salary, one suit, two ties, two pairs of shoes, and a very happy young wife.

It was getting cold in the hotel room. I turned down the air-conditioning and sat on the edge of the bed. I got my wallet off the nightstand and hunted through the pictures until I found one of Nora and me. It had been taken shortly after we moved to New Hampshire. I took a sip of my drink and gazed at the picture, then put my thumb over her image. I felt as though I ceased to exist. I put the wallet back on the nightstand, turned off the light, and tried to sleep.

I couldn't. The early years at Leland-May rolled through my mind. I'd finish work, change into running shorts, put my teaching materials and clothes into a suitcase, and jog the three miles home. Nora and I would play a set or two of tennis in the summer, make dinner together, eat, and then make love, sweet and gentle or wild and crazy. We were so happy.

Except for once a week. Once a week we would get together with another faculty couple for an evening out. Nora looked forward to these forays, but I didn't. I tired of hearing about colleagues' wealthy families and the wonderful universities that multiple generations of their kin had attended. During my recruitment I was required to give my complete biography and it became known that I had been raised on a farm. Also, that I would become the first of Leland-May's Jewish-sharecropper professors. Negative comments about scholarship students' backgrounds bothered me, and I heard a lot of them when I ate lunch at the faculty club.

"You know, Samuel, if the O'Brian kid doesn't make it here, he can always tend bar for his father. There's something to say for being a Boston Southey."

I brought my lunch after a few faculty club lunches and ate in my office. I never told those stories to Nora.

And then there was the research my colleagues were publishing. A reworking of previously plowed ground, fodder used to swell their curriculum vitae for advancement purposes. Their work rarely took on difficult issues, which in retrospect was not my affair. Yet I found the self-serving mediocrity intolerable. I said nothing at the time, but I put a lot of effort into making the kids I taught think, instead of just parrot back my ideas.

And the academic backbiting. One of the couples we socialized
with most frequently was James Northwich (of the Philadelphia
Northwiches) and his wife, Deanna. James was older than I and
had just made tenure. All tenured faculty sat on the tenure-track
committee, and James immediately began wielding his power to its
fullest extent. For example, one of the qualifications for tenure at
L-M was punctuality. It was obviously meant by the authors of the
document as a means of dealing with chronic offenders. You always
knew the candidates James didn't like because he would comb the
file for evidence of noncompliance. If he found anything that could
be so construed, he would write a letter to that point and have it in-
corporated in the applicant's permanent file—regardless of whether
tenure was offered! It quickly became known to the junior faculty
that James Northwich was not a man to be crossed if you wanted
to make tenure. Nora liked Jim and Deanna, so I said nothing to
her about the situation and suffered through our evenings with the
couple.

For the most part, I spent as little time with the faculty and
administration as possible, choosing instead to concentrate on my
teaching and budding research.

Nora, without knowledge of the facts, considered my colleagues to be "normal." A little arrogant perhaps, but not bad
people. "You," she said, "are too judgmental." As a consequence of
my being "judgmental" we had few real friends, just acquaintances.

Nora knew some of the things that had happened to me and my
family the last three years we sharecropped, because Dad would
answer her questions about our years in Kentucky (although he did
it in his own political fashion to protect me). As a consequence of
Dad's disclosures, Nora wanted me to return to Kentucky and "ex-
orcise my demons," which she felt were the cause of my solitary
ways.

I didn't think I had any demons. I had put Kentucky behind me
and saw no reason to dredge it up. Besides, Nora could never tell me
why I should go back, only that she thought "my problems" lay in
Kentucky and a return visit would benefit me.

I didn't think I needed benefiting. What the hell, I didn't hate my colleagues, I just didn't think they were all that much. I couldn't relate to them. They weren't bad people. They were just . . . different from me. So much so that I felt uncomfortable around them. Somehow our ways of looking at things were not the same, and I had a right to my way of life! I was happy with my work. I was happy with Nora. We had each other and that was all I needed.

Then again, I hadn't had a real friend since Fred and Lonnie. I missed them, especially Fred. Lonnie and I had been friends but Fred and I had been *best* friends. At one point, I decided to go back and see him, but a lot of time had gone by and I wasn't sure he'd be all that happy to see me again. Somehow, I never got around to making the trip.

The clock on my nightstand said it was after three. I swallowed the remainder of the whiskey in my glass and got further under the covers. Nora had been gone over a year now. Somehow, the core of my soul had been buried with my love and what remained was a purposeless shell. Did she know that I would feel this way? Was that the reason she made me promise to return to Kentucky after her death . . . to find a reason for living?

12

I woke up thinking about Fred. There had to be some way to find him other than just checking mailboxes in the area where we once lived. I got an outside line, then dialed information. There was nothing for a Fred Cody Mulligan, or for any of our other neighbors who might have known the Mulligans. How could people just vanish in two generations? To my astonishment, Google was no help. The earth seemed to have swallowed everyone I knew from my childhood! I began getting hunger pangs and went to the hotel restaurant for breakfast.

That breakfast was the kind of feast that, had my daughters been present, would have led them to faint. Four pieces of thick-cut hickory-cured bacon, three eggs sunnyside with plenty of pepper and salt, grits, and two biscuits with heavy butter and lots of honey. Big Southern biscuits, by God, not those skinny little Yankee things. Biscuits that stuck to your ribs, and, of course, coronary vessels, which my nervous physician was vigorously treating with prophylactic drugs. Furthermore, the food was chased with four cups of coffee. What the hell, I was seventy-two years old and I was going to go out with a smile on my face.

While I ate, I people-watched, especially the kids. They were well-scrubbed, well-fed, probably well-educated, and judging from their behavior, spoiled rotten. I wondered if, by age ten, they had ever performed a day of hard physical work. I thought about my comments to Candy and Penny concerning my years in Kentucky. I really had worked as I had described. I was expected to contribute to the family's quest to make a living. Sharecroppers' kids never even thought about it, they just started doing. Then again, we had something these kids didn't—a degree of freedom they never even knew existed. Everything was planned for the modern day kid. I doubted that any of them ever knew the joy of making a slingshot, going barefoot all summer, making their own fishing pole, or being out of sight of their family for days at a time. Free! Free as though floating in warm, breezy air. Even though what we did was often risky.

Ben Begley came to my mind. Had it not been for Ben, someone other than Samuel Zelinsky would have gotten the Johnson-Goldsmith Prize, because I would have been dead. The thoughts of that fall and winter long ago came to my mind . . .

. . . We had a light snow in early December and it got below freezing for the first time. Everybody was busy stripping tobacco and on the way to school we would see big trucks heaped high with burley all covered with a tarpaulin and going to Lexington to be sold. We were more than three-quarters done with our tobacco stripping and Dad had sold the first half. It weighed out a ton to the acre and averaged fifty cents a pound, which was tops for the market. Every evening, Mom and Dad would sit side by side in the living room going through magazines about farms for sale and talk about what kind of place to buy in Indiana. Dad said that if the second half of our tobacco crop sold as good as the first half, we'd have almost enough money for a big down payment.

That kind of talk really shook me up! I was happy Mom and Dad were going to get what they wanted, but buying in Indiana meant leaving Fred and Lonnie and LD, and I'd never had so many close friends. I didn't feel bad too long though, because our Christmas school break was coming, which meant three weeks to have a good time. I had some money too. I'd been getting fifty cents a day for doing up all the chores after getting home from school so

Mom and Dad could keep stripping tobacco. With that money, I could buy Christmas presents. I wanted a Lash LaRue neckerchief for Fred, things for my family, Lonnie, LD, and something really nice for Ben Begley. I hadn't seen Ben since that day he kept me from drowning. I liked him too, and felt sheepish about not having gone to see him. I couldn't figure out what to buy him though. Then one day Dad had to go into Spears where there was a general store and I grabbed my money and went along. Wandering through the store I saw a three-bladed knife behind a glass case. The longest blade was four inches and heavy. There was a three-inch middle blade and a little blade about two inches long that was skinny and come to a point. I had never done any fancy whittling but you could tell the blades were perfect for working wood. It was eight dollars. While Dad took care of his business, I saw other presents I wanted and decided to go ahead and buy now. The storekeeper's wife kept following me around.

"Do you want somethin', young man?" she asked finally.

"Yes, ma'am," I answered. "I'd like this stuff I picked out."

"Hmm," she said. "That costs money, y' know."

That burned me. She was lookin' down her nose at me! "I got plenty money," I said, stacking my presents on the counter. "How much is this?"

"Let's see your money first," she said, and I started digging in my pockets and making a pile of dollar bills on the counter. While I was piling, her husband come in and said, "You're Mr. Zelker's boy, ain't you? You buyin' somethin'?"

"I was thinkin' 'bout it," I answered, "but don't nobody want my business."

"Huh!" he said, and looked at his wife, who smiled kind of funny.

"Why sure we do," she said. "I just didn't know who you was, honey. I thought maybe you was some of them riffraff comes in here," and that just burned me more.

"I'll total this right up," she said, and then did. "Yes, sir. Is they gonna be anything more?"

"I'll give you five dollars for that three-blade knife in th' case."

The woman glanced at her husband, who was frowning. "Uh, well, that's about an eight-dollar knife, honey," she said to me. "We can't sell hit for five."

I checked her total and saw it would take two and a half dollars more than I had. The store owner stood at the cash register while I looked for something else.

"Tell you what," the owner said. "It's Christmastime. Sell it to you for six."

"Five-fifty," I said, and, man, I couldn't believe I said it. Neither could he.

Then he laughed and said, "Okay, hit's a deal," and that's how I got Ben's knife.

13

I was busting to give those presents to everybody and the week before Christmas, when all the family was together, I gave them out. They were the first presents I had ever given and I felt great saying, "Merry Christmas and Happy Hanukkah" and Mom said just "Happy Hanukkah" and I said, "Yeah," and everybody laughed. It was a good time, boy, especially for Dad and Mom who had just shipped the last of the tobacco. We kept hearing on the radio how the tobacco crop was short and how the price was gonna go up. Dad said that with a little luck, this coming year would be our last on somebody else's place.

The next morning, Fred come over and brought me a birch flute he made and I gave him his neckerchief. He really liked it and it looked fine hanging down over the top of his shirt, cowboy-style. We were out in the front yard where Fred was trying to teach me how to play my flute when up our lane come a hunched-over man. We knew it was Mr. Shackelford from the way he walked. When he got to our front fence he said, "Hello boys, how y' doin'?" and before we could tell him he said, "Samuel, where's your pa?"

"In th' kitchen," I answered.

Then Mr. Shackelford said, "Would you go inside and get him for me?"

I was about to say he could go on in, but Mr. Shackelford knew all he had to do was knock and his asking me meant he didn't want the women to hear. When I told Dad, his eyebrows rose, then he stood up. Mom didn't say anything, but as we went out the kitchen door she and Naomi were heading toward my bedroom window. Fred and me followed Dad to the front yard gate, where he and Mr. Shackelford shook hands.

"How y' doin', Ed?" said Dad.

"Pretty good 'til this mornin'," Mr. Shackelford answered.

"What's wrong?" and Dad got a worried look on his face.

"Morse, I just found the damned'st thing in my back sheep pasture. One of my bucks was killed."

"Dogs?"

"Naw, hit wudn't dogs. No dog ever done nothin' like this."

"What?" said Dad, and his thumbs went into the belt of his Levi's.

"Well, hits neck was broke and th' hindquarters taken. Carcass was cut with a knife."

Dad's eyes kind of squinted, then he said, "Sounds like you got a thief on your hands, Ed. Wonder who it could be. Most folks around here won't eat mutton."

"Yeah, I know. Anybody around here was in hard straits, they'd take chickens or hogs or maybe a calf. Nobody'd take a buck."

"Must be somebody from Lexington."

Mr. Shackelford glanced at Fred and me and his voice dropped lower. "Morse, that ain't the strangest part. Hits eyes was gouged out. Hits male organs was taken too."

Dad stiffened. "What!"

"Swear t' God. Both eyes gouged plumb out and nuts cut off."

"Crazy man," Dad whispered, and him and Mr. Shackelford stared at each other.

So did Fred and me. The Shackelford place wudn't far from the river and a straight shot to the cave where we found the bones and bloody stick.

"Come see hit, Morse," said Mr. Shackelford, and they started toward our car.

Fred and me followed, but Dad motioned for us to stay. "Tell

Mom I have something to take care of with Mr. Shackelford," he said. "I'll be back in a little while. Oh, and Samuel, don't mention anything about th' sheep. I'll tell her, okay?"

"Okay," I called, and they drove off down the lane.

When they were gone, Fred took a deep breath and blew out slow through his puffed cheeks. "Hun'ney, hit's a crazy man what was in th' cave!"

"No it ain't," I said. "It's th' Devil!"

Fred shook his head. "Can't figure hit that way. Devil don't have t' eat mutton."

I looked away, not wanting him to see how scared I was. "It's th' Devil!"

Fred didn't say nothing for a while, then asked, "Why you think hit's th' Devil?"

I was stuck. I couldn't tell him Ben told me. "I just know is all," I said.

Fred didn't ask again because he knew I'd say if I could. He kind of moved his no-heel around in the grass and waited for me to say something else.

"You figure we ought to let our folks know about th' cave and th' dog?" I asked.

"Hit ain't up t' us alone," he said. "Before we go tellin' anybody we got t' talk hit over with LD and Lonnie. 'Specially Lonnie. We'll get a hiding, but his pa might really give him a beatin'. When Mr. Miller gets drunk, he beats up on everybody. He knifed a man once when he was drunk. My ma won't let me go t' their house."

I could see his point. "I didn't know it was that bad. Maybe we could leave Lonnie out of it. It happened a while ago and nobody will remember he was with us."

Fred mulled that over, then scraped his no-heel around. "That's a good idea, but we still got to get together and talk. LD and Lonnie'll be in church Sunday and I'll get a meetin' time set up for early next week. How's that?"

"Sounds good t' me," I answered, then I thought about Lonnie's present. "Hey, will you take Lonnie's present t' church with you so he'll have it in time for Christmas?"

"Sure. You got one for LD too?"

"Yeah, but I'm gonna deliver it personal. I hope Lonnie won't get sore about me not givin' his th' same way."

"Lonnie'll understand. Don't nobody go t' their house less'n they have to."

After Fred left, I got LD's present, stuck Ben's knife in my pocket, and took off, after telling Mom what Dad said and promising to be back to do my chores. She didn't say much about my leaving, which was odd, because I hadn't gotten to do much since the trot line thing.

I had never been to LD's house before but knew where it was from talking to him, so I took a shortcut across the back of Cummings Hill. When I got to the top, I was looking down at the last valley before the Big Bend bottoms. There, in an open field, stood a little white house with a lot of oak trees around it. Smoke was pouring out its chimney. In back of it was an outhouse, a toolshed, a smokehouse, and a stock barn. On the other side of the oak trees I could see their tobacco barn with stalks piled around it from stripping and the bare field where they had cropped. Everything was covered light with snow. I couldn't see anybody but the Ford was in the yard so they had to be home. I knew dogs were somewhere too, so when I got to the last big tree before the yard with a low limb I could jump up to, I started calling.

The second I called, two dogs run to the front of the house barking their heads off. I kept on calling and soon a tall man come to the door. He shushed the dogs and yelled for me to come on down. When I got there, LD was beside him.

"Pa, this here's Samuel I been tellin' you about," said LD, and Mr. Howard shook my hand and said to come in.

Inside, it was hot, and there was a great smell of hickory burning in the fireplace. There was a pine smell too that come from the Christmas tree in the corner.

"Sarah, come here and meet a neighbor," Mr. Howard called.

I could hear dishes rattle in the kitchen, then a round-faced, kind of fat lady, wearing a red apron with flour dust handprints on it and a yellow dress, come in smiling, her hands still having little bits of bread dough on them.

"Mama, this here's Samuel," LD said.

Mrs. Howard smiled, and her whole face lit up. "Well, land sakes, I was about t' think I was never gonna meet you people. I've been meanin' t' get over a dozen times. LD talks about you every day. How'd you like some biscuits and honey?"

I was about to say, *Hi* and *Yes ma'am* to the biscuits, but Mrs. Howard had already rustled back into the kitchen, talking as she disappeared.

LD and his dad and me sat in the living room. It was a nice room with a linoleum floor and lots of chairs and a table. There were pictures on the walls of Jesus and things from the Bible everywhere and some other people. One of them was a little girl. LD saw me look at her.

"That's my sister," he said.

That surprised me since LD never mentioned he had a sister.

"She's gone home," Mr. Howard said, and I knew what he meant. "She got th' typhoid back about ten year ago and went home. I almost went too but Jesus didn't want me yet."

Mr. Howard kept talking about going home and I just sat not knowing what to say.

"Your pa finished strippin' yet?" he asked, finally.

"Yes, sir," I answered. "He just finished."

"Going to be a good sale, praise th' Lord. Th' Lord's providin' for us, son. This here's one of them fat years. They'll be lean years comin'. That's what old Daniel told th' King, and hit's been like that ever since. You know about Daniel and th' King?"

I answered that I'd read a lot about Daniel and Nebuchadnez-zar, which I had in my book *Heroes of Israel*.

"You read a lot from th' Old Testament?" he asked.

"Yes, sir."

"That's good, that's good," he said.

Just as Mr. Howard was about to say more about the Old Testament, LD's mom stuck her head in and said our biscuits and honey was getting cold.

In the kitchen, Mrs. Howard began talking to me and I thought she'd never stop. I didn't think I was ever going to get LD alone to tell him about the sheep and give him his present. After what seemed like forever, Mrs. Howard went to the living room with some wood for the fire and I grabbed my last biscuit, tucked the present under my arm, and nodded at the kitchen door. As soon as we got outside, I started walking toward the tobacco barn.

"What's wrong?" LD asked, as we trotted along together.

"Tell you at the barn, and Merry Christmas," and I handed him his present.

"Why, Samuel . . . I thank you. I . . . I don't have one for you. I asked Mom and Dad and they said y'all don't give Christmas presents."

I could tell he felt bad and was wanting to give me something so I said we take them but for another reason and that if he wanted to, he still had time. He perked right up until we reached the barn, where I told him about Mr. Shackelford's buck.

"Lordy, what we gonna do? Hit's a crazy man and he could kill somebody!"

"Huh-uh. It's th' Devil," I said, and I was positive the way I said it. LD turned pale as a ghost. I really shook him up bad and had to calm him down.

"What makes you so sure hit's th' Devil?" he asked, after we had talked awhile.

Suddenly, I realized how dumb it was saying that and was mad at myself for making the same mistake twice. I moved over to a pile of tobacco stalks and sank down on them. "I just kind of figure's all," I answered. "You said it first, y' know."

LD came over and sat on the pile, beside me. He pulled up a cuff of his Levi's and scratched, then looked at me kind of sideways. "What you think we ought do?"

"Fred says th' four of us need t' talk about it. He's gonna meet you and Lonnie after church and make a time when we can all get together."

LD's eyes opened kind of wide. "That's a good idea. Man, I'm gonna get a hidin'. Pa'll razor strop me somethin' awful. Reckon hit's comin' t' me, though," and he seemed to feel as bad about not having told as about the licking he was gonna get. Not me, boy! If the Devil done it, I knew wudn't anybody going to do anything about it because a human idn't going to win against the Devil. I was going to say not to tell anything.

14

LD and I walked back to the house, where I thanked his folks for the biscuits and honey, then I headed to the Big Bend bottoms. The hills were clean and quiet with tracks everywhere, mostly fox, bobcat, and rabbit. Patches of rabbit fur said some critters got their bellies full.

A hundred yards or so from Ben's house, Cain and Abel came for me and I was scared until their chains stopped them. I kept coming until I got close, then stood talking to them. They just kept on barking. Nobody come out so I yelled, "Mr. Begley!" and let a few seconds go by.

"It's Samuel, Mr. Begley!"

The dogs were barking so loud I thought he couldn't hear, so I kept on trying. I was about to quit when the door opened and there stood Ben in a checkered blue shirt and Levi's. "Cain! Abel!" he said, and the dogs trotted back to him and sat by his legs. "Come on in, Samuel."

I walked to the door, took off my muddy shoes, and went inside.

"How y' been?" he asked.

"Okay," I said. "You been okay, too?"

"Yep." We sat down, him in the big chair and me in a small one. He grinned. "You get a hidin' from your folks when you showed up with new clothes that day?"

I grinned back. "They were put out, and I haven't gotten to do much since."

"What'd you tell them?"

"I said I got 'em from some people down on th' river I didn't know."

He laughed. "They knowed that was a lie."

"Yeah," I said, "but I couldn't think of nothin' else," and he really laughed.

"I can see how that might be hard t' explain. Anyways, it's good t' have you here. You're good company. Most folks just bother me. You havin' a nice Christmas?"

I said yes and noticed a Christmas tree in the corner about four foot tall hung with popcorn chains, pine cones, painted carvings of animals, and a big carved wood star at the top. About the prettiest Christmas tree I ever seen except there wudn't nothing under it, which struck me as lonesome. I reached in my pocket and pulled out the whittling knife. "Merry Christmas."

Ben got up and stood rock-still, not saying anything. I was beginning to think maybe he wudn't going to take it, then he swallowed and spoke so quiet you could hardly hear him.

"Thank y', Samuel."

I don't know how long he rolled the knife around in his hand, then he put it under the Christmas tree. "I'll open th' blades Christmas mornin'," he said, then began looking around.

I knew he was searching for a present for me and figured it was going to be one of his wood carvings. If that was so, I wanted the mallard duck and let my eyes fall on it long enough to tell him that was it but not so long he'd have to give it if he didn't want to. He did, and we shook hands, and I said, "Thanks."

That duck was something to see, boy. It looked like it would take to wing in a second. It was as big as a live duck, which was going to cause a problem at home since I couldn't tell Mom and Dad where I got it and a wooden duck a foot long is hard to hide.

We sat by the fire for a while, then I brought up the buck. He didn't seem at all surprised.

"You say hits eyes was gouged out."

"That's what Mr. Shackelford said. Eyes gouged out, nuts and hindquarters cut off."

"Hmm," he said, and lit his pipe again, which kept going out. "You say this happened inside a mile from th' river?"

"Yeah, I'm pretty sure."

Ben kind of sucked his teeth. "Be a long way t' get there from th' low bottoms if you didn't go up th' cliff, wouldn't it?"

"Aw, yeah," I said. "It's three mile anyway down to where the sand-bar starts, then you got t' double back. Maybe seven mile that way."

"Any footprints around th' carcass?"

"Mr. Shackelford didn't mention any."

"Don't make no difference," Ben said, getting up from his chair and standing with his back to the fire. "Hit's moving inland from th' river. Hit can climb th' cliffs again."

"Th' Devil's got t' climb cliffs?" I said, that not making any sense to me.

"Two-legged ones does."

He meant a man! That was what he meant last time! "You think a man done this?"

"Man, or somethin' like it, anyways."

"Why you think that?"

"I know th' river. I've been livin' here over ten year and I seen his tracks down on th' Little Bend. Big man. From his footprints, he's bigger'n me, and I'm six-three and two hunnert. He never left th' river until a few year ago, then he began goin' over th' cliffs until, somehow, he got hurt and just stayed on th' bottoms. His tracks have changed."

"Cloved," I said.

Ben's eyes widened. "You been foolin' around that water hole, ain't you?"

I told him the whole story from start to finish, the blue hole, the dog, the cave, how we got away, and even about burying the fish. "It happened before you told me not t' go there," I said, "and none of us been back since."

Ben sat back down in the chair and threw a leg over one of the arms. "Samuel, you better tell your pa about this. I don't know for sure, but this fellow may start t' come further inland from th' river if th' winter gets rough. Hit's a lot easier t' kill a sheep than get rabbits and squirrels when you got a gimpy leg. Besides, most of th' game has left th' Little Bend. If he comes out further, I'm afraid of what he might do. Ain't nothin' in him but hate."

"Has he killed anybody before?" I asked, thinking about the people that was drowned or maybe, I thought, found dead in the Blue Hole.

"Don't know. I heard the same tales you probably have about th' Blue Hole. One thing I do know is he does crazy things. I seen his doin's before on some animals down near that water hole. Nobody's done nothin' about th' goings-on 'cause up to now hit ain't bothered them directly. Hit's like any other kinda evil. Folks will let hit grow until hit gits t' be a monster, then hit's too late t' do anything without a lot of people gettin' hurt."

He was still talking about evil and it scared me. "LD said his pa wanted to float a Bible out on th' Blue Hole. He said it would drive th' evil out of th' water."

Ben shook his head. He had started shaking it the second I said, "float a Bible" and kept on shaking it until I finished, which surprised me because up to now I'd never seen him do anything without thinking it through first.

"Naw, you don't fight evil holdin' prayer meetins. Ain't nothin' wrong with that pool of water. People say all sorts of fool stuff. Never let fear rule you, Samuel. Someday, when this is all over, you need t' go out and swim in that thing. Show you're not afraid of th' stupid things people say. But, when it comes t' evil, you got t' face hit down, and you got t' do hit just soon as you know for sure hit's evil. There's lots a signs whoever's doin' this is crazy. Mean crazy. If nobody does nothin', he's gonna hurt or kill someone. I hope your pas don't wait that long."

I knew what he was driving at. We had to tell. Man, were Dad and Mom going to be mad. I'd never get to go anywhere and might lose my friends. Fred would get a licking, but LD would get razor stropped and it would be a real bad one. That brought me to Lonnie. I remembered what Fred said about Mr. Miller when he got drunk. I wondered if maybe he was the one doing everything when he got liquored up. He had already knifed somebody. Even if he wudn't the crazy man, he still might hurt Lonnie real bad if we told.

By this time, I had been sitting and thinking just like Ben. I decided to ask him about Lonnie's pa being th' crazy man, and th' problem with Lonnie even if he wudn't.

"Lafe Miller's a mean drunk," he said when I finished. "He might kill somebody when he's boozin', but he ain't your crazy man. He don't have a cloved foot."

I felt like a fool for not thinking of that. "Mr. Miller might still hurt Lonnie, though."

Ben sighed. "Yeah, he might. Y'all better not say Lonnie was along. But you got t' tell about what you saw. Hit won't wait, Samuel."

I knew he was right and it was going to spoil everything. I kept trying to figure some way around it, but nothing come to mind. By this time, it was nigh two o'clock and I had a long walk ahead of me and stood up. "Well, gotta go. Be seein' you, and Merry Christmas," I said.

Ben got up too, but he didn't say Merry Christmas. "Got a gun at your house?" he asked.

"Dad has a shotgun, and Bob has a .22."

When we got to the door he put his hand on the latch, then stopped. "Ever shoot 'em?"

"Shot th' .22."

"Shoot pretty often?"

"Once," I answered, beginning to feel funny at his questions.

Ben kind of sucked his lips, then went over to a long box all shined up and opened it. Inside were three of the prettiest guns you ever lay your eyes on. There was a 12-gauge shotgun with the stock carved with birds and rabbits, a .22 carved with squirrels, ground-hogs, and trees, and another rifle of some kind that was the prettiest of all. It was carved with deer and a wild boar with his head down coming at a hunter, its tusks white ivory.

"Come on," Ben said, pulling the two rifles out of the box along with a couple boxes of shells. "It's time you got a little more shootin' under your belt."

We walked outside and the dogs growled. He shushed them, then put a cardboard box against a tree and smeared some mud in a little circle four or five inches wide on its bottom. We backed off about a hundred foot, and he handed me the .22.

"Put one in the middle of that mud," he said.

The rifle was a single shot just like Bob's with the sights the same and all, but from a hundred foot I just ticked the box edge. Ben watched for four or five shots, then said I had a good eye, but there was a couple of little things he had picked up would help and for me to watch. He shot four times and trimmed out a hole in the center of the mud no bigger than a dime. Then he showed me how to relax and a bunch of other things and pretty soon I was hitting the mud circle almost every time. We shot up the whole box of shells. Then he picked up the big rifle and fired. Man, it was loud. I asked what kind it was.

".30–30," he answered. "Deer rifle. You like to shoot it?"

I sure did. It was a lot heavier than the .22, and I had trouble holding it. When I shot, it kicked like a mule. Dang nigh deafened me too. "Wow, that's sure some gun."

He laughed a little short laugh. "Ain't much use around here, though," he said. "No deer, no hogs. I keep it oiled and cleaned. Just in case."

"In case of what?" I asked.

He kind of squenched his mouth. "Anything . . . what kind of shells you got for your .22?"

"Shorts," I answered.

When we got back to the cabin, he took out a box of .22 long-rifle hollow points.

"Shorts is for practice," he said. "I want you t' take these with you. A .22 short won't stop nothin' unless you hit it in th' head. A long-rifle holla point will spread and take down a big critter. You understand what I mean?"

I did. It scared me and he could tell. When he spoke again, his face and voice was hard. "Samuel, I want you t' clean that rifle and put it where you can get hold of it quick. Hide these holla points near it. If some night your daddy ain't home and somebody tries t' break in, aim like I showed you and shoot right at th' center of his chest. Then put in another shell and keep shootin' 'til whoever it is has gotten away or is dead."

I felt weak all over and Ben could see it, but his face stayed hard. "I know what I just said is awful, but that thing down on th' river is gonna hurt lots of people if he ain't stopped. I don't want you t' be one of 'em."

I understood, but I knew I couldn't do it. Wudn't any way I could shoot anybody.

It was past three o'clock by this time, so I said goodbye, put my duck under my arm, and headed for home at a trot. The cows were in the field where the Dry Branch Road turned off the Cuyper Creek Pike, and since I had to get them up for milking anyway, I decided to go home by that direction. As I trotted I thought about Fred. I had to tell about the crazy man not being a devil but I knew he'd ask me how I knew. I couldn't tell him that Ben Begley had told me. And another thing, I was going to have to change what I said when the four of us met. Thinking got to bothering me so much I decided to quit thinking.

When I passed the Mulligans', I took to the hollows, not wanting to explain my duck. Things were going well for the Mulligans. I could see the edge of their strawberry patch. It had really taken off. Dad and Alfred had made a deal so Alfred could have a share in an acre of tobacco by working some for us and got Mr. Berman to say it was okay. Mr. Berman also let Alfred make a garden and grow a couple of acres of corn so he could feed some hogs. Alfred's sows had pigs and they were really growing. As soon as the pigs were weaned, Alfred killed one of the sows, and they had lots of pork to eat. They had a great show going.

The closer I got to home, the more I worried Dad or Bob would see the cows and come out to meet me and ask about the duck. I needed time to think what to say. I couldn't tell them I got it from Ben. When I got to the last pasture before the stock barn, I ran ahead of the cows and hid the duck in the hayloft.

That night I got out the rifle. Since Bob was home, I had an excuse to clean it, and asked him in front of everybody if I could keep it in my room. He said sure, then Mom got upset and said she didn't want me fooling with guns, and Dad and Bob said all the ammunition was in Mom and Dad's bedroom and it couldn't hurt anything. She didn't like it, but she finally agreed. As I curled up under the quilts that night I had a funny feeling, boy. I had a rifle in the corner just six foot from me, and a box of fifty long-rifle hollow points hidden about a yard away. If the crazy man busted in, I was set to kill him and I knew I couldn't do it.

15

Monday morning, which was the day before Christmas, I got up extra early. There was a lot of stuff to do. First, I had to get a safe place for my duck. I couldn't leave it in the hayloft since Dad was helping with the chores now that stripping was over and would find it if he threw down hay. The second thing I had to do was go to the Mulligan house and find out when we were going to meet with Lonnie and LD. The duck problem got solved when I remembered a loose plank in the barn's feed room. It was a perfect hiding place.

When the chores were finished, I grabbed a handful of biscuits and took off for the Mulligans'. Fred was out splitting up kindling and wearing his Lash LaRue neckerchief.

"Hidey, Fred Cody," I said, and he grinned, letting the hatchet dangle in his hand.

"Hidey, hidey, Samuel. What you doin' here so early?"

"You know dang well what," I said, and we both laughed.

"Tomorra afternoon," he said, and picked up another chunk of wood and split it.

"Christmas Day? What about LD? His dad and mom ain't about t' let him go anywhere on Christmas Day except church."

"That's why we're meetin' in th' Howards' tobacco barn. Lonnie asked his ma if he can visit me, and she said yes, so we'll come together. One o'clock sharp. Wanta come in for a while?" and he sunk the hatchet in the end of a log.

"Naw, got t' get back. Don't want Mom missin' me t'day if I'm gonna be gone tomorra."

"Wonder what she'll say when she finds out about th' Blue Hole," Fred muttered, and he sounded like he had made up his mind about how he was going to vote.

"It won't be good," I answered. "She's just gettin' over th' trot line thing."

Fred sighed. "Hit's a bugger."

On the way back home, I got to thinking about my duck. A pretty wood duck under a plank floor was no fun. I might as well not have it. On the other hand, one more big lie to the folks that they figured out was a lie was going to be bad, especially if I had to tell about the Blue Hole. The more I thought, the more it was plain that if I was going to get my duck into the house, it had to be done honest. I wudn't going to tell about Ben though, no matter what. I'd give up the duck first. The only thing to do was go man-to-man with Dad about secrets and see if a boy had the right to keep one, then let him take it up with Mom. If he said yes, everything was okay. But if he said no, I didn't know what I was going to do.

That afternoon, Dad and Bob went into the living room after dinner and left Mom, Naomi, and Debby washing dishes. That was about as clear a chance as I was going to get. When I got in the living room Bob was reading a book and Dad was in his easy chair and had just finished filling the bowl of his pipe from his Prince Albert can.

"Dad, do you think it's okay for somebody to keep a secret from even people in his own family?" I asked.

Bob looked up from his book for a second, then started reading again, but Dad kind of looked at me funny.

"Well . . . I haven't really thought about that. Never came up before. What kind of secrets we talkin' about?"

"There's a Christmas present I got and I don't want t' tell who gave it. Everybody's gonna ask so I want t' know before bringing it in th' house. Th' person who gave it don't want me t' tell who they are."

"You're goin' to open it here, huh. We all get t' see what it is?" and he was looking at me suspicious like and I was getting more nervous.

"Yes, sir," I said, and swallowed.

Dad lit his pipe and I could see that he was thinking while he did it. "Well . . . if it isn't somethin' that we don't approve of, I don't see why not. I'd never ask you to break your word," and he started puffing and picked up his newspaper. "Fine with me under those circumstances. Wha'd Mom say?"

My heart sank. "I . . . didn't ask her. Thought maybe you would for me."

"I think you should," he said, turning a page.

He had me. Now, I wudn't ever going to get my duck in the house. The tears started coming into my eyes, and I fought back crying.

Dad blew out some smoke, then looked at me again. "Your mom's a fair woman, Samuel. If you'd come forward instead of tryin' t' get around her, you'd find that out."

I nodded, but I didn't say anything. After a while, I wandered out to the lane and threw rocks at the fence posts. Finally, I went to the barn and took out my duck. It was the prettiest thing I ever owned and I wudn't going to get to keep it. It was my duck, and I had a right to keep it. I was going to tell her that too.

Mom, Naomi, and Debby were all sitting at the kitchen table when I come through the door. "I want t' keep my duck, Mom," I said. "It's a present, and it's mine, and I don't want t' tell who gave it t' me."

"Your what?" she asked, and everybody stared at me.

"My duck. He was a Christmas present, and it's not right not lettin' me have it."

Mom's face was a blank. "I didn't say you couldn't have a duck," she said slowly. "It's okay by me. Why are you so upset?"

"I'm not upset!" I shouted, almost crying.

"Then why are you yelling at your mother?" come a voice, and there stood Dad behind me, his eyes turning pale blue and his temples starting to beat. "From now on when you want something from your mother, you ask, young man. And you do it in a decent tone of voice. Now go put your duck in th' backyard with th' chickens. After you apologize t' your mom! And don't worry, nobody cares where you got it. I'll tell you something, though. A duck won't live alone with chickens unless it's raised with them," then he went back into the living room and rustled the newspaper.

I stood there for a while trying to hold back the tears, but it wudn't any use. Mom put her arms around me and pulled my face against her chest and talked soft while I held on and sobbed. When I quit crying she said not to worry. If we fed the duck well, it might be okay.

"It's a wood duck," I said.

Her eyebrows went up. "Oh, a wild duck. Well, still, if we treat it well, maybe . . ."

"No, no, it's made out of wood. It's carved."

"Carved!" Naomi yelled, and everyone started laughing, including Dad and Bob in the living room.

"I'll go get it," I said, and went racing out the door. You should have heard 'em, oohing and aahing and running their hands over it and saying how beautiful it was. Nobody asked where I got it and that was one thing nobody was ever going to find out.

The next morning drug by slow. I spent a lot of time with my duck, learning the little grooves and bumps and feeling the beady eyes. After dinner, I asked about taking off if I got back in time for chores. There was no problem, because Mom didn't want my feelings hurt again.

By 12:30, I was at the edge of the Howards' oak grove, circling downwind to keep the dogs from catching my scent. That brought me to the barn's back door. Inside, it was just like all the other tobacco barns in our parts, with a big center driveway. From there, it was forty foot straight up to the coxcomb roof. There were sheds on both sides about as wide as the center but not as tall since the roof had a steep slope.

Everything was sectioned off into fourteen-foot squares by twelve-by-twelve oak beams, which reared clear up to the roof. Crossbeams of the same size were stacked one above the other every five feet inside the big squares. From the crossbeams, wooden two-by-fours were spread apart, and it was on these that the tobacco was hung.

Most of the Howards' tobacco was stripped except for half of one shed. I climbed to the highest spot where unstripped tobacco was still hanging and sat on one of the beams. I was starting to get cold and lonesome when there were sounds of the front barn door being pushed on its slide. I slipped between the hanging tobacco. The door slid shut again, and LD come into view in the center of the driveway.

"Fred . . . Samuel . . . y'all here?"

I snickered, but I didn't answer.

"Anybody here?"

I stayed still.

"Whoa . . . Fred . . . Samuel . . . huh, ain't nobody here yet," and he walked over to a cultivator and sat down on the seat.

I whistled softly, and he jumped.

"Fred?"

I didn't make a sound, except to giggle.

"All right now, y'all come on out. I know you're here. Fred?"

Just then a ventilator panel opened. It was Fred and Lonnie.

"LD, that you?" called Fred.

"Yeah, hit's me. Old Samuel's here, too, but he's a-hidin' some-wheres."

"Samuel," Fred called soft.

"Lookin' for me?" I said, and stood up on the crossbeam.

They laughed, and I said I'd be right down.

"Naw, stay there," said Fred. "Hit's a good place t' hide if anybody comes."

Pretty soon all four of us were sitting on a big beam talking. For a while we just talked, then it turned quiet. It was Fred who got down to business.

"Well, boys, what we gonna do?"

Nobody said anything until LD choked a little and said, "About what?" and I almost fell off the beam laughing.

Fred didn't laugh. "About what we know . . . th' Blue Hole 'n' all."

LD shrugged his shoulders.

"You think we ought t' tell, don't you?" I said, looking at Fred.

"Yeah, I do," he said. "Whata you think?"

"I think so too. We wait 'n' that crazy man might kill somebody."

LD stiffened on the beam and stared at me. "Crazy man!" he shouted, and Fred went, "Shhh, somebody'll hear you."

"Reckon they will," LD went on. "Day before yesterday, Samuel was a-sayin' hit was th' Devil. T'day hit's a crazy man. If I'm tellin', I want t' know what's goin' on. What made you change your mind t' hit bein' a crazy man, Samuel?"

He had me. I couldn't think of a thing. "I just changed it," I said. "A body can change his mind, can't he?"

It got quiet for a while, then LD said, "What good's hit gonna do t' tell if hit's a crazy man or a devil? Ain't nobody goin' t' do nothin' about it. Everybody's scared t' go around th' Blue Hole. If hit's a crazy man, he don't hurt nobody but what goes around th' Blue Hole. Ain't ever hurt anybody we for sure know. Killed one or two old bucks. If he is a crazy man, somebody will see him one of these times and shoot him. If hit's th' Devil, then you know dang well nothin' we say's gonna make a difference." LD looked around at Lonnie and Fred, then said, "Ain't no reason t' tell."

"We don't tell and hit is a crazy man, he might hurt somebody," said Fred.

"Don't nobody know that," said LD, shaking his head. "Folks been tellin' about him for years and ain't anybody but old man Hackett seen him. Nobody believed what old Hackett said. He was out of his head half th' time. Everybody knows that."

"That old crazy man's movin' inland from the river," I said, kind of hot.

"He comes out one time," said LD, "and you don't even know if hit was him. Hit could've been anybody makin' hit look like a crazy man. I don't want t' get tore up for nothin'. What about Lonnie if we tell? You know what his pa might do t' him?"

"We don't have t' say Lonnie was with us," said Fred.

"Yeah," I said, "we can say it was just th' three—"

"Aw sure," yelled LD, and it sounded like he was starting to cry. "My pa asks me was that so, and hit'll mean I have t' lie some more. I won't just get a lickin'. My pa can beat just like Lonnie's when he's mad, and he don't have t' get liquored up."

"My pa don't beat!" come a hot voice. "Y'all can do what y' want far as I care. But if'n hit's really that much of a bother t' LD, I'm ag'in tellin'!"

It was Lonnie. In the argument we clean forgot he was there.

LD calmed down after Lonnie spoke and we just sat there, Fred and me wanting to tell, LD and Lonnie not and them with the most to lose.

Fred kind of shook his head. "Supposin' he kills somebody, then we'll have t' tell. We'll really be in trouble."

"We don't never tell!" said LD. "We just forget about hit. If we hadn't gone fishin', we wouldn't have seen th' dog or cave or nothin' and he'd still be comin' out just th' same. That would be just like us knowin' now and not sayin' nothin'! Wouldn't it? Wouldn't it?"

LD's face was set hard and he kept looking back and forth from Fred to me, then said loud, "Well . . . wouldn't it?"

Fred scraped his no-heel on the beam and muttered, "I reckon."

I didn't say anything. After Fred spoke, LD quit looking back and forth and just looked at me. His eyes felt like they were shoving me off the beam.

"Supposin' he does kill somebody," I whispered. "It would be our fault."

"He ain't a-gonna kill nobody," LD said. "He ain't ever that we know of for sure and ain't no reason why he should now."

"He . . . he's . . . all hate," I said, and I was choking on the words.

Fred had been eyeing me suspicious since LD started in on me.

He knew I wudn't telling everything and it bothered him. "How d' you know that?"

This was it. I had to tell about Ben or give in. Since we had been on Berman's I had heard several people say they wondered why Ben was like he was, why he didn't let anybody in his cabin and only come out to take your money for melons or go to the store for supplies. He didn't have a mailbox. He was a loner and lots of folks didn't like him. If I said what I knew, everybody would be down there in no time and I didn't know what they'd do to Ben.

It was dead quiet, everybody waiting for me to say something. I had promised Ben. Given him my word. He had saved my life and was my friend and all he asked from me was not to tell I knew him. No real man would tell after that. Dad would never do that, or Fred, or Lonnie. I started shaking so bad I almost fell out of the barn. "I just know's all," I whispered.

"Then why don't you say?" barked LD. "You know so much whyn't you tell us!"

"I can't!" I answered loud. "I won't!" I straightened up on the beam, reached one hand around a two-by-four, and began swinging down. "Don't say nothin'. I wanta keep it a secret."

16

For the next few weeks, things were kind of cool between the four of us. I was uneasy being around Fred because I always figured he was wondering where I got my information. LD never asked again either, and he really didn't seem to care now that he got his way. Lonnie . . . well, Lonnie was Lonnie. He wudn't going to worry about nothing until he had to. No more sheep got killed, and people seemed to forget about what happened. I started thinking about why I was still sore and decided that what was bothering me was LD won the argument fair and square and done it so well even my best friend sided with him. After that, I done all I could to make us all friends again and it worked.

It had been an easy winter, and it was going to be an easy year. You could tell by the signs. The rains come early, the grass followed soon, and the cows began pouring milk. In the fields, volunteer crops started growing anyplace that had been planted the year before. That was the big sign. When the croppers saw that, you couldn't keep the smiles off their faces.

We had some luck too. During the winter, Dad bought three sows. They had twenty-five pigs and only one of them was a runt. By May, the pigs were on their own so we shipped the sows to market and they brought a big price. Dad said if hogs just stayed around twenty cents a pound until we were ready to sell the pigs, we'd make enough money to keep a lot of sow pigs for breeding, and if the price anywhere near held for pork we would have a few thousand bucks coming in two years down the road and be able to buy a real place instead of just a little rock pile. Every day he'd call the hogs at slopping time: "Whooee, pig, pig, pig. Come here you sweet-smellin' down payments," then he'd laugh like crazy. Mom was happy too. It was the same thing each night. They'd go over newspapers that advertised land sales and Mom would see one that said things like four bedrooms with two baths and shower and built-in appliances, and Dad would look and say things like "Yeah, and it's got a thirty-foot silo that could let a man really feed and do it cheap."

The talking didn't stop there either. Sometimes I'd wake up at night and hear strange sounds out of their room that didn't make any sense to me. Everything was great except when they brought up moving to Indiana. That was the only place they seemed wanting to buy.

In May, Bob's college let out and something happened that changed the whole summer. One evening in early June, I come home from the Mulligans', and Bob's old bicycle was sitting outside the kitchen porch. It didn't look at all like the beat-up wreck we'd kept for him while he was at war. Now it was perfect. It had new tires and fenders, and its chrome shined, even in the twilight. A back carrier had been added too. It was beautiful. I run my hands over it and measured the height from the seat to the pedals against my body. It was a tad long, but if the seat was lowered I could pedal it if I knew how, which I didn't. Inside the house everybody was sitting around the kitchen table. Bob grinned at me.

"Whadyasay, stranger?" he asked.

"Hi," I said.

Dad kind of leaned back in his chair. "You see how Bob fixed up his bike?"

"Yeah," I said. "Looks great."

Bob stuck his hands in the pockets of his Levi's. "I added a light up front, and a rack in back. It's gonna make gettin' back and forth t' classes a lot easier."

"Yeah," I said again, turning sideways and looking out the screen door. "It's really nice. How 'bout givin' me a ride?"

Bob looked out through the twilight and said, "Well, guess I could. We got a headlight if it gets too dark. Let's go."

I ran outside and got on the luggage rack and waited. Man, he was slow. When he got there, he said to hop off until we got out in the lane because he didn't want to risk chipping the paint on the yard gates.

The minute we were through the front yard, I got on the luggage rack again.

Bob shook his head. "You can't ride there. Get on th' seat."

"Where you gonna sit if I'm on th' seat?"

"I'm not," he answered. "I'm gonna help you learn t' ride. It's your bike, Samuel. Happy tenth birthday, six months late. Have a good time this summer."

I couldn't believe it! Then I saw the whole family standing behind us and I let out a yell and grabbed Bob around the waist and gave him a hug and everybody started laughing and saying, "Congratulations!" and "Mazel tov!" and "Happy Birthday!" We had a big old time.

Learning to ride took longer than I figured because it was a man's bike and it really stretched me to reach the down pedal even with the seat low. I took a hundred spills. I didn't worry about the skinned knees and hands, just about hurting the bike. I couldn't wait to tell Fred but I wanted to be able to ride before I showed him. In a couple of days I could stay up. Then, in just a few hours, it seemed like I could do everything.

The next morning, Saturday, I headed for the Mulligans'. Climbing the big hill from our gate to where it got easier was tough, boy. I had to stop beside the sweet apple tree and push. When I reached the top of the hill it was pretty much flat to the Dry Branch turnoff, then downhill steep for a ways, then it flattened to the Mulligans' gap. I come down that last stretch flying. Fred was on me before I scooted to a stop.

"Samuel, where'd you get that bike?"

"It's mine," I said, trying to catch my wind. "Bob give it to me. Want a ride?"

"Lordy, yes, hun'ney," he yelled, and got on the rack.

It was mid-afternoon before we got back to the Mulligan house. When we pulled into the yard, Fred went inside for a drink of water and I sat on the bicycle puffing. Thelma Jean came out and walked to just in front of me.

"Hidey, Sam," she said. "Your new bike's not very purty. It shoulda been brown 'stead of blue. Old blue bicycles got by everybody. You ought take hit back and make them paint hit brown. You know, that old headlight of yorn ain't nothin' but a flashlight all fancied up. Hit won't be a month 'fore the batteries go dead and leak. You better take them out right now," and she reached down to take hold of my headlight.

I caught her hand and said, "Leave it alone. If it needs fixin', I'll fix it!"

That was the only thing wrong with going to the Mulligans'. You had to put up with Thelma Jean. She was dumb and stunk all the time. Just then Fred stuck his head out the door and said his ma wanted me to come in and say hi.

I parked the bike against the house and followed Thelma Jean inside.

The living room was crowded. It was small to begin with and Mamie and Alfred's bed filled a quarter of the space even though it was shoved into a corner. There were only two chairs, one being Mamie's rocker, and the other more of a stool than anything else because it didn't have a back. Alfred was sitting on it. Bea and Pers Shanks were there and they were using the two kitchen chairs. That didn't leave me anyplace to sit because Fred, Annie Lee and her new boyfriend, WK Lensfort, and Thelma Jean took up all the space on the bed.

I was pooped, boy. I leaned my shoulder against the wall and sort of catnapped. Pers and Alfred were talking about crops and things and Mamie talked with Bea and kept an eye on WK and Annie Lee on the bed. Fred had told me Mamie didn't like WK being around Annie Lee because he was twenty-five and Annie Lee was only fourteen.

"Yeah," said Alfred. "That's right, three hundred dollars' worth of strawberries, and they didn't take but a little while t' pick. Old Berman, he brought th' crates, and th' kids and Mamie did most of th' pickin'. Got one hundred and fifty dollars for my part. Easiest money I ever made."

"Boy, boy, Alfred, that's great," Pers whispered. "Y' know, them berries ain't done yet."

"That's what I think too," said Alfred. "With the hog and to-bacco money, I'll have enough for my mules, a plow, secondhand disc harrow, and maybe a few other things. I can't make all I need for rentin' for two years, but that's okay 'cause old Red Bill says he'll wait."

"Red Bill sure can be a cuss though, can't he? An' that idjit boy o' his gives me th' willies."

Alfred laughed. "Red Bill's meaner'n a by-God's fifth cousin. Hit's just good bidness makes him want me t' crop his place, though. Idjit don't bother me. Five, six years from now I'm gonna own a little piece a land just like you."

"I hope so, Alfred. I sure do."

During the next week, I taught Fred to ride. He caught on quick and we would take turns pedaling. Trouble was, we didn't have any-place we needed to go. Somehow just pedaling lost its fun and in a couple weeks we found ourselves doing the same things we were doing before I got the bicycle and wishing we had a reason to use it.

17

I was no longer acclimated to the Kentucky heat and humidity and was exhausted by the time I returned to my hotel room, having driven to Clay's Ferry, then around Bourbon County. I ordered a burger and fries from room service, ate them with bourbon on the rocks, and fell asleep with my clothes on.

I awoke at three in the morning feeling restless, and decided to go for a drive. Once the lights from Lexington were behind me, I was enveloped in darkness, save for my headlights and the awakening in the east. There was no one on the road, so I slowed to thirty and opened the front windows. The air was warm and fresh, and smelled of newly mown hay.

Nora would have loved this ride, I thought. For all her feisty nature, Nora had the soul of a poet. She used to write me letters for no particular reason. I would come home tired and discouraged, go into the bedroom to change into casual clothes, and there on my pillow would be a handwritten note expressing the depth of her love and belief in me. Frequently there would be a P.S.: "Tonight I'm going to test your manhood." She would, too! Sometimes after a rousing liaison, while we were still gasping, she would say: "Brooklyn did this to me." Nearly a half century of marriage and I never cheated on my wife.

Tears began to blur my vision. She had pushed me into this odyssey, but now, instead of lessening my pain, the journey brought it back, along with memories better left forgotten.

Nora would never have known anything about my years on Berman's if it hadn't been for Mom and Dad. In retrospect, this trip began during our first visit to the farm in Indiana. Nora had asked Dad about our years in Kentucky, what it was like being a Jewish sharecropper, about the people we lived among and how they related to Jews. She listened with fascination as Dad claimed that he faced very little anti-Semitism among the Kentucky farm folk. The always inquisitive Nora had countered: "Tell me about your life in Kentucky."

Dad had been born in Eastern Europe and, at age twelve, was sent by my grandfather during a pogrom to live with an uncle in America. Dad never returned to the old country. Over the years in Kentucky, he had acquired the great Southern art of storytelling. Nora was fascinated, and the more stories he dredged up, the more Nora wanted to hear. Eventually, of course, they came to the time we lived on Berman's.

I never spoke to Nora about my years on Berman's. Whenever she asked about Kentucky, I always finessed her in my best hillbilly drawl, insisting that I made the best moonshine of any twelve-year-old in our parts. During that first visit to our farm in Indiana, I was standing behind Nora in Mom and Dad's kitchen when she asked Dad for stories about me. Dad saw me shake my head and treaded very carefully.

"Did he get the scar on his arm on Berman's?" she asked.

My father smiled at her. "Nora, I'm going to have to plead privacy here. Samuel is a man now. You'll have to ask him about those years. I hope you understand."

Nora turned immediately toward me.

"We'll discuss it later," I said, hoping that she would forget.

I should have known better. After we pulled away from Mom and Dad's gate to begin our journey home, she looked across the front seat. "Tell me about your life on Berman's."

I must've sighed very deeply because her eyes searched my face in obvious wonder. I asked what was bothering her. Why should she want to know about my childhood? She already knew about my years in high school. Why was Kentucky important?

"Because I'm getting ready to marry a man who is hiding three years of his life."

I answered that I didn't ask about her personal life and that she was the woman I was going to marry. Her response: "Ask anything you want."

I didn't want to know about Nora's personal life before she met me. "Do I have to?"

We drove about twenty-five miles in silence. It wasn't deep-freeze, arm-folded silence, but it was unsettling. I decided to tell her some, but not all. She sensed that the rendition she was hearing had been abridged but already understood enough about her man that she was willing to proceed in bits and pieces over the years.

One night after Mom died, I was having difficulty getting through the loss, and with a few stiff drinks in me, I brought several things into the open. We had been married quite a few years by that time and Nora knew me well. When I finished my story, she told me there was something I should do. I thought she was talking about seeing a psychiatrist and before she could continue I told her that it would be a cold day in hell before I went to a shrink.

Nora laughed. "That's not what I want you to do. But I do think you have a problem. You need to go back to Kentucky, Samuel. You need to go back to Berman's."

I asked her why. How was going back to Berman's going to help me get over my mother's death?

"Probably nothing to get over your mother's death. That will come with time. But I don't think you've made peace with things that happened on Berman's. It's going to make loss of any kind more difficult for you. Fred was your friend and you really cared about him. He's gotten word to your father more than once that he wants to see you, yet you refuse to go."

I told her there was nothing in Kentucky for me now and going there would be a fool's errand. She replied that I was unhappy with people in my field of work, that we rarely saw other faculty members, that I was becoming a recluse at my beautiful little college, and finally, that my problems, which she felt were partly due to my past, weren't going away until I dealt with them.

I resented that assessment. I replied that my students liked me, my family loved me, and I didn't give a diddly damn about the pompous asses on the faculty. If my colleagues in the world of comparative English literature didn't like me, that was just tough!

Nora was at least partly right—I got over Mom's death, Dad's death, and the deaths of my siblings. Each was devastating, and through it all, the love and support of Nora and the girls kept me sane. Now, Nora was gone. I still had the girls and I loved them, but my rock had disappeared. And here I was, back in Kentucky, looking for . . . what? I didn't know.

By the time I reached Old Cuyper Creek Pike, the glow in the eastern sky had lit up the clouds. A couple of miles down the pike, I recognized a small, redbrick building on the right side of the road that I had missed previously. Sixty years before, it had been taller and had a belfry. The Colored Baptist Church. I stopped and began wandering the grounds. The building was in disrepair and looked abandoned. I rounded a wall and walked to a window to see inside.

"Who you is, and whatchu want'n in our choich? We still owns this choich 'n' you trespassin'."

I jumped. In the window I could see a form behind me. I turned toward it. The speaker was a black man I judged to be about ninety. He was nearly six foot, skinny, and dressed in jeans, a T-shirt, and a sweater. His shoes were high-top work shoes, nearly identical to those worn by the farmers of my childhood. There was now enough light to see a Cincinnati Reds baseball cap and snow-white, extremely short, wiry hair extending below the cap's rim. His face was dark brown and deeply wrinkled, as were his hands. The right hand was missing a thumb.

"I'm sorry," I said, "I didn't mean to be trespassing. I lived in this neighborhood many years ago and I have fond memories of this church."

The old man stared into my eyes, unblinking and suspicious, and came forward to within a couple of feet. "When you lives heah?"

"Over sixty years ago."

The wrinkled head raised but his eyes never left mine. "Yo daddy a croppah or lan'lawd?"

"Cropper."

"Who you crops on?"

"The landlord's name was Berman. Farm was about a mile past the Dry Branch Road."

The thumbless hand rubbed the white stubble chin with its knuckles. "Don't know no Berman. I crops all time ovah 'round Spears. Who you is?"

I extended my hand. "My name is Samuel Zelinsky. My father was Morris Zelinsky. Did you know anybody who lived down toward the river?"

The unblinking eyes under the baseball cap continued to stare and ignored my hand. Then, slowly, he raised his own hand and we squeezed a handshake since he was thumbless. I could feel calluses. He was still doing rough work at an age when most men just slept through the day, if they existed at all.

"I's Ruggles White. Whatchu doin' heah at our choich this time of th' mawnin'?"

"If I told you that I was just looking for where I came from, would you believe it?"

The old man smiled, exhibiting a mouth that still had a lot of teeth. "Yeah. You old. Lookin' all you and me is good fo'. Too old fo' mischief. I come t'day t' see my mama. She back there," and he pointed the absent thumb toward a graveyard. "What you knows 'bout this choich?"

"Sometimes on Sundays I would stand on the edge of the road and listen to the singing. It was beautiful. I was just a boy, but I loved it. Couldn't go in, of course."

The baseball cap nodded up and down. "Yeah, we could sing it out. Whatchu like best?"

" 'Go Down, Moses.' You had a man whose voice was so deep

it sounded like faraway thunder. *Go down Mo-o-oses,*" I began and we continued together. "*Wa-a-ay down in Egypt's la-a-an'. Tell old Pha-ar-o-o-oh . . . let my people goooo.*"

We both started laughing.

"That Collis Yates. He had a ches' on him big as a barrel. Man, he could sing it out. Lawd himself prob'ly like listenin' t' Collis. He gone now. They all gone. Ain't no peoples come here no mo'. Everybody go to de new choich in Lexington. This here property bein' sold. Dey gone even move de graves. Ain't right." He tilted his head and lifted his saggy eyebrows. "You finds anybody you huntin' fo'?"

I shook my head. "I've checked a lot of mailboxes . . . about ready to quit." Then I reeled out a dozen or so names to see if he knew them. He shook his head until I mentioned Bert Raney.

"Mistuh Raney! Yeah, I knows him. He own that farm 'cross d' road. He full o' mischief, but I likes him. He dead now. He own right over deah," and he pointed.

Bert Raney's old place! I knew precisely where I was now. I could feel my skin tingle. A hundred feet beyond that fence I had forged one of my earliest links with Christianity.

I said my thanks and goodbyes, then crossed the road, climbed the fence, and walked to a mystical spot. I reached up and clutched the air. Sixty-odd years previously, my hand could have been wrapped around a tent pole. It was about this time of the year. What a day that was . . .

18

J ust after the Fourth of July, Fred come over all excited. There was going be a revival near Harper's Corner.

"Hit's gonna be great. We just got t' go, hun'ney!" he said, sitting down on our front lawn and checking his slightly stubbed toe.

"What's so special about this one?" I asked. "There's always revivals goin' on."

"Hit's Holiness! Th' Reverend Joe Don Baker's gonna be th' preacher!"

Fred could tell that I didn't know the name and was disappointed. "He's the one on radio . . . WLEX . . . don't y'all never listen t' WLEX?"

"Sure we do. We get all our market reports on WLEX."

"Well, th' Reverend Baker comes on on Sundays. I'm surprised you ain't heard of him. He's gonna to be there in person! Everybody's goin'."

It sounded like fun. "You, me, Lonnie, and LD?"

Fred shook his head. "Oh no, they ain't Holiness. Lordy no! LD's pa'd beat th' stuffin's out of him if he went t' anything but First Christian. Lonnie's ma won't go neither."

"Don't your folks care if you go?"

"Naw," Fred answered, picking at a callus on his heel. "Mama said she figured she'd rather have me in church than anyplace else. Figure you can go?"

That was going to be hard. When we first moved in, a preacher had come over to see Mom and Dad about Naomi and me going to the regular church meetings and Dad had told him that when we come of age we could go if we wanted, but not until then. "I don't know," I answered slowly. "Prob'ly not."

Fred snorted. "Your folks just like LD's and Lonnie's."

"No, they're not," I said. "Mom and Dad don't care if I visit somebody's church."

"How come it is then you can't come? You ain't never gone t' church at th' First Christian with LD and Lonnie and me."

It was true. Boy, was Mom going to get upset when I asked her. Maybe Dad too. I would have to really work to get a yes out of them. "When's it start?"

"Thursday at eight. If it don't rain. Hit'll be called off if'n hit rains. Samuel, we just got t' go!" he said, getting up and adjusting his Levi's.

"I'll ask, but I'm pretty sure Mom and Dad will say no."

"Shoot," he sighed, getting up. "First time we get a chance t' use your bike t' really go somewheres, and we can't do hit." Then he slipped through the hole in the backyard fence and left, kicking little sprays of dust with his bare feet.

I waited until after supper to ask Dad. He was reading his newspaper and smoking his pipe.

"Dad, Fred said there was gonna be a revival."

"Eh," he grunted, and didn't look up from his reading.

"He said there was goin' t' be a revival soon."

"Who did?"

"Fred."

"Did, huh?"

Nothing happened. He just kept reading with the smoke from his pipe billowing around his head. "Fred wants me t' go with him to th' revival."

"Does, huh?"

"Uh-huh. Can I go?"

"Oh, I don't think so this time," he said, moving the paper closer and frowning.

"LD and Lonnie's folks won't let them go either since it idn't First Christian. Fred says we're just like th' Millers and Howards."

"Huh!" Dad said, and looked at me over his paper.

"I said . . ."

"I heard you. Samuel, I don't let you go to the Christian Church because I don't want a lot of pressure put on you to convert. Now, that's different than Lonnie and LD's thing."

I nodded and started toward the door to the kitchen. "Fred says that's why Lonnie and LD's folks won't let them go either. They don't want them t' be Holinesses."

Dad's newspaper come down and his body jerked up. "You wait right there! That's ridiculous," he said, pointing his pipe stem at me. "They're Gentiles. We're Jews. There's a difference," and he put the pipe back in his mouth, ruffled his paper, and began to read again.

I thought about what to say next. If he got real mad, I'd never get to go, but if I stopped now, I wudn't going anyway. "I can't see any difference," I said. "Nobody wants t' take a chance on anybody convertin'. I think Fred's right."

Dad stiffened. He knew I was conniving. Still, there wudn't much difference between what we thought from the Howards and Millers. It turned out Dad was thinking the same thing.

"You really wanta go?"

"Yes, sir," I answered.

"You got any idea what they're gonna do? I don't want you handling snakes! If they're gonna be foolin' around with rattlers you're absolutely not goin'! Understand?"

"Does that mean I can go if they don't handle snakes?"

"That means I'll think about it again when you find out what's happening there. *And*, if Mom says yes."

The next morning, I went over to Fred's. "They ain't gonna be handlin' snakes, are they?" I asked, as we wandered through the strawberry patch eating what had been missed at the last picking. "Dad told me I couldn't go for sure if they handled rattlers."

Fred straightened up and stuck his thumb in his Levi's. "Aw, naw, hun'ney," he said, popping a handful of berries in his mouth. "These here are Holy Rollers. I don't go t' no revivals that handles snakes. These folks rolls and talks in tongues."

I had heard a lot about tongue talking at school, but wudn't quite sure what happened. "What's tongue talkin' like, Fred?"

"Why, hun'ney, don't you know what it is talkin' in tongues?" and he grinned.

"Huh-uh."

Fred's grin got bigger. "Well you can see when we get there. Figure you'll get t' go?"

I jammed my hands in the pockets of my Levi's, "Don't know. Helps they won't be handlin' snakes. Dad ain't hot on it, but I think he'll go along if Mom will."

Fred slipped the stem of a big red strawberry between his toes and jerked upward with his foot. The strawberry flew up in the air and he caught it, plucked off its little green seat, and popped it in his mouth. "Just like Lonnie and LD," he said.

I shook my head. "If I tell you tomorra, is that time enough?"

"I reckon. Long as I know in time t' slick my hair down. We got t' leave by 7:30."

When Mom heard about it that night, you'd have thought the Holinesses were going to cut my throat.

"A tent revival! Holy Rollers! One of those wild-eyed, arm-waving, screaming preachers! People rolling around, babbling like idiots! No! Absolutely not! It's bad enough that you run around God knows where with those crazy friends of yours! The next thing you know, you'll be going to church meetings on Sundays, marrying some shiksa, eating *traif* . . . ham, bacon, making moonshine with Bess Clark! No! You're a Jew. Enough already!"

By the time Mom finished yelling, Dad was laughing so hard his neck veins were bulging and Mom, who had been drying dishes, was standing in the middle of the kitchen floor with an iron skillet in her hand that had been waving all over the place. Naomi was at the sink, and I could tell by her face that she was dying to laugh, but holding back. I wanted to laugh too, but I knew if I did wudn't no way I was going to the revival.

Finally, Dad wiped his eyes and said, "M'dom, it's just a tent revival. In the last twenty-five years there've been hundreds around us. Nobody's going to convert him. So far these people have been very careful with us when it comes to religion. Samuel knows who he is. Let's let him see what's goin' on out there, get an understanding of the world that surrounds him."

Mom seemed kind of confused because she put the skillet in the pots and pans cabinet instead of hanging it on a hook where she always did. She had closed the door to the cabinet when it hit her what she'd done and she took the skillet out and hung it up. Then she shook her head at Dad and laughed. "You'd let him go anywhere."

"Now, you know better than that," he answered, and laughed too.

The night of the revival, I started chores early. By the time Dad got in from the field I was finishing up and my hands were killing me from squeezing tits too fast.

"Gettin' done early t'night, huh?" Dad said, leaning against the main post to the stock chute and scratching his back.

"Yes, sir," I said.

"Wanta be there from the start, eh?" He chuckled.

"Yes, sir."

"Ought to see quite a show. Alfred said Mort Thomas was gonna be there."

When Dad mentioned Mort Thomas, I almost jumped off the milking stool. I had only seen Mort a few times, and when I did, he didn't do nothing. You had to get him riled before he'd do anything and Mort always tried to stay calm.

"Alfred said th' preacher tonight's a real Holiness disciple. If anything can rile anybody, it oughta be a real Holiness preacher. What time you go?"

"I got t' pick up Fred at 7:30," I answered. "The tent's down at Mr. Raney's."

Dad ricocheted off the stock chute. "Bert Raney? Bert's one of those people that tease Mort. If that preacher don't rile Mort, Bert will." He stopped talking for a few seconds, then said, "Samuel, if anything happens, you got sense enough t' get out of that tent, don't you?"

I said I did, but what I didn't say was that if Mort started doing it I wudn't about to leave without seeing at least some.

"You stay close to old Fred," said Dad. "He's got a head full of common sense. You do like he does. Fred Cody's not goin' t' get into anything he can't get out of."

The clock said ten minutes after seven as I pushed down the last biscuit and honey and ran out to my bike. I pedaled hard, and when I got to the Mulligans', Fred was waiting by the road. He was so excited he was jiggling.

"Let's go, hun'ney, we're late," he yelled, and jumped on back as I turned around.

It was a hard pull back to the main road because I was already tired, so I turned pedaling over to Fred from there. He took off, being fresh, and all I had to do was sit on back and let the wind fly though my hair and listen to the tires sing. In a few minutes, we come over a rise and there, about a mile away, we could see the tent lit up with people walking in and out in the twilight and the sounds of "Shall We Gather at the River" as we coasted down through pockets of warm and cool air, and went boiling into the gap that Mr. Raney had cut in his road wire fence.

The tent looked like the pictures I had seen of circuses, with a pole up the middle and shorter poles around the sides so people could set out toward the edges. It must have been awful old because the canvas was full of little tears and some of the seams was split. You could see lantern light shine through in lots of places.

When we pulled up, Fred was off the bike in a hurry. "Come on, hun'ney," he said. "Th' preachin's gonna start soon. Come on!"

Inside was maybe a hundred people. Only half of them had

chairs and the rest were standing. Most of those were in the back near the opening, and it didn't look like we were going to see anything until Fred began wriggling between people. The preacher saw us and said, "Let them young'uns up front." It was a great spot. We could see everything. The only bad part was a fat lady behind us that kept farting. Right in the middle of "Old Rugged Cross" she let a whopper. Finally, the singing was over and the preacher started. He was a big man in a brown suit and he had a white handkerchief in his hand that he kept wiping his forehead with. He wiped it a lot too, because it was hot in the tent, and all crammed together like we were it was sweltering. Nobody seemed to notice though because we were all listening. The preacher talked slow at first and I could tell he was warming up like Fred had told me he would. Then he speeded up some. A lot of the time he was looking right at me, and his eyes were big and I began to feel a little shaky. It was like he was reaching inside me and moving stuff around.

"Jesus wept! And when you read the Gospel it ain't hard t' see why. Each of us knows what he said when he was alive, yet we keep on doin' what we're doin' like it don't mean nothin' 'cept in church. But that ain't what he asked of us; he asked that we do right like he taught us t' do right all the time. How many of us are gonna go home t'night, right after this meetin', and start doin' th' same things we been doin' before we came here?"

He stopped talking and looked around and I guessed nobody thought it was a question. When he started again it was like that made him mad because he come at us like a mean bull. He talked about living like Jesus said. He didn't want us to live any lies, he wanted truth!

"You can't go 'round keepin' th' truth inside you and lyin' on th' outside. That's sin! Sin just as sure as tellin' it!" he shouted at us.

I thought about the crazy man and us knowing and not saying nothing while bad stuff was happening to peoples' stock. I looked over at Fred and I could tell he was a little shook up by what the preacher said too and figured it was probably that.

But the preacher never let up and I could hear a few folks talking out loud and then all of a sudden Fred punched me in the ribs and I looked to where he was nodding. There, across the open space in front of the preacher, stood Mort Thomas and right next to him was Bert Raney. Bert was saying lots of "Amens" and "Yes, Lords."

The preacher was getting to going good now, and more people was talking. The loudest voice of all come from the fat lady behind us. It got higher and higher and louder and louder. Suddenly, she grabbed Fred and me by our shoulders, throwed us aside, and staggered into the little clearing, where she fell down jabbering like a fool.

Nearly everybody was talking now, especially Bert Raney, and several were using words that didn't make any sense and falling down, knocking over chairs, and praising Jesus.

All at once, there was this high-pitched scream like a blue jay, and Mort Thomas fell in a heap. He started twitching and quivering all over. Then the quivers turned to jerks, and he began slobbering at the mouth. The more he jerked, the more everybody went crazy, calling and babbling in tongues and flailing their arms and legs with the preacher going strong.

Then somebody hit the center post. I saw it tilt and so did Fred and he grabbed my arm.

"Hun'ney, let's get outta here," he said, but the way out was blocked with people falling and flailing all over the place. Just then, the center post was hit again and slowly tipped sideways. Fred headed for the only canvas we could reach, flopped down on his belly, and tried to squeeze under. He wudn't making much headway until I grabbed the edge and yanked. We were at a seam and it ripped and gave enough room to get through. We got out just as the center post went down. Folks was crashing and yelling, then the sides began to give way, and people started crawling out of everywhere like cockroaches from a breadbox.

Fred and me jumped on the bike and I took off, him hanging on behind. We started laughing so hard, I thought we'd die. It was so bad that a couple miles down the road we had to stop. We were still laughing when I dropped Fred at the Mulligans' and headed home.

While I was pedaling, I got to thinking about the revival. What the preacher said about the truth was right and I knew it and we were lying like mad about the crazy man. I wondered what God was going to do to us unless we told. The strangest thing though was the preacher's eyes and the way I couldn't get away from them and the jiggling feeling they made inside me. The revival was really different from what went on in shul. Everything we did was kind of mournful. The Holiness people had a lot more fun than we did, but they were really scary about all the fire in hell and how if you didn't do what the preacher said, you were gonna burn in it. That really got to me. I figured I'd had enough of Holinesses. I was just gonna be a Jew.

19

I was wore out by the time I got to our gate and couldn't wait to go to bed. As I pedaled up the lane, I got the feeling something was wrong. All the lights were on, and I could make out Bess Clark's pickup in the barn lot.

When I pulled into the yard, a wave of people come out to greet me. Mom and Naomi kept saying, "Thank God! Thank God!" but nobody would say what they were thanking him for. The third or fourth time I asked, Bess Clark answered.

"We had a little excitement t'night . . . matter of fact, your pa and me was 'bout t' come lookin' for you."

"Why?" I asked.

"Come on in, and we'll talk about it," said Dad.

We went in the kitchen and the men sat down at the table while Mom and Naomi started making coffee and putting baked stuff on the table. Dad leaned toward me. "Samuel, did you and Fred have any trouble tonight?"

I thought about how the meeting ended and told what had happened. Soon, everybody in the house was laughing, especially Bess Clark, who doubled up when I got to the part about Mort's fit and the tent falling.

"Any other problems?" Dad asked, when things calmed down. "Did you and Fred see anything strange on th' way home?"

"No, sir. Wudn't anything strange that we saw. Why?"

"Just after you left, Mr. Clark found the carcass of one of his bucks," said Dad. "It was in the field next to Shackelford's and had been hacked up like the other one."

"Its male organs and eyes?" I asked, trying to keep my voice calm.

"Yeah, tongue too, this time. It was a pretty bad sight," said Dad.

"Hit was a awful sight!" said Bess.

There was a rap on the kitchen door, and I heard Mr. Mac-Werter say hello to Naomi.

"Hello, Morse," Mr. Mac said as he come to the table. He was wearing a slicker which I thought was odd because it wudn't raining.

"I got t' worryin' after you checked for Samuel at our house and decided t' come over. Good t' see he's home," and he put his arm around my neck and squeezed and something hard pressed against my head. He opened the slicker to sit down and pulled the longest barreled pistol I ever saw out of his belt and laid it on the table. "What all's happened?" he asked.

"Another sheep killin', George," Dad answered. "By th' time Bess got here, it was pretty dark. We grabbed our guns and lanterns and picked up Ed and his dogs, but by th' time we got there it was pitch black. The sheep had been dead for about a day as best we could tell, but th' dogs were goin' crazy. They cut right through Shackelford's place, then seemed t' lose th' scent at Cuyper Creek. Whatever or whoever did th' killing knows how t' fool a dog."

"Movin' toward th' river, wudn't he," said Mr. Mac.

"Oh yeah," said Bess. "Ain't no doubt 'bout that. Headin' toward them cliffs. He's got t' get outta that stream someplace, though, and that's when we're gonna find where he went."

"Better do it t'morrow early or th' trail's gonna be cold," said Mr. Mac. "Only thing you're gonna have left t' follow that long after th' killin' is some tracks. Unless you had a bloodhound. Ordinary dog won't pick up a human scent after two days."

"Sheriff's bringin' three of them tomorrow," said Dad.

"Sheriff's goin' out with ye?" said Mr. Mac, and his eyes lit up.

"Sheriff, Morse, Ed, me, 'n' Rags," said Bess. "Wanta join us, George?"

"Hell yes! Whoever's doin' this is closer t' me than he is t' Rags! What time?"

"Just before dawn," said Dad. "Meet here at th' house."

"I'll be here 'n' have old Betsy," said Mr. Mac, and he patted his pistol.

"Doubt there'll be a need for guns," said Dad. "Hope no one gets an itchy trigger finger."

I could tell Dad was trying to cool things down before the crazy man was shot to pieces. Mr. Mac nodded that Dad was right, but Bess didn't. He sulked awhile, then looked at Dad with his eyebrows raised. "Morse, y' know this old boy coulda done th' same thing to Samuel there he done t' that sheep," and he pointed his chin at me. "You was worried a few minutes ago when he wudn't home. I say we got t' do somethin' 'bout this old boy 'fore hit's too late."

"You're right," said Dad, strong. "The only thing I don't want is a killin' unless we have no choice. If he came for me or mine or a neighbor, I'd shoot him if I had to, but so far, he's only killed stock, and no matter how terrible th' way he did it, it's not enough t' shoot him. I've seen too much killin' in my life, Bess. I don't want to see any more of it unless it's life or death."

Bess got up from his chair and stretched. "Wouldn't even go along with a little tar 'n' feathers, huh, Morse?" and we all laughed.

As soon as all our company was gone, I started thinking. What I had to do was go with the posse and lead the dogs to the cliff bottom. Soon as the men saw the cave, and the dogs started going wild, they wouldn't have any trouble figuring out where the crazy man was and we wouldn't have to tell about that day at the Blue Hole. Boy, did I wish Fred could go, but it was already late and if I asked to go over to Fred's now, Mom and Dad would think I was crazy. Besides, I wudn't about to go out alone again tonight! That meant I was going to have to handle it myself. I just had to get Dad to take me along. I decided to wait until the next day to ask about going so that Mom wouldn't have all night to talk Dad out of it. With a little luck, I thought as I crawled into bed, Fred, Lonnie, LD, and me was out of trouble.

I didn't know how long I had been asleep when something woke me up, then I heard the telephone ringing, Dad's footsteps, and then his sleepy voice.

"Yeah . . . yeah . . . okay . . . g'bye."

The phone hung up and there were more footfalls and a squeak as Dad got back into bed. Then, kind of foggy-headed, I wondered why somebody was calling in the middle of the night. Something else was wrong too. There was a sound like bacon frying. Rain!

I come full awake in a flash, flung off the covers, opened the door that went out onto the screened-in porch, and dang nigh went sprawling on the gut-slick, water-soaked deck. Rain by the bucketful was pouring down. The telephone call was probably the sheriff. Hard as this rain was falling, all the scent would be warshed away. Even deep tracks would be gone. The posse'd been rained out! Nobody would show up because they would know it was a warshout.

I set up and thought for a while and listened to the danged old gully-warsher. The only thing that kept coming back time after time was a new meeting with Fred, Lonnie, and LD. That meant I had to talk to Fred tomorrow since the best place to set up a meeting would be when he saw Lonnie and LD at church. As soon as I figured out what I was going do, I felt better and slid back under the covers. The covers smelled musty and good, and the patter of rain on the roof and slosh at the side of the house drained the wake out of me and in a few minutes, I was asleep.

20

I t rained hard all the next morning. I didn't want to rust my bike
   so I walked to the Mulligans' and got soaked. Fred laughed
   when he saw me. I must've been some sight standing at the front
door draining all over the place with cockleburs hanging here and
there.

"What you doin' all wet, hun'ney? Don't you know 'nough t'
stay out th' rain?"

"Had t' talk t' you," I said.

"Must be mighty important," he said, and laughed again, but
I didn't, and he looked behind him and stepped outside and closed
the door. "Somethin' happen?" he asked soft.

"It ain't good," I answered. "Where can we talk?"

"Can't inside," and I could hear voices. "We can sit in th' shit
house . . . or walk."

"Why don't we walk."

We went down the road to where we could watch the Dry
Branch pour over the blacktop. The water was moving fast and
making an awful noise.

"Some rain, wudn't it?" he said, as we watched.

"Yeah," I answered. "Few minutes was enough for us. Crazy
man killed a buck night before last over on Bess Clark's. They found
it just after we left for th' meetin'. Dad and Bess and a bunch of
others were supposed to meet th' sheriff and have bloodhounds and

everything this mornin' and track him down but the rain warshed out the tracks and scent. Wouldn't you know it, I could've led them to th' cliff and we'd've been out of trouble."

Fred turned toward me quick. "You were gonna lead them t' th' cave without me!" he squawked, then started walking around in a little circle glaring at me.

"I didn't want to," I answered, kind of apologizing. "Wudn't anything else I could do, Fred. I couldn't get here late as it was, and we were leavin' before daylight. I didn't even know if Dad would let me go, much less wait on you."

Fred kept acting mad for a while, then picked up a rock and threw it in the roaring Dry Branch. "Now what we supposed t' do?"

"We better get together and talk again," I answered. "He's comin' further and further in from th' river."

"Yeah, and lots of time's passed since we've knowed. And we've lied our fool heads off. He's killed two sheep and everybody's gonna blame us. We in for hit now."

"We just got t' tell!" I said. "He's gonna kill somebody!"

Fred squatted down and watched the roaring water. "Samuel, you know somethin' 'bout th' crazy man I don't and you won't tell me?"

"I can't," I said. "You're my best friend and all, but it's like a blood oath."

Fred kept looking at the branch, then said, "Figured hit was like that. Lonnie'll go along with tellin' even though he's got more t' lose than any of us, but LD won't."

"We got t' try," I said. "Fred, that crazy man is gonna hurt somebody! When we meet, I'm gonna tell LD whether he wants me to or not, I'm tellin', and that he better leave Lonnie out of it. Fred, we got t' tell! You still want to . . . don't you?"

Fred didn't answer right off and the longer he took, the more worried I got. I was about to say something when he sighed. "I reckon. Ain't gonna do any good, though. LD ain't about t' go along with hit or lie for Lonnie."

I was really getting mad. "I'm gonna bust old LD Howard right in th' nose!"

Fred just kept squatting, picking up little rocks every now and then and pitching them underhand into the stream. "What good's that gonna do? Problem'll still be Lonnie gettin' beat up . . . maybe killed."

"Damn old LD, anyhow!" I yelled, standing up. I picked up a big rock and flung it as hard as I could at the water, which hardly splashed it was moving so strong.

"I'll set up th' meetin' when I see LD and Lonnie at church tomorra. Maybe if we push LD hard he'll come around. Hit's hard t' blame him though if he don't. His pa is downright scary when he's mad."

Sprinkles of rain started falling, and Fred stood up. "We better git, hun'ney. Whyn't you come up th' house and sit a spell."

I didn't want to be around anybody. "Naw, I better be gettin' back. Little more rain ain't gonna get me any wetter."

"That's th' truth," he said, and laughed. "Where you wanta meet, Sunday?"

"How about our stock barn? Th' four of us haven't gotten together at my place for quite a while. We can flop around in the loft on the fresh hay Dad just put in."

"Okay, see you about one o'clock, unless LD and Lonnie can't make it."

"One o'clock Sunday in the hayloft," I said.

Saturday was bad enough, but Sunday morning didn't ever seem to end. About a quarter of one, I went out to the barn and up the ladder to the loft. While I was waitin', I hollowed out a place we could all lie down in without sliding off the edge, then I flopped back and waited. It wudn't long before I heard whispers and the back barn door being pulled out. I peered over the edge of the loft and there was Fred and LD.

"Hi," I said.

"Hidey, Samuel." Fred grinned and headed for the ladder.

LD didn't say anything, and he wudn't smiling. Matter of fact, he looked like he was ready for a fight. That was okay, because I was ready too.

"Where's Lonnie?" I asked when they got up the ladder.

"He ain't coming," said LD, kind of snotty.

"Why?" I shot back.

"Lonnie's pa's on a drunk," said Fred. "Miz Shackelford told LD's ma that Mr. Miller beat Lonnie's ma t' pieces day before yesterday. Beat up a couple of his sisters too. Th' whole family is scared t' death."

"How's Miz Shackelford know that?" I asked. "Nobody visits th' Millers!"

"One of th' little girls run away to th' Shackelfords last night," LD answered. "She said he'd been drinkin' hard. Th' Shackelfords brought her to th' preacher and he's gonna keep her until Mr. Miller sobers up. Fred says you wanta talk!"

"That's right," I snapped back, "and you know about what."

Fred raised his hands upward and talked soft-like. "I think first we ought have a prayer for Lonnie. Let's all bow our heads and pray," and LD did, but I didn't. First place, I didn't want to, and second, I wudn't sure Jews ever bowed their heads to pray.

Both Fred and LD had their heads bowed and LD's eyes were closed. Fred's must've been open some, because he said, "Samuel?" and I still just stood there, and he said, "Lord, we gathered here . . . Samuel . . ." and I bowed my head, but I didn't close my eyes. "Lord, we gathered here t' talk about doin' right. Now, you know what th' problem is. The four of us . . . it was four anyways . . . found out about a crazy man or somethin' lives down on th' Little Bend cliffs who is just plumb mean. We didn't tell our folks 'cause we wudn't supposed t' be there, then we lied a little . . . quite a bit . . . maybe more, I guess. Along about last year, th' crazy man started killin' stock. Now we're afraid t' tell 'cause we're going t' get a real lickin' for not tellin' before now. The worst part though is that Lonnie's pa is on a drunk and will beat him t' pieces or maybe kill him if we tell th' whole truth. LD says he won't lie and leave Lonnie out of hit if we tell 'cause his pa will find out if he does and really give him a stompin'. Hit's a bad problem, Lord."

Fred kind of stopped there and I was about to raise my head when he started again.

"Well, that's about hit, Lord. What we need you t' do is two things. First, help Lonnie so's he don't get beat t' pieces, then find us a way t' get th' crazy man caught."

Fred quit praying and I could see him start to say, "Amen," then stop.

"There's one more thing, Lord. We know th' talkin' we're about t' do ain't gonna be easy, but remind us that we all friends and children of God and got t' love each other and talk peaceful t' one another. Without fightin' or yellin'. Teach us they ain't no way fightin' is gonna help and that we got t' do what's right peaceful. We ask in Jesus' name. Amen."

It kind of bothered me like always when Fred said "in Jesus' name" but since that was how everybody down home but us ended a prayer, I knew he didn't mean anything against me. The prayer helped a little. Some of the fire was gone from LD's face when he opened his eyes. He stood there not quite knowing what to do. The prayer had done something to me too, but the first time LD opened his mouth, I was back wanting to put my fist in it. After we set down in the hollowed-out place I made in the hay, LD spoke:

"Fred, I don't see why we had t' have this meetin'. Y'all know how I feel. If we tell, I'm gonna tell everything and that means th' part about Lonnie being with us."

I was really burning. "Lonnie didn't tell most 'cause we didn't want him to," I said. "It ain't fair t' tell on him. Anyway, we got t' get th' crazy man caught. That's what we ought talk about and not waste time on th' other."

"What you got in mind?" asked Fred, leaning back on the hay with his hands behind his head and legs crossed.

I had done some thinking but knew my answers wudn't good.

"Well, why don't we say we saw buzzards circlin' th' cliff? That'll get people thinking about th' cliffs."

"What good'll that do?" asked LD. "There's a sheep carcass less than two mile from there. Every buzzard around's gonna be circlin'. Besides, old Shackelford'll be lookin' that way hunnert times a day and he'll know if buzzards been circlin'."

I started to say something back to LD but Fred raised his hand and I stopped. "Hit's not a bad idea," he said. "Hit's a pretty good start. What else can we do?"

"Well"—I swallowed—"we can walk over t' th' top of the cliffs again, and maybe find some bent-over weeds and tell our folks about them. We can say we saw what might be a cave down below where somebody could be hidin'."

"Go down't th' Little Bend cliffs again by ourselves!" said LD, and his face was white. "After what's happened there! And after what our mamas said this mornin'! You're crazy!"

"I am not!" I yelled. "I just want th' crazy man caught. What's he blabbin' about, Fred?"

LD jerked stiff the second I said, "blabbin'" and I started getting up.

Fred jumped to his feet. "Now, wait a minute, boys," he said, raising his hands. "Y'all quit now. Let's just talk some more. Samuel, this morning after church, th' women all got t' talkin' about Lonnie's pa and about th' buck. Before they left, Miz Wallace said hit was dangerous on that stretch of river, and our moms said maybe hit was, and that's when LD's ma said, 'LD, don't you dare go down there, y' hear?'"

"And I said y . . . yes," LD said. "And Fred's ma said she d . . . didn't want F . . . Fred t' go neither! So there!"

I looked at old LD and just got madder and madder. No matter what I did, he always foxed me. He was winning again too, and taking my best friend with him. *Okay*, I thought, *it's my turn.* "Y'all can do whatever you want but I'm tellin' and I'm gonna say th' reason we didn't tell sooner was 'cause o' you, LD Howard!"

LD's face went bleach white, then come a big sob and here he come, both fists just flying. In a second we were rolling around on the hay, first him on top, then me on top, pounding away at each other and Fred trying to pull us apart, saying, "Stop . . . come on, you guys . . . y'all stop now . . . Samuel . . . LD . . . y'all stop hit right now," but we kept swinging and rolling and kicking and grabbing hard as we could, and cussing up a storm. All of a sudden the world turned upside down and the wind just gushed out of me.

We had fallen off the loft. I thought I was dying. I couldn't get my breath, and barely struggled to my feet. While I was gagging, I could see that LD was bleeding from a big cut on his forehead and his mouth was open trying to cry with nothing coming out. Something finally did, though. "I hate you!"

Just then I got a gasp of air and went for him again, but Fred grabbed me around the waist and held on. LD started running, hit the back barn door with his body, knocking it open, and shot out before it fell shut.

As soon as LD was gone, Fred let go of me, then stepped back and let his arms drop to his sides. I guess he thought I was going to come for him and he didn't want to fight. It wudn't because he was scared. Fred would fight anybody, but he didn't want to fight me. I didn't want to fight him either, and I just stood there wanting to cry. Little time passed and he said, "You ain't really gonna tell, are you, Samuel?"

I shook my head. "Don't see any way I can."

"Your mouth's bleedin'. You got any broke teeth?"

I tried to spit on the barn floor and instead of it coming out like a wad, it splattered. I felt around with my fingers which come away all bloody.

Fred moved up close. "You got a busted lip."

"Yeah, I guess," I sputtered.

He looked real close, then said, "Hit's swellin' up like a poisoned pup."

"Damn old LD! Damn him!" I spat out. "Now I got t' lie about how I got it and Mom's gonna raise all kinds of hell."

"Aw, hun'ney, tell her you fell," he said, chuckling. "Hit's the truth, ain't it?"

"Yeah . . . I guess. Aw, Fred what we gonna do?"

Fred moved his bare heel around in the barn dust and shook his head. "Don't know, hun'ney. We can't tell now. Old Lafe Miller might kill Lonnie if we do, and LD will tell for sure. I wish they was somebody we could talk hit over with."

"Yeah," I said.

"Well, got t' be gettin' back. Hey, let's do some fishin' this week, get a bunch of frogs and stuff. Hit's gonna be okay, Samuel, you'll see," and he threw an arm around my shoulders and we walked together to the back of the barn, where he squeezed out the door and disappeared.

21

After my fight with LD, I stayed out of sight for the rest of the day hoping my swollen lip would go down. Mostly, I lay by the creek with a piece of wet tobacco canvas on my mouth. It didn't do any good. I could see my reflection in the stream and I looked funny. My face was long and skinny and I had this real black hair and black bushy eyebrows, big eyes and nose, and my ears stuck out. With the fat lip my head kind of looked like one of those bushmen I had seen in a magazine, except I didn't have a ring in my nose.

At milking time, I kept my head in the cow's flank so nobody knew anything until I went inside for supper. Then Mom saw me.

"Samuel, what happened?" and the way she said it everybody at the table stared.

"Fell out of th' loft," I muttered.

"How could you fall out of the loft? What were you doing there?" Mom asked.

"Just foolin'."

"Let me see," and she rolled back my upper lip and I jerked away. "You didn't get that falling out of any barn loft, young man. Which one of your crazy friends hit you?"

"I fell out of th' loft," I said, acting kind of mad.

"Is that how you talk to your mother?" said Dad, and he was giving me that stare.

Tears come rolling and I bawled as bad as LD. I don't know how long I cried, but when I finished Mom had her arms around me and Dad was picking at his food.

"You okay?" Dad asked me sharp.

"Yes, sir," I answered.

"Got anything you wanta talk t' me about?"

I almost choked as I shook my head.

"Then it's closed," he said.

Everybody started eating again, but the clink of the knives and forks on the plates sounded ten times louder than usual. "It's been a bad day," Dad said to Mom. "Remember that guy who said he would be able to help us house tobacco? He took a job in Cincinnati."

Mom's mouth fell open. "How'll we get the tobacco in the barn?"

Dad shook his head. "I don't know. Everybody's huntin' for help. I just don't know, M'dom," and how he said it was real down.

I knew Dad was right. We had to have another hand because we had so much tobacco that even swapping work with Mr. Mac and Babe wudn't enough.

Mom shook her head and looked worried. "There has to be someone else we can get."

"I wish I knew who," said Dad with a sigh.

Mom thought for a minute, then said, "Jennie Dee Wallace said a man came by the other day looking for a house to rent."

"What kind of man?" asked Dad, and his eyes widened.

"Jennie Dee thought he was a mountaineer," said Mom.

"Where is he?" asked Dad, kind of excited.

Mom shook her head. "I don't know. Rags might know."

"Ring him up for me!"

A couple of days later, Dad come into the yard with what was a mountaineer. He wudn't very tall and was real skinny. He had a quiet about him that was scary. Dad rapped at the kitchen door, and Mom and I come outside.

"M'dom, this is Mr. Ervin Cross," said Dad.

"How do you do?" said Mom, wiping her wet hands on her apron.

"Hidey," the skinny man said, then looked down.

"This is Samuel, my youngest, Mr. Cross," said Mom. "Say hello, Samuel."

"Hello," I said, and Mr. Cross nodded.

Mom asked, "You have a family, Mr. Cross?"

"Yep," said Mr. Cross, still looking down.

Mom kind of stared at him. "Are they with you?"

"Nope."

Dad shifted his weight and I could tell he didn't exactly cotton to Mr. Cross.

"You have a boy, sir?" I asked.

"Two," he answered, and looked at me.

"They my age?" I asked.

"Reckon Radar is," then he looked at Dad. "We ought see t' th' house."

"Sure," said Dad, and they took off for the house in the hollow with me tagging along.

The house wudn't much, just wood floors and whitewarshed walls, but it had two rooms, a kitchen, an outhouse, and a chicken coop. It needed windows put in and Dad told Mr. Cross that Mr. Berman could get them for him.

"Hit'll do," said Mr. Cross, finally.

"You need help movin'?" Dad asked.

"Nope."

"You got a lot of stuff?"

" 'Nough."

When we got back to our house Dad told Mr. Cross that if he needed milk for his family he could have some whole milk for drinking and lots of skim milk from the separator for making stuff. Mr. Cross acted like he hadn't heard a word.

"Can I keep chickens?" he asked.

"Sure," said Dad, "What kind you got?"

"White Legurns and three fightin' roosters."

"Fightin' roosters?"

"Yep. And you ain't never seed any better. Kill any chicken fools with 'em."

Dad squinted one eye. "Can I carry you t' your family?"

"Nope," Mr. Cross answered, then struck out walking down our lane.

A week went by and we had pretty much given up hope that the Crosses were coming. Then one morning Dad come in from milking and said they had moved in during the night.

"During the night?" said Mom, stopping her work and looking at him.

"Smoke's coming out of th' chimney. I can't figure out who else could be there."

"Why did they move in at night?"

"Why do mountaineers do anything?" Dad muttered, then he answered himself. " 'Cause they're crazy's why! We have to have him though, so let's make the best of it."

At first, the only Cross I saw was Ervin. I wanted to go down and meet the rest, but Mom and Dad said no. I could go down if they asked, otherwise no. Nobody asked.

Things were pretty much back to normal now. Just like before, everybody seemed to forget about the crazy man except Fred and me, but pretty soon even we were back to having a good time, mostly trying to see what the Crosses were doing. There'd be smoke coming out of their chimney, but no people in sight. I began to wonder if anybody else lived there, and Fred and me talked about maybe Mr. Cross was mixed up with the crazy man. A brother or something. I didn't meet the Cross boys until the first day of school. They were already at the bus stop, when Naomi and I got there. I knew they had to be Crosses because they looked a lot like Ervin. One was a couple years older than me and the other maybe a year younger. We stood there, together, nobody saying anything, then I picked up a rock and threw it at a fence post and hit it dead center. The older Cross did the same thing, only a lot harder. Soon, we were peppering away.

"Hey, I bet you're Radar," I said to the older one.

"Yep," he said, "and hit's spelled th' same back'ards as fo'ards."

"What's his name?" I asked, pointing toward his brother.

"Billy Bacon Jacob."

" 'Lo, Billy Bacon," I said.

"Hidey," he answered.

"Hello, Billy," said Naomi, and Billy didn't say nothing back.

When Rosemary showed up, she and Naomi acted like they hadn't seen each other in years, hugging and squealing and jumping up and down even though they spent half the summer together. Rosemary was prettier than ever and when I looked at her, I felt weak. By the time the school bus come, I was back to where I was when we first met. I just really loved Rosemary.

22

Tobacco housing went easier than anybody figured even though Ervin was slower'n molasses in th' wintertime. We swapped work with Mr. Mac and Babe, which meant we had twenty-five acres to house. Things went well, though, and by mid-September, we were finished.

Fred didn't start school that fall. Nobody said anything because the teachers figured he was helping with the tobacco, but soon as housing time was over the truant officer come down to see Alfred and Mamie and told them if Fred didn't show up they were going to put Alfred in the pokey. Alfred got mad and told the man to get his ass out of his house. The truant officer said, "Okay, buddy, but you just wait. You goin' t' jail!"

That scared Mamie and she told the truant officer that the reason Fred couldn't go was he didn't have any clothes and wudn't any money to buy them with because they had to save up to buy salt butts for winter. The truant officer said he didn't give a damn about their butts and if Fred wudn't at school in a few days Alfred was gonna be busting rock on a chain gang.

The day after it happened, Alfred was still sore and asked Dad what he ought do.

"Tell him to send Fred to school," Mom said when Dad brought it up at supper.

"I did," Dad answered, heaping stuff on his plate. "He sends th' girls."

"What did he say?"

"Said he was saving up t' buy mules and farm equipment. He wants t' crop Red Bill Rogers' place year after next."

"What's that got to do with sending the girls to school and not Fred?" Mom asked.

"Well, they got Purina feed sacks and Mamie made clothes for Thelma Jean, and WK bought dresses for Annie Lee, so Alfred wasn't out anything. But Levi's and shirts cost money."

"So Alfred will buy his mules a week later," said Mom.

"You know Alfred," said Dad, chuckling. "Stubborn as those mules he's gonna buy."

"Then let them throw him in jail," replied Mom. "Serve him right!"

Dad didn't answer. He just raised his eyebrows, then winked at me.

Lonnie didn't start school either, and since LD and I had fallen out and Fred wudn't there, I didn't have any close friends to pal around with. The Langleys were nice, especially Melvin, but he was serious all the time. I tried to get friendly with Radar, but it didn't work out. He couldn't talk about nothing but chickens. After a week or so you can't say much more about a chicken. Billy Bacon Jacob never said anything, he just kind of hung around. I was lonesome. The only time I had fun was on the weekends with Fred. He was happy being out of school and said he didn't want to ever go back. He planned to help his dad crop and buy a .22 rifle. Alfred told him that if he put his back into the work, they might buy their farm in as little as four years, then the two of them could crop it together and sharecrop another farm until Fred could buy his own land. The only thing they had to do now, Alfred said, was keep the goddamn truant officer off their necks.

Just as I was about to be bored crazy at school, Lonnie showed up. It was great to see him, but real sad too. His eyes and face were light greenish-red-purple and he limped. His sisters were marked up a little, but not as bad as Lonnie. When I got on the bus and saw him, I didn't know what to say. About all I could get out was, " 'Lo, Lonnie."

" 'Lo, Samuel," he said so soft I almost couldn't hear it. "How y' doin'?"

"Okay," I answered, and moved over to sit beside him. Everybody who got on the bus after that stared at Lonnie and his sisters. When LD got on, he turned white and didn't even say hello.

The first chance Lonnie and I got to be alone was at recess. While the other kids went out to the big open field, we leaned up against the rock fence and talked.

"How y' doin'?" he asked again.

"Okay, I guess."

"Anything happen in th' past few weeks?"

It hit me then that Lonnie didn't know about anything since July. "Yeah," I answered. "Lots of things. The crazy man killed another buck and there was almost a posse and I almost got t' go on it but it was rained out and after that we got together t' talk about fightin' and LD tellin' . . . I mean us tellin' and LD and me had a fight and . . ."

I was talking a mile a minute and Lonnie laughed and said to slow down. I did, then I told the whole story.

"You 'n' LD made up yet?" he asked.

"No!"

"Goin' to?"

"No!"

Lonnie looked out across a barbwire fence on the other side of the road to a bare field where somebody had just finished cropping. He didn't say anything else.

"Think I should?" I asked.

"Hit's up t' you," he said, twisting his nose and sniffing.

I wudn't sure what he meant. "If we told about th' crazy man and your pa found out . . ."

"Go ahead and tell," he said, hunching his shoulders. "I don't care."

"I'm afraid you'll get beat up again."

"My pa don't beat!" Lonnie said, turning toward me and answering quick and hot.

I didn't know what to say. He glared like he was going to come for me. I just stood there. "I only wanta be your friend, Lonnie," I said.

Big tears welled up in Lonnie's eyes, and he turned toward the field again. We stood a little more, then he croaked out, "Thank y', Samuel."

I left because I knew he wanted to be alone. I thought about the problem all through geography and missed hearing a few questions because Miz Callen yelled at me.

It was early October by this time, and Fred still wudn't coming to school. The truant officer went to the Mulligans' again and Alfred run him off. That was a mistake because before the day was over, a deputy stopped by and told Alfred if Fred wudn't on that school bus the next morning he'd be back before noon with handcuffs.

The next day, when the bus pulled up in front of the Mulligans', Annie Lee and Thelma Jean were there waiting but no Fred. You could hear screaming and yelling inside the house. One of the voices was Fred's and the other was Mamie's.

"G'won!" said Annie Lee. "Hain't nobody else comin'."

"Not what it sounds like t' me," said the driver.

"I don't care what hit sounds like t' you. Hain't nobody else comin', so g'won."

The driver grinned and threw it in low, grinding the gears. Like usual, we drove to where we picked up LD and the Langleys, then turned around and headed back. As we neared the Mulligans', Alfred stepped outside waving his arms and Mamie pushed Fred out the door. He stumbled toward the bus like a drunk. Didn't nobody say nothing when he got on, they just looked. The second he was inside he headed for the backseat and hid in the corner. He was crying but not making a sound. I wanted to go back and say something but I was afraid it would just make things worse. God, it was awful. I knew what was going to happen and did happen the second the Flickums got on. They took one look and started laughing and pointing.

"Fred's a flarred feed sack . . . Fred's a flarred feed sack . . ." and Fred lunged out of the backseat, but I'd already hit a Flickum before he could get there. In a flash, Fred and Annie Lee and me just started beating hell out of every Flickum in sight with the bus driver trying to stop us and everybody all wrapped up together.

The driver couldn't pull us apart and began hitting me to make me let go. Then Naomi screamed for him to take his hands off me and pulled me out of the tangle. All of a sudden the bus started to roll backward, and the driver, who had finally got Fred off somebody, run to the wheel. Fred saw his chance and made a beeline for the door. I looked out the window and saw him jump over the fence and tear out through a pasture.

When Naomi and I got home that night I found out about more trouble. One of Mr. Mac's bucks had been killed on the back of their place. It was the same deal as before, only this time it had been dead for several days and there was no trail. As soon as I heard, I got scared and at supper I couldn't eat. Like always, Mom was watching and asked what was wrong.

"Nothin'," I said. "Just ain't hungry."

"Aren't. Is that all?"

"Yes, ma'am."

Dad had a little smile on his face. "Couldn't be because you were in a fight on the bus today and worried what your mom and I are gonna say, could it?"

"A fight!" said Mom. "With whom?"

"Those trashy Flickums called Freddie a feed sack," said Naomi. "Samuel was right."

"Naomi!" said Mom, and it surprised me too because Naomi didn't like fights.

"Naomi's right," said Dad. "This is one fight Samuel can be proud to have been in. He stood up for his friend." Then he told the whole story. It was pretty much like it happened except I come off a real hero, how I saw injustice being done to a friend and how I had backed him even though there was more Flickums than Fred and me and I had waded in anyway. After a while even Mom, who hated fighting, said she knew she had a courageous son who did his duty.

I felt awful. Wudn't any doubt in my mind the crazy man thing was a lot more important than that old fight on the bus. Things wudn't quite right about that either, because Annie Lee had got into it, and when she got mad she could stomp the whole Flickum family herself. They were praising me and I was lying my fool head off about the important problem.

"Yeah," said Dad. "Alfred said Annie Lee told him it was something t' see, old Samuel there punchin' away on any Flickum he could find. Just like Barney Ross or Benny Leonard, I bet," and he laughed, and I made myself grin.

"And he's so modest," said Mom. "What's our hero have to say about all this?"

"Wudn't nothin'," I muttered, and Dad looked at me like I had just been made captain of the Kentucky Wildcats football team and I felt worse than ever.

After dinner, I took a walk to the tobacco barn. I wanted to go see Fred but I knew he wudn't going to let me get anywhere near him while he was hurting. That was how Fred was, and he wudn't about to change. Walking at night scared me now, but my problem bothered me more. To the tobacco barn and back to the house, tobacco barn and back to the house; I don't know how many times. My thoughts went in circles. I had to talk to somebody and there was only one person I could think of to trust. That Saturday, I took the Cummings Hill route to Ben's.

It was real pretty out with all the leaves green, yellow, red, and brown on the oaks and hickories. Squirrels were everywhere storing nuts and things for winter. The groundhogs were so fat they waddled and the little animals born in the spring were sleek and near full-sized, drinking at the shiny clear pools of the slightly running creeks, with the sun hanging in the sky like a yellow ball, filling the air bright and fall-smelling, with duck families flying overhead.

I come out of the last grove of trees onto the bottoms and

there was Ben gathering pumpkins and stacking them in piles so
the trucks could pick them up. Cain and Abel were near him so I
stopped and yelled.

"Mr. Begley."

He looked up and shushed the dogs, then called, "Come on in,
Samuel."

I walked up grinning and set one bare foot on a warm pumpkin.
"Hi," I said.

"Hi, yourself," he answered, and grinned back. "Whatcha up
to?"

"Come t' see you."

"Reckon y' did." He laughed. "Don't nobody else live here. You
like pumpkin pie?"

"If they have ciminon," I answered.

"Well, I got one up th' house with cinnamon. Think that'll do?"

"Yeah."

"Then let's go have some pie and a cup of coffee, them here
pumpkins can wait." He stuck the machete he was holding in the
ground, and we walked to his cabin.

The pie was great. "You cook this yourself?" I asked.

"Yeah. Whatcha think?"

"It's really good. Where you learn how?"

"Just picked hit up."

"You cook lots of things?"

"Everything I eat," and he laughed.

When we finished the pie, we set and drank our coffee. He
didn't ask why I came or anything. I didn't know how to bring my
problems up without getting all shook and crying. I didn't want
that in front of Ben so I waited for my feelings to get right.

There were some new carvings since my last visit. He had a quail
with six little quail strung out behind her on a shelf over his bed.
The mama quail's head was cocked to the side, listening like a quail
will do. In one corner, several blocks of walnut, some three foot
square, were stacked up. There were mink and rabbit and muskrat
pelts around. From the way his scissors and rawhide were laid out

on the table, I was sure he was making other things too. Looking at Ben's stuff made me feel good and pretty soon, I started talking. "I got a problem, and I was wonderin' if you'd help me with it."

"I can try," he answered as he refilled our cups from his speckled black and white coffeepot. Then he sat down in his easy chair.

"Crazy man's killin' lots of stock now," I said. "Dad and th' sheriff tried to get up a posse with dogs, but the rain washed out th' scent." I tried to think of what to say next. It was hard to just come out and tell him I'd ignored his advice. There had to be an easier way than blurting out, *I didn't tell.*

I started feeling nervous again, so I looked around some more. The trunk Ben got my clothes out of that time had been moved to the foot of the bed and on top of it was a pile of leaves and twigs. They were pretty, but it didn't make sense to bring that many leaves into the house. Then I made out what looked like the upper part of a boy. The leaves had been put so the light-colored ones made the face, and deep red leaves the hair. The shoulders and chest were dark oak tan and fixed like a little open-neck shirt.

When I looked back toward Ben, he was slumped in his chair, with a leg thrown over one of its arms. "I didn't tell," I said.

There was a "blump" from the coffeepot, which was putting out some steam.

"Lonnie's pa got on a drunk and nigh beat his mom and sisters and him t' pieces."

This time Ben took a sip of coffee. He still didn't say anything, though. I was wishing he would, but I knew he wouldn't until I talked it all out.

I shifted in my chair and took a sip of coffee. The sun coming through the window half blinded me, so I shifted back and looked at the big pin oak that shaded that side of the cabin. Two squirrels were playing on a limb.

"LD says if I say anything he'll tell th' whole story, Lonnie 'n' all. We had a fight, LD and me. If I d . . . don't tell, somebody is gonna get killed by th' c . . . crazy man and, if I do tell and Mr. Miller finds out Lonnie knew and didn't tell, he might kill him," and the tears come rolling and I hated it. I seemed to be crying all the time now and here I was, crying in front of Ben. I got up, and he got up with me.

"Don't cry, Samuel," he said, and his hands went on my shoulders. "Maybe I—" and he stopped, then said, "Samuel, couple weeks ago a fella come here t' buy melons and was talkin' 'bout your pa. One of th' things he said was he was a good man. An educated man. He ain't gonna tell on Lonnie if you tell him why he shouldn't."

"It don't make any difference if he don't tell," I said, sniffling. "Any time old LD hears th' crazy man's been caught, he'll tell everything. He's scared t' death of his pa findin' out he lied. He'll tell everything th' second he hears, hoping he can make things easier on hisself!"

Ben sighed. "Samuel, I'd like t' step forward . . . I'd do most anything for you, but I can't. Talk t' your pa. He'll work it out. He'll help you, Samuel. Trust him a little. He's your pa, and this is really important."

Ben put his arm around my shoulders and I started toward the door. The arm felt strong and warm. It was an arm a body could trust. I wanted to twist around and squeeze his waist, but I had never done that to a man outside my family, so I didn't.

The dogs snarled as usual when we stepped out, and Cain bared his teeth. When the growling was shushed, Ben spoke. "Samuel, I've lived a lot longer'n you and I've learned a few things. One of them is, you don't let somethin' important fester. You do, hit'll build up until hit's so big can't anybody handle it, then your whole life will change. Don't let that happen. Do somethin' now, before hit's too late. Lafe Miller's mean when he's drunk, but I . . . I don't think he'd hurt Lonnie about this."

The second Ben's voice stumbled, fear went through me. He wudn't sure! And he wouldn't lie. No matter what he or Dad did, LD was so scared he was going to tell the instant he heard the crazy man was caught, and it would be all over for Lonnie.

The walk home was awful. I kept thinking about Lonnie's face and limp when he come back to school, and how I'd feel if he was killed and I was at his funeral. I couldn't tell about the crazy man. I just couldn't.

23

It was now many hours since I had driven away from Bert Raney's field. I'd been all over the heart of the bluegrass, finally following the Elkhorn Creek into Georgetown. I was born near Georgetown in a little white farmhouse during what my father described as the coldest damn winter since hell froze over. I don't know whether it was an omen, but until a half hour before I was born Dad was "sitting up" with the corpse of the "meanest white man in Scott County." Incredibly enough, the little white house that witnessed my worldly arrival was still occupied. Not far from it I saw a diner and remembered that I hadn't eaten. It was one o'clock and all the tables were filled, so I climbed onto a stool.

"Hi there," said the pudgy, middle-aged, pink-uniformed waitress as she put a menu in front of me. "Care for somethin' t' drink? Just made some iced tea."

"Biggest glass you've got."

The waitress laughed and began fixing my tea. "Haven't seen you in here before. You travelin'?" she asked, her back toward me.

"New England," I answered. "I was born here, though."

"How many years you been gone?" she asked, setting my iced tea on the counter.

"Sixty."

"Before my time," she said, grinning. "My folks been here since before th' war though."

I knew the joke. "Which war?"

"Between the States, o'course. What's your name?"

"Samuel Zelinsky."

The waitress thought, then shook her head. "My daddy'd of remembered but he's gone now. Anything look good on th' menu?"

"What do you recommend?"

"Fried chicken. That's all ole horse feathers back there can cook."

"I'll have the fried chicken. I take it mashed potatoes and gravy come with it?"

The waitress winked at me. "Some things never change, do they?"

After lunch I decided my odyssey was over for the day. I drove from Georgetown to Lexington and began winding through the city to my hotel using the vehicle's GPS. I turned a corner and almost wrecked the car. There was the old conservative synagogue where we had gone to shul. I wasn't certain, but it looked like it was now part of a strip mall. I parked and began walking. Everything was different except for the names of the streets. Mom-and-pop businesses were crammed together, helter-skelter. I tried to remember what the buildings had originally been used for as I passed them. I was unsuccessful until I came to:

SAIGON SUE'S
VEGETARIAN RESTAURANT

Instant recognition. Mr. Gollar's butcher shop! How many times had I walked up those three concrete steps to deliver produce? Eggs, vegetables, fresh milk in mason jars that Mom reserved special for bringing milk to our kosher friend. In return, we left loaded with deli and halava, a kind of sugary candy. That was for me. Mom never told him I didn't like halava.

I walked in to see what the place looked like and the proprietor descended, forcing me into tea and soup. I tried, but my mind refused to bridge the gap between a kosher butcher shop and a Viet-namese restaurant.

When I finished eating, I walked to the front of the shul. My memories of those times weren't negative, but they held little mean-ing for me. Judaism to me as a child was more historical than re-ligious. In fact, a book entitled *Heroes of Israel* was my religious training. It was an accumulation of biblical stories for Jewish children in need of heroes who won great battles instead of being slaughtered in concentration camps.

My experiences in shul had been empty as a kid. Partly because my father became agnostic after our family was murdered in WWII, and partly because as dirt farmers we were looked down upon by the Lexington Jewish community. In my adult years I came to greatly admire my little ethnic group but sadly never got past a secular-intellectual concept of Judaism. And yet, in adolescence and young adult years, anti-Semitism was to play a dismal role in my life.

I had encountered anti-Semitism as a child before we moved to Berman's. The comments made about Jews got me into several fights, but it wasn't too bad, and there was very little anti-Semitism among the hill people. My adolescent years in Indiana brought about my isolation, a more subtle form of anti-Semitism. For a while that experience caused me to reject all religions.

Until Nora.

Nora didn't profess a strong belief in Judaism, but she was ex-tremely proud of her heritage. We argued the value of the traditions from the start of our relationship. Why, I said, should one prepare Shabbos meals or celebrate the enormous number of Jewish holi-days if they didn't believe in God? Her answer sounded like Tevye in *Fiddler on the Roof*.

"Tradition!"

"And what am I to get from 'tradition!'?"

"The wonderful comfort of being a part of the whole."

"Nora, I have read dozens of books on Judaism, and other reli-gions . . . Buddhism, Islam, Christianity. All have wonderful things in them, all are important as bulwarks of civilization, but the vast majority require belief in a supreme being. That's fundamental. I have my own concepts of God and they don't fit with organized religion. I'm a Jew by birth and very proud of my roots, but it will be a cold day in hell when some rabbi directs my life."

While Nora wasn't a strong believer, her parents were, and she had spent two summers on a kibbutz in Israel. She spoke pretty good Hebrew and knew the services for Shabbos and a couple of Jewish holidays. At the start of our marriage the only Jewish tradition we observed was the Passover Seder with her parents. Every year we went back to New York for Passover. I enjoyed the service. It was fun. That was especially true after the kids were born and they could join in the first Seder. I surprised everybody by getting tapes and learning some Hebrew. The results made for some great scenes.

Nora: "Chu . . . chu . . . not, huu! Hebrew is not spoken with a hillbilly dialect!"

"That's bigotry," I'd counter. "You wouldn't say that about Russian, Spanish, German, Mandarin, or Urdu. Hillbilly is my language! I will not be discriminated against!"

The kids were preteens by this time and would join in the arguments. Some of the most outrageous religious discussions would take place among us. Nora, the teetering-agnostic traditionalist, raised the kids Jewish, and I did my best to help. Whenever they asked the big question, however, I told the truth as I saw it. I didn't believe in organized religion. I told them that they should believe whatever they wanted, believe what they felt in their hearts. Also, that I thought their mother was right, tradition was important. Every few weeks Nora would prepare a Shabbos service and I would join in, yarmulke and all. The girls would laugh that I was trying to cover up my bald spot.

Both girls wound up marrying Gentile boys. One of the boys converted to Judaism and became the first devout Jew in the Zelinsky clan since my grandfather.

Though a nonbeliever, being Jewish did provide me with a temporary respite once, when the weight of the world seemed to be crushing my skinny shoulders . . .

. . . I didn't tell. I was almost certain I wouldn't when I left Ben's, and by the time I got home, I was dead sure. Not being able to talk about it made things awful. It was a long Saturday night and Sunday. Monday morning, though, I started feeling better. It was Rosh Hashanah, and I figured nobody tells something like that on Rosh Hashanah or Yom Kippur. I heard Dad say to Mom one day that he figured all our relatives was dead and wudn't any reason for it. He said Jews better plan to make it on their own because wudn't anybody above or below gonna help. We were still going to shul on Rosh Hashanah and Yom Kippur though.

Mr. Mac and Babe agreed to milk for us on both holy days. I was in the front yard trying out my new shoes when they come rolling up in their black '32 Ford coupe. Babe was driving like he always did unless Mr. Mac had a snootful, then he was "gonna by God drive!" As the Ford pulled up, I went to meet them. Mr. Mac come flying out of the car, flung open his fleece-lined coat, and folded me inside. He squeezed so hard I couldn't breathe.

"How ye doin', Samuel!" he roared.

The sound rolled like thunder in his bony chest, which was crushing the side of my head. He smelled good of tobacco and liquor. When he quit squeezing, he took hold of my shoulders, leaned back, and looked at me. "Hey, you look spiffy, boy. Hot dog, you're shined up enough t' go courtin', ain't he, Babe?" Babe grinned and said he reckoned I was and that it wudn't going to be long before I was doing it.

Just then, Dad come out of the house, putting a tie around his neck. "Come on in, George," he called. They did and stood by our Warm Morning stove which we had just lit for the first time since spring.

"What kind of religious doin's is this, Morse?" asked Mr. Mac.

"New Year's," said Dad, finishing his tie in front of a little buffet mirror.

"What kind of celebration you have?" asked Mr. Mac.

"Oh, we thank th' Lord for all he's given us. And pray for th' dead folks."

"Way th' world's treated your people, you must have a lot of faith, Morse," said Mr. Mac, opening the door to the Warm Morning and shoving the coals around.

"My daddy'd of wanted it," said Dad and it got quiet for a few seconds.

"You know he's gone for sure?" asked Babe.

"They're all gone," said Dad. "Brother, sisters . . . everybody. Gone."

Mr. Mac nodded kind of slow, then he turned to Babe and said they better get started milking because it was getting late.

After some yelling by Dad that it always took Mom and Naomi forever to get ready, we got in the Ford and started for Lexington. The air coming through the Ford's broken back window was cold, boy. Naomi and I huddled together on the good side of the car to keep warm.

Mom kind of shuddered. "Morris, when are you going to fix that window?"

"You want me to stop tobacco housing t' fix a car window?"

"We finished housing a month ago."

"Stop with the nagging," said Dad, his voice sounding tired.

"I'm not nagging," said Mom. "The children will freeze. They'll catch a death—"

"All right, I'll fix it. Just stop nagging," and we went along a little way in quiet.

"Do you know who's going to be president of the shul next year?" Mom asked.

"No, who?"

"Guess."

"Pope Pius the twelfth," Dad said, and laughed.

"Oh, Morris, guess right."

"Okay," he said, and quit laughing. "Uh . . . Isadore Gold."

"No."

"No? Then who?"

"Guess."

"Dammit, I guessed. Now, who's gonna be president of th' shul?"

"Your cousin Henshy," she answered, kind of meek.

"Henshy!" Dad boomed.

"Henshy," she said.

"My God! What's he doing president of a synagogue?"

"Henshy," Mom said again, like she knew everything.

"But . . . it can't be Henshy! Henshy runs a whorehouse! Everybody knows—"

"Morris, the children!" Mom yelled.

"But Henshy! I can't believe it! Not even those schlemiels could elect Henshy. It's an . . . an . . . It's an abomination!"

"Henshy," Mom repeated.

"Now, that's a sin. If you believe, that's a sin," and he was all over the road.

"Morris, watch where you're going," yelled Mom, and Naomi and I grabbed each other as the car skidded on the shoulder and tore up gravel.

When things calmed down, Mom said, "You know who's going to be an officer?"

"Hermann Göring!" Dad screamed, and threw his arms in the air.

"Nate Berman," Mom said, and her voice had a little laugh in it.

Dad thought that over for about five miles. It started to drizzle, and the one old wiper that worked made a little pin streak out of which Dad could see the coming cars, but the rest of us could only see moving blurs of light. Every now and then, the road would bend a certain way, and the drizzle and the smell of damp night would fill the backseat.

"Nate ain't bad," he said, finally.

"No," Mom answered. "Nate ain't bad."

"He don't know Judaism from a hill of beans, but he's okay. What's Abe Gollar?"

"Nothing. I guess he'll still be cantor, but nothing. No officer."

"Humph," come out of Dad, and he didn't say anything for two more miles.

In the back, it was getting cold, boy. I mean, I was freezing. My teeth started chattering and I couldn't stop them.

"How come Abe Gollar is nothin'?" Dad asked.

"Morris, he's so old-fashioned."

"How much Torah does Nate know? He'd eat a pig's ass if it chewed a cud."

"Morris . . ."

"What's so old-fashioned about being able to read Hebrew? What's old-fashioned about having read th' Talmud? What's the matter, don't they want a Jew for a president?"

"Morris, he's—"

"—old-fashioned," said Dad. "He don't play golf. He's a butcher. He didn't make a million during th' war. His boy fought in th' Battle of th' Bulge and was decorated."

We drove a couple more icy miles, then Mom said, "The women don't like Abe."

"Why don't th' women like Abe?"

"He calls them names. They go in for meat and he cuts everything off the same piece. He'll say, 'You want chops? Chops! Bam! Flank? Flank! Bam! Roast? Roast! Bam!' And they can't argue with him. He's the only kosher butcher in Lexington."

Dad chuckled. "What's he call them?"

"Old yentas."

"To their faces?" and he started laughing.

"Yeh," and her voice laughed too.

Dad sighed. "Well, maybe Abe is a little hard t' get along with, but he and I don't have any troubles. He always looks me up and talks t' me and makes me feel like I belong a Jew. He's not ashamed to say 'Good yontiff' to a dirt farmer like me. You watch the rest of them t'night, how many greet me and talk t' me when I speak t' them."

"Morris, they know you don't like them."

"How th' hell can you like people that make a white slaver head of a shul!"

"Morris, the chil—"

"It's the truth! It's Rosh Hashanah. We need to tell the truth! They shouldn't even take Henshy's pledge until he quits. It's wrong. M'dom, don't you see it's wrong?"

"Yes, it's wrong, Morris. I know it's wrong," and we pulled into the shul parking lot next to a big Cadillac.

At the door of the shul somebody gave me a yarmulke and we went inside. It was like it always was, with the women on one side and men on the other. I stood beside Dad, who had on his suit and felt hat. He never wore a yarmulke or tallis, but he read the prayers, which he understood even though the Hebrew letters looked like hen scratching to me.

The rabbi up front was chanting, and every now and then Mr. Gollar would walk up all grizzled with a black and white striped tallis with fringes around his shoulders and start singing. When he did, tears come rolling down his cheeks and soaked into his salt-and-pepper beard. His voice made me sad because it sounded like he had a rock on his heart.

Pretty soon, I noticed Stacy Kalman and some other boys walk toward the door. I looked at Dad and his face said if I wanted to go out, go ahead.

In the parking lot I saw Stacy and the others and walked up to join them. Just as I got there, they stopped talking.

"Hi," I said, and somebody said, "Hello."

There was this little quiet period, then they began talking about bowling and how Stacy had just bowled 180, and was good enough to bowl in a league next year.

"You gonna bowl in a league?" I asked, trying to sound like I knew what I was talking about, which I didn't because I had never seen anyone bowl in my life.

"Yeah," said Stacy, and it got quiet again.

Then they started talking about going next year to Henry Clay Junior High.

"Y'all goin' to Henry Clay Junior High next year?" I asked, figuring that ought to get me into the conversation.

"Yeah," said Stacy. "Where you goin', Middletown?" and they all laughed.

He knew dang well that's where I was going to go someday. I had been looking forward to going to Middletown too. It sounded like nothing when Stacy said it.

"Middletown can't beat anybody. They never make it past th' first game in th' basketball tournaments," Stacy said, snickering, and the rest of the boys snickered too.

"There ain't anybody but goyim at Middletown," said Martin Millheim, and everybody snickered again.

"I ain't goyim and I'll go there," I said, and they snickered louder.

I could feel the hot come into my face as they made fun of me. Then Stacy motioned with his head and the whole crowd walked off, leaving me standing there. It was cold and lonely, so I went back inside the shul.

At last they got to the part I liked best, blowing the shofar. Mr. Gollar would stand there and say something in Hebrew and the rabbi would blast away on the ram's horn. It was really pretty to hear and I couldn't help thinking how much it sounded like the fox horns around home. Over and over the rabbi blew it, and each time power rushed up into my chest. I felt like I could lick the world. I even felt like I could lick Lonnie, which was dumb because wudn't any way I was ever gonna lick Lonnie Miller.

The rain that was falling on the way in started again on our way back, only this time the wind had shifted and some come through the broken-out window onto Naomi and me. It felt like it was going to either sleet or snow and we were shaking so bad we almost couldn't stand it, all wrapped up with our arms around each other and faces stuffed against one another's necks. I looked up once as a car come past and almost screamed. Naomi's hair had turned white! Just before I yelled, I realized that it was water drops glistening in the headlights. It was pretty. Naomi was pretty. Not as pretty as

Rosemary, but kind of like Joy West. I was about to compare her to some of the other girls when she pulled my head back toward her neck.

"For criminy's sake, Samuel." She shivered. "Stop lettin' cold air in on me."

I put my head down and listen to the Ford's engine and the tires on the wet highway and the sounds of cars passing us. That's all I could hear until I heard Mom say:

"We are going to get rid of this car!" and her teeth were chattering.

"What for?" come out of Dad. "This is a good old car."

"You may think it's a good old car, but I think it's a sh . . . shitting car. The window is broken out. It doesn't have a heater. The windshield wipers don't work so someday we won't see somebody and have an accident and kill us all. The wadding is coming out of the seats and a spring jabs me in the tuches every time I sit down. The brakes are almost gone. It won't go in the backup gear. It drips oil . . ."

"It doesn't drip oil," said Dad.

"It drips oil!" yelled Mom. "I've seen it on the ground every time you move the car!"

"A quart of oil lasts me almost two weeks, M'dom. That's not a bad leak."

"A shmozzle of your leak! Get a new car!" Mom yelled.

"Aw, naw. I'm not makin' Mr. Ford any richer. That Bundist bastard!"

"Then get one from General Motors. Maybe they're patriotic enough for you!"

Nobody said anything for a minute, then Mom started talking again, her teeth still chattering. "Someday . . . someday I'd like to have just a little something good. A decent house with water, a bathroom I can walk to without stepping in chicken manure. I'd like a cooking stove with gas instead of building a coal fire each morning. I'd like a decent refrigerator, a few of the things that make life easier. And not secondhand like this shitting car! New things!"

About then I heard Dad laugh softly.

"It's not funny, goddammit!" said Mom, and she almost never said that.

"I didn't mean that it was, M'dom," he said. "It's just that you're carryin' on so."

"Carrying on! I don't have a decent dress to my name. My children are going to die of pneumonia from riding in an open wreck. I won't know it, I'll have already died of the same thing. What will you use for caskets, Morris, cardboard boxes!"

"Now, M'dom . . ."

"M'dom nothing! I want a decent car!"

"Okay, okay, I'll see about gettin' a heater and th' window fixed."

"Heater and the window fixed? How about a new car!"

"I told you, I'm not makin' General Motors or Ford rich. That kind of money is a down payment on a place . . . almost."

"So! We're going to ride in dreck and walk in rags while you skimp for a farm. You're just like Alfred. Why don't we make Samuel's pants from flowered feed sacks?"

Dad's head kind of shook a little. "M'dom, that is not fair."

"Oh, it's not fair! It's fair that I'm deprived of any of the comforts that make life a little easier. That I never get to see any of my Jewish friends. That if I didn't like Lisa Shackelford, I'd die of loneliness. But what Jewish things can I talk about with Lisa? She's Christian!"

"And she's a heck of a lot nicer than those Lexington trash!" said Dad.

"And just what makes you such a judge?"

More quiet, and the road sounds returned. I started to raise up and look, but Naomi's hand grabbed the back of my head and pulled it against her. I let out a muffled "Ow" as my nose hit her collarbone. I was about to say, "Quit it" when from the front seat come Dad's voice.

"Who should I talk to in Lexington, M'dom?"

"I don't know. What's wrong with Isadore Gold?"

"What have I got in common with Isadore Gold? He's not bad, but he doesn't know anything but runnin' a hock shop."

"What's wrong with Joe Blumberg?"

"Same thing, only clothin' instead of hock shop. He's dumber'n owl shit too."

"And Hyman Millheim?"

"Same thing. Dry goods. He doesn't know the slightest bit of literature. He thinks Tolstoy sells ladies' ready-to-wear. They're all greenhorns. In th' old country their families were illiterate, poverty-stricken, and hungry."

"Oh, so, they're too dumb for you. Maybe you'd like Justice Brandeis."

"Justice Brandeis, I'd talk to," Dad said with a laugh.

"Hooray! You know, I just noticed tonight that there were windows in the Millheim Cadillac. Sarah Blumberg was wearing a hundred-dollar dress. The Gold children are in a private school. Their boy, Shecky, is going to be a doctor."

"Shecky's eleven years old. What makes you think he's gonna be a doctor?"

"Because he's getting a good foundation. He's going to a private school so he can get into a top university. Then he can get into medical school. It's hard to get into medical school if you're a Jew. What's my son going to be, Morris, a tobacco yap?"

There were sounds of crying from the front seat and Naomi could hear it too because I heard her say, "Ohhh" real soft.

Poor Mom. I didn't know who was right or wrong. Everything seemed okay to me. Other than I was cold, I mean. But we'd be home soon and I'd warm up. I never thought about Mom as unhappy. It made me sad thinking about it.

"M'dom," said Dad, so soft I could hardly hear him, "I'm just not like those people. I know there's a lot of things you'd like to have and we'll have them someday. After we get our own place. Put things off just a little longer. Trust me."

It was quiet for a while, then I heard Mom say, "You know, Morris, I must really love you. We've been married for twenty-five years, and that's how long I've been waiting. I must really love you, you know," and I could hear her laugh between her sobs and I knew she was wiping her eyes with a tiny little handkerchief.

The car slowed as Dad pumped the brakes five, six times then turned right. We were at the gate to the lane. We were home.

24

The cold snap ended after Yom Kippur and Indian summer returned with its warm weather and trees all colors and sky October blue. Through the long open ventilator panels, you could see tobacco curing in the barns golden brown, and smell its warm spiciness on any road you cared to walk. It was good curing weather, and people would start stripping early. It was great fishing weather too, and the first nice Saturday I grabbed my pole and a pocketful of worms and took off for the Mulligans.

It had been over three weeks since the flowered pants thing and I hoped Fred was cooled off enough to see me. It looked like he was going to get his way about school. One of the sheriff's deputies told Dad that when Fred didn't show at Selby the truant officer went to the sheriff and asked him to put Alfred in jail. The sheriff told him that if he locked Alfred up the kids would starve so he wudn't gonna do it. The truant officer got hot then and said it was his duty to lock Alfred up and the sheriff told him he didn't give a shit what anybody thought, he knowed his duty and it wudn't to starve kids.

There was nobody in the yard when I got to the Mulligans so I climbed up on the gate by the hog lot and yelled, "Fred!" Nobody answered.

"Whoa, anybody home?" Still no answer, so I started across the yard to the pond.

"Hidey, Samuel. Whatcha want?" come from the upstairs window.

I turned and there was Annie Lee. Her hair was mussed and she was wearing a man's white shirt. It didn't have nothing under it neither because her tittie nipples showed. "I'm lookin' for Fred," I said. "Figured him and me'd go fishin'."

"Don't know if he's ready t' see you yet," she said, leaning her elbows on the windowsill, which caused the shirt to pull tight and her nipples to stick out more. "He's still real down. You know how he gits . . . won't eat, up half th' night."

Annie Lee started to say something else when this hairy arm reached up and got her shirt. The hand had a big square ring on its middle finger and I knew it was WK's.

"Gitchegoddamnhandsoff'nme. I'm a-talkin' t' Samuel," she said, and a low voice said something and she slapped at him. There was a "pop" then an "oow" from below.

"He's down't th' pond, Samuel," she said, getting back into the window. "He's still spooky, but he might talk t' you. He's been actin' a little better last couple days."

I said, "Thanks" and took off, just as WK's hand reached up and got Annie Lee by the shirt again. She fell over this time and I heard her giggle.

All the way to the pond, I thought about what to say to Fred. I had to say it right or he might not see me for weeks. Fred couldn't stand it if he thought you were doing something because you felt sorry for him. I thought about turning around and going back because maybe it was too soon, but then old WK might tell Fred he saw me and he'd know I was hunting for him and figure I was worried about hurting his feelings and he sure wouldn't have anything to do with me after that so I better go on. Suddenly I was at the pond. It was too late now because I knew Fred would've already spotted me.

I searched the brush-hidden banks with my eyes but couldn't see him, so I walked through the brush and there he was at our favorite spot beside a big sycamore log. He glanced up, then turned back toward his bobber. I waited, then crawled over the log, unwound my pole, and baited up. For some reason wouldn't any fish bite. Finally, I thought of something to say.

"Got any makin's?"

Fred didn't move nothing but his hand and it reached inside his shirt pocket and pulled out the Durham sack.

I opened it and stirred the fluffy gray stuff with my finger. "Got any wrapper?"

He reached inside his shirt again and out come several pieces of brown paper sack. I took one and he put the rest back. "You not smokin'?"

Fred barely shook his head.

"You gonna make a man smoke alone?" I said, trying to sound half mad.

Out come the slips again and I handed him the sack. He took some and put the sack back in his shirt. I just sat because I hadn't ever rolled a cigarette.

A little grin come on Fred's face. "You gonna roll hit or dip hit like snuff?"

"I ain't too good at cigarette rollin'," I said, and spent the next ten minutes pasting together a bulging mess and held on while we smoked. Boy, it was bad. I was trying to get a best friend back though, so I talked about how good it was and how it opened my bronical tubes.

"Hit'll do hit ever time," said Fred. "Uncle Charlie says they give it t' people with numone and hit brings 'em back t' life."

"It's good all right," I said, nigh puking.

"More rabbit tobacco this year'n I can remember. Hit's gonna be a bad winter."

"Figure it will, huh?"

"Hun'ney, hit never fails if they's a big crop of Life Everlastin'."

Then we just set. The sun glinted off the water next to my bobber, making it hard to see, and I squinted. "We ain't had a bite in an hour," I said.

"Been that way all week. Fished hard yesterday and only caught two little brim."

"Why don't we do somethin' else?"

"Whatchawantado?"

I thought for a minute. "Don't know. What about gettin' some hickory nuts."

"Ain't ready yet, hun'ney," he said, scratching his toe. "Ain't been enough killin' frosts. Besides, they's a poor crop. Let's ride up t' the sweet apple tree on your bike, get some apples and eat 'em with that coarse salt in y'all's feed room."

"Let's go," I yelled, and we took off. I felt good. I had my best friend back.

Skinnying up the sweet apple tree was hard, but when we got up it was loaded. We filled the basket on the front of my bike, then headed for the feed room.

Sweet apples taste awful unless you know how to eat them. We spread these out on a bale of straw, put a little mound of coarse cattle salt in the middle, then lay back on some sacks of bran, licked the apples, and dipped them in the salt. They wudn't bad like that.

"You want any more, Fred?" I said, eyeing the pile that never seemed to go down.

Fred was lying almost flat with both hands over his bulging belly. "Hun'ney, if I et 'nother apple I'd puke."

"Me too. Let's throw these t' th' hogs?"

We were almost at the hog lot with our arms full of apples when Fred pulled up short. "Hun'ney, I got a great idea! You ever make a deadfall?"

"No."

"Well, that's just what we're gonna do, and we can use these here apples for bait."

"You know how t' make a deadfall?"

"Deadfall? I make dandy deadfalls," he said. "Let's go cut some triggers."

Before we got the triggers cut I was about to go out of my head as Fred tested limb after limb, but by milking time, we had enough for several deadfalls. The next day we barked them and carved the notches. I lay on a feed room sack and watched.

"How's this kind fit together?" I asked.

"Just like any old deadfall," he said with a laugh.

It kind of hurt my feelings being made to look dumb, and Fred could tell it.

"Soon's I finish, we'll find a flat rock and I'll show you," he said quick.

The rock Fred picked must of weighed twenty pound. "Hold hit there, hun'ney," he said after we had it up on its edge.

I held it up and Fred went around to the front of the rock and knelt down. "When I tell you, let her down reeeal slow," and he started fitting the little pieces of wood together. When the trap was set, the rock was leaning against one stick, which was triggered against another that had the apple on its end and was stuck in the ground.

"Hot dog," he said, squatting down on his haunches. "Hit's just right. Old rabbit comes along and says, 'Now, that's a purty apple a-layin' there. Wonder how come hit's way out here?' "

While Fred was talking, he was bouncing around the deadfall like a rabbit, and you never saw anything funnier. His nose was nigh to the ground and his butt was up in the air and he was wiggling it like a bunny.

" 'Hit's shore odd hit a-layin' here with no apple tree. Maybe I can just sneak up and nibble a little,' " and he began sneaking up to the deadfall and acting like he was nibbling the apple.

" 'Man, that's a sweet apple, and hit's a good one!' " he said, and acted like he was nibbling harder, and wiggling his nose. Then Fred reached in with his finger and pulled the trigger. Kawam! The rock come crashing down so fast he barely got his hand out.

"Got him!" I yelled.

Fred's eyes lit up. "We gonna catch more rabbits than a hog's got fleas."

"Where we gonna set 'em?"

"Why not near th' fence by th' Dry Branch Road turnoff?"

"That's a far piece," I said. "How come we don't just go down by that blackberry patch near Ervin's house?"

"Hun'ney, you want th' Crosses t' rob our deadfalls?"

"I don't think th' Crosses'd do that," I answered.

Fred kind of cocked his head. "Ain't what I heard. Heard the Crosses'd steal th' hat right off'n your head."

"Radar'd do that? Aw."

"Don't know about Radar or Billy Bacon Jacob, but old Ervin might. Bill Lamb told my daddy couple days after Ervin moved in that Ervin done time for stealin'."

Somehow, I couldn't figure Ervin for a thief. "You really think he done time?"

"Hun'ney, a Lamb never lies!"

It was true. A Lamb'd die before he'd tell anything but the truth, and he'd kill you if you called him a liar. Nobody in our parts ever doubted their word. "What'd he steal?"

"Chickens. They put him in th' pokey for just a few days th' first time, but he kept doing hit 'til they sent him up for two years. Let's not put our deadfalls there."

We set the traps near where the Dry Branch Road turned off from the pike and rubbed them with wild onions to kill the people smell. The next morning, we had a rabbit. We caught four more that week. Since we didn't eat rabbit, I gave my half to Mr. Mac and Babe. We were really having fun. Everybody was, because most of the fall work was laid by.

One Sunday, the Shackelfords and Clarks came over, which usually bored me silly. This visit turned out different, though. I was in the yard with the men, sitting on the grass and leaning against a big maple half asleep, when Dad brought up the sheep killings and said he thought they were the work of a crazy man. That woke me up quick.

"I dunno, Morse," said Bess, straightening up in one of our rickety old lawn chairs. "This old boy's too smart at coverin' his tracks t' be crazy. I think hit's one of them smart-assed niggers come down here from Lexington."

Dad kind of cringed when Bess said "nigger" but he didn't mention it. "I've been thinkin'," said Dad. "He might not be anything but a thief, but he always heads for th' river. Now that's a slow, hard way of gettin' out of here. A thief would want t' get out quick."

"Could be he's tryin' t' scare us into thinkin' he's crazy," said Mr. Shackelford.

"If that's th' case, why don't he leave just th' head of an animal with its eyes gouged out?" said Dad. "He only takes th' hindquarters and nuts off th' carcass."

Bess laughed. "Th' hindquarters are th' best parts, Morse. That old boy just knows what's good. He can't carry a whole sheep. Each a them bucks would weigh a hunnert and a half. Hindquarters ain't even seventy."

Dad sighed. "Y'all are probably right, but supposin' it really is a crazy man?"

"What are you drivin' at?" Mr. Shackelford asked.

"Well . . . we're alone in these fields. He could come up t' us like any number of strangers who stop by asking questions and get you with that knife he uses before you could defend yourself. He could get at your house while you were workin' too. Kill everybody there. You'd never hear screams above the sounds of a mowin' machine."

It was true what Dad said, and it really scared me. Fred and LD and Lonnie and me knew everything and we wudn't saying and somebody might get killed!

Nobody spoke for a few seconds, then Bess got up from his chair and went over to his Ford. When he come back, he had a mason jar full of moonshine. "We gonna talk about things like this we can't do hit on a empty stomach," he said.

Mr. Shackelford and Dad laughed, then they all had a drink from the jar.

"What if he is a crazy man, Morse?" Mr. Shackelford said. "What can we do?"

"Go after him now! Stop things before somebody gets hurt," said Dad.

They quit talking then and everybody just kind of set. "You know, there is somebody," said Mr. Shackelford. "He might not be crazy, but he's mighty peculiar."

"Who?" Dad asked.

Before Mr. Shackelford could answer, Bess said, "You talkin' about Begley, ain't you?"

I got an awful feeling. I had heard at school that one of the people who didn't like Ben was Mr. Shackelford.

"What's peculiar about him?" Dad asked.

"You ever meet him?" asked Mr. Shackelford.

"No," Dad answered.

"Lots of folks ain't met him," said Mr. Shackelford. "Come here about ten, twelve year ago and bought that place down on the Big Bend from th' Cummings. Hardly speaks except t' sell his pumpkins and melons. Nobody knows anything about him."

"And he's got th' meanest goddamn dogs since Creation," said Bess. "Ain't anybody ever seen inside his cabin. Ed's right. We ought have th' sheriff do some checkin' on him."

I was shaking inside now like a bowl of jelly. I had to do something. There was only one thing I could think of. "Mr. Begley lent Bob his boat for fishin'."

Everybody turned and looked at me, and the shaking inside me got worse. I knew they were going to ask questions and I had to be careful what I said.

"You ever meet him?" asked Mr. Shackelford, looking at me suspicious.

"No, sir," I lied.

"Bob ever tell you about meetin' him?" Mr. Shackelford asked Dad.

"Yeah, he did, now that you mention it," Dad answered. "I remember Bob saying Begley lent them his boat. Bob thought he was just a man who wanted t' be left alone."

"Samuel, you ever see him?" Mr. Shackelford asked, turning back toward me.

"No, sir," I lied again. "But he never bothered us when we run th' trot line."

"I don't think he's our man," Dad said, kind of musing. "All this stuff has happened over our way. Hard to imagine he'd come all the way over here t' kill stock."

"Not if he's crazy like you say," said Mr. Shackelford. "I don't like Begley. Went down there one time t' see him about truckin' some of his melons into Lexington and he just left me standing outside callin' with them damn dogs raisin' hell."

Dad thought about that too. "Did Begley ever hurt anybody or steal anything?"

"Not that I know of," said Bess. "Sure is peculiar, though."

"I'll ask Bob more about him th' next time he's home," said Dad. "Meantime, I think we need t' get a posse together and comb th' Little Bend. Thirty or forty men with dogs. Maybe th' sheriff can get Lexington to provide us with a search plane."

"You really that worried, huh?" said Bess, screwing the top back on the jar after everybody had taken a second drink.

"The more I've thought about it, the more worried I've become," Dad answered.

Bess puckered his mouth. "Whatcha think, Ed?"

Mr. Shackelford raised his eyebrows. "Well, hit's an idea, but it won't work."

"Why?" Dad asked, sounding kind of upset.

Mr. Shackelford tilted his head to the side as he answered. "'Cause folks around here won't have nothin' t' do with hit, Morse," and he stuck his hands in the pockets of his Levi's.

The look on Dad's face said he thought that was the stupidest thing he'd ever heard. "I can't understand that. They got family and property at stake too."

Bess chuckled. "What Ed's drivin' at, Morse . . . they's been strange goings-on around th' Little Bend bottoms for years. You heard of th' Blue Hole, ain't you?"

"You mean that story about Collins," said Dad. "My God, you guys don't believe that, do you? That a ghost haunts a pool of water and kills people who come around?"

Bess didn't answer for a while, then he said, "Well . . . no, but lots of folks do. You ain't gonna get no posse from around here t' go down on that stretch of river."

I was busting. We had a chance again. If they did get a posse together, Fred and me could lead them to the cave. I wanted to yell, *Yeah, do it!* But I knew better.

The next day, Dad called the sheriff, who said it sounded serious and if we could get as many as ten men together, he'd come with his dogs and try to get Lexington to send a plane. Dad and Bess talked to everybody around. Bess even talked to Mr. Miller. It turned out the only people who would join the group were Alfred, Rags Wallace, Mr. Mac, and Babe, and Rags backed out the next day. The police in Lexington told the sheriff that the whole idea was crazy, going out for something that probably wudn't there to begin with, and even if it was, a handful of men couldn't cover an area that big, and without men on the ground, the search plane wouldn't help. The sheriff said he had to agree with them and under the circumstances he wudn't coming.

That wudn't the worst part, though. The worst part was that after Dad and the other people got together and said they were going regardless, they wouldn't let Fred or me come. When they got back from the search, Dad was in a bad mood. They hadn't found anything and from what I could tell, hardly spent any time around the Blue Hole or the cave. Mr. Shackelford said that it was the last wild-goose chase he was going on, and Bess laughed and said maybe they'd get hired by Mr. Hoover and his F.B.I.

Generally, I'd have been down about how things worked out but I was getting used to stuff going wrong about the crazy man. Thanksgiving vacation was coming up, and it was too good a time to waste feeling bad.

25

We had our first light snow the day before school was out for Thanksgiving. The next morning, Fred come by so we could run the deadfalls together. During the week he did the trapping alone, but on weekends I was always with him. Our rabbit catching had slowed a lot. If we caught two a week, we were doing well. We were sitting at breakfast when there was a little peck at the kitchen door.

"There's your sidekick," said Dad. "Come on in, Fred."

I could hear a strange muffled sound like feet stomping on a pillow. When Fred come in I saw why—he was wearing gunnysacks around his shoes.

"Hi," I said.

"Hidey, hidey," he answered, and walked past me to warm up by the stove.

I started eating in a hurry when I heard Fred take a deep breath and say, "Shuee."

Dad looked at Fred out of the corner of his eye.

"Shuee," Fred said, again, and squirmed a little like his clothes itched.

"Aren't you going to invite Fred to have a bite with us, Samuel?" Dad asked.

In my hurry I had forgotten to ask. "Yeah, Fred, how about some biscuits and jam?"

"No, hun'ney." he said, shaking his head. "I just et. Thanks anyway."

Dad kind of eyed Fred. "Think your daddy'd like it if he knew you turned down somebody's vittles after they were offered?"

Fred's eyes got wide. "I didn't mean nothin'! Sure, yeah, I'll have some," and he come to the table and sat down.

"M'dom, fix Fred a couple of eggs. You got any more biscuits?"

"Sure I do," said Mom. "There's a whole pan full. Do you like coffee, Fred?"

"Yes, ma'am." Fred said, and started eating biscuits and jam.

I never saw anybody eat faster. He didn't say anything, he just ate, maybe six or eight biscuits, and when the eggs got there he put them inside biscuits, covered them with jam, and ate that. When there wudn't anything left, he looked around and said, "Shuee."

"How would you like some hard candy?" said Dad, who had been eating slow.

"I'm pretty full," said Fred, then he laughed and said a man hadn't ought eat two breakfasts, on account of it would spoil his dinner. Dad said that every now and then it was good to do that and let the belly rest and if he didn't want any candy would he take some back to the rest of the family. When we left the house, Fred was carrying our whole big bag of hard candies.

Outside, it was warming up fast. Snow was falling off bushes and trees and I knew it was going to be muddy. The morning was nice, though. Crisp and clear. We got two rabbits and set the deadfalls again for the next day. The next morning, we run them before the ground thawed, but we didn't get anything. That was odd, because there was fresh blood all over one rock.

"Wonder what happened?" I said. "Don't make any sense there bein' blood on that rock and th' trap not sprung. Wudn't any blood on it when we set it, was there?"

"Umm, don't know. Prob'ly was though."

"Naw, I remember now, they were clean. Besides, that's fresh blood."

"Yeah, hit does look fresh," said Fred. "We better watch from now on. Apple looks good, though. If th' trap sprung, how come it ain't squarshed?"

He had me there. We talked about it for a while, then spent the rest of the day sliding down the volcano hill on a sled we made out of some old roof tin.

That night after supper I got to thinking about the deadfalls. It wudn't right those apples not squarshed with blood being on the rock. Somebody was stealing our rabbits. That was why we wudn't catching many. First, I thought maybe it was the crazy man, then I decided he didn't do things that way. He'd kill a sheep, but he never took something already dead. Besides, he wouldn't set the dead-falls again after he robbed them. It had to be one of the Crosses. I had told Radar about the deadfalls and how many rabbits we were catching and he must've watched where we went and stole them. They had apples from the sweet apple tree too because I saw him and Billy Bacon picking them. The more I thought, the more I was sure it had to be Radar. Since Radar wudn't too smart he might've left tracks around the line fences where there was still snow and maybe I could track him back to their house. But if the wind come up strong or it snowed again, it would cover any footprints. If I was going to look, it had to be tonight.

Later that evening, I told Mom and Dad I was tired, then went to my room, took off my shoes, and crawled under the covers still wearing my clothes. I lay there for what felt like forever waiting for everybody to go to sleep. Finally, I heard the door to Naomi's room close, and a few minutes later, the squeak of Mom and Dad's bed. They talked for a while, then it got quiet. As the minutes went by I could feel my heart pick up and by the time it was safe to start out it was pounding like a sledgehammer. I put on my shoes and macki-naw and got my Eveready. I kept thinking about the crazy man and getting more and more scared. I sat down on the edge of the bed and tried to calm down. Outside I could hear the wind and knew that soon all the tracks would be gone. That's when I thought about the gun. If I took it along, I'd be plenty safe.

The rifle felt icy cold and slick from a little layer of dust. I wiped it clean, then set down on the bed again until I got up enough nerve to reach behind the dresser for shells. My hands was shaking so bad I was afraid of dropping the shells so I put the whole box in my pocket, then left the house through the door to the screened-in porch.

It was cold and the little snow that was left crunched under my feet. There was a full moon which made it light enough that I didn't have to use the Eveready. I climbed the hog lot gate, then loaded and cocked the .22. I was scared to death.

There wudn't anything in the first trap or the second, but in the third we had a rabbit. The rest of the traps wudn't sprung and looked okay and the only tracks were mine and Fred's. Old Radar was smarter than I thought. He didn't leave any clues.

I hadn't gone but a little ways toward home when I stopped. If Radar was smart enough not to leave any tracks near the traps, he was smart enough to circle around by the Dry Branch Road to get there so nobody could see any signs leading up from our direction. That's what he must've done and the wind covered his tracks near the traps because they were made earlier than ours. I went back past the deadfalls to the main fence that separated our pasture from the road, then turned on the Eveready. On the road side of the fence there was a steep bank that faced north and was covered heavy with blackberry briars and two, three inches of snow. I hadn't gone more than a hundred foot when I noticed where briars had been pushed aside. I pressed up against the fence and shined the light on the ground. My heart stopped. There wudn't just footprints, there were gunnysack footprints!

Fred robbed our traps! Couldn't of been anybody else. My best friend! He took them and lied about it. He could've had them all by asking but he stole them. Didn't care about me, he just wanted the rabbits. Fred wudn't nothing but a thief and a liar!

By this time, I was running and the light from my Eveready was a bouncing blur as the cold and tears blinded me. Fred and me wudn't friends no more. I wudn't ever going to have anything to do with him again. He was just trash. All the Mulligans were.

Suddenly, my foot snagged on something, the flashlight flung up in the air, I turned head over heels and the rifle went off next to my face.

I lay there for a while shaking, then I got the flashlight and looked around. The rifle was leaning against a little bank and there was a hole blowed in the ground inches from where my head hit. I had forgotten to put the safety on. My pants were torn at the knee and all bloody and I could hardly bend my leg. I got up and started for home. As I walked, I thought about Fred. He could see signs of me if he run the line and he'd know that I knew. I hoped he did.

The next morning, I woke up stiff and achy. My knees and palms were skinned and there was blood all over the sheets. I hadn't fixed anything when I got in and had to clean up in a hurry. I really moved, boy. Pretty soon everything looked okay except for my torn Levi's and the blood on the sheets. I was just going to have to tell Mom I fell. I hated to lie again, but I'd lied so much already I figured one more didn't matter. I got out clean Levi's and went to breakfast. I didn't feel hungry and Mom kept asking why I wudn't eating, then she felt my forehead.

"Morris, he's getting sick," she said. "He was running around outside in the snow yesterday with Freddie and came in soaking wet. Look at him."

"You feelin' bad?" asked Dad, and I told him no.

"Just not hungry, huh?"

"Yes, sir."

"How about helpin' me feed th' cattle?"

"Morris, he's sick," Mom said again. "He could be getting pneumonia. I don't want him running around outside."

Dad thought for a while, then said, "Maybe Mom's right. It snowed last night and th' way th' wind's whippin' it, you probably wouldn't have any fun anyway."

After Dad left, I went into the living room. Through the window, I could see snow everywhere. It was winter, boy, and the Warm Morning stove sure felt good as I curled up in a chair and read some of my *Heroes of Israel*. Pretty soon, Dad come back from feeding and sat down in his chair and picked up his newspaper.

"I saw Fred," he said. "I told him you were sick and he ran th' deadfalls himself. You all got two last night. I put yours on the fence post by th' backyard gate."

"I don't want it," I said.

"He brought it to you. It's yours."

We sat there for a while and I listened to the dishes clink in the kitchen as Mom and Naomi washed them, and to the fire crackling in the Warm Morning. Outside, the sun was shining and everything was white. It should have been a nice time.

"What happened?" Dad asked softly. "You and Fred have a fight?" And he struck a match on the stove to light his pipe.

Instead of answering, I shrugged and kept looking out the window.

He took two or three big puffs and smoke come rolling out as he said, "How come you don't want th' rabbit?"

"Because it's a lie."

"How so?" and he unfolded the paper and started looking at the headlines.

" 'Cause he's been robbin' our deadfalls."

Dad stopped reading and turned toward me. "How do you know that?"

I told the whole thing. Except for the gun part.

"I wondered how come you were limping this morning. I won't say anything to Mom about your goin' out last night but I don't want you doin' it again, understand?"

"Yes, sir," I answered, and a little time went by.

"What you gonna do about Fred?"

"Nothin'! And I ain't havin' nothin' t' do with cheap white trash again!"

Dad looked away from me a little, then said, "You think Fred's cheap white trash?"

"Yeah."

"Some folks think Jews are trash," and he began reading the paper and puffing his pipe.

That bothered me. We were different. "Well, he is!" I said.

An answer came quick. "Cheap white trash? No."

"Well, what is he then?"

"What do you think he is?"

"A thief and a liar."

Dad lowered the paper and looked at me. "I don't agree, Samuel. Fred's proud, and his family don't have enough to eat. You didn't need th' rabbits. You gave them to Mr. Mac and Babe. They eat rabbit because they like it, but they have a smokehouse full of meat. Fred and his folks are hungry. The only thing they have left are a few salt butts and some water-made cornbread because Alfred won't kill a hog. If I know Alfred Mulligan, that family will starve before he spends any money because he's savin' for mules and equipment."

I was boiling by this time, and I was going to say how I felt no matter what. "How come you're takin' Fred's side? You're th' one always talkin' about doin' right. How come you're so happy with Fred when I'm right? He was my best friend, and he stole my rabbits, and you're my dad and you side with him."

Dad didn't get mad. He just nodded toward my *Heroes of Israel* lying on the arm of my chair. "David forgave Saul, didn't he?"

I wondered what that meant. "Yeah."

"Saul did more than just steal rabbits. He was gonna kill David."

"Yeah," I said, not knowing if it was a question or not.

It was quiet for a while and we both stared out the window. The sun was fierce bright and everything sparkled. There was a good smell from the kitchen, and the teakettle whistled.

"Well, he's your best friend," Dad said, finally. "You do as y' like," and he picked up the paper and started reading and puffing on his pipe.

I knew what Dad said was true . . . about the Mulligans being hungry and needing my rabbits, but I still couldn't be Fred's best friend. I figured I'd be friendly but that was as far as I could take it, and that's the way it was all the rest of the winter.

26

After the stolen rabbit thing, I just stayed down in the dumps. Christmas and Hanukkah and my school vacation were coming up, but Bob and Debby couldn't make it home and I didn't feel like celebrating. In December, we went into Lexington and I found a present for Ben, a pair of light steel traps. They were $9.50, and this time I had to pay full price. After getting my folks' stuff, the traps took all the chore money I had left. They were beautiful though. A mink's picture was etched right on the jaws.

I gave out everybody but Ben's present early and had Fred take Lonnie's to church for him. I bought Fred a pair of Tougher'n Nails work gloves, and he gave me a box he made that I could lash to the carrier rack of my bike. It was nice and I thanked him but I didn't feel nothing for it. I didn't give LD anything.

The day before Christmas, I headed across Cummings Hill to Ben's. It was cold, and by the time I dropped onto the bottoms, the smoke from his chimney looked good. Nothing was changed. Ten steps out of the oaks old Cain and Abel come barking and snarling. I was pretty sure they knew me now though, because they whined a little and Abel showed less teeth, but when I tried to come closer than usual, they both went crazy. That brought Ben to the door.

It was great to see him. When I handed him his present he put it under his little tree like the year before, then handed me my gift. It was prettier than any Christmas present I ever saw. The wrapping was only brown paper sack, but it was decorated all over with ginger-bread Santa Clauses. There were two Santa Clauses on top and one each on the sides and ends. They had red sugar hats and coats and pants with white trim. Between them were little pine sprigs and cones and they'd been dusted white like snow. The present was shaped like a long box of candy, but the second I picked it up I knew it was wood. I loved gingerbread and was wanting to open the package anyway, so I asked if we could have some of the Santa Clauses with coffee?

"Sure," he answered. "Why don't we eat th' ones on th' ends. That way hit'll still be pretty when you open it tomorra."

It wudn't what I had in mind but it was enough. The Santas were really good, and after we wolfed down the end ones, we finished off the sides.

"You havin' a nice Christmas?" he asked.

"Okay, I guess. We call it Hanukkah."

"Get lots of presents?"

"Quite a few. You really like Christmas a lot, don't you?"

Ben smiled. "Reckon I do."

"Did you use t' have big Christmases when you were my age?"

He didn't answer, and it hit me I was prying. Before I could say I was sorry he said, "Christmas has always been my favorite time of year. When I was a boy we'd go huntin' after church, then have a big dinner. All my kinfolk would gather. It was like that for most families in th' Smokies. Ever'body was nice t' ever'body else."

I felt warm and good and leaned against the table with my chin in my hand. Ben was by the fire and kind of draped over his easy chair. I watched his red flannel shirt move in and out when he breathed and noticed where the shirt gapped a little that his chest hair was part gray. Dad's was that way too. I wondered if they were the same age, then decided Ben was younger, maybe forty-five. It was always hard for me to tell about a grown-up. Pretty soon, I was in the mood to talk about my problems.

"Dad and some neighbors tried to find th' crazy man and didn't," I said, then went on and told him the whole story. It come out easy, and it was nice not blubbering for a change.

"Fred and me tried everything we could t' go along, but Dad wouldn't let us. Him and Mr. Shackelford got mad at each other after they didn't find anything. Mr. Shackelford said it was a wild-goose chase."

Ben gave a short laugh that made his head and chest bounce.

"Y' know," I said, "nobody's had any stock killed for quite a while."

Ben sighed, then got up and walked to the window and stared out at the bare oak tree. "He's prob'ly scared now, but he'll be back," he said soft, then turned to look at me. "You got t' deal with him, Samuel. He ain't ever goin' away on his own."

"I can't tell," I whispered. "I just can't."

He nodded, then went back to his easy chair and fired up his pipe. I knew he was disappointed in me. He thought I could do anything and I kept letting him down.

"You done a good job," he said, finally. "That was a damn good try. If your daddy knowed, he'd be proud of you."

I felt better right off.

Ben filled the coffee cups again and we talked more about when he was a boy growing up in Tennessee. His daddy was a cropper too, only they raised cotton instead of tobacco. We did all the same kinds of stuff, except he played the guitar. When I asked if he still played, he reached under the bed and pulled out this beauty. Boy, he could play.

When he quit playing, I decided to talk about the stolen rabbits. It would be nice having somebody on my side for a change. I brought it up and he listened quiet like always.

"You seen him since then?" he asked, after I finished.

"Oh yeah. We even got each other Christmas presents."

"Hmm. Whatcha gonna do?"

"Nothin'! He's a thief 'n' a liar."

Ben sipped some coffee and picked at the crumbs on his shirt. "You like some hick'ry nuts? Short crop this year, but they got a fine taste."

I said I would and he got up and pulled a flat rock and hammer out of a drawer and brought over about fifty little nuts. We pounded away, and the more I ate the more I wanted.

"Don't you think he's a thief and a liar?" I said, working on a nut.

"I think he stole and lied, yeah."

That wudn't what I had asked. "Yeah, and he's a thief and a liar."

"Think so, huh?"

"Yeah! What else could he be?"

"Well," he said, raising his eyebrows. "He could just be somebody who stole and lied. Everybody who steals and lies ain't necessary a thief and a liar."

I couldn't believe it. I didn't expect that kind of stuff from Ben. I stared at the fire and thought about what he said. "What would you do about it if you were me?"

Ben stretched and yawned. When he did, he looked like a big cat. "I'd forget th' damn rabbits. Fred'd be my best friend if I was you, and a bunch of rabbits ain't worth losin' a friend over. 'Specially if he's a best one."

We talked a little longer, then I took off for home. On the way, I got mad at Ben and everybody else. I hadn't done anything wrong! Fred stole the rabbits and lied, not me. If somebody stole Ben's pumpkins or Dad's tobacco, they'd know whose side I was on, but nobody give a shit about my rabbits. Okay, fine, they could just be that way!

I stayed mad all that night and lay in bed and ate the last of the Santas. The next morning, which was Christmas, I unwrapped the present. When the brown paper come off I forgot about being mad. It was a walnut box and carved like the stocks of Ben's guns. There were birds and deer and squirrels and some animals I had never seen in real life, like moose and bear. It was polished so good the shine seemed to go way down in it. I took it to the living room to open the box and everybody gathered around.

"My goodness," said Mom. "What a beautiful box! What's inside?"

I lifted the lid and inside was a pair of bedroom slippers, only they wudn't like any other slippers I'd seen. The outside was mink and muskrat and the inside was rabbit. The bottoms were real soft leather and everything was lashed together with rawhide.

"Samuel, who . . . ?" said Mom.

Dad shook his head. "It's Samuel's secret as long as he wants t' keep it."

27

I was hot, sweaty, tired, and hungry as I drove back to my hotel. I took a shower, slowly turning the tap to cold. When I got out, a crisp, frosty, fall-in-New-Hampshire sensation invigorated me and with it, my appetite. I headed for the hotel's restaurant.

The restaurant was spacious, with white tablecloths and uniformed waiters. It was still early and there were only a few diners, one table being occupied by a family. I was thirsty and ordered a beer. As my thirst slaked, I became aware of things occurring at the family's table.

The two adults were early middle-age and with them was a girl who looked to be in her late teens. I didn't catch all the conversation, but I could tell they were arguing. From their accents they were not of Kentucky.

Suddenly the man opened up on the girl, who was trying to defend herself but couldn't because the man wouldn't let her. The mother proved an unsuccessful diplomat as the man railed on. I could make out a few words, "expect," "pregnant," and "Ronnie."

Suddenly, the mother threw up her hands. "I can't stand this," she said loudly, "I'm going back to the room." In a few minutes the table, thankfully, was empty.

By the time my steak, baked potato, salad, and another beer arrived, the argument at the table had evoked memories of Dad and Ben. I learned a lot about parenting from them. Ben was my friend but he had advised me in some ways like a father. He didn't become angry with me. Frustrated, perhaps, but he listened to my arguments. Dad was a little more volatile in his approach to rearing his most difficult son but was also willing to consider my thoughts when they differed from his. He never hit or ridiculed me. They let me make mistakes, provided logical guidance, then let me learn from my mistakes. In some of my darkest moments, their views, taught so long ago, allowed me to persevere, to think my own thoughts and stick to them until I was proven wrong. Their simple lessons continued to influence me as a father.

Raising daughters isn't easy. Everything goes well until they turn about twelve, then they discover, or perhaps are discovered by, the opposite sex. My traumatic introductions to the maturing female brain came at 1 a.m. one morning when sixteen-year-old Penny hadn't arrived home from a date with a seventeen-year-old "hunk" who was the star running back of her high school football team. He was supposed to have had her home by midnight! Nora tried to keep me calm.

"Samuel, they're only an hour late and I know this boy's mother. He's a good kid. They'll be home soon. They simply lost track of time."

I squirmed about on the living room couch where we were sitting, Nora stroking my hand. I was mad and getting madder. "When she gets in, she's grounded! For a month! And when I get my hands on that kid she's with, he's gonna be the only one-legged high school running back in the nation!"

Nora laughed. "You men amaze me. From puberty, the only thing you have in mind is sex. You hatch an infinite number of schemes for sleeping with girls. Then, after trying to deflower every virgin around, you turn into puritan preachers the moment you have a daughter."

I gave Nora a baleful stare. "I did not deflower every virgin around!"

Nora laughed again, slipped her arms around my neck, and planted a big kiss on my mouth. The kiss was nice. I kissed back and pretty soon we were necking. One thing led to another . . . then we heard the door close. This required some rapid rearranging of clothes before I confronted Penny.

"How come you're an hour and fifteen minutes late, young lady?" I asked.

Penny held up her hands. "Rita Adams' date's car went on the fritz and Charles and I had to take them both home. I tried to call but our line was busy. It was a long way to their houses, but it would've been twice as long for their parents, so I insisted that we take them. I knew I was supposed to be in by twelve but I thought I was doing the right thing. Did I do wrong?"

I reached over and picked up our downstairs phone. Our youngest daughter was talking to her friends. At past one in the morning! Nora gave me a shot in the ribs and I grinned, sheepishly.

"You did right, Penny. I apologize for doubting you. When you get upstairs, tell your sister Candy to hang up the damn phone and go to bed!"

Candy proved to be a handful. Boys again. Times changed, but I hadn't. I didn't have a problem with premarital sex (how could I?), but I did have problems with promiscuity.

Candy was not promiscuous, but her sexuality was being . . . expressed . . . by her senior year of high school. She and I had always had a close relationship and we frequently trout-fished together in the summers, even during her years in college. One day when we were fishing a beautiful stream and had caught several nice trout, Candy waded out of the river and sat down on a large rock. It seemed odd to me that she would leave the water when fishing was hot, so I swam over and sat down beside her. I said nothing.

"Dad, I'm pregnant."

That is not an easy thing for the father of an unwed daughter to hear. Not me, anyway. I tried to think what to say, then I remembered Ben's technique. I didn't say anything, choosing instead to nod and let her tell me.

"You're probably wondering how this happened. I've been dating a boy named Boyd Iversen for about four months. He's a year ahead of me at Dartmouth . . . a senior. He's really cute and we've been sleeping together. I ran short of money and didn't buy my birth control one month, and, well, I'm pregnant."

It was obvious some shoes had yet to fall, so I nodded again.

"When I told Boyd, he got really angry and said it was my fault. He's starting law school and says he doesn't want to be burdened with a child. He says I should have an abortion."

My gut reaction to this news was to ask for Boyd Iversen's address and the whereabouts of the nearest sporting goods store that sold baseball bats. Instead, I nodded.

"I don't know what to do. I'm so miserable," she confided as the tears and sobs came.

We sat on the rock for a long time with our arms around each other. I decided her statement about not knowing what to do was a request for advice. "Have you thought over what you might do?"

"I've barely thought about anything else the whole three weeks I've known. I don't love Boyd and he doesn't love me, so marriage is out. Everything comes down to having an abortion or a baby, then deciding whether to keep it or let it be adopted. I can't make up my mind."

"Which way are you leaning?"

Candy clutched my arm so hard it was painful and tears streamed down her face. "I don't think I could live with myself if I had an abortion, Dad. I want to have the baby, but I don't know if I'll be able to give it up for adoption once it's born. My insurance only pays for part of this. I'll need help. I swear I'll pay you back. There's another thing, I'm going to be pregnant and hanging around the house. Your colleagues will know your daughter got knocked up."

It was time to be a man. "Candy, whatever you choose, I'll support. As for my colleagues, they can go pound sand. If you decide to keep it, your baby will be my grandchild and I'll treat him no differently than any of my other grandchildren. As for what it costs, don't you worry. Half the money is going to come from young Mr. Iversen. You can tell him that from me. He either—in advance—

pays half the calculated cost for the entire pregnancy and delivery, or I'll write a letter to the dean of his law school concerning the issue. He has three weeks to get me that check before my letter goes out. Does your mother know?"

"Yes. She thinks I should have the baby."

I chuckled. "I'd have bet th' farm on that."

The hug I received from Candy nearly crushed my ribs.

I grunted. "Tell Mr. Iversen one last thing. Tell him if we ever meet, he had better be wearing pillows over his cast-iron jockstrap."

Both of us laughed.

A week later, Candy miscarried. Still, she had made a life decision. And I had been a real father. I remember thinking that Dad and Ben would have been proud of me.

28

We finished stripping just before New Year's, and got on the first tobacco sale after the Christmas break. Dad and Alfred set Fred and me up on their worst baskets of burley so that the buyers would think it was given to us and maybe bring a better price. It was fun sitting on the baskets of burley. You could see the whole warehouse. The tobacco was in rows about four foot apart that stretched from one end of the building to the other and down these come the buyers. It was Fred's and my job to sit on the baskets twice, once when the government man came around and put his government price on it and once for the buyers. The government man didn't speak, he just grabbed a few hands of burley out of the stack, glanced at them, then threw them on top of the stack and wrote a number on a paper slip and walked on.

Finally, the auctioneer came around going a mile a minute, saying things couldn't nobody understand except the bidding price and who bought it. The buyers walked along behind, pulling tobacco from the stack, then bidding by making secret signs. The crowd was moving about half as fast as folks walk and it was hard to see how anybody made sense of the buying.

Old Alfred stood behind the basket Fred was on and when the buyers got close he yelled, "Bid her up, boys—hit's the young'uns." The buyers eyed Fred, then me a little further down the row, and just kept moving.

Both our crops sold good and when we headed home everybody was rich and happy. We had to stop at two filling stations on the way for Alfred to pee though, and he kept saying he felt weak and it was easy to see he'd been losing weight. Dad told him to start eating better now that he had money, and Alfred said he wondered if that was why he was getting puny. Dad said sure, that if a person didn't eat, he'd get weak and lose weight and why didn't he kill a hog. Alfred said he didn't figure they needed any full hog and would just buy a few more salt butts.

It was a good winter, but a rough one. Nights would go down to four, five above and warm up in the daytime to the high twenties. It was bright and clear though, and I spent as much time outside as possible on the new sled I got for my eleventh birthday.

In February, the six gilts we saved from our last bunch of hogs found forty-six pigs. With the six sows we had fifty-two head of hogs. Alfred had great luck too. He was really happy, especially when the price of hogs jumped.

Winter just didn't seem to want to quit, though. In late March, when it was usually rainy, we had a cold spell that lasted until the second week of April. It was scary at the Mulligans'. Everybody was skinny and moved real slow. We caught a few rabbits, which helped, and Mamie cut the salt butts thin. They were ready to start eating the starved old hens when a miracle happened: spring! It come overnight. Birds sang, flowers bloomed, everything living felt happy. And Alfred bought his mules and equipment.

The late spring picked folks up and flung them into a new crop year. Everybody was behind and working seven days a week, daylight 'til dark. I didn't see a single neighbor until late May and the only reason I did then was because of heavy rain. I went over to the Mulligans'. It wudn't I wanted to see Fred so much as I didn't have anybody else to visit. I couldn't go to Lonnie's, Ben's was further than I wanted to walk in the rain, and I only spoke to LD if I had to.

It was a warm rain and smelled like spring rains always smell and trickled in little rivers two, three inches wide over the yellow dandelion and short young bluegrass fields. By the time I reached the Mulligans' hog lot, I was soaked. From the top of the gate I could see secondhand equipment everywhere. Next to the yard fence on Cummings Hill, two young mules swished their tails. They were big, boy.

I jumped down on the other side of the gate and knocked on the front door. Thelma Jean opened it about a foot.

"Whatchawant, Sam?" she asked, looking at me, skinny, dumb, and ugly.

"Samuel," I said. "Is Fred home?"

"Reckon. Whatchawant?"

"T' see Fred!"

"Aw. Okay. Fred, hit's Sam!" she yelled.

"Samuel," I muttered, and I could hear stomping around, then Fred come to the door. He was skinny like Thelma Jean but not quite as bad.

"Hidey, Samuel," he said, and stepped out and closed the door. "What you up to?"

"Foolin'," I answered. "Figured I'd see what you were doin'."

"Just kind of restin'," he answered as we walked into the yard and picked our way through the farm tools. "Whata y' think of our stuff?"

"Looks pretty good."

"Yeah. Hit's a lot for th' money, Pa says. All we need now is a tobacco setter and mowin' machine and we can crop anywheres."

"Looks that way," I said. "Your mules are mighty pretty."

"Wanta go see 'em?"

"Sure."

We started past the kitchen and Alfred come out to join us. He was terrible skinny, and he looked like he'd kept on losing weight since we sold the tobacco.

"Hidey, Samuel," he said. "What you think a them mules?"

"They're a pretty team, Mr. Mulligan."

"Yeah, them's as purty a team a mules you'll ever see. Look at them backs and chest. They can pull anything. What's old Morse doin' today?"

"Restin', mostly."

"Yeah, that's what I been doin' too. We needed that dry spell, y' know. Weather broke just right to let us catch up some. You see my strawberries?"

"They're coming on fast, ain't they," I said, and they were white with blooms.

"Hit's gonna be 'nother great year," Alfred said, not paying any attention to my answers. "See them pigs?" he half shouted. "Not a runt in th' bunch. Hogs is at twenty-eight cents. Shit, them'll be ready for market in a few months. Folks didn't think we could make last winter with no more'n we had. Reckon I showed them."

After he said that, Alfred kind of half staggered back to the house. When he got to the door, he turned around and yelled for me to say hey to old Morse for him if I saw him. I thought that was an odd thing to say since Dad and me lived in the same house.

Fred and I fooled around for the rest of the day. I had a good time until right in the middle of talking about making new slingshots I remembered the rabbits and something inside me just sagged. A little while later, I headed for home.

We finished setting around the first of June and we were further behind than ever because all the other work, like corn planting, hay baling, sheep shearing, hadn't been done. It wouldn't have been so bad except Alfred just kept going slower and slower. Ervin was worse. One afternoon, while I was getting some stuff for Mom from the feed room, I heard the back barn door squeak and Dad and Alfred come in arguing. I looked through a crack and I could see Dad half dragging Alfred to a stall, where he set him down and leaned him against a beam. Alfred looked awful.

"How long you goin' before you see Doc Culbert?" asked Dad, resting on one knee in front of Alfred.

"I ain't seein' no doctor, Morse. My daddy got puny and went to a doctor and he died. Ain't none a them sonamabitches gonna get me."

"I wouldn't worry about doctors killin' me if I were you,

Alfred." Dad said. "You're dyin' now th' way you're goin'. It's just possible he could still do somethin' for you, though."

Alfred shook his head. "Ain't payin' out my tobacco or strawberry money!"

"Aw shit, Alfred, you could cut him some wood this winter. I'll help you. Besides, what good's your mules and equipment if you're too sick t' work 'em?"

"Supposin' I die before winter?"

"Then I'll cut th' wood for you. You won't be a charity case."

Alfred's face squenched up. "What if somethin' happens 'n' you can't do it?"

I could see Dad was fed up. "Then Culbert's outta luck! Goddammit, Alfred, I'm through talkin'. I'm takin' you in and you can't stop me because right now, I'm stronger than you. Sling an arm around my shoulder or I'll carry you like a goddamn baby."

"I'm gonna die, Morse," Alfred said, trying to push Dad away. "You take me t' that doctor and I'm gonna die!"

"Bullshit! You'll be burying stiffs in no time. Mamie'll have a smile from ear t' ear."

"Huh, hit'll have t' improve, 'cause she ain't had nothin' t' smile about recent."

Finally Alfred quit struggling and he put his arm around Dad's shoulder. They stood up together and walked past the feed room, where Dad saw me and flushed red.

"How long you been there?" he asked me.

"Awhile," I answered.

He stared for a few seconds, then said Daisy and Gabe was hooked up to the cutting harrow and for me to disc until he got back, or near dark, then get in the cows and start milking because he was taking Mr. Mulligan to the doctor.

It was real late when Dad got back, and Naomi, Mom, and me sat at the kitchen table with him while he ate. It turned out when he got to Culbert's, the doctor just sent them on into Lexington and that's what had taken so long.

"How bad is it?" Mom asked.

"They don't know," Dad answered. "They put him in the hospital and said they had to run tests and would know in a couple of days. Some organization's payin' for it."

"What did Culbert say?" asked Mom.

"He said Alfred was a sick man."

Mom wouldn't leave it alone. "Didn't you ask what was wrong with him?"

Dad gave a big sigh. "He said Alfred was in bad shape."

Mom kind of slumped in her seat. "How'll we get everything done? What about the tobacco crop?"

"I'll have to do it with Samuel and Ervin. Fred will have to handle most of Alfred's stuff. We'll help him when we can."

"What about housing time?" said Mom. "What then?"

Dad didn't answer for a while, then said, "Maybe Alfred will be back by then."

It was a week before Alfred got home. The doctors told him he had the sugar diabetes and had to take imulin shots for the rest of his life. Alfred got mad and told the doctors he wudn't taking imulin shots after he got home because he couldn't afford it and even if he could he wudn't going to let some sonamabitches stick him with needles and that they better come up with something else fast because he had to get back to work since work was his bidness. The hospital gave him a piece of paper telling him the things he could eat, but the Mulligans didn't have anything on the list. Without the imulin and right victuals, Alfred started getting sick again. Finally, Dad talked to Doc Culbert, who said if Alfred would tell him what they had to eat, he'd try to write out a new list. That worked pretty well and before long, Alfred was back in the fields. He wudn't the hand he had been though, and got down on himself something awful.

It was July before the spring work was finished. Dad told me to just take off and do whatever I wanted until tobacco housing. I was all set to try making friends with Fred again so I could enjoy the rest of the summer, when Rosemary come over to see Naomi. She was all dressed up in a blue skirt and white blouse and a little heart cameo necklace. When she came inside there was this great smell of perfume.

"I have something t' show you," she said to Naomi, then she stuck out her left hand. There was this big diamond ring on her finger, and Naomi screamed, "Rosemary! You're engaged!" Then they both started jumping up and down and hugging each other and laughing and talking about who it was, and when she was going to get married, and where she was going to go on her honeymoon, and how happy she was and all.

This feeling come over me. I wanted to run but my legs wouldn't move. When things got to where they halfway worked, I went to the tobacco barn and crawled up on the mowing machine seat and bawled until there wudn't any tears left in me.

29

I awoke late the next morning and spent an hour in bed reading a novel that had won the Man Booker Prize. It was typically British, meaning that it moved at the speed of a crippled snail. Heresy, I know, for a professor of comparative English literature.

After breakfast I started driving. I had no plans, but apparently my subconscious did, because when I reached the entrance to the old Shackelford place, I stopped. What sixty years before had been a rutted lane ending at a farmhouse in need of paint, was now a two-hundred-foot blacktop driveway to an antebellum-style mansion. This was sacred ground. Rosemary Shackelford, the first woman I ever loved, lived where that elegant home now stood.

Until this moment I had never really considered the move from Kentucky to Indiana as a watershed event in my life. Once in Indiana, however, I found myself excluded from the mainstream community, especially when it came to girls. I had exactly two dates in high school. The girl's name was Kendra and I had just gotten my driver's license. We had fun, but when I asked her for a third date, she refused and said her father didn't think it was right for her to go out with a boy who wasn't Christian. That was a moment of real pain. Since I wasn't a good athlete and was considered a hillbilly, I was pretty much at a loss for male companionship as well. I retreated into our farm and into reading, which I came to love because books afforded me a form of friendship and gave free rein to my imagination. During my senior year, one of my teachers insisted that I apply for a scholarship to an elite New England liberal arts college known as Collingwirth. How I got accepted is still a mystery to me.

My luck with girls was no better in college than in Indiana. Collingwirth was populated by the children of the rich. There were five Jewish kids there, all rich except me. And all male. I didn't have a date in two years and eventually quit trying. Then a miracle happened.

Cheryl Marie Smith was a waitress at Tulley's, my college town's least favorite coffee shop. Tulley's was perfect for me because it was devoid of Collingwirth students, whom I detested. It had four tables, twelve red plastic counter stools, two waitresses, one cook, and few customers. Cheryl was blonde, cute, divorced, a part-time student at a local college, and about twenty-three. I frequented the coffee shop as often as possible, sat at the counter chatting with her and trying to work up the nerve to ask her out on a date. One day she asked if I had seen the movie at the town's only theater. I hadn't, and she said, "If you're free tonight, let's go." I had three papers due in two days. "Not doing a thing," I answered, and a few hours later I indulged in the first non-self-administered sexual experience of my life. I almost didn't. Apparently none of Cheryl's previous lovers had been circumcised, and while guiding my clumsy attempts at penetration she squealed, "Oh my God, part of it's gone!"

I thought she was referring to size and became instantly flaccid. A few minutes later Cheryl remedied that malady and I declared my manhood. I was a novice but a fast learner. Of the now nine Jewish kids on campus, I was comforted by the belief that I was the only one getting laid. Then tragedy struck!

I was dating Cheryl on Wednesday and Saturday nights. One Monday evening I had exciting news to impart. I raced to her little apartment with a bottle of cheap wine, quietly used the key she had given me, and entered. Sounds emanated from her bedroom. I was certain she was struggling with someone and burst through the bedroom door to rescue her, only to find Cheryl and my philosophy professor deeply involved in hedonist studies.

I received an A in philosophy that semester.

The good news I had been in such a rush to tell Cheryl concerned reviews on a paper I had worked on for an English professor. As a research assistant, I was studying the effect of Charles Dickens' visit to the United States in 1842 on his future work as editor of the British newspaper, *The Daily News*. During that trip Dickens had become bitterly opposed to slavery and shifted the direction of the newspaper after he returned to England. That was well-known, but little had been written about the effect of the American trip on Dickens' later work. My observations were not totally new, but offered my professor an exhaustive review of the topic. The academic accolades got him tenure and he wrote me a glowing recommendation for NYU's graduate program. A few months later, I met Nora.

I was jarred from my musing about Collingwirth when a man of about forty came out of the mansion that had replaced the Shackelford farmhouse and walked briskly toward me. I exited the car. Once he saw my age, he dropped his aggressive posture.

"Can I help you?"

I laughed. "Not unless you can tell me where Rosemary Shackelford lives."

It was obvious from the look he gave me that he found this a little strange. I quickly made an effort to remedy the problem. "I'm revisiting places I lived as a child, and the love of my juvenile life lived where your house now stands. The family name was Shackelford."

The man smiled. "Carry a torch a long while, don't you?"

We both laughed. I recognized his accent. "Have you lived here long enough to trade in your Red Sox tickets for field-level Cincinnati Reds?"

The man shook his head. "I plan to have my ashes scattered in Fenway's outfield. We've lived here three years and I don't know any of my neighbors." He smiled and started to turn away, then turned back toward me. "Sorry I can't help you with Miss Shackelford, but I'm sure you'll meet another girl soon. Have a nice day, sir," and he walked toward his house.

I backed out of the driveway thinking about Rosemary. I wondered if she was still alive. If she had children. If her life was happy with the man she had chosen. The words of my undergraduate psychology professor ran through my mind: "You never forget your first love." Apparently, he was right.

What was I going to do today? I had no idea, but then it didn't make any difference. I was retired. An abandoned derelict floating on an irrelevant sea. I decided to go back to my hotel and spend the day soaking in the swimming pool.

As I started driving, I looked to my left toward the ridge where our tobacco barn had set. I found myself upset by its absence and felt an urge to explore where it had stood. I parked at the fractured old gate, then walked to the top of the ridge and followed the creek toward the volcano hill. When I was abreast of "our house," I began my search. The bluegrass was so tall that what I felt with my feet was as important as what I saw. I wandered in circles until I tripped over the remnants of a ventilator panel, one of many such planks that could "open the barn up" to the air. This would aid in curing the tobacco after it had been harvested. When rain threatened, of course, it could be closed. It was obvious to me where I stood. In 1946, I would have been standing in (or beside) the tobacco barn. I searched, but found no further remnants.

The distance between the tobacco barn and the sheep barn was perhaps two hundred feet, and I walked toward the site. Halfway there I discovered part of a weathered, creosoted plank. The distance from both barns put it exactly in the neighborhood of the corncrib. Perhaps this piece of wood had witnessed an event that deeply affected my life on Berman's. At the time I was having difficulty coming to grips with Rosemary Shackelford's engagement. Indeed, I . . .

. . . didn't want to be around anybody but Ben. Every morning I'd take off across Cummings Hill to the Big Bend bottoms. Finally, I just left my fishing pole at his cabin. That ten-mile round trip was the only bad thing about visiting Ben. It was worth it, though. I could be lower than a snake's belly and Ben would make me feel better. Third or fourth time I visited, he brought up the crazy man and about my talking to Dad. I told him I wudn't up to it at the moment and it would have to wait until I was over my problems with women. He grinned and said I'd better not figure on waiting that long. I told him it shouldn't take more than a couple weeks and he really laughed.

We talked about all sorts of things, or sometimes just sat on the riverbank and fished in dead quiet. Man, did he know stuff. He talked a lot about his family . . . he was the youngest, same as me, and had the same kind of troubles with one of his sisters I had with Naomi. He'd even been in love with a girl Rosemary's age when he was eleven, and the same thing happened to him that happened to me. Everything was going great until one day I asked where he got the clothes he had lent me. He got quiet, but it wudn't like our usual quiet. When I left that evening I took my fishing pole.

Truth was, I was getting lonesome for a friend my own age. That was a problem because I didn't want to see Fred very often, and Lonnie didn't come over. Mostly, I just took my slingshot and wandered the hills. I was a good shot, boy. I was better than Fred now, and a couple times in the past I let him know it by plunking a sparrow at forty, fifty feet. Fred never said anything, but he never took a shot unless he was sure he wouldn't miss.

You can learn a lot wandering hills if you already know some and Fred had taught me lots. I'd go down to the creek in the morning and study tracks. It was fun putting together what went on during the night. Like one day I found the tracks of a mama coon and some little coons that had come down for a drink. The babies wandered ahead, and suddenly there was a set of fox tracks moving on the other side of the creek. This went on until they come to a narrow spot and the fox made his play. There was mud tore up all over the place with lots of gray-red fur and just a little coon fur and some blood. I could see where the fox run off limping. He must have been a young fox to be dumb enough to tangle with a mama coon. Ain't a fox in Kentucky can lick a mamma coon with babies.

One day, I decided to follow Cuyper Creek. It was awful hot and when I got to a deep hole I shucked my clothes and went for a swim. When I got out, my clothes was gone. I was shook up because I thought maybe a goat got them. I couldn't go hunting for them since I was naked as a jaybird. Then I heard somebody laugh and Lonnie stepped out of the bushes.

"Lookin' for these?" he asked, holding up my clothes.

We had a good time swimming and squirrel hunting with our slingshots. I got a couple and then Lonnie asked me to their place. I was kind of scared, but figured he wouldn't ask me if he was worried about his pa.

We crossed Cuyper Creek and walked through the cornfields along the high bottoms. From where we crossed the creek it wudn't far to the crazy man's cave. That gave me the willies. After a while we come to a bluff. You could see a long stretch of river from there. The channel got wide, then the stream narrowed and deepened and started the Big Bend turn.

Just below the bluff we were on was another cornfield, and below that, in a little hollow, was the Miller house. It was small and white with the grass clipped short in the yard and some pink roses climbing along a wood-rail fence. Mr. Miller wudn't there, but everybody else was. The house was neat and had some real pretty furniture, most of it made out of walnut. One of the kitchen chairs was sitting in the corner though and was kind of broke up. I wondered why it hadn't been fixed because with five kids the Millers needed it. Turned out Mr. Miller made all the furniture and even built the house. I had dinner with them.

Before the day was out, it got tiresome. Lonnie just didn't say much. Finally, I told him I had to get the cows milked before Dad got in and took off, leaving the squirrels for him.

When I got home, Naomi and Mom were standing by the cistern, and Mom said I had better get started doing chores because Fred had hurt his hand and Dad took him to the doctor.

"Hurt his hand? How?"

"He cut his finger off. He was acting meshuga with the corn

sheller and cut his finger off," said Mom, shaking her head. "Dad and Alfred took him to Dr. Culbert."

I felt awful. "Dad said that Culbert's a quack and Fred's gonna die!" I yelled.

Then Mom and Naomi started talking to me together, telling me it was just a finger and you didn't die from a cut-off finger.

I did the chores but I couldn't get Fred out of my mind. Why the heck had I gone on so about the rabbits? Fred and them needed the rabbits and I just gave them away. I could've told Fred that I didn't want them and he ought take them because it was a sin to kill them and throw them in a ditch to rot. He might have taken them. But no, I had to give them away to people who didn't need them. Boy, I was dumb.

Dad got home as I was finishing milking and told us all about what the finger had looked like. That made me feel even worse. I wanted to go see Fred. Mom didn't like the idea of my walking at night, but she didn't want to upset me again so she let me go.

I was really feeling low. Fred and me wudn't best friends anymore but he had been my best friend. He taught me everything I knew about slingshots and frogging and fishing and reading signs. I hated them damn rabbits!

The night was hot as I walked through the big field toward the hickory and locust thicket. The moon looked like a pumpkin, and swallows flitted in and out across the twilight sky. When I slipped through the barbwire gap, somebody come out of the kitchen door, saw me, climbed the hog lot gate, and ran my way. I could tell it was Thelma Jean by the milk-cow way she ran.

"Fred cut his finger off!" she yelled, when she got close. "Fred cut his finger off!"

"Yeah," I said, and kept going.

Thelma Jean walked along beside me, jabbering as she gasped for breath. "In th' corn sheller! You know how hit gets jammed with cobs . . . all plugged up? Well, Fred always reaches and pulls 'em out and today they was this one wouldn't come and he reached in further and hit cut his finger right off! Spurted blood all over th' corncrib! Bled like a stuck hog! Finger just laid there a-twitching. You ain't ever seed so much blood! Hurt somethin' awful. Fred was a-squallin' and runnin' 'round with his finger stickin' out and hit just a-pumpin' blood all over th' corn! Some places hit looked like Injun corn! You shoulda heard him squall! Old Radar heard him down in th' holler, I betcha," and she kept on and on.

Poor Fred. It must've hurt terrible. He was always fiddling with that damn corn sheller. As we neared the house I kept going faster and faster and feeling worse and worse and by the time I got to the front door, I was nigh crying. Thelma Jean stood beside me while I knocked. Pretty soon, Annie Lee come to the door.

"Hidey, Samuel. Well, Thelma Jean, what you knockin' for? Whyn't you just come in?"

"I wudn't knockin'. Old Sam there was a-knockin'," and we both stared at her.

"Who is hit, honey?" Mamie called.

"Sam," Thelma Jean yelled.

"Samuel," I said, and went inside.

30

Wudn't any lamps in the front bedroom where I entered, but it was bright in the living room beyond, which made the bedroom half light. There, on the bed, in a bunch of covers, still wearing his Levi's, was Fred. One of his feet was sticking out from under a quilt, its big toe wiggling.

"Hidey, Samuel," he said soft, waving his bandage-covered hand.

"H . . . how you doin', Fred?" I croaked, and went to the side of the bed.

"Tolerable," he said holding his hand in front of him and looking at the bandage. "Hurts like farr sometimes, but hit don't hurt right now."

I didn't know what to say so I just said, "Will you still be able to shoot a slingshot?"

"Well, hun'ney, reckon I will. Ain't gonna be th' man I used t' be, though," and he kind of shook his head.

"Maybe you can learn t' shoot left-handed," I said. "Yeah, that's it, you can learn t' shoot left-handed," and I set down on the side of the bed.

"Hun'ney, I'm right-handed," then he cocked his head to one side like he often did and said, "You think I could learn t' shoot left-handed?"

"Hit ain't likely," said a voice behind me. It was Thelma Jean.

"Will too!" I said, mad.

Fred called out, "Mama, Thelma Jean's a-botherin' me."

"Thelma Jean, you git in here and close th' curtain," Mamie yelled.

When they closed the curtain, most of the light was gone. Fred's face was dark, but the light that was there shined on the whites of his eyes and I could see them good.

"Think I could learn t' shoot left-handed?"

"I know you can," I said. "Nothin's ever kept you down. You'll be a left-handed gun. Like Billy th' Kid."

Fred set up in the bed. "Maybe I could. I've got some blood for hit. Uncle Charlie's left-handed."

"See there," I said.

He thought about it for a while, and then asked what I'd been doing lately.

"Not much . . . saw Lonnie today. Him and me went squirrel huntin'."

"Get any?"

"Two."

"You did, or Lonnie?"

"Me."

Fred thought a minute then said, "What else y'all do?"

"Went down t' his house."

The white in Fred's eyes widened. "You did!"

"Yep. Lonnie asked me and I did. Ate dinner there too."

"Wudn't you scared?"

"Yeah, a lot at first, but they were real nice. Mr. Miller wudn't home."

"Huh. What else you been doin'?"

"Fishin' and stuff."

"Me too. 'Til today, when I cut my finger off. Not much fun in that."

Neither of us spoke for a while after that. We could hear people talking on the other side of the curtains but you couldn't make out more than a word or two. I felt so bad about Fred. Dad and Ben were right and I was wrong as I could get. I was about to tell Fred what a fool I'd been when he swallowed and moved a little on the bed.

"Samuel, I . . . I've done somethin' real bad," he said soft. "I . . . I . . . stole your rabbits. I feel awful about it. I'm just terrible. I ain't no good. I'm just terrible . . ."

There was a choking sound and I knew he was getting ready to cry and I couldn't stand it. "It was nothin'," I said quick.

"Was too. When a body's somebody's best friend, he don't steal his rabbits. I feel awful what I done. I have ever since I did it. I just ain't no man at all."

The choking sound turned to squeezin', and I felt worse and worse. I didn't know what to say, so we just set, him cryin' squeezin' tears and me struck dumb as a board.

"I don't care about th' damn rabbits," I said hard. "I just want us t' be best friends again. I ain't been much of a man neither. I figured out you done it but didn't have th' nerve t' say anything. I just walked around mad. That ain't bein' a man."

Fred snuffled and wiped his eyes. "Figured you knowed. You ain't been the same 'round me since Thanksgivin'."

"I found your footprints along th' fence th' night after we saw blood on that trap."

"You went back that night!" he said quick. Then there come a look on his face. "It snowed and drifted before mornin'. That's why I didn't see any sign of you."

"Yeah."

Fred sighed. "I'll never do nothin' like that again, Samuel. Maybe God's punishing me for what I done. Can you give me a forgiveness?"

"It wudn't nothin', Fred. It's me that's been lonesome and hateful and I feel awful. You got all my forgiveness. Let's be best friends again."

"Shake," he said, and stuck out his wrapped-up hand.

I took his wrist and we shook and I felt peaceful for the first time in months.

"Come on in here, Samuel," Mamie called. "I ain't seen you for a spell."

I rolled over to the other side of the bed and went into the living room. It was jammed with people. Mamie asked me about the family, then said, "What you think of that boy of mine cuttin' his finger off?"

"It was terrible!" I answered, and a flash of sick feeling shot through me again.

"Hello, Samuel," come from behind me.

I turned around and Annie Lee was sitting on the bed beside WK. She had on a new red dress and high-heeled shoes and a red ribbon in her long black hair.

WK scowled, then moved his big leg next to hers.

Everybody talked for a couple of minutes, then I heard a noise on the stairs that led up from the front bedroom to the bedroom at the top of the stairs. There was a whisking sound as the curtains pushed to one side and Alfred walked through.

"There's our Alfred," said Mamie.

Alfred had gained a lot of his weight back, but he still didn't look good. His face was long and his eyes were sunk back in his head and he didn't smile.

Annie Lee bounced off the bed and took him by the arm. "Lie down here, Pa," she said, and Alfred looked toward WK, who didn't seem like he wanted to move.

"Get your ass offn' th' goddamn bed and let Daddy lie down," Annie Lee blazed.

WK made a face then scooted off the end of the bed. Then he kind of smiled. "I'll fix th' pillow for you, Alfred," he said, and he began fluffing it. When he finished, he turned to Annie Lee and said they ought take a walk and let Alfred get a little air.

Annie Lee said there was enough air, then Alfred said maybe it was a little close. She glared at WK, then moved toward the kitchen door in a huff with WK following.

"How you doin', Mr. Mulligan?" I asked.

"No good," he mumbled, lying down. "Sugar's got me. Gonna die with hit, I reckon."

"I don't think so," I said. "Dad says if you just stay on your diet, you'll be okay."

Alfred's face turned darker and he started muttering. "Can't eat nothin'! Won't let me eat nothin' n'more! Shot two groundhogs last Sunday and couldn't eat more'n a few bites. Ain't no way for a man to live. Don't wanta live like this n'more."

Everybody started talking then, telling Alfred how good he looked and how well he was going to be, and it began to bother me so I went back into the front bedroom with Fred. We talked about river fishing with Lonnie and catching some big cats instead of little brim like we had in the pond, and how we would cut new poles, and maybe buy some cane poles if we could get some work, and how nice everything was going to be when the Mulligans got a place of their own. Before I left, I gave Fred my arrowhead that Dad turned up in the flint-rock field. We were best friends again, Fred and me, and it was gonna stay that way.

Going back, it was almost light because of the full moon. It was still warm too and the grass felt like the sun had just gone under a cloud. Wudn't a drop of dew. Crickets were everywhere and from the pond I could hear bullfrogs bellowing. I leaned my head back until my eyes saw straight up. I felt dizzy and good and staggered like a drunk holding my arms out until I felt like I was wallowing in an ocean of air, then just spun in circles all the way to the barb-wire gap. As I was closing the gap I thought I heard something. I held my breath and listened. Nothing but the crickets, so I started walking. Then all of a sudden I heard a man's voice. My hair stood up and my heart started pumping. The voice come again out of a little clearing on the other side of some hickories, along with a girl's voice. I circled the thicket and come up behind a big hickory tree. There was WK and Annie Lee. They were about thirty foot away, and she was lying down, leaning on her elbow, and he was next to her drinking from a pint. He took a big swig and offered it to her but she didn't want any. He took another big swig, then put the top back on, and kissed her hard and put his hand on her tittie.

"Don't, WK, I don't want to," and she pulled his hand off.

"Why not?" he grunted, and reached up and got the zipper on the back of her dress and pulled it down and then pulled the top of her dress off one shoulder.

"WK . . ."

"What," and he bit her on the shoulder and pulled some more on the top of her dress until I could see her bra strap, then he shucked the whole top of the dress off and pulled her up against him. She wudn't helping him, but she wudn't fighting neither.

"WK, I don't want to. Hit's a bad time, WK. We said we wouldn't this time of th' month. You'll get me with a baby," but he reached up under her bra and got hold of her tittie with his hand and squeezed it working his hand back and forth, then he pushed up on her bra and pulled her tittie out and put it in his mouth and started sucking while he pulled the rest of her bra off and began playing with the other tittie. Then he switched titties again.

Annie Lee was kind of half pushing him away, but he kept it up and started kissing her on the neck and pulling on her nipples. Then she put her hand around his neck and he reached down and went under her dress and started working up.

"WK . . . don't honey . . . honey, don't. I don't want to t'night."

But WK kept on and lifted her skirt, until I could see her panties, then he put his hand where her legs come together and started moving it back and forth and grabbing the inside of her leg and digging his fingers into her hard, and she squeezed his neck.

"Don't baby . . . baby . . . let's not t'night."

He kept it up and started pulling the elastic around the legs of her panties until I could see something dark, then he dug his hand in again. She squeezed his neck hard, and he reached up and got the top of her panties and pulled them off.

"WK . . . don't honey . . . not tonight."

WK didn't stop. He began kissing her hard all over and tried to pull her legs apart. He managed to get his finger against her black place and rubbed her, and she squeezed his neck and swallowed like there was a big lump in her throat. Then all of a sudden she spread her legs and he took down his pants and his tool was as big as a corncob and he rolled over and stuck it up her and started pushing back and forth. She was pushing too and they were thrashing up and down and sideways and then he started going hard and grabbed his hands around her rump and jammed up against her so hard she scooted forward again and again and wrapped her legs around him and he kept shoving and then she kind of tried to get away then shoved back up against his tool and then they just went plumb crazy.

I wanted to leave, but I couldn't. I felt something down in me and I didn't know what except I wished I was WK. Just then, I remembered the time and slipped away.

It was about 10:30 when I got back, and Mom was pretty sore. The four of us sat in the living room and talked for a while and Dad asked about Alfred and Fred.

"They're doin' okay," I said. "Mr. Mulligan's talkin' funny, though."

"How so?" Dad asked.

"He says he don't want t' live like this. He says he can't live on what they let him eat."

Dad nodded. "On a strict diet. I saw Doc Culbert in Spears. He said Alfred oughta be takin' insulin." Then Dad turned toward Mom and said, "You know that quack asked me for money. Turns out the organization that paid his bill before doesn't help but the one time. Wanted me t' pay th' Mulligans' other doctor bills too."

Mom's eyes got big. "What did you tell him?"

"I said I wasn't th' Mulligans' banker. He got mad and said why did I keep bringin' him in then, if I knew Alfred couldn't pay?"

Mom shook her head. "Some nerve!"

"I said Alfred would pay him when he got some money set aside. Then we had an argument and he walked off in a huff. T' hell with him!"

When Dad cooled off a little I said, "Mr. Mulligan said they'd only let him have a couple of bites of groundhog."

Dad laughed. "Not many doctors figure groundhog into a diet."

That seemed dumb to me. Maybe they were all quacks.

That night when I went to bed I could hardly sleep. I kept thinking about WK and Annie, and what they were doing, and how pretty Annie was naked in the moonlight. When I fell asleep I had a dream about Rosemary, and we were in the same little clearing in the moonlight.

31

I flipped the remnant of the corncrib back into the grass and started down into the small valley. The tenant house the Cross family had occupied was gone. Above it, the volcano hill rose in green splendor. When I crossed the creek, I angled for the sheep path, which, had it been there, would have risen upward along the base of the volcano hill. The path was gone but I could have made this walk with my eyes closed.

The base of the volcano hill rose gently from the valley to a point that had allowed a distant view of the Mulligan house, as well as the thicket situated in front of the pond. Thicket and house were both gone. One landmark still loomed high above everything: Cummings Hill. I walked toward the pond and discovered it had been replaced by bulrushes. I circled the bulrushes and came to the base of Cummings Hill.

The path from the pond to the Mulligan house was also gone, and getting to where it had set became a matter of exploration. Eventually, I topped a rise and saw the Dry Branch Road. My eyes followed the black ribbon until it dipped toward the Dry Branch Creek. Now I knew exactly where the house had stood. The entrance to the Mulligan yard from the road had been fifty feet before the drop-off. I wandered the area but found no evidence of the house.

I was getting tired and decided to return to the car by what had been my favorite route, past the hickory and locust grove. I hadn't gone far when I remembered something and turned back to look at Cummings Hill. I wondered if they were still there, waiting for Fred and me to show up. Then my memories broadened in a rush. The rabbits, the corn-sheller accident, and all the guilt I felt when I learned of Fred's injury. The evening at his bedside when we each confessed our deceit. All the things that happened that year before my family left Berman's. Fred was my best friend. The best friend of my life! *And I never saw him again after we left Berman's!*

I choked up. Why hadn't I contacted him? I couldn't remember another person in my adult life, other than family, who wanted nothing more from me than friendship, who supported me in the face of adversity. None of my colleagues fit that description. When Dean Simmons received an angry letter from an advisory board member objecting to my unorthodox teaching methods, he called me in and demanded that I give didactic lectures. I told him my pedagogical approach was a matter of academic freedom. This was true, and it was important to the entire faculty, but not one professor in the Leland-May English department stood up for me. When the issue resulted in my being passed over for promotion to full professor, a committee of my colleagues—all of whom knew how important my teaching was to me, and to the issue of academic freedom—advised that I "reassess [my] teaching techniques."

The more controversial my stand on teaching became, the more the faculty distanced themselves from me. Tolliver Atwood, a professor with whom I played tennis, found another tennis partner. How many letters had I written for his advancement? If I hadn't come through for him, he would never have progressed as rapidly in rank.

Thoughts of Fred had gone through my mind frequently during that particular brouhaha. Fred would never have deserted me in the manner of Atwood, and he was a child when we were together. I was willing to bet he would have called the dean and my faculty peers sonamabitches. I wanted to see Fred, but so much time had passed since he last had tried to contact me and I hadn't responded.

I couldn't face him. Dad had told me in high school that he had run into Babe MacWerter, and in the course of the conversation, learned that Fred had wanted to see me. I didn't go, because I was afraid someone at Harlan Jeffords High would find out and new jokes would arise about me being a Kentucky clodhopper and my life would become even more miserable. It was, perhaps, forgivable for me to have erred at that time, because I was a young teenager and desperate to be accepted by my peers. But Fred had tried to contact me again in later years and I never responded. Somehow, I just couldn't. Fred had meant so much to me; he had come through for me when grown men might have left a friend twisting in the wind.

I scanned Cummings Hill. *It's been a long time, Fred*, I thought, *but I'm going to find you. When I do, I'm going to tell you the truth and let you decide if you want to tell me to go to hell, or try to resurrect our friendship.*

I began walking again and was soon in the hickory and locust thicket. I wandered into the interior and tried to get my bearings. Most of the locust was gone, but the hickories were now very large. True to the Kentucky farm folk, they had cut the thorny locust, leaving the hickory trees to produce their sweet nuts to crack and eat on a cold winter night. I sat under a hickory and lay back with my hands under my head and stared at the canopy. The leaves were beautiful, deep green and so thick that I was completely shaded. The wind rustled them and the odor of soil and grass wafted about. A few minutes later a squirrel leaped from one limb to another, then scampered back to the trunk. It was a big fox squirrel, and he turned his head to look at me. Suddenly there were more squirrels, all gamboling about on the tree trunk and peeking at me. I was an intruder. I rose and started walking, then I suddenly realized the significance of this spot. It was here I saw Annie Lee and WK together that night. I chuckled, then continued on to the car, thinking about Fred.

That was a tough summer for Fred. I did everything I could to help him deal with his injury but I was only partly successful, because some tasks became difficult for him to perform. Perfection was the only goal Fred accepted for himself. Being with him every day, however, strengthened our friendship.

The problems he would suffer from the loss of his finger became clearer when . . .

. . . August come around and that meant tobacco housing. Like always, we were short of help so I stayed home after school started. Fred and I were made full-fledged tobacco hands, breaking out suckers, handing sticks of tobacco up from the wagon to the man on the bottom rail and even hanging some burley ourselves when we got to the sheds, where it helped to be short because the barn's roof sloped and bent a grown-up over. We also learned to cut tobacco. That's when Fred found out he was going to have big trouble from his hand. He dropped things. And even when he didn't, he was clumsy. We both learned cutting at the same time and in just a little while I was hacking my stalk of tobacco off with a tomahawk and ramming it over a spear and onto my stick. Fred could cut his plant off okay, but he had trouble hitting the spear. Before I knew it, I'd be ten, fifteen sticks ahead of him. It made me feel bad to be ahead of him, but we had to get the tobacco in the barn so I kept cutting as fast as I could. Fred never mentioned it because he knew that was what I had to do. When we finished housing, he told me that if he couldn't figure out how to get the job done with three fingers and a thumb, he and his Pa might have trouble on Red Bill's because he didn't think Alfred could go hard for a full crop year. It was true about Alfred. He tried, but by mid-afternoon he'd run out of gas.

The Sunday after I started back to school, I rode my bike to the Mulligans' for a visit and found Fred awful down about his hand. Alfred was down too, talking about how the goddamn sugars was holding him back and how some days he wudn't worth a diddly shit. I kept telling Fred he was worrying about his hand for nothing because we had just read in the paper where a fellow lost a whole arm and leg during the war and was running a four-hundred-acre farm with just him and his woman and that Fred was in a lot better shape than that old boy. Fred sighed and said, "Yeah . . . maybe." When I left the Mulligans that Sunday, I knew something had to be done to cheer Fred up, but I couldn't think of a thing until it dropped right in my lap.

It come about when Melvin Langley lost his lunch box at school and I found it. It didn't surprise me he lost it because Melvin always looked up. He'd talk to you and it was like he was looking at the top of your head. I couldn't figure how he found anything. Anyway, my finding it made Melvin happy because everybody knew how Miz Langley made her boys walk the straight and narrow and if I hadn't found it he'd have got a licking. That evening on the bus, he invited me over for a fox hunt. I was surprised because the only person the Langleys ever took with them was their dad's friend Mr. Rick. Fred had told me once that he would give most anything to go on a fox hunt, so I asked Melvin could I bring him. He said he'd check and the next day he said yes. I thought Fred was going to do cartwheels when I told him.

I left our house about 7:30 the evening of the fox hunt. The radio said rain, but it was warm and wudn't a cloud in the sky. It was hard biking to the Dry Branch Road, but after that, it was all downhill to the Mulligans'. When I got there, Fred was antsy.

"Hun'ney, you better hurry or we're gonna be late! It's two, three mile to that bluff!"

"We'll make it okay," I puffed and took off pedaling hard.

We scooted down past where the school bus turned around, then a way further we turned up a gravel lane overhung by hickory and elm. This made it darker and in the early twilight I could hardly see where I was going. It also got steeper. I thought about slowing down but figured if I did Fred would yell so I just let her rip. Pretty soon, we come to the gap Melvin told me about, then pedaled across a field until we come to a big open meadow with just a few trees on top and a thicket at the bottom. We could see four, five people and some dogs.

"Hit's them!" yelled Fred.

Melvin came over to meet us as we pulled up. "Hidey, Samuel, Fred. Y'all just in time. You bring some victuals?"

"Sure did," I said, and Fred held our sack up so Melvin could see it.

"When we startin'?" Fred asked.

"Just a few minutes," said Melvin. "Pa and Mr. Rick will take th' dogs down by th' thicket so's they can get a scent. Soon's they pick one up, him and Mr. Rick will come back up here and we'll lay around and talk and eat and listen to 'em run."

Just then, Mr. Langley got his dogs by their neck chains and started down the hill followed by Mr. Rick with his three. The two men and the dogs faded into outlines against the thicket, the dogs jumping and yelping. One of the yelps got kind of excited, and Melvin grinned.

"Hit's Maude," he said. "She's on t' somethin'."

I could see Mr. Langley's form bend down and turn one of the dogs loose, then the other dogs started going wild, rattling their chains and barking. All the dogs were turned loose then, and I watched their ghostly bodies snuffling and twisting and turning. Then one of the dogs began trotting, then loping with all the others following, and the barking changed into a "yaaap, yaaap, yaaap" as they disappeared into the early dark. Mr. Langley and Mr. Rick floated back toward us, then Mr. Rick built a fire.

The rest of the evening was spent lying on the ground and listening to the dogs bay. We ate our sandwiches while Mr. Langley and Mr. Rick drank. I was bored silly, but Fred loved it. I pretended like it was great because I wanted Fred to have a big time. The only real fun I had though was looking into the fire and watching the clouds light up from lightning in the direction of the Little Bend. It was far-off weather, but as the evening wore on, the lightning turned to small streaks and you could hear low thunder.

"Looks like we're gonna get that shower they predicted on th' radio, Frank," said Mr. Rick as the lightning got closer.

"Yeah, sure could use a shower. Wish I had my rye sowed. Wouldn't you know, I just finished discin' that field. Now I'll have t' do it all over again."

"Right now, though, we better get outta here before that old truck of mine gets mired down on a muddy hillside," said Mr. Rick.

Mr. Rick got to his feet and stretched, then picked up his big horn, which was shaped just like the shofar Mr. Gollar blew at shul. Everybody stood around while he wet the end with spit and took a deep breath.

"Burrrup . . . burrrup . . . burrrup," then he listened to the dogs. "Burrrup . . . burrrup . . . burrrup," and this time there was some quiet, then a few barks. "Burrrup . . . burrrup," then quiet.

Fred was still having a big time but I was wanting to go because the lightning was brighter and the rumbles deeper. You could tell that there were clouds gathering too because the stars had gone out in that direction. It was going to pour and I was going to get soaked.

Soon, the dogs came running in, shaking and panting, their tongues hanging out and giving off heat and grass smell and pushing up against our legs, tired and happy.

"Good girl, Maude," said Mr. Langley, kneeling down and patting her.

Maude flopped down on her back and lay panting while Mr. Langley scratched her belly and took out the pint again. "One for th' road, Carl?" he asked after taking a big snort.

Mr. Rick nodded. "Just enough t' kill," he said, looking at it through the firelight, then drained the bottle and put it behind the truck seat.

Going back wudn't nothing like as easy as coming down, and we were already tired. By the time we got to the Mulligans', I was beat and the storm was closer.

I rested a couple of minutes in front of the Mulligan house. I thought Fred wouldn't ever stop thanking me. It was good to see him happy.

The air was dead calm as we said good night, but the thunder and lightning was coming every few seconds. I started pedaling as fast as I could. About halfway to Cuyper Creek Pike the trees began moving, slow at first, then quick with rustling leaves as the wind rose. It was coming straight at my face and getting harder by the second. To make any headway at all, I had to stand on the pedals. I was giving out fast, gasping for breath, my legs aching so bad I thought they'd explode. Little flashes of lightning were coming between the big flashes now, and the road kept going from half dark to real bright like somebody turning a switch off and on. Finally, I could see the hill to the pike and knew the turn was a couple hundred feet up the grade. That seemed to give me new power. I reared up on the pedals, cramming them down with all my might, sometimes almost freezing straight up because I didn't have enough weight to turn the wheels against the wind.

Finally, I made the turn and stopped. My breath cut my lungs. A giant lightning bolt split the sky and hung there. I could see the thunderhead clear, boiling and coming straight my way, and I could smell the rain. The wind was to my left side now instead of my front and the road was flat at the start, then downhill, which really helped. I began pedaling like mad, my body stretched out over the handlebars.

Then the rain hit. It came in mighty sheets, cold, like somebody throwing buckets of ice water at me and getting in my eyes. It got hard to see, and the old batteries in my headlamp didn't help much. The wind kept gusting up and letting down, then got terrible hard in little short puffs and once I thought it was going to blow me off the road. The trees were going crazy. A limb as thick as my leg blew across the road just missing my back tire. I knew I had it made, though. I was going into the steepest part of the hill, which meant that the sweet apple tree was just ahead and beyond that our gate. I was giving it all I had when a lightning flash lit up what looked like a great, towering man staggering out of the brush, waving four arms and coming straight at me. I screamed and swerved. The bike skidded and I almost went down, then my foot bounced off the road and I got control.

When I reached the house I was numb. I couldn't remember opening the gate to the lane or yard. I just stood on the screened-in porch and shook and cried. Mom and Dad were waiting up. They'd been worried. They thought I was crying because I'd been scared by the storm and I didn't tell them any different. Besides, the more I calmed down, the more sure I was I hadn't seen anything but tree limbs. People didn't have four arms. Not even crazy men.

32

The fox hunt was just like a tonic for Fred. Friday night was foxhunting night for a while. I didn't look forward to it, but the Langleys were nice, so it wudn't too bad.

We had a cold snap the last week of October, and a lot of time that Sunday was spent inside the Mulligan house. It was bad, boy. The problem was Alfred. He was way down on himself and would sit and sigh and say how weak he felt and how the goddamn sugars was getting him just when he was about to have it made and how he never did have no luck and wished to hell he'd either get better or die and get it over with. Fred would be feeling good, then Alfred would start in and Fred would get big tears in his eyes. I felt sorry for the Mulligans, but I couldn't wait to leave.

The next Sunday I decided that I'd go see Ben. Like usual, I cut across Cummings Hill. It was Indian summer, but the prettiest part of fall was gone. A killing frost had stripped the trees, making them look like wood skeletons. It wudn't cold, but I still wore my mackinaw.

I walked out of the oaks into Ben's clearing just as he stepped through the cabin door, carrying his .22. I cupped my hands and yelled, "Mr. Begley!" Cain and Abel, who had been jumping up on him, whirled in mid-air and started barking.

Ben shushed the dogs, then waved to me. I walked up and we shook hands.

"Howdy, stranger," he said with a big grin. "Been a long time . . . missed you."

"Missed you too," I said, sheepish. "I don't know exactly how come I haven't—"

"You're here now and that's all that counts," he said, cutting me off. "Let's go get a couple squirrels for dinner."

We went back into the oak grove and sat down and waited. Pretty soon, two fox squirrels come out and started running down a limb maybe a hunnert foot off. Blam! Blam! And they both flew up in the air and come crashing down with their heads blown off.

"Whooee," I said. "That's some shootin'."

"Hit's nothin'," he said, and grinned. "Let's go back t' the house and fix these two for dinner, then we'll shoot up a box of shells and see how your eye's comin'."

While Ben worked, I checked his carvings. In the corner, where the two big blocks and five little blocks of walnut had been, set a bobcat, mother coon, and five baby coons. The bobcat was reared slightly on its back legs for the attack and the mama coon had her teeth bared and was scooched down, ears laid back, ready to fight to the death for her cubs, which were huddled wide-eyed behind her. I run my hand over the brown oil-smoothed wood and said, "Wow."

"Like it?" said Ben, flouring up the squirrel parts.

"Aw, yeah," I said soft.

Ben laughed. "Hit's my masterpiece. Don't reckon I'll make a better one. Gonna set it in a spot in th' corner I can see from anyplace in th' room." He warshed his hands and dried them, then picked up the .22, which was leaning against the table, and nodded toward the door. "Let's you 'n' me do some shootin', then we'll dig some worms and fish . . . after we make a pumpkin pie and eat some squirrel, a'course."

I shot up two new boxes of shells after finishing off the one he had already started. Ben either stood or lay right beside me and after every shot told me what I had done right and how to make it better. I couldn't believe how good I was. I could hit the circle in the box eight out of ten times from a hundred feet, and he made it smaller than usual.

By two o'clock, we had dug our worms, eaten the squirrel, made the pie, put it in the oven, and started fishing. Man, did the catfish bite! Real beauties . . . channel cats and blues, a foot long, fatter than moles, maybe fifteen, twenty, almost as fast as you threw in. One cat would have gone ten pound for sure, but he got away.

About four o'clock, we quit fishing and had pie and coffee. I ate half, and Ben ate the other. When we finished, I let out a big burp and we both laughed, then kind of melted into our chairs. We just sat like that, like we had so many times before, only this time we fell asleep. When Ben woke me up, it was twilight.

"Time t' go," he said, and I jumped to my feet.

When we got outside, I picked up the stringer of fish and wound them around my fingers. The fish were heavy even though I only took a few. "Well," I said, "you take it easy."

"I'll do that . . . Samuel," he said soft, "come back sooner next time, huh."

"Okay," I said. "Say, why don't you come over to our house sometime?"

His face went blank, then his arms went around my shoulders and hugged me up against him. He had the same smell as when we first met . . . warm, good, a little bit of stale hog meat thrown in. After he quit squeezing, he stood back with his hands on my shoulders, and said that, yeah, maybe he would, one of these times, when we had the tobacco stripped and sold, and before spring work started. Outside, I patted Abel for the first time. I tried to do the same thing with Cain, but he snarled and backed off.

It was deep twilight now as I trudged along, the stringer of fish slapping against my leg. The moon was coming up and I stopped and watched as it turned from orange to pumpkin yellow, then walked on as it turned whiter and gave off more light. It was going to be later than I'd hoped when I got back and I thought about Mom. If I hurried, I could be there about thirty minutes late and since she was used to me being fifteen behind, she'd just raise a little hell.

Halfway up the back side of Cummings Hill I could hear dogs barking from the direction of LD's house. That was rotten luck because it meant I had to circle an extra quarter mile down toward the hollow to keep from being seen. It was going to cost me time. I began running and finally dropped into a low place that was shielded from view. It was harder going now because I was in the middle of an elm thicket and trees were closer together than the oaks and there was more brush in between. Finally, I come to a fence I knew. I smelled some kind of stink, real strange, and thought about going further down to cross but I was in a hurry. I unwrapped the fish from my hand, slung them over to the other side, then put my pole next to them. As my foot touched the bottom wire to start climbing, I raised my head. Standing uphill, ten foot in front of me, was a wild-headed giant. He looked half a foot taller than Ben and the stuff he was wearing was falling off. His eyes somehow glistened in the moonlight, and his chest billowed in and out. I froze. Slowly, he raised his arms, then I knew what it was. The four-armed man! His dangling rags looked like the two more arms I saw near the sweet apple tree, and there was this big knife in his right hand. I tried to scream, but couldn't.

"Vengeance is mine sayeth the Lord!" he roared, and staggered toward me until his whole body towered over my head. Then he must of tripped because he come crashing down across the fence and the knife blade buried to the hilt in the ground next to my foot.

Screams come out of me I didn't even try to yell, and my body turned to jerks, leaping this way and that way until my legs started running, just pumping away on their own and me screaming like I'd gone crazy. I didn't know where I was going until suddenly there was a clearing and two dogs bounding toward me in the moonlight. I swerved as they come, trying to get out of their way. Then, all of a sudden, giant arms were around me and I was fighting, and kicking, and thrashing, but the arms had me tight. Then I smelled stale hog meat.

"It's okay, Samuel . . . it's okay, Samuel . . . you're all right . . . just relax . . ."

Something hot and wet wiped across my face and the voice said, "Go way, Abel."

I was back at Ben's. I opened my eyes and there he was, his long face just a few inches above my nose in the moonlight. We were about fifty feet from his cabin. Every part of me that could move had an arm or a leg wrapped around it. I wriggled and the coils relaxed.

"You okay, son?" he whispered, and I turned my face into his chest, put arms around his body, and bawled. I must've cried five minutes, Ben just stroking my back. When I stopped we went to the cabin and I told what happened, much as I remembered anyhow, and drank coffee while he filled .30–30 clips.

"Hit's our ole buddy from th' Little Bend," he said. "Your gettin' away was a miracle."

"Yeah," and I shuddered when I thought what the crazy man done to the bucks.

Ben laid the clips on the table and came over and gripped both my arms. His hands was so strong they hurt and his eyes were wide and scary and his voice was hoarse. "Samuel, you got t' tell your pa. You got t' tell him tonight! Understand?"

Fear went through me. "What about Lonnie?"

Ben rolled his head. I never seen him do that before, and he kind of shook my shoulders and his voice rose to almost a shout. "How long you figure hit'll be before that maniac kills somebody! Hit could be Lonnie! His whole family! They're only three, four mile from that cave!"

Fear shot through me again. "Yeah, I . . . I know."

Ben turned away from me, picked up the .30–30, then turned back, put a clip into the rifle, threw a shell in the chamber, set the safety, then stuffed the other clips in his pockets. Then he stared for a few seconds like he wudn't sure what to do and said: "Samuel, th' next thing th' crazy man kills could be your mom or dad or sister."

Suddenly, his face got real hard, and he shoved it only a few inches from mine. "You got t' tell, Samuel!" he said real loud. "You gotta forget this thing about Lonnie and tell! T'night!"

I was shaking when I nodded, and then I thought of something.

"Suppose'n nobody believes me. Crazy man ain't done nothin' for a long time. They'd believe you. You're a grown-up."

I was trying to get him to come in the house with me because I was too scared to tell by myself. I hated myself for being a coward. Still, there was some chance they might not believe me, and he was considering it. He run one hand through his hair and looked at the door, then at me, then reached over and picked up his big flashlight.

"I'll think about it," he said. "Come on before your folks go outta their heads."

We took the lane to where it turned to blacktop, then circled behind Pers Shanks' house and crossed Rags Wallace's place. About a hundred yards below Dillard's, just about where Fred and me had set the deadfalls, we crossed the road into our field and headed for the stock barn. We'd noticed a glow in the sky, but it wudn't until we come over a rise that we could see what it was. The MacWerters' barn was on fire.

We started trotting. I could see Ben's eyes shift back and forth in the moonlight. His finger was on the trigger guard of the .30–30 and his thumb was lying on its safety. When we got to the hog lot we hugged the barn until we come to its gate, then scooched down and looked at the house. Three people were standing in the dim light of the kitchen porch. I could tell two of them were Naomi and Mom from their size, but the third was a man. It couldn't be Dad because the man was too tall. There was something in his hand. Then he turned sideways and I could see a long-barreled pistol.

"Mr. Mac," I whispered.

Ben put his hand on my shoulder and I jumped. "Listen," he said soft but strong. "You go in there and you tell your folks what happened. Th' whole thing! Don't leave nothin' out except about me. You got t' do it, Samuel, and you got t' do it now! People's lives depend on this! No more stuff about Lonnie, y' hear?"

"You ain't coming in with me?"

"Not t'night. If they won't believe you, come see me tomorra and bring your pa. Just your pa! Nobody else! Get him t' promise he won't tell about seein' me, okay."

"But Ben, I thought you were goin' t'—"

"I can't, Samuel. I just can't."

"All right," I said, disappointed.

He knelt down and squeezed me 'til I was almost crushed, then leaned back and said: "When all this is over, we'll get in some huntin', do lots of stuff t'gether, okay?"

"Okay," I said, and started to reach for the gate.

Ben's hand grabbed my wrist. "Whoa! You don't walk up on a guy in th' dark when he's holdin' a gun and his barn's just been fired. Start callin', and as soon as your ma or sister recognize your voice, go. I'll wait here until you're inside th' house."

"Okay," I whispered. Somehow, I didn't realize he meant for me to start calling right then and I kind of just stood there.

"Go on and call!" he said, and his voice was a little mad.

I yelled as hard as I could. "Mom . . . Mom . . . it's me, Mom!"

Everybody's head turned toward the barn and Mom started to move. Mr. Mac grabbed her arm and his pistol pointed toward where he heard my voice.

"Samuel!" Mom yelled.

"Yeah, Mom . . . it's me, Mom!"

"Samuel . . . Samuel," and it was Naomi's voice.

I could see Mr. Mac's gun point down and I began climbing the hog lot gate.

"Bye," Ben whispered. "I . . . I love you, Samuel."

I started to say I loved him too, but somehow I just couldn't. I ran. When I reached the yard, Mom's arms wrapped around me squeezing so hard I almost smothered.

"Where's Dad?" I yelled, then I remembered the flames shooting up from Mr. Mac's place. "Your barn's on fire!"

"Too late for th' barn. Almost too late for me," said Mr. Mac, and he pulled back a flannel shirt that I recognized was Dad's. There was white gauze all over the left side of his hairy chest and up toward his neck. Blood was soaking through in places making little patches of red.

"G . . . gosh," I stammered.

"Your father's out looking for you," said Mom. "So is Edwin. Mr. MacWerter is guarding us while they're gone."

"Terrible things have happened tonight," Naomi gasped.

"There's a crazy man out there! He tried t' kill me!" yelled Mr. Mac.

"He . . . he . . . tried to k . . . kill me too!" I stammered.

"What!" Mom screamed. "Oh my God!" and she started breathing fast.

We went inside the kitchen, Mr. Mac holding Mom up. He grabbed the first chair he come to and pushed it under her. She flopped down, white as a sheet, then leaned forward and put her arms and head on the kitchen table.

"Get some of your dad's whiskey," Mr. Mac snapped at Naomi.

Naomi seemed to spring in the air and suddenly there was the bottle.

Mr. Mac got out the cork and started to push the pint to Mom's lips, then stopped. "Get me a glass," he snapped again, and it was there in a flash. He poured some whiskey in the glass and put it at Mom's white lips. "Drink some, Liz," he said, and she took some in her mouth and swallowed, then coughed and waved her hand over her chest and head. Mr. Mac pushed the glass toward her again and she shoved it away.

"I'm all right," she gasped.

Mr. Mac looked at the half-full glass, wrinkled his forehead, then downed it in one gulp. "What happened t' you, Samuel?" he rasped.

"I was comin' home from fishin' and started to climb a fence near Cummings Hill when this great, tall, raggedy man screamed, 'Vengeance is mine, sayeth th' Lord' and staggered out with a knife maybe two foot long and tried t' stab me. He tripped and fell before he could do it. Just missed me. I took off runnin' before he got up."

"My God!" said Mom, turning pale again, and Mr. Mac reached for the pint. "No, I'm okay," Mom said, raising her hand.

Just then I heard the yard gate squeak and the sounds of a bucket being kicked. Mr. Mac turned white and cocked the pistol he was holding in his shaky hands. "St . . . stand and identify yourself or be kilt!" he boomed in a quaky old voice.

"It's me, George . . . Morris," Dad answered, and Mr. Mac uncocked the pistol.

"Come on in, Morse!" Mr. Mac called.

Dad came in carrying the old 12-gauge. His eyes were wide, and his short, big-shouldered body filled the entrance. Mom shot out of her chair toward Dad. "He's home, Morris," she yelled just as her body slammed against his chest.

I had moved beside the kitchen stove and Dad saw me for the first time. He come toward me dragging Mom with him. With his free hand, he took my head and squeezed it against his cheek. "Thank God!" he croaked, and it sounded a little like he was crying but he wudn't.

"He almost got killed," said Mom.

Dad's head jerked back but before he could say anything I yelled, "Crazy man tried t' kill me with a knife!"

Dad's hands were shaking as he propped the 12-gauge against the refrigerator.

"Where's Babe?" asked Mr. Mac.

"Warning neighbors who can't see your fire and don't have a telephone. Only four, five families can see your flames down in the hollow. God knows where that nut's headed next!"

"Fine place," said Mom. "Four telephones between here and Harper's Corner, and three of them within a mile of each other. Fine place!"

Dad lifted his hands a few inches, let them flop against his thighs, then set down in a chair, his legs sticking straight out. Suddenly he looked at me. "What happened to you?"

"I was climbin' a fence by Cummings Hill and th' crazy man stepped out of th' bushes and tried to stab me with this great long knife. He fell and missed and I run off."

"Where were you, anyway?" asked Mom, and she was getting hot.

"I went fishin'."

"Where?" asked Dad.

"The Big Bend bottoms."

"Big Bend bottoms!" said Mom. "That's miles from here!"

"Where you, Bob, Alfred, and Fred ran that trot line?" asked Dad.

"Yes, sir," I answered.

Dad opened his mouth to ask another question when the telephone rang. He jumped to his feet, ran into the living room, and lifted the receiver off the wall box. When he answered his voice was almost squeaky. "Hello . . . he's home, Edwin. Crazy guy almost killed him, though . . . yeah, he's okay too . . . yeah, many as you can and tell 'em t' move their families together quick as possible. Split up th' work. Get Shackelford t' warn people down toward the Millers. Get Rags t' work on down th' Dry Branch. You and Bess cover Cuyper Creek Pike toward Harper's Corner. That bastard is on a rampage and this time it ain't sheep. Have one man guard each group of people and all th' other men assemble at my house . . . Sure they need to bring a gun. I'll call the sheriff. We got to make plans tonight. If this goes wrong, and we don't find him, he'll get another crack at us, and I'll guarantee next time somebody's gonna get killed. G'bye, Edwin." Click.

The room fell quiet, then Dad lifted the receiver again. "Operator, get me Sheriff Wilkers. This is an emergency."

While Dad was talking to the sheriff, I thought about Ben. There had to be a reason he wouldn't come forward. He was scared of something, most probably the sheriff. That meant he had done something wrong sometime or other and was worried about being put in jail. I already told that I was fishing on the Big Bend bottoms, and that the crazy man had tried to stab me coming back from there. They'd search the Big Bend, maybe Ben's cabin. The sheriff might recognize him. Somehow, I had to keep the sheriff away from the Big Bend bottoms.

33

I stopped at the crest of the hill during my walk from the hickory and locust thicket to my car, and looked back. There was an area I hadn't explored. I hesitated, but it was as if some invisible force were drawing me. I moved by instinct through some of the wildest briar-, thorn-, mosquito-, and tick-infested land in Fayette County. Vines grabbed at my feet. Wild blackberry briars were so thick as to be impenetrable; they were, however, loaded with berries. The briars demanded tribute for their fruit and received it in the form of my ripped skin.

The further I went, the more uneasy I felt. The heat was stifling and I had no more water, only the sweet blackberries to replenish my fluids. Sweat was pouring off me. I reached the top of a ridge and looked about. Primitive country in all directions. Then I saw a sliver of what I was relatively sure was river. It was a long way off. It occurred to me that if I injured myself, I was in trouble. Not a soul knew my whereabouts. Which direction should I go? In the course of wandering I had lost my bearings, and thirst was becoming an issue. Yet there remained within me this strange need to continue a journey to—nowhere.

I was moving downhill through some briars when I thought I heard running water. I stopped, held my breath. There was a definite trickling sound over the hum of insects. I moved toward it through brush and locust. The trickle grew louder until I came to the source.

I had stumbled upon a small, spring-fed creek. The water was clear and cold and good.

With a belly full of water I wandered on, up one hill and down another. My uneasiness increased. I was crossing a small ravine when I tripped and fell forward. Luckily, my face landed on soft ground. My right ankle wasn't quite so lucky and blood ran from a two-inch rip in the skin. The bleeding was fairly brisk and I decided to pack dirt around it. I commented to myself how fortunate I'd been to keep up my tetanus shots. As I was packing on dirt, I saw what I had tripped on—a piece of rusty barbwire was sticking out of the ground. I began to tremble, then calmed myself.

The bleeding stopped and I considered my choices. I decided the best thing to do was retrace my steps back to the hickory and locust forest. I had a belly full of water, plenty of blackberries to eat, and the land that I had crossed, while rough, was passable. I sensed that if I went straight ahead, I faced more than I was capable of enduring.

I checked the sun. There were at least four hours of light left. If I had to spend the night in the open, it wasn't going to kill me. I could sleep until dawn, then keep moving until I made contact with people. Then I came to the top of a rise and recognized a landmark. The effect was so overpowering that I had to sit down. There was no way I could spend the night here.

I began moving again, slower than before and extremely fatigued, but in a direction that I was certain would eventually get me back to my car. The crack of a .22 rifle revived me. I walked toward the sound and came upon a boy of about sixteen. He was wearing jeans and a Cincinnati Reds T-shirt, and carrying a .22. I felt profound relief.

"Hi," I said.

"Hidey," he answered, giving me a look that told me my appearance was frightening.

"Doing a little huntin'?" I asked.

"Just shootin'. Target practice."

I looked at the rifle. "Whatcha shootin'?"

"Winchester .22."

I smiled at him. "I used to live around here. I shot a Winchester. Mine was single shot. I was pretty good once."

His eyes played me up and down. "What's your name?"

"Samuel Zelinsky. What's yours?"

"Edgar Krauthammer. Am I on your property?"

I shook my head. "I'm just wandering. Know th' way t' Cuyper Creek Pike?"

He stared at me, then pointed in the direction I was almost certain was correct.

"Long ways t' Cuyper Creek Pike. You're gonna be mighty tired by th' time you get there. Stay near th' big trees and you can cut th' distance."

I looked in the opposite direction. "What you come to if you go that way?"

"That's th' Big Bend bottoms a few miles down. You don't wanta go that way."

Now I knew for certain where I had been. I felt weak and the boy sensed it.

"You okay, sir?"

"Yeah. You got any more shells for that rifle?"

"Half a box."

"I'll give you five dollars for five shells if you'll let me shoot your rifle."

A suspicious look returned to his face. I was a stranger who looked like he'd wandered through hell. He had no idea what I would do once I had the gun in my hand with a bullet in the chamber. Then again, five dollars for five bullets was a hell of a deal. I decided to make him feel safe. "Suppose you pick out a target and I lie down on my belly. Then you give me th' rifle and stand behind me while I shoot. You can give me one bullet at a time."

He thought for a few moments, then said: "Okay, but I want m' five dollars first."

I reached into my wallet and handed him a five. "What's my target?"

"See those three big toadstools at th' foota that oak?"

The toadstools in question were about the size of a large saucer and slightly more than a hundred feet away. "Tough shot," I said.

"That's it though. Want your five dollars back?"

I shook my head, bellied down on the ground, and reached back for the rifle. When I was ready he handed me a bullet. I checked the open sights, cocked the gun, took a deep breath, blew half of it out, and squeezed off the shot. A small piece of bark flew off the oak about six inches above my target. I reached back and got another bullet. "Your sights are off."

The boy looked offended. "No such a thing."

"Yeah they are. Watch this." I compensated for the sights and squeezed off my second shot. The toadstool exploded. "Your sights are high. Bet you missed a bunch of squirrels with your sights like this. When was th' last time you zeroed this thing in?"

A look of disgust crossed the youngster's face. "Never zeroed it in. Don't need t' be zeroed in. They do that in th' stores before you buy them nowadays. Not like when you were a kid."

"All right," I said, "let's see you put one in that second toad-stool."

He lay down beside me and said, "Gimme my rifle." His shot kicked more bark off the oak. Six inches above the toadstool. He looked at me. "You know how t' zero in a .22?"

"Yep." And I did, knocking down the second toadstool when the sights were correct. "Care t' check my work?" I said, handing him the rifle.

He shattered the last toadstool, then looked me up and down. I felt as though I could read his mind. *Who is this old fart?*

He sniffed, then said, "Need a ride t' th' Pike? Got m' dad's tractor."

I hadn't ridden behind someone driving a tractor since Mom and Dad died and the farm was sold. Holding on to the boy's shoul-ders made me remember how thick and powerful Dad's shoulders had been even as an old man. A lump developed in my throat and I could feel myself tear up. Naturally the kid picked that moment to look back at me, see my wet eyes, and ask if I was okay.

"Little dust in my eyes, nothin' t' worry about." Then I looked behind me. I knew that this would be the last time I saw that unearthly vista. Sure to God, it would be the last time!

34

It wudn't long before our living room was jammed with men. There were so many Mom put out piles of sweet rolls and made coffee in our canner. It was strange how they ate, kind of ripping the bread with their teeth like a dog killing a rabbit. There was a stink too, mixed in with the smell of sweat and tobacco. I'd smelled it before, but I couldn't remember where. Cigarette smoke was layered out in the living room and parted in swirls as people walked through. Everyplace you looked there was a gun stuck in a man's belt or a rifle or shotgun beside him. The talk was low, muffled, and constant, mostly about Mr. Mac, who had to show his bandage to everybody. All the close neighbors was there. Mr. Mac, Babe, Mr. Shackelford, Bess, Mr. Dillard, Mr. Lamb, Pers, Alfred, Rags, Mr. Langley, LD's dad, Ervin, Mr. Hickman, who we never saw much but who lived near the Langleys, and several men I didn't know.

Somebody yelled that the sheriff's car was coming up our lane. I ran to the window of my room. There it come, splashes of red and white light flying. As it got near our yard, its high beams showed cars and trucks all over the place. Old Fords and Plymouths and Chevys were standing every which way, and the police car had to twist and turn to make it through. It pulled in beneath the biggest maple, then seemed to sit exploding color every half second. Finally, the door opened and three men got out. I figured the one driving was the sheriff, and the other two were deputies.

As the sheriff and deputies started up the rock walk to our door I raced back into the living room and found myself an empty spot in a corner. Pretty soon the room was jammed again with standing people. You couldn't move. When somebody wanted coffee, they passed it one man to the next. It was stuffy, and even though a window was open, the air was still.

I had picked a bad place to stand. People filled the area around my corner, and I couldn't see the lawmen, who were in a little clearing in the middle of the room. I wriggled between one pair of Levi's-covered legs after another until I was behind a man standing near the sheriff. I could see pretty good if I moved my head when the man moved his legs. Everybody talked at the same time for a while, then the sheriff raised his hand and said that, okay, he wanted to take it from the top, and for the people who had got attacked to step forward.

Mr. Mac pushed into the clearing. His creaky old body looked wore-out next to the broad-shouldered, barrel-chested, young lawman who was wearing crisp brown law pants and brown shirt with a big star on his chest. It hit me then that I'd been attacked too, and I wriggled between the legs of the man in front of me and stood next to Mr. Mac.

"That it?" asked the sheriff, looking around.

"Hit's 'nough," said Bess Clark, and he wudn't grinning like usual.

"Okay, sir," the sheriff said, talking to Mr. Mac, "what happened to you?"

Mr. Mac looked like he was trying to figure it out, then he said, "Well sir, hit happened s' fast I hardly even know. 'Bout six this evenin' Babe went out for groceries and I went out t' milk. I hung my lantern in the rafters like always and went at it. When I finished milkin' I left th' lantern in the barn 'cause I had slops t' carry back and needed both hands. While I'm on my way from th' house with th' slop I hear horses whinnyin'. When I got t' th' barn th' insides was burnin'. I dropped the slops and run t' open th' stalls. Fire was ev'rywhere 'cause th' hay caught fire. Somehow I got th' stalls open and all th' animals out, then I run out th' far end. All of a sudden, through th' smoky light, I see this . . . thing. It was covered with rags and hair, and the second I see him, he yells, 'Woe to the wicked!' That's what he yelled, and staggered toward me. I managed t' just make hit a little out th' way of his big knife . . . blade maybe a foot long and two inches wide . . . come slashin' down at me and sliced through th' hide of my chest. I yelled and stumbled around hardly knowin' what t' do, then here he come again and I took off runnin' through th' flamin' barn toward th' house. How I made hit I'll never know," and he shook his head. "Flames was everywhere. Only burn I got was on my hand. Think I was just too damn scared t' burn if y' ask—"

"What did you do then?" asked the sheriff.

"Why, I run in th' house and got old Betsy," and he patted his long pistol.

"What did you do next?"

Mr. Mac looked at the sheriff like he was crazy or something. "Headed back out t' th' barn. I was gonna blow his ass off. Just as I got t' th' yard gate, here come Babe in th' Ford goin' like sixty. He was headin' straight toward th' fire. I went runnin' toward him hard as I could, yellin', 'Babe . . . Babe . . . look out, Babe, there's a crazy sonamabitch out there with a knife, son.' When I got up t' Babe, he grabbed me and yelled, 'Pa, you're bleedin' like a stuck hog.' I looked down, and by God, I was. Babe yelled, 'Let's get t' Zilkner's, and get some help!'

"I jumped in th' car and we went racin' over, me holdin' some rags against th' cut. When we got to th' pike, here come Morse, roarin' down his lane in his Ford t' help us. I leaned out the window and yelled hit was too late 'bout th' barn and I'd been stabbed by a crazy man and needed help. He yelled t' go on up th' house and Liz and Naomi would work on me and that Samuel was missing and for Babe t' go down toward th' Little Bend bottoms lookin' after he dropped me off, and he'd drive down th' Dry Branch Road."

"What happened then?" asked the sheriff.

"Well, they patched me up some while Babe and Morse did what they was s'posed to. Short time later, Samuel come home. When Morse didn't find him, he come back here t' check. Then Babe called and Morse sent him and others to warn th' neighbors. Morse called you 'bout then. Reckon you know th' rest."

When Mr. Mac said that everybody started talking to each other, at first just muttering, then it started getting louder.

"What happened t' you?" the sheriff asked, looking at me, and the room got quiet again.

My heart sank as I thought about Ben. I couldn't answer for a moment, then I blurted out, "I was comin' back from fishin' and th' crazy man tried to stab me with a knife this long," and I held my hands about two foot apart.

The sheriff's eyebrows rose. "Where?" he asked.

"In th' heart, I think."

Everybody laughed, and th' sheriff said, "Naw, I mean where'd this happen?"

I told the story, being careful not to mention Ben but still not lie. It was hard and a couple times I got the feeling that the sheriff smelled a rat, because his face looked like he was kind of wondering as I talked. That scared me and my voice started shaking and my knees got jelly. I kept thinking he knew I wudn't telling it all and he was gonna get Ben. Dad was beside me like a shot with his arm around my shoulders.

The sheriff stared at me for a while, then he turned back to Mr. Mac. "Sounds like he hit you first then caught th' boy while he was makin' his way back t' wherever he holes up."

"Shit, that's down my way," muttered Mr. Hickman, who had been cleaning his long, dirty fingernails with a pocketknife. His eyes were wide now, and his black sailor beard tilted sideways as he squenched his mouth and twisted his big heavy shoulders, causing the straps of his bib overalls to wriggle. Muttering started again and was getting louder.

"A body could hide out forever in some of them Big Bend cliffs," Mr. Langley said, and people shook their heads yes. "Them cliffs got a cave ever hunnert foot."

Bess Clark had been standing with his back against the wall not moving anything but his eyes while the different people spoke. When Mr. Langley finished, he stroked his mouth and chin with his hand and spoke to Mr. Mac. "Wha'd he look like, George?"

People stopped talking.

"Just by God awful," Mr. Mac answered. "Must've been six-foot-four or -five and had a chest on him an ax han'le across. Hair everywhere. Face like a bear. Rags just hung offa him 'n' stink, goddamn!"

"Yeah, I smelled him too," I broke in, suddenly remembering. I could still smell it, but nowhere near as strong as at the fence. Nobody in the room seemed to notice but me.

Bess lit a cigarette and kept looking at Mr. Mac as he blew out smoke. "You say he staggered, and Samuel says he fell. Either of you see how he walked?"

Mr. Mac shook his head. "I was tryin' t' stay alive! Wouldn't of knowed if he flew."

Bess looked from Mr. Mac to me and I shook my head too.

"What you gettin' at, Mr. Clark?" the sheriff asked.

"Well . . . I was wondering if he was lame. A fisherman few years back said he was chased out of th' Little Bend bottoms by a wild man with a limp. They's always been strange sightin's down there . . . tracks and things . . . some of 'em crooked. Especially around that water pool they call th' Blue Hole. We were close to it when we went huntin' for that sheep killer. That's the place they found the Collins woman and her two little girls."

Suddenly, everybody was talking. The sheriff held up his hands and Bess stopped. "I never heard any of this before. Who are th' Collinses, Mr. Clark, and what happened t' them?"

"They were bottom farmers," Bess answered. "Lived just before th' Little Bend turn of th' river. They built a house above th' flood line . . . leastways that's what everybody thought until one spring ten, twelve year ago there was a flood. The river crested short of their cabin, then some terrible rains come upstream. A wall of water musta hit th' Collinses in th' dead a night. Looked like they lashed themselves together and tried t' swim for hit. They found th' woman and kids and th' loop that went around Ralph in that Blue Hole, but they never found Ralph. Since that time, strange things have happened on that stretch of river."

"Like what, Mr. Clark?" asked the sheriff, and he had to hold up his hand again because everybody started telling him about things that had happened.

Bess thought for a moment, then said, "Well . . . like animals have left there. Couple years later two people drowned in th' Blue Hole. Two, three years after that an old trapper claimed he was chased up th' cliff by somebody callin' in th' name of th' Lord. Said he was almost had when this guy fell back down th' cliff."

"Where's this old man now?" the sheriff asked.

"Aw, he died three, four year ago," said Bess.

Mr. Shackelford laughed. "Shit, Bess, old man Hackett was crazier'n a hoot owl. He was always talkin' about findin' that Dutchman's mine out West, and bushels of gold, and Indians doing sacrifices by cuttin' people's hearts out. He even claimed he talked to th' Devil."

The sheriff raised his eyebrows, and Mr. Shackelford said, "Yeah! Crazier'n hell!"

"I don't think that's crazy, Mr. Shackelford," come a voice from the rear, and without looking I knew it was LD's dad.

"Aw, come on Zack. That wudn't no Devil out there tonight," said Bess.

I turned around and saw Mr. Howard standing near the kitchen door. He raised his right arm and pointed at Bess. "You don't know what it was," he said, his voice rising. "I say that place in th' Little Bend bottoms is evil. It's got th' mark of Satan. I've tried t' get th' people in this community t' have a prayer meetin' at that Blue Hole and float a Bible and a cross on hit, but everybody's too scared or has too little faith. They'd rather make th' Devil's brew."

I turned and saw Bess Clark lurch forward. He spoke quick. "Now, you just wait a goddamn minute, what other folks do is none of your bus—"

"Hold it, boys. Hold it," said the sheriff. "We're trying to catch a suspect who is still at large and dangerous and we can't do it fightin' among ourselves."

Bess relaxed some, but ever' now and then he glared at Mr. Howard. The sheriff went on. "I want to know if any of you have any hard evidence that a dangerous man lives on that stretch of river. Now, I want real evidence. First, did any of y'all see those two drowned people and if you did was there any evidence of foul play?"

There was movement in the back of the room and a skinny man who was just a little taller than Dad worked his way forward. His hair was straight and black and hung to one side like he'd taken the time to comb it. His denim pants and light blue work shirt were neat and clean. When he got to the center of the room, he stopped and spoke to the sheriff. "I seen 'em," he said real soft. "I found 'em. I had some stock out and saw buzzards circling down that way. Thought some of my animals might of died there."

The sheriff looked at the skinny man for a moment. "Who are you, sir?"

"My name's Lafe Miller. I live down on th' Little Bend bottoms."

35

I felt numb when Lonnie's pa said his name. It was strange. He didn't look mean. He just looked like a skinny farmer.

"Okay, Mr. Miller," said the sheriff. "What did they look like?"

"They was swole up like poisoned pups. Naked as jaybirds. Meat was falling off th' bone. They stunk so bad you couldn't breathe."

"So you couldn't tell if they had been hurt in any way."

Mr. Miller shook his head. "I couldn't anyways. People from Lexington come down. They just pulled out what they could and wrapped hit in sacks. Don't know what they done with th' stuff they sacked. Couple darkies done hit."

The sheriff thought, then looked around the crowd. "Who in here knew Mr. Hackett?"

"I did," said Rags. "He lived in my attic in winter. I kep' him 'cause I liked his stories about th' West. I found out a lot of them was true. He was a scout for th' cavalry back in th' Indian wars. He'd been a gunfighter too. You ought seen him draw his old six gun. Must've been nigh ninety and could still clear his holster quicker'n my boy. He could shoot too, by God."

"Did you think he was crazy?"

Rags tilted his head to the side a little. "Well, Sheriff . . . most of the time he made sense, but now and then he'd say outlandish things. I . . . don't know. I wouldn't stake my life on him."

The sheriff stared at Rags in what I was learning was his way, then kind of squenched his mouth. "Did he describe him? The guy that chased him, I mean."

"Just a wild man like Bess said," Rags answered.

The sheriff thought again, then said, "Anybody got anything t' add t' this?"

"Yeah," said Dad. "What about the stock that's been killed? He's probably the guy that did it. Everybody says there's no game on that stretch of river. It makes sense he'd kill what he could get easiest if he had a bum leg. He always killed a buck sheep. A buck's slow . . ."

"We looked once, remember?" grumbled Mr. Shackelford, and Bess snickered.

Dad turned red in the face but kept looking at the sheriff. "You wanted evidence and those mutilated carcasses are evidence. Everything that's been said t'night dovetails with it. This guy is some nut that's been livin' down there for years. Our posse must've scared him. He's probably still there, though, if he hasn't taken off for th' Big Bend."

When Dad mentioned the Big Bend, I felt sick.

The sheriff looked at Dad for a second, then at Ed and Bess. "How come you people didn't tell me all this when you wanted to go lookin' for that stock thief a year back?"

Nobody spoke for a while, then Bess shrugged. "People around here don't talk much about hit. We told you we had a hard time gettin' a posse."

"Just sounded like mumbo-jumbo," said Dad, when the sheriff's eyes fell on him.

"Mumbo-jumbo?" said the sheriff raising his eyebrows. "Several people found dead in a waterhole? An old man who says he's been chased by a nut? A stretch of river without any animals? A fisherman chased away? You got any more mumbo-jumbo?"

Everybody kind of looked sheepish at everybody else, then Mr. Miller asked, "Who'd be down there all these years we wouldn't of found long ago?"

"Satan," come Mr. Howard's voice from the rear.

"Satan, shit," said Bess real quick. "Clean him up and he's Ralph Collins."

"Run that by me again," said the sheriff.

"And you can keep your godless meetin' too," yelled Mr. Howard, and from the shuffling sound I knew he was moving toward the door.

"Stop right there!" said the sheriff. "I'm investigating the attempted murder of two people, and it's gonna be done right. I come from parts just like these down in Harlan County. Lexington doesn't give a damn about y'all, but I do. When I got out of th' service I went to th' police academy. I ran for sheriff of this county because you people said you wanted a Real Lawman. Well, I am a Real Lawman and this investigation is gonna be professional."

Nobody spoke for a few seconds and the only sounds came from one of the big deputies moving to guard the door. The next thing I heard was Dad saying to the sheriff in a soft voice, "Does what you just said mean we get no help at all from Lexington?"

"That's what it means," said the sheriff. "Not even a pair of handcuffs. Now, before we go any further, I want every man in here to raise his right hand and take a deputy's oath. Those who won't swear for religious reasons just say 'I promise' at th' swear part." Then he reached in his shirt pocket and pulled out a piece of paper, and everybody started to say what he said. I was just standing there when the sheriff stopped reading and looked at me. "You too, son," he said. I looked at Dad, and he nodded, and I raised my right hand and started saying along.

I was scared again, but they were on the right track and it sounded like they were going to figure everything out for themselves. If they were going to do that, I sure didn't want to tell what I knew about the crazy man and the Blue Hole. Not with Alfred, Mr. Howard, and Mr. Miller in the room. I wondered what the sheriff would do to me if I didn't tell. I knew what would happen if I did tell. Mr. Mac had almost got killed and his barn fired, I was almost killed, and maybe somebody else would get hurt or killed or their barn fired before the crazy man was caught and us knowing all the time. I began to shake and Dad's arm went around me again and I pressed against him.

When the oath was finished, the sheriff looked at Bess. "Okay, Mr. Clark, you were sayin' the attacker might be this Collins fellow. What makes you think so?"

"Ralph Collins and his family met me and my family several times. The Collinses was loners. Moved into th' upper Little Bend maybe six months before that flood. Ralph was big. I mean, he was a good six-foot-five and had th' awfulest pair a shoulders I ever saw on a man. He knowed more 'bout livin' off th' land than anybody I ever met too. If he hid out back in them cliffs, you'd play hell findin' him."

When Bess finished, the sheriff turned toward Mr. Mac with a questioning look.

Mr. Mac shook his head. "Can't say if it was him or not, Sheriff. I knowed of Collins, but we never met. Like Bess said, he was a loner."

The sheriff's steady blue eyes fell on me for an instant, then passed on as he realized I was too young to remember Collins.

"Was Collins lame?" he asked, turning to Bess again.

"Naw," said Bess. "Ralph had two good legs."

"And was a God-fearin' man," come Mr. Howard's voice. "I remember Ralph Collins too 'cause he come t' church. He hardly ever spoke outside church, but he talked plenty in God's house. Ain't hit true he tried t' convert you, Bess Clark?"

Mr. Clark's face turned sour and he muttered, "Yeah."

"Sheriff," Mr. Howard went on in holy tones, "I say that Ralph Collins was a man of God, and that he drowned in that flood and that his body swept on downstream. What we're dealing with here is Satan!"

"Aw, come on, we're dealing with a maniac, not a devil," said Dad.

"As a Christian I say we are!" Howard boomed back, and Dad's head whipped around.

Just then, Mr. Mac reached inside the flannel shirt he was wearing and ripped back the gauze, taking gray hair with the tape and popping two buttons. "Devils don't do this! Steel does this!" he yelled, and blood started oozing from the cut on his skinny old chest that was an easy eight inches long and gaping to where you could see red meat.

It got quiet.

The sheriff sniffed, then spoke. "Well, so far we don't have much," he said. "Mr. Zilkinsky, I agree with you about it possibly bein' th' same guy that killed th' stock because of th' crazy way he butchered them. Trouble is, you looked like hell for him once, and didn't find him. As for its bein' Collins, I can't see how anybody would be able to hide out that long and escape detection. This is probably some nut that moved in about th' time Mr. Hackett was chased. As far as devils go, Mr. Howard, I'm just a plain old lawman and I got t' deal with people. I'm lookin' for a man. It sounds t' me like he was headin' toward th' Big Bend bottoms when he tried t' stab th' boy. From what y'all have said, there's a lot of caves in those cliffs. Who of you people live on th' Big Bend?"

Mr. Langley and Mr. Hickman raised their hands.

"That's all, huh?"

"Yeah," said Mr. Langley. "Only other people living down there is th' Cummingses and Ben Begley."

"The Cummingses? Who are they?" the sheriff asked, and everybody laughed as Alfred told how they owned almost all that land at one time and were touched in the head and maybe ninety years old.

The sheriff kind of give Alfred a look, then said. "What about this Begley fella? How come he ain't here?"

A shudder went through me when the sheriff mentioned Ben's name. Dad felt it and looked down. He was about to speak to me when Mr. Langley said, "Begley don't have anything t' do with people, Sheriff. He's lived on the Big Bend bottoms ten, twelve years now. Sells pumpkins and melons. He'll only speak if you speak first, then he'll walk away."

"Was he warned tonight . . . and these Cummings people?" asked the sheriff.

Rags Wallace kind of hung his head. "I moved th' Cummingses to Alfred's, but I didn't go t' Begley's."

"How come?" asked the sheriff, kind of hot.

"Well . . . it was dark, Sheriff, and Begley's got these dogs. They're real bad."

The sheriff frowned. "Bad enough you wouldn't go close enough to call in a matter of life and death?"

"He won't generally come out for a call, Sheriff," said Pers, and his Adam's apple was jiggling up and down a mile a minute and eyes popping. "The road runs out a mile or so before his cabin and them dogs is killers. I mean, they'd tear a body's throat plumb out."

"That's right, Sheriff," said Mr. Dillard. "I wouldn't have gone there neither."

"Wouldn't of neither," said Mr. Lamb, then everybody muttered the same thing.

The sheriff glanced at one of the deputies, then asked, "Y'all know anything about this Begley?" They shook their heads and my heart started pounding.

"Hit wudn't him, if that's what you're drivin' at," said Mr. Mac. "I seen Begley couple times since he's been here and I'd of recognized him in th' firelight."

My heart started slowing down as the sheriff nodded. "All right, back to where whoever it is might be. Now, y'all say there's lots of caves around th' Big Bend."

"Aw, yeah," said Mr. Langley. "After the sandbar, th' river narrows, then cliffs begin again and goes all th' way around th' turn. Matter of fact, hit's cliffs for miles after that with little flat breaks in between. They's a million places he could hide."

"What about the Little Bend bottoms?" said Dad. "He could be down there too!"

I was about to breathe a sigh of relief when the sheriff said, "I don't think so. You searched that area once before and didn't find anything."

"Yeah, and we went all over that place then too," said Bess.

"But, Bess, all th' things have happened up this way," said Dad, and his voice was half pleading. "There's never been an incident in th' Big Bend. And we didn't have bloodhounds with us that time."

Mr. Clark shook his head slow. "Sorry Morse, I got t' go with th' sheriff. I figure this old boy was a-headin' home when he attacked Samuel. We got t' look in th' most probable place and do hit quick, 'n' that means startin' from that fence and try to track him. Boy, Sheriff, if we ever needed bloodhounds . . ."

"No chance. After Mr. Zilkinsky called me I got in touch with Lexington PD and they said no to a search plane and that th' dogs were already bein' used."

"Well, that leaves us in one hell of a fix," said Dad. "We got th' Little Bend, and th' Big Bend to search. We may as well be huntin' for a needle in a haystack, why—"

The sheriff cut Dad off. "We got t' do with what we got, and right now I think we ought t' start searchin' at that fence where your boy was attacked. Everybody leaves a trail sooner or later and that's how we're gonna find him. We're gonna search every cave in th' Big Bend cliffs and move over that land with a man every ten foot. We'll talk t' this Begley fella too."

The sheriff kept on talking, giving instructions, with everybody's eyes fixed on him to make sure they got every word.

I didn't hear a thing he said. My mind raced in a jumble. They were going in the wrong direction and they were going to get Ben. I stared at Mr. Miller. He seemed just like anybody else now, but I remembered how Lonnie and his sisters had looked after he beat them up. I looked at Mr. Mac too with his chest all bandaged and bloodied and imagined the big knife coming down and slashing through him and about my own fear when the crazy man tried to knife me. I thought about Ben again and how he believed in me, trusted me, and how he expected me to tell, and how I said I would. I started shaking inside. I had to do it. I had to do it and I had to do it now. "I know wh . . . where th' . . . c . . . crazy man's at," I croaked.

36

People seemed to freeze; then everybody turned and stared at me.

"Samuel . . ." and Dad's voice was strange. I was shaking all over and trying to keep from crying. I must have looked pretty bad because the sheriff spoke next, and his voice was soft.

"Calm down, son, you're okay. Just tell us what you know."

I tried to put stuff together but my mind was in too much of a jumble. So much had happened. I had to keep Ben out of it too. I thought about Lonnie. Poor Lonnie. Mr. Miller might get drunk and kill him. My mind was flip-flopping and when I tried to speak, I couldn't.

"Go on, Samuel," said the sheriff. "Nobody's gonna hurt you."

I didn't know what else to do so I told about us finding the dog and the cave and running up the cliff. I left out everything else.

"You claimin' my boy was with you?" Mr. Howard asked, and his voice was hot.

"Fred, too?" said Alfred, who sounded more took back than mad.

Mr. Miller just stood there, his eyes strange and cold.

Dad was staring too, but his face wudn't mad, just question-ing. "Samuel, why didn't you say this when the animals were killed, or when we organized that posse . . ." and his voice trailed away. "That's why you wanted to go. You wanted to show us so you wouldn't have t' tell."

"You mean Fred Cody let all this happen and didn't say a dad-burned thing!" barked Alfred. "He's gonna get a hidin' like he never did when I get home!"

"That boy's lyin'," said Mr. Howard.

Dad whipped around toward Mr. Howard. "Samuel don't lie!"

"I'm gonna get LD and we'll see who's lyin'," Mr. Howard shouted, and moved toward the door. One of the big deputies was in front of him in a flash.

"You can get him soon," said the sheriff. "Right now, we're goin' t' hear Samuel."

Things seemed to hang in the air, Mr. Howard trembling mad, his hand at the gun stuck in his belt. Four, five feet in front of him was a deputy, legs spread, shotgun chest high and slightly forward with the safety off. People were scattered back against the wall and scooched down, their eyes wide. The deputy and Mr. Howard each looked like they were waiting for just a slight motion and they would do something terrible. Slowly, Mr. Howard's hand dropped to his side, his body relaxed, and the deputy moved back.

The sheriff glared at Mr. Howard, then slid his hip onto the arm of Dad's big chair, letting one leg dangle. He leaned forward until he was only about a foot from me. His face was almost soft, and his eyes deep blue. It was a nice face, real honest, and any other time I would have felt calm around him, but now I just kept getting more scared.

"Samuel," the sheriff said, raising his eyebrows, "there's a mad-dog killer out there. We have t' know everything that happened in order t' track him down. If we don't get him, he's gonna kill a lot of people. Now, whatever it was you boys got into that time can't be as bad as you think. I promise you I'll talk this whole thing over with your folks afterwards. All of y'alls folks," and he looked around, then back at me. "I can't say you won't get punished, maybe even a lickin'. Nothing worse, though. The law calls you boys minors. That means you ain't accountable like a grown-up. Now, this is a matter of life or death. And you're a deputy."

The tears started pouring. I felt Dad's hands squeeze my shoulder, then a voice yelled my name and Mom come crashing through the crowd, her fat little body turning and shoving, making people stumble all over the place falling out of her way. "Leave him alone! You all leave him alone," she screamed, and her arms went around me and I never felt anything so good. I cried for a while, then Mom dried my tears with her sleeve. I felt like a coward, bawling and hanging on to my mama, but I was sure glad she was there.

"M'dom, we have to know what happened," said Dad softly.

"You'll know," she snarled. "But you won't badger him . . . none of you! You bullies and your damn guns and redneck yelling!" And her eyes were blazing. Nobody spoke, then I heard a kitchen match scratch on Levi's, flash alive, and smelled its sulfur.

"Miz Zilkinsky," the sheriff said as he cleared his throat, "would you ask Samuel why they didn't tell about th' cave and th' Blue Hole 'til now?"

"Yes, I will," she said, still hot. Then she turned toward me.

Mom standing there made me feel safe and I decided to tell everything. Except about Ben. "We were scared about what would happen t' Lonnie," I said toward the end. "We were afraid Mr. Miller would beat him up. May . . . maybe kill him. Not at first. At first, we just didn't want a lickin' for bein' around th' Blue Hole, then sheep started gettin' killed, and we held this meetin' and Fred and me wanted t' tell and leave Lonnie out of it but LD didn't because his dad would beat him up bad for goin' against what he told him . . . goin' around the Blue Hole, I mean. LD kept sayin', if we told, he was gonna tell about Lonnie too. Then Mr. Miller . . ." I quit there because I knew it was going to be bad if I said the rest.

"Go on, son," said the sheriff.

"Mr. Miller b . . . beat Lonnie t' pieces on a drunk and I was sure he'd kill him if we told and he went on another. We couldn't tell unless we left Lonnie out of it, and LD wouldn't. Him and me, we had a big fight about it. The crazy man just kept killin' stock, and things kept gettin' worse and worse until we were too scared t' tell. Then after th' posse, he quit killin' so we didn't see any reason t' tell. Then everything just went crazy with him."

Mr. Miller had stopped staring and just stood looking at the ground. Alfred didn't say anything either, but Mr. Howard's face was wild.

"I'm gettin' m' boy," Mr. Howard said under his breath.

The sheriff stood up. His face was drawn tight and I didn't know what was going to happen. Then he nodded real slow. "All three of you men get your boys," he said, and people started to move. "But y'all hear this," and people stopped. "When you get back here, those boys better be in one piece. Any of those kids been beaten, I'll see his pa does six months!" He let a couple of seconds go by, then said, "Just one hair out of place," then he said, "Okay, go get 'em. Be back here in less than an hour."

While they were gone, the sheriff and some others started questioning me again. It was easier to tell the truth now, but my big problem was keeping out any hint of Ben. I was doing a good job, but I was worried Dad would remember my Christmas gifts. My duck and slippers had to be made by a grown-up and I had always refused to tell who had given them to me. If Dad brought it up, the sheriff might think I was hiding something and go get Ben. I started shaking again as I thought about it. Ben had saved my life. I couldn't let him down. I just couldn't. What was I going to do, though, if Dad asked? What was I going to say? Dad was my dad, and awful things had happened. But Ben was my friend and I owed him my life. I owed him so much, and he acted like there was a terrible reason for people not knowing anything about him.

I was still shaky when LD, Lonnie, and Fred walked in led by their dads. LD was crying and white as a sheet. Fred was white too, but I knew his head was thinking. Lonnie didn't show any fear. His face was calm as the river in pool. He was the only one who spoke to me.

"Hi, Samuel."

"Hi, Lonnie," I kind of whispered back.

The sheriff scooted half of his rump onto the chair again and called for quiet. "Boys," and he looked at the four of us, "y'all come sit here in a row on th' floor."

We shuffled forward, and LD began crying harder.

"Whoa, no more cryin'. Nothin' real bad is gonna happen t' you kids. I promise y' that. All I want t' know is th' full truth about your findin' th' cave and tracks down on th' Little Bend. Samuel there says y'all found them and didn't tell. Is that so and if it is, why?"

"We didn't tell 'cause old Samuel there didn't want to!" yelled LD. "He kept us from tellin'. We wanted t' tell. He's just a liar . . ."

"That's a damn lie, LD Howard," I shouted, and started to leap over and hit him in the mouth, but the sheriff shot his finger out at me and I sat down.

"He's a liar . . . he's a liar!" LD yelled, pointing at me, then he looked at Lonnie and Fred and said, "You know he is. You were there when he told us t' lie. You know he did!"

"I did not," I screamed. "LD's lyin'! He's lyin'!"

Fred was death white. I knew what was going through his head. If he said it was my fault, I'd get most of the blame and he and Lonnie and LD would be off nigh free. The other way, they'd all be in trouble.

"I wudn't afraid t' tell," said Lonnie, looking straight in the sheriff's face. "They could tell anything they wanted far's I cared. Nobody made me do nothin'."

That really fired LD up. "Naw, we didn't tell because old Samuel there kept us from tellin'. We wanted t' tell and leave Lonnie out of hit but he kept sayin' if we told he was gonna tell about Lonnie and then he'd get beat t' pieces by his pa. Samuel stopped us from tellin'!"

"LD's lyin'!"

It was Fred.

LD jumped up and started to yell and the sheriff pointed his finger at him real quick and LD sat down.

"Go on, Fred," said the sheriff.

Fred turned his face up toward the sheriff and his eyes looked real sad. When he spoke, his voice was soft and sad too. "Samuel said he wanted t' tell and leave Lonnie out of it. It was LD said if we told, he'd say Lonnie was with us."

"I ain't lyin'! I ain't lyin'," LD sobbed. "They are . . . they are, Pa, they are," and he jumped up and ran to Mr. Howard, whose right hand come slamming down across LD's face sending him sprawling, his head crying, but not making a sound.

The sheriff leaped off the chair. "Stop that!" he yelled at Mr. Howard, and his voice shook. "Howard, I told you once I wouldn't put up with that kinda stuff. So help me if you hit that kid again you're gonna be talkin' to a judge!"

Mr. Howard stuck his chin out. "Your judge can't judge me. Only He can judge me," and he shoved his finger at the ceiling.

"Call it whoever, but I'll see Judge Fraser gives you six months!" the sheriff shot back.

It got quiet again, except for LD, who was bawling against the wall. Mom walked over and knelt beside him. He started to push his bloody, swollen face against her, then saw who it was and jerked away quick. Mom got up and turned toward Mr. Howard, her mouth all squenched. "You bastard," she whispered in a little hoarse voice.

"Call me a name, you heathen woman!" Mr. Howard yelled, and Dad yelled something back and started toward him. People scattered, then both deputies came between them in a flash.

"Knock it off!" the sheriff shouted. "Give those guns to th' deputies."

Dad showed with his open hands that he didn't have a gun, while the bigger deputy snatched Mr. Howard's out of his belt.

LD was still crumpled on the floor, bawling so hard his neck veins was popping out when the sheriff said, "Come here, son."

LD didn't know what to do. He glanced at his pa and kept on crying.

"Come here!" the sheriff said again, this time loud, and LD struggled to his feet and stumbled over, still bawling. The sheriff put one hand around LD's arm and began talking soft while he used his handkerchief to wipe away the blood from his mouth and nose. "Things are gonna be okay. This whole thing is gonna be over pretty soon and everything is gonna go back t' normal. What we have to do now is catch this old boy who's causin' all th' trouble. We need your help . . . all you boys' help. Now, tell me th' truth."

LD did. There was a lot of sobbing, and some of the time you couldn't understand what he said and he had to say it again, but when he finished it was all out. Lonnie tried to break in twice and each time the sheriff held up his hand and he stopped. Finally, when LD finished, the sheriff nodded at Lonnie, who was sitting with his legs crossed and his face stiff as a poker. "What y' wanta say, Lonnie?"

Lonnie looked the sheriff right in the eye and spoke soft, but strong. "My pa is a good pa. If they didn't tell, it wudn't because I was afraid of what my pa would do. My pa is a good pa," and for the first time his voice broke, but he was damned if he was going to cry.

There was a shuffling sound and Mr. Miller come to the sheriff's side. His lips were white and tucked together so you couldn't see anything of his mouth but a slit in the skin. His eyes were full of tears, and his face wrinkling in and out. He kind of lifted his open hands just a hair in front of his Levi's and Lonnie shot into his arms.

"You m' boy," Mr. Miller said husky. "Ain't nothin' gonna happen t' you. You m' boy."

The sheriff glanced at Mr. Howard and Alfred and Dad, not saying anything, then slid off the chair, checked his pocket watch, and motioned to a deputy to give back Mr. Howard's gun. "It's gettin' late and I've gotta make plans," he said. "Everybody be back here at four tomorra mornin'. These boys are gonna lead us t' that cave. If we don't find him there, we head for th' fence where Samuel was attacked. Get some sleep. Gonna be a long tomorra."

37

By the time I got off the tractor, I was exhausted. I said good-bye to my young driver and entered my own vehicle. I had no idea how much ground I had covered during the day but I knew it was a lot. I considered curling up and sleeping in the car but rejected it. *Hopefully*, I thought, *there's enough adrenaline left in me for the drive to Lexington.*

I became a little less sleepy as I drove, but more anxious. I knew what was happening but was powerless to stop it. I was still dealing with the event sixty years after the fact. Sweat trickled from my underarms even with the air-conditioning on high.

Suddenly, I could smell the odor. The same odor I had smelled in our living room that night. Pungent, undeniable, terrifying. My car swerved and a motorist honked at me. I steadied the car, made it back to my hotel room and lay down on the bed. I was trembling and felt weak, and it took a while before my body and psyche relaxed, and I was rational enough to think.

I began considering my mission. What was the point of going on? I couldn't find any evidence of the people who had lived in my community. I wondered if anyone who had participated in that long-ago manhunt was still alive. Fred? Lonnie? Visiting my past had not turned up even a mailbox with a familiar name. People were more mobile today than in the past. Perhaps they had moved by necessity. Certainly, none of the croppers I knew could have become owners of the estates that had replaced the farmland I once roamed.

Death, dispersion, and gentrification, slayers of my salad years.

I had given Nora's request that I return to Kentucky to shed light on my early life a legitimate try. There were still a couple of things I wanted to do, but they wouldn't take long. Then there was going to be a be-all and end-all to this odyssey.

I considered calling the airline immediately and asking for an earlier return flight but rejected the idea. I was tired and didn't have the energy to go through the inevitable stream of questions that would follow. I would do it when I was fresh.

I thought of calling Penny, then decided against it. Both of my daughters were sensitive to my ways and it was getting late back East. If I made the call now, they would be in Lexington in a matter of hours.

That time, that day, the significance of it in my life, rolled and churned through my mind. The love of Lonnie for his pa, a man who nearly beat him to death. LD! He was just a scared kid with a lunatic for a father. I hated LD then, and it bothered me that now, though I could rationalize his behavior, my emotions still wouldn't let me say truthfully, "I forgive you, LD."

But Fred dominated my thoughts. I could feel the stifling heat and hear the rustle of Levi's. And I could hear Fred's voice.

"LD's lyin'!"

Fred had come through for me in my hour of need. My friend, maybe the only real friend of my life. I owed him so much.

But it wasn't all one way. I had come through for him too, for the whole Mulligan family back when Fred really needed me. "You did a lot for the whole Mulligan family!" I said aloud.

I did do things! Important things! But for sixty years I had totally avoided Fred. That was the way it was, the way it would always be. What was I trying to prove by wandering through my memories? Yet, I could not stop thinking about that night . . .

. . . I tried hard but I couldn't sleep although a couple times I must have been close because my body would give a jerk and the whole bed would squeak. It wudn't just because I was excited; somehow I was too tired to sleep. Tomorrow we were gonna be finished with the crazy man and I could go back to being without worry.

I thought about Mom, and how people went flying as she come busting through to get me. She wudn't scared of nothing! I mean, she stood up to men with guns! I thought about how much I loved my mama and hot tears come up in my eyes.

I tossed and rolled, then I heard the sound of tires on gravel and a light come through the window. I jumped out of bed and ran to look. It was a car, okay. Out on the pike I could see other lights. In just a few minutes a bunch of people were at the house and Mom was heating coffee and letting everybody through the door. The smell of the crazy man was there again.

By a quarter after four, everybody was back except LD and his pa. Fred and Lonnie looked like they hadn't slept either. We greeted each other with hi's, squeezes on the arms, and nervous grins. Even Lonnie looked nervous. We waited until 4:30 and when the Howards didn't show, the sheriff said we couldn't wait any longer.

We were going to split into three groups. One group would be led by a deputy and Fred and go straight to the top of the cliff above the cave. Another deputy would lead my group and go up the river above the cave and walk downstream. The third group would follow Lonnie upstream from below the Blue Hole. It was this last group that had the hardest walk and was most likely to hit trouble. The sheriff was going to lead that party himself. The first group on the low bottoms that got within a hundred yards of the cave was to stop walking, give a whippoorwill call, then wait for it to be answered. When that happened, we were to come forward and join up. This way we would have swept the territory from above and both sides of the cave and the escape from inside it would be blocked.

"What happens then?" asked Bess.

"Then you people cover us while my deputy and me go in and get him."

"Nobody else goes with you?" asked Dad.

"No, you all are our cover. All hell breaks loose, I expect you people with rifles t' pick him off while he's on th' cliff face. Those with shotguns will move in and finish him off if he makes it down before a rifleman gets him. Now, you men remember we're up there, and nobody fires unless the suspect has made it *past th' mouth of th' cave!* I don't want my carcass full of lead again . . . had enough of that at Anzio. I don't expect him t' get out of th' cave, though."

"Just plan to go in shootin', huh?" said Dad.

"That's not so," said the sheriff. "I don't do things that way. When we get t' th' cave, I'm gonna call on him t' come out. Shootin' is a last resort."

When Dad spoke again, he had a softer voice. "What I had in mind was George and Bess goin' along. George can identify him, and Bess knew Collins. If it is him, maybe Bess could talk him into comin' out and you wouldn't have t' shoot."

The sheriff thought for a moment, then looked at Mr. Mac. "Can you climb that cliff?"

Mr. Mac answered hot, "I can climb hit as well as you can."

"I'm right with y' too, Sheriff," said Bess.

The sheriff turned toward Dad. "That suit y'?"

"Yes it does," Dad answered, and they kind of gave each other a look.

After that, the sheriff turned to the deputies. "Check everybody's guns to see they're unloaded. Load up when we get out of the cars and order safeties on. After that, nobody's thumb touches a safety and no finger gets inside a trigger guard unless you plan t' fire. And when we're on th' cliff face, *nobody fires* until one of us says fire."

Each group drove fairly close to their spot near the cliffs, which meant they were about a half mile from the river, then they turned off their lights. Mr. Shackelford led the way to the river for my group since he knew the area best. I walked beside Dad and a deputy. It seemed like we went forever, then Mr. Shackelford said, "Okay, we can get down t' the river easy at this spot."

The deputy spoke: "Load your guns and put th' safeties on. *Be certain those safeties are on!*" And everybody did.

In the east, it was getting light and I could make out the trunks and branches of trees that just a little while before had been blobs against the skyline. Somewhere on the bottoms, an owl was calling *whooo . . . whooo . . . whooo*, and it echoed against the cliffs.

It was tough getting down the slopes even though they wudn't real cliffs. You couldn't walk, you had to climb, and everybody slipped at least once, getting skinned up and cussing under his breath. Finally, we were on the bottoms and moving downstream. The closer we got to the cave, the quieter we walked. When we had about three hundred yards to go, we were brought up short by a whippoorwill call. It was so perfect I couldn't tell if a bird or a man did it. It come again, and this time, the deputy answered just as perfect as the one from downstream.

The first I saw of the other group was a flash of skin, then a flannel shirt and some jackets appeared through the head-high, twisted and bent river brush. On the top of the cliff, a deputy rose out of nowhere looking like he was carved out of the sky, his feet wide apart, rifle in his arms. Then three or four more people appeared beside him. One of them I could tell was Fred from his size. When I looked ahead again, we were about thirty foot from Lonnie's group, and people were nodding.

The sheriff walked in front of us and motioned Bess and Mr. Mac and the deputy to join him. Chills were running up and down my back. Lonnie looked excited too, standing there beside his pa, who had an arm around his shoulder.

"Okay," whispered the sheriff. "Lonnie, Samuel, and Mr. Zilkinsky, you come with us and show us th' path up the cliff. After that, Mr. Zilkinsky, you bring th' boys back here. You other men, spread out wide and lie down. I want th' safeties left on on every firearm. Nobody takes his eyes off th' mouth of th' cave. When we get on th' cliff face, keep our position in mind every second. Do-not-fire-your-weapon-unless-the-suspect-is-out-of-the-cave-and-coming-down-the-cliff-face. If the suspect makes it out of th' cave and you hear our order t' fire, shoot and keep shootin' until he stops movin'. He-is-not-to-escape! Everyone understand?"

There were more nods, then the sheriff and deputy and us started slowly moving forward. The lawmen were in front, Bess downstream, and Mr. Mac upstream, which made a little pocket, and it was in this that Dad and Lonnie and I walked. We crept along half bent, the scraggly river brush pulling at our clothes and water-bared roots tangling our feet. The deputy stumbled and the sheriff gave him a dirty look. It was two hundred feet or more to the bottom of the cliff and my back began to hurt from being bent over. A couple of times I glanced up toward Fred. I knew he had to be dying, wanting to be down here with us. Suddenly, the sun peeked over a hill shedding its blinding light on the cliff face, making shadows from rocks that jutted out. I could see and hear everything so clear, the sound of feet on the sand, little twigs that brushed our bodies and flipped back, and the breath moving in and out of the sheriff's windpipe.

We were only a short way from the path up when I saw a smear of red on the cliff face. Then another, and another. I stopped and pulled at Dad, who looked at me, then to where I pointed. Lonnie had stopped too by this time, but the sheriff and everybody else kept walking.

"Sheriff!" Dad whispered.

The sheriff whipped around. There was fire in his eyes, and he motioned us forward like he was mad. Dad didn't speak, he just pointed and the sheriff turned back toward the cliff. He stood for an instant, then he saw the blood and swapped his rifle for the deputy's scattergun and flicked off the safety. "Cover me," he said softly. "Rest of you hold your fire 'til th' deputy says shoot. Let him do any shootin' my way."

It took the sheriff forever to move that thirty, forty foot. His head was fixed straight in front, but I knew he was seeing everything. The deputy was near him clutching his rifle and little catches were happening in his breathing. He was scared. The second I saw that, I was scared too.

Finally, the sheriff waved us forward. When we got there he pointed to the ground. There were drops of blood, and footprints heading toward the river. They were big and straight, and made by work boots.

"He's hurt and headin' for th' river," the sheriff whispered.

"His footprints at th' Blue Hole was bare and one was crooked," Lonnie said soft.

"Well, they're straight now, son, and covered with shoes," said the sheriff. "You men go with th' deputy and take th' boys back t' th' group. I'll join you soon."

We did that and the sheriff followed the tracks. I watched him until he neared the river, then lost sight. He was gone a long time and people started looking worried. Boy, I was tired. I hadn't slept since the night before last. My eyes burned and my head felt fuzzy.

"Hit's not th' crazy man," Lonnie whispered to me. "He was barefooted and one foot was cloved. Bet I know who it is though."

"Who?"

"LD's pa," he whispered again. "He was all het up last night and didn't show this mornin'. I bet he come here before we did and got hisself knifed."

It made sense. LD must have told his pa where to find the cave. Wudn't any tracks going to the path so he probably climbed down to the cave from above, found the crazy man, got stabbed, and made it down the cliff face to the bottoms. He was probably hurt too bad to get back up the cliff and headed for the river. It was the only way out for him. But where was the crazy man? He could be anywhere by this time. A twig snapped, and I jumped.

Lonnie laughed. "Hit's th' sheriff. You think hit was th' crazy man?"

I sure had.

"What'd y' find?" asked Rags, when the sheriff got close.

The sheriff had a half-mad look on his face. "Dead end. Tracks end at the water's edge. Whoever it was went into th' river and didn't come out. Something strange is goin' on here. I don't think those tracks were th' suspect's. Th' only guy who could've known where th' cave was other than th' people here is Howard, and he's th' only one missin'."

"Where's th' crazy man then?" asked Pers, popping his eyes.

The sheriff squenched his mouth. "Good question. Probably in some other cave by now, wilder'n ever. He could still be in that one though. Let's do everything just like we planned. Mr. Clark, you and Mr. MacWerter come with me and th' deputy."

It was something to see old man Mac climb that cliff, his long-barreled pistol in its holster. When they reached th' cave, they spread out on the edge of its mouth.

"You, in there," the sheriff boomed. "Come on out. You're surrounded!"

Nothing. About ten seconds later, the sheriff called again. "Come out with your hands up and you won't be hurt. This is your final warning!"

Another ten to twenty seconds went by, then the sheriff waved to the deputy, who went in the downstream lip of the cave, while the sheriff leaped in the upstream edge. They stood there for an instant, pointing their guns, then the sheriff called for Bess and Mr. Mac. All four went inside and disappeared.

They were gone maybe five minutes. The first one out was Bess. He clambered down the cliff like a cat, half falling the last twenty feet. Everybody broke and run in his direction at the same time. Bess' eyes were wider than I ever saw when he got to us.

"Hit's Collins," he gasped. "Deadest man I ever saw. Somebody shot him to pieces. Must've pumped two-three magazines int' him . . . .30–30s," and he opened his hands and showed spent cartridges. "Tore him to pieces . . . knife's up there covered with blood . . . place looks like a slaughterhouse . . . God, hit's awful," and he kept babbling.

.30–30s! Ben! It wudn't Howard, it was Ben! And he was hurt! Knifed! He knew somebody would find the blood and tracks so he headed for the river. He was bleeding bad but if he got a log and made it to the sandbar he could cut across country and maybe make it home. I had to get to Ben! I had to help him! While everybody was squeezed in around Bess I slipped away and headed downstream.

38

I ran bent over until past the Blue Hole, trying not to be seen, then straightened up and took off. This was a part of the bottoms I'd never seen before and it was hard going. I was already getting tired when I come to a big marsh. The only way across was to slog through since the marsh backed up against some bluffs that looked like they would crumble if I tried to climb them. The muck sucked at my legs, pulling me in up to the knees. By the time I got on solid ground I felt weak. The sandbar had to be a coming up soon. There was no choice after that but to turn inland because a little further on, the Big Bend cliffs started and they come right down to the water's edge. I knew there was wild country ahead and I wudn't sure what to expect. I kept on running, and when I come over top of a little mound, I saw a flattened gentle beach with big willow trees behind it and knew that was the sandbar. I went past it, then ran into the trees and away from the river.

The land went up quick, the high bottoms where running was easy only lasting about a quarter mile. Then came hills, mostly brush covered, but in places thick with blackberry and raspberry briars that ripped at my long-sleeved flannel shirt and Levi's and pulled their thorns across the backs of my hands, leaving white tracks that popped out in blood. I kept watching for broken brush and blood, but there were no signs.

I thought about Ben while I ran. He'd saved my life and I had never done anything for him. Couple old presents he could've bought easy hisself. There were long stretches when I hardly even visited him. He'd always come through for me, though. If I had done what he told me to a long time ago, he wouldn't be hurt now. Lonnie was my friend and I didn't want him beat to pieces, but it was Ben who saved my life. All this stuff was my fault. I wudn't a man like I should've been, and Ben was maybe dying because of it.

I was sucking wind when I come into taller timber. There were fewer briars, but still a lot of locust, which is worse than briars with its long needles. At the top of a hill, I got my first clear shot of the land ahead and stopped.

The river had made about half its big bend and stretched out straight into the distance. Great forests of trees and brush hid the haze-covered ground. A couple of spots looked familiar but only the river was certain. My eyes went blurry and my face felt drawn. I hadn't slept in a long time. When I saw clear again, I took off downhill.

At the bottom of the hill was a ravine with a hickory grove. The ground flattened out into what looked like a silted-in creek bed with heavy dead grass and great high iron weeds with thick stalks. I raised my arms up to keep the leaves from hitting my face and crashed on through, but with my face covered like that I didn't see th' slanting barbwire fence until I ran into it. The top wire caught me just below the neck, then all the strands jabbed barbs into me as I spun down them like a corkscrew, their dragon's teeth eating me alive.

When I got up, I hurt every place the barbs had touched. My left eye blurred, and I rubbed it with my shirttail. There was blood, but I could see clear again after I wiped it. Turned out my eye was okay, the blood was coming from my forehead and trickling down. I dug around one of the fence posts where the ground was loose and packed dirt from my eyebrows to my hair. That stopped the bleeding and I stood up and checked myself. There was mud nigh to my hips, my clothes were tore to pieces, and I was bleeding everywhere. Oozing though, not gushing. My left knee was a little stiff too. All in all though, things wudn't bad. They just looked bad.

I was climbing the fence when a noise froze me straddle the

wires. I held my breath and listened. Quiet. Then a squirrel leaped from one hickory tree to another. Wudn't any other sounds but the breeze, so I figured it was the squirrel. It still bothered me because the sound seemed like it come from the ground. When nothing else moved, I swung my other leg over the barbwire and started running. It was uphill and down again and the ache that started in my upper legs sank to my calves. My side began bothering me, a real running side ache. Funny things started happening too. Trees and hillsides were stretching out of shape. I thought maybe it was more blood in my eyes and I put my hand to them but the only thing that stuck to my fingers was mud.

The hills got steeper and seemed to go up forever. At the top of one hill, the hickory trees quit and it was back to brush, locust, and blackberry briars. They took a lot of hide.

At the top of another hill, I come to an oak grove. By this time my forehead was really bleeding again, making it hard to see, and my legs and side were killing me. I just couldn't go further without stopping and fell on a heap of dead brown leaves gasping for air. Two, three minutes went by while I got my breath and the side ache eased, then I set up and dug some more loose dirt and packed it on my forehead. It was quiet in the big oaks. Something was going on; I could feel it. I thought about LD's dad. He could've followed the posse and saw me slip away. Maybe he was after me because I told. I was really scared and took off down the hill after glancing back.

It was good running now, steep, smooth, with big oaks and no scrub. My body was flying, taking great glomping, floating steps into soft, windless air like leaping off little cliffs into pillows. On my last leap my foot come down on sand. Bottom land!

A new rush of strength filled me and I poured it on, coming at last to the far edge of the melon patch. I quit running and stared across the open field. The cabin looked deserted. I raced toward it. About forty, fifty foot into dead melon vines, I thought about Cain and Abel and pulled up. If Ben was in the cabin the two of them would be outside and they'd tear me to pieces if they got surprised, especially if Ben was hurt.

I began walking slow, and at a spot just beyond the length of their chains, I called. Around the house they come, barking like devils. My knees shook as their big yellow bodies scooched down and streaked toward me, jingling their link chains which yanked them upright at the end. I had to stop being scared if I was going to get to the cabin. They could smell fear. Looking at Cain, I knew things wudn't going to be easy.

"Abel . . . Abel . . . it's me, boy, Samuel. It's Samuel, Abel."

They stood there, ears laid back, barking and snarling while I kept talking soft and squeaky. "It's me, Abel . . . it's me . . . good boy. It's me, Abel . . . good dog."

He quit snarling, and his tail wagged a little, but Cain barked as hard as ever. I walked forward and kept talking soft.

My hand touched his short yellow coat and head. I knelt down to rub his back and let him smell me over. "Good boy," I kept saying, and he licked at my face and shoved me with his head.

Cain had backed away and stood snarling. It was strange, he looked exactly like Abel, so much from a distance it was hard to tell them apart, but he wudn't like Abel at all. Cain hated everybody but Ben. Especially me.

"Cain . . ." I said, stepping in front of Abel, but still holding on to his neck. "Hi, Cain . . . you're a good dog, Cain."

Cain stood his ground, giving a low growl that got deeper. I kept coming, fighting to keep from being scared, but it wudn't any use. "Good boy, Cain, good boy," and his upper lip curled back showing his fangs. Looking at him was terrifying, but I had to find out if Ben was in the cabin.

Suddenly, there was another growl, and it come from behind. I looked around and Abel was growling. His head was cocked at an angle, watching the two of us. I wudn't sure if he was growling at Cain or me. The insides of me was jelly so bad I could hardly stand it. I looked to the front again, and suddenly I shouted, "Get out of here, Cain!" hardly realizing what I said. "Get out the way, you sonamabitch!" and I started straight at him.

Cain backed up a step and I come faster, "Get the hell out of the way," I shouted.

Cain turned his shoulder to me and began half trotting toward the cabin, his big body jogging sideways, head and eyes still watching me. Twenty yards behind, Abel was sitting on his haunches like he didn't know what to do. I stopped and yelled, "Abel, come here!" and he did and let me pet his neck. "Good dog, Abel, good dog," I said.

I started walking again, straight toward the cabin, acting like I did it every day. Cain kept trotting ahead and to the side, a constant growl coming out of his throat.

I was so busy with the dogs that the blood smeared on the cabin door didn't catch my eye until the last ten, fifteen feet. He was in there! Maybe he was alive! I had to fight to keep from racing ahead, and almost wrenched the knob off when I got there, causing a deeper growl from Cain. The door was locked. I stood for a few seconds, then pecked on the wood and whispered, "Ben?"

Nothing.

Behind me come another growl and a bark. "Ben, you in there?"

Dead quiet.

"Ben," and my voice raised, and I gave a louder knock. The growls got louder, followed by several barks and a snarl. I turned and looked at the two dogs. Cain had taken about all he was going to. "Come here!" I yelled, and Abel walked up three or four foot from me and whined, barely wagging his tail. He wudn't sure anymore. Cain was. In just a little while he was gonna tear me apart. I stepped up to Abel and rubbed his neck while he whined again and snuffed my pants. He liked me, but not what he smelled. Fear. And it was getting worse.

"Ben," I yelled, moving back to the door, and pounded. "Ben, it's Samuel! Open th' door, Ben. Cain's gonna get me, Ben!"

The snarls grew a lot louder, causing me to whirl around. Cain was ready to come. "Get back, you sonamabitch!" Cain didn't move. "Get back, damn you!" and I took one step toward him. He stayed put, little tufts of yellow back hair standing straight up, and he snarled harder, his fangs looking like white daggers in his brown-red mouth.

I turned back to the door. As my fist rose to pound, it hit me Ben might not be inside. He could have gone for help. I could be pounding on an empty cabin. I had to get to the window. I moved ahead slow, one hand on the wall. Cain was going crazy, and making little motions in and out toward me. Abel was starting to snarl now too and I knew it wouldn't do any good to call him. I stretched and peeked in when I was close enough to see inside. "B-e-e-e-n," my voice quaked.

"Sa . . . Samuel," come a weak answer, and I stretched up and looked through. Ben was pulling himself up by the table edge.

"C . . . Cain . . . b . . . back, Cain," he called, and somehow Cain heard him over all the barking and froze. You could see the hate in his eyes and it was terrible.

This time I ran to the door and grabbed the knob. It was still locked. "B-e-e-e-n! B-e-e-e-n," and I was so scared I could hardly say the words.

"H . . . hang on . . . Samuel . . . be there . . . m . . . minute," and there was a sound of scooting furniture, followed by a softer thump of a body.

A lock clicked. I shoved hard and it gave a little then pushed back shut with a rap. He was lying against it.

"Wait," he gasped, and there was more sound, then another thump.

I jammed my shoulder against the door, fell through, then kicked the door shut.

What I saw was awful. Ben was on his back, his legs kind of curled under him, face death white and sweaty. He was soaked in blood and so was everything else. The room seemed to spin, and the carvings wavered around like they were moving. Somehow, things was getting warped. I rolled onto my knees beside him, grabbed his shoulder, and bawled.

"Don't cry," he whispered, and raised his hand from his belly to my head.

There was a long rip in his pants and blood poured out. He was hurt so bad! I looked back to his face. "You got t' get help! You been stabbed! He stabbed you, didn't he?"

"Y . . . yeah. Went t' c . . . cave after I dropped you o . . . off. Afraid you might not t . . . tell. Dark . . . didn't see him. Got m . . . me before I shot. Shot time after time . . . kept comin' . . . kept shootin' . . . Did posse f . . . find him? . . . He dead?"

"Yeah. How'd you get home? I didn't see any signs."

"River. Found log. Lil' currents if y' know . . . how t' find."

"You got t' get to a doctor, Ben!" and I started to get up.

"Huh-uh. No doctors."

"Ben, you'll die if you don't get a doctor!"

"No doctors . . . Samuel. Can't . . . some water."

I jumped up and got the dipper from the water bucket, and he drank a little sip at a time. He had to struggle to keep his head up, so I grabbed the blood-soaked pillow off the bed and stuffed it double under his neck. He looked terrible. His eyes were pale blue, white and strange. "Ben . . . you got to have a doctor!"

He looked up at the ceiling. "Can't . . . doctor'll call police. I've killed . . ."

"But it was a crazy man," I said, loud. "They'll let you go. He almost killed me and Mr. Mac! They'll let you go, Ben. You're gonna die here!"

I tried to get up but he grabbed my wrist.

"Not . . . talkin' 'bout . . . crazy man."

I stared at him, and he looked into my eyes. "Who?" I asked.

"Long time ago," he gulped, and looked back at the ceiling.

"I don't believe it," I yelled, and tried to pull away, but he hung on.

"Begley ain't . . . my name. N . . . name's Willis . . . Ben Willis. Everything I told you . . . true. Left things . . . ou . . ."

He looked like he was fading, and I tried to get free, but he clamped down hard.

"Back in . . . Depression had a little . . . little money. Made a lot with it . . . married prettiest woman in Higgins County . . . had a boy. Worked all time . . . drank hard. Come home . . . no Jimmy . . . w . . . wife with another man. Killed them both . . . grabbed clothes chest . . . guns . . . other stuff . . . started driving. One night . . . wound up . . . Spears . . . loafers laughing about Cummings . . . sold me this land. Drove . . . car into a sinkhole . . . twelve years ago."

His hand dropped off my arm, and his eyes rolled back. I didn't know what to do so I put my hand over where the blood was coming out of his belly to stop it. He opened his eyes and touched my hair, and I put my arms around his neck and hugged.

"Don't die, Ben. I love you, Ben. Everybody thinks you're Ben Begley. They'll never know. I'm going to get a doctor."

I jumped to my feet and started to the door and he grabbed my ankle. I could have pulled loose because there was no strength in his grip, but I didn't.

"No. They'll . . . send me to . . . electric chair . . . druther die now."

"No!" I yelled, and jerked my foot loose, then grabbed for the door.

"No, Samuel . . . No . . . Sam . . . ," but he was too weak to stop me and I belted out of the cabin and ran. A yellow blur come at my head and my arm went up and great, slathering, brown-red jaws with white ripping teeth clamped down three, four inches above my wrist. I felt my bones snap as I flipped and went rolling and screaming to the ground with the snarling, tearing Cain on top of me. Between his legs, I could see Ben hanging on to the doorknob, his body half outside. He was yelling and Cain quit biting.

I crawled out from under Cain and started running. Blood was pouring from my floppy right arm and me trying to stop it with my left hand. I was screaming like I had after the crazy man tried to stab me. Then, out of the corner of my eye, I saw something, half running, half floating. It was yelling, but I couldn't hear what. I must have gone couple hundred yards before I knew it was Fred. He caught up and grabbed at my arm, but I pulled away.

"Hit's bleedin' bad," he yelled, whipping off his shirt. "We got to wrap hit!"

"Ben's dyin'! Ben's dyin'! We got to get help!" I screamed, and Fred grabbed again and got me, pushing his shirt against my arm, and tied it with the sleeves.

We started running as hard as we could, tearing up the gravel lane, leaping tire and water ruts, both of us yelling, and me holding my floppy arm. Dad's car was in the Mulligans' yard so I ran to the door and started pounding until it flung open and there stood Dad and Alfred.

"Samuel! My God!" Dad yelled, and he grabbed for me and I pulled away.

"No . . . No . . . Ben's hurt . . . dyin' . . . help me," but Dad didn't understand, then Fred yelled.

"Hit's Ben Begley. He's hurt bad! He's dyin'!"

Dad kind of acted confused then said, "Your arm . . ."

"It's okay! It's okay," I yelled. "Help Ben! We got t' get t' Ben!" and I went running to the Ford, pulled the door open, and climbed in back. Alfred and Fred and Dad were there in a flash.

Then here come the sheriff's car down the pike and Dad jumped out and ran to the Mulligans' gap and started waving his arms. The sheriff's car seemed to rear on its back wheels and streak toward us, then screech to a stop in front of Dad.

My heart sank. He was telling the sheriff about Ben! "Leave him alone . . . leave him alone!" I screamed.

Dad ran back to the car as I was trying to get out. "Stop it, Samuel. We'll help him."

"No, no, not the sheriff!" I yelled.

"Get back in th' car," Dad shouted, and pushed me through the open door. "Alfred . . . hold him," and Alfred grabbed my Levi's and pulled me over Fred and into his arms.

"Where's Begley?" Dad yelled, slamming the door and getting behind the wheel.

"Down past Langley's and keep a-goin' toward th' river!" Alfred yelled.

"Tell the sheriff t' go away," I screamed, twisting and trying to break Alfred's hold, but I couldn't. Finally, I was so wore out

I couldn't fight anymore. We were tearing down the Dry Branch Road now with the sheriff's siren wailing behind us, whipping around curves that Dad didn't know well, our tires just squalling. Strange things were happening to me. First, the trees on the lane flashing past started bending from side to side, their limbs moving like arms in water. Then Alfred's nose started growing. When his mouth fell open on a sharp curve, the inside looked like a red cave with big white rocks in front. His wild hair and black and white stubble beard began to grow out of his face and turn to grass and briars and bushes and I shuddered as his arms squeezed me tighter and a voice from his mouth said hollow like an echo, "Hit's okay, Samuel. We'll be there in a minute."

Then Fred reached over and squeezed my good arm. His eyes had grown big and were made up of little circles in a pool. His cheeks sucked in and the top of his head began to get wide and flat, his hair turning to grass, green and brown, and I could feel his hand squeeze my arm, off and on like milking a cow, while the siren behind us wailed, first just a wail, and then started making sense calling Ben's name, its voice going up and down like a Holiness preacher. "Sinner . . . sinner, hit's the day of judgment and you ain't been saved . . . Jesus don't want you, sinner, he's going to cast you out and away from him and your soul will burn in hell's fire through everlasting time," up and down and up and down the words wailed, then the inside of the car started changing, the seats turning to hills and the fuzzy brown seat covers green with grass and I reached out to touch it, soft and lush and cool, and saw Dad's bald spot in the back of his head getting bigger and bigger until it turned into a rock with bushes growing around it and moss covered, then suddenly the sky turned red and through the opening in front of our moving ground I could see smoke and flames leaping high into the air, red and yellow dripping hungry tongues jagged on the edges licking the roof of Ben's cabin like they come from the mouth of a hundred-headed snake, black smoke curling around and pouring through the roof and out the window and door and little chinks in the walls, the melon patch around it not dead, growing and green with little melons everywhere being crushed as we rolled over them while a great shining, floating chariot flashing red and white fire pulled by a team of black and white flying horses, their manes and tails of gold and up on top at the rains was God and next to him the Devil all racing toward the roaring, leaping flames and smoke. Then I saw God and the Devil get down from the chariot, and I screamed, "Wait, God, wait," and pushed on the side of our rolling ground and it opened and I struggled out, while branches and trees kept snagging at me until I tore away and went running toward the fire and God and the Devil, the flames leaping higher and higher as I got nearer and nearer, and a voice, Ben's voice, come out of the flames, and him and Cain and Abel walked out and stopped in front of me, and Ben said, "Forgive Cain. Forgive Cain," and I screamed "I do! I do! I forgive you, Cain!" and then Ben pointed toward a spot on the ground and there was the bobcat and mother coon and her babies, all watching Ben and Cain and Abel as they got into the back of the chariot, then God and the Devil drove off and it got dark.

39

It is rare to be able to state unequivocally that one has just awakened from the worst nightmare of one's life. There is no question in my mind, however, that I had just achieved that state of certainty. The sheets were wet with sweat and I was more exhausted than when I had lay down to sleep. I definitely needed a drink and took one.

My God, I thought, that was exactly the way it had happened. I felt amazed that I had come through my break from reality. After a half dozen more deep swallows of some sort of alcohol, I felt better. I laughed when I remembered the Hebrew prayer thanking God for giving the Jews the "fruit of the vine."

"You are indeed a wise God," I said aloud. I began to wonder if I was turning into an alcoholic, then it occurred to me that I rarely drank. I thought about Ben, wondering if he had been drunk when he murdered his wife and her lover. I had my problems, but where did he stand on the great scoreboard of life? He murdered three people and left a son without a father or mother. But he died because he didn't want to chance my not telling the adults what I knew. The truth was, he also died for our community because they didn't have the courage to face up to their responsibilities and take on the crazy man years before the disaster happened.

They embraced Ben after he died heroically. They wound up building him a monument; a huge stone that took them days to move into place. Would they still have erected the monument had they known of his past? I didn't know. Would I have told of his murderous past had I learned of it after he saved me from the river? I decided I would not have told then and still would not tell. Was my decision the correct one? I didn't know and wondered what the great philosophers would have done if they had faced that question in real life outside their ivory towers. I suddenly remembered my philosophy professor who had been sleeping with my college girlfriend. He was married and the subject he taught was ethics. So much for an unlived philosophy!

The big question, I thought, was what would have happened if everybody had just told the truth. Fred, LD, Lonnie, and I would have gotten in trouble (in the case of Lonnie, perhaps horrible trouble) but I doubted that the community would have gone after the crazy man. They were too scared of the unknown. Ben was a triple murderer and they surely would have executed him if they had known about him before the crazy man incident happened. Instead, ignorant of his previous murders, the neighbors said prayers for Ben, built him the best monument they could, and began turning him into a legend before we left Berman's.

"Being a human is difficult," I said aloud. "Common decency is the greatest quality to which one can aspire and the hardest to practice." I had never expressed that thought before. Maybe I was learning something after all.

Fred returned to my mind along with a lump in my throat. I thought again about the night Fred had backed me against his own interest. How much we shared before our family left Berman's. It kept revolving through my brain like an endless computer program. How do you come to grips with the fact that you abandoned your best friend? The first time might be forgivable because as a teenager I was worried that if I returned to the hills to see him some of my high school classmates would find out and return to their "hillbilly" hazing. That was spineless of me, but like LD, I was a kid. In later years I just didn't have the guts to face him. "You weren't a man," I said very loud.

I thought of Ben again and his final gift to me that lay in boxes in our attic. I had never discarded the wood carvings but I never displayed them either. Why? I knew the answer: I didn't want questions asked about them, didn't want to see them every day and be reminded that I was in large part responsible for his horrible death. He had saved my life, and maybe the lives of others; his thanks was to die alone with his dogs. I took another drink.

Nora. What of Nora, the woman who loved me so much that she put up with my bullshit. What the hell did she see in me? She was ten times the person I was, and yet she saw me as "her Rhett Butler." Her hero? Some hero.

She believed in me! She understood somehow the effect my past had on my life. She said one time that the hill people I described to her had instilled in me a sense of Old Testament honor and its attendant rigidity. Combined with the scholarly bent of my ethnic group, these values had somehow merged to produce a being who fiercely demanded total intellectual freedom, yet sought absolute truth! I didn't believe any of that mumbo-jumbo but maybe it was true. If so, it was an unfortunate coupling that had haunted my life.

I was drunk but I refilled my glass with ice and booze and settled into pleasant memories of the early years of my career. Things had been going great for us those first six years at Leland-May. Nora got pregnant. I had a great wife, was starting a family, my students loved my classes, and I was moving along professionally. I didn't, however, particularly like the Leland-May faculty and they didn't care much for me. It started innocently enough. I was on the student affairs committee to which most young profs were assigned at L-M because you couldn't do a lot of harm as a member of SA (as it was called). SA was run by Tolliver Atwood, who wanted the kids to adhere to a dress code. I thought it was stupid, especially given the temper of the times, and disagreed. Unfortunately, I made the mistake of calling the idea ridiculous during a meeting of the committee and embarrassed Atwood. Shortly thereafter, several members of the faculty began subtly critiquing my academic endeavors in unflattering ways. I was pretty sure the instigator was Tolliver, who remained cool toward me for months after the committee incident.

Life stayed sweet, but my tenure hearing was looming and I had only published a few scholarly articles. I loved teaching, but a tenure committee wants to see some creativity. I was due for sabbatical and had a chance to go to England and do some research.

The sabbatical was in Cornwall, only a few miles from Land's End. Our daughter was toddling and repeating Gaelic words to the delight of the town's women. Nora and I loved it there, and I got a lot of great work done. I discovered that English scholars had largely ignored the fascinating field of Cornish fiction. By the time we returned to New Hampshire I had compiled enough research to write a major tome and several articles. I made tenure. We got the house painted. Nora was ecstatic.

Then came the James Wallace episode. James Cacey Wallace was a bright young man who had done well in my classes. One day, in our Charles Dickens course, he turned in an essay on Joe, the *Pickwick Papers* character who keeps falling asleep. Something about it was familiar. A few days later I remembered where I'd seen it before: my undergraduate years when I cowrote my paper on Dickens. I confronted Wallace and he confessed. His excuse was that his grades in the current semester were good, but not good enough to keep his full scholarship. He needed an "outstanding" in my course since it was his area of concentration or he would lose his funding. That night I talked it over with Nora.

"What will the administration do if you report it?" she asked, stirring the beef Stroganoff.

I knew exactly what the dean would do. "Kick him out of Leland-May," I answered.

Nora continued stirring the Stroganoff, casually sipping a glass of wine. "What would you like to do?"

My mind flashed on Fred and the stolen rabbits. "Give the boy another chance. Wallace isn't a liar and a plagiarist; he's just a kid who lied and plagiarized."

Nora, who by this time was accustomed to hearing such logic

from me, answered in a matter-of-fact tone, "Then why don't you give him another chance?"

I did, but I made sure he earned it. Wallace worked in my courses like a field hand.

For days after that, I thought about Fred, but as the time approached to buy my plane tickets to Kentucky, I developed a sinking feeling. What would Fred and I talk about? So much of what had happened on Berman's was traumatic and in the years since, our lives had been totally different. I didn't go.

The Wallace episode wasn't the end of that issue, even though the kid went on to graduate with honors. Nothing ever seemed to be the end of an issue with me. Occasionally, I got to Nora. I remembered how exasperated she became when I refused to meet with the committee about my refusal to give didactic lectures.

"Samuel, meet the schmucks' demands partway," she said. "Give a few lectures, then teach the way you want. For God's sake, the faculty understands this is about academic freedom. Why do you have to drink the hemlock?"

Her argument made sense, but I couldn't do it. Didactic lectures had been shown to be an ineffective way to teach. The way to transmit knowledge was by challenging students. But Dean Simmons was not open to challenges of any kind, especially to his preferred pedagogy.

I paid a price for continuing to teach my way. The committee on academic advancement declined to recommend my promotion. And who was a power on that committee? Tolliver Atwood! Salaries in academic literature departments are not high, and I needed the money that promotion afforded. We had an eight- and a twelve-year-old. Nora had to take a part-time job in a bookstore to build up their college fund instead of staying at home until both children were in high school.

The attack on my teaching was the beginning of an academic nightmare. I seemed to be criticized by every professor on campus. While annoying, it was still just criticism.

Then James Wallace, who was now a young professor at a little

Ivy League college, gave amnesty to a student who cheated. He told him why, naming me as his mentor. The student told his friend, who told his father, who was on the Leland-May Board of Trustees. The father, of course, told Dean Simmons. A firestorm ensued. Tolliver's attack was overt and I became ostracized by my colleagues. I was again passed over for advancement.

Then the last shoe fell. Anton Cathcart, editor of one of the most important literary journals in my field, wrote a scathing review of one of my publications. The result was disastrous. I was attacked now for both my teaching and my creative work. It was obvious that I would never make full professor at Leland-May and the odds of getting another academic job were slim, given the negative comments I was accruing. I was fifty-six, had one child entering graduate school and a second entering college, was ten years from retirement, facing old age with inadequate financial means and poor job prospects because my curriculum vitae was less than sparkling.

Then came the miracle of Cyrus Whitley-Jones. The old Oxford don, who rarely said anything good about anyone, went so far as to use the term "significant" in regard to my work in one of his articles on writers of the Cornish region. Within a month, four major universities contacted me regarding positions at the full professor level. Even better, I could teach as much or as little as I liked, provided I taught "some."

I contacted Dean Simmons by letter, asking for a short leave of absence to "investigate other academic positions" and copied it to the department chair. Leland-May's faculty was composed of superbly educated, adequate teachers (depending on your point of view), but far from creative. If they lost their one internationally recognized scholar, it would not go well with the Board of Trustees. Especially if it appeared that I had been driven out of town.

The dean and my chair made an offer. I thanked them, but replied that in the interest of my family and career, I had to investigate other institutions. The next day, the committee on academic advancement voted to raise my rank to "Distinguished Professor,"

let me determine which courses I taught, and assured me my pedagogical technique was a matter of academic freedom.

I stayed. Every fiber of my body wanted to write an open
letter to the faculty, who had made my life miserable. Nora advised rapprochement and a new attempt at social interaction. Rapprochement, I could do. See them socially? I would have preferred
dining with Faulkner's Snopes family. A few years later, I won the
Johnson-Goldsmith Prize. I developed a cult following. Nora developed cancer.

40

The blow delivered by the memory of Nora's death brought a draining of the alcohol in my glass. Again, I lay on the bed and waited for the pain to ease.

Ease, the pain did not; change my reference point, it did. It moved back to the time I left the hospital after my arm and emotional upheaval had improved and I returned home. People treated me like a returning hero. I felt drenched in guilt. The next few weeks . . .

. . . went hard. I just couldn't get over Ben. Fred come to the house every night and told me what happened while I was sick. Having him there helped. He said he seen me slip away from the group in front of the cave and followed me. He wanted to stop me lots of times but could tell I didn't want anyone to know where I was heading so he hung back. The times I thought somebody was behind me, he was only a hunnert or so foot away. He stopped just inside the oak grove and watched as I went to Ben's cabin. When the dogs come, he said he didn't know what to do. He knew they were killers, but after I pet Abel, and Cain backed off, he figured everything was okay. By the time they turned on me, it was too late for him to do anything and he just stood at the edge of the oaks scared to death. He said he felt bad he didn't run to help me but he thought it might make things worse since the dogs didn't know him. I told him I would've done the same thing, knowing Cain and Abel.

Everybody around that had known Mr. Collins saw the body. What was left of him, I mean, 'cause Fred said he was really shot up. Wudn't any doubt in anybody who it was and the sheriff said the case was over. They held a funeral at the church for Mr. Collins because the preacher said Christ would have wanted that, since Collins was a good man before he turned crazy, and asked that he get forgiveness from everybody, which I suppose he got. He didn't get forgiveness from me though. I hated the sonamabitch and hoped he went straight to hell!

Poor Ben. After Fred and me ran for help, Ben shot Cain and Abel and drug them inside the cabin, then doused it all over with coal oil and shot hisself after he lit the fire. He put the bobcat and coons and the Christmas knife outside. Dad said he saved them since he figured they were for me.

Fred said the church held a funeral for Ben too, right where the cabin stood, and buried what parts they could find. The preacher said Ben had laid down his life for his friends and that the name Begley would always live in our parts and in the house of the Lord. After that, all the men got together and hauled the biggest rock they could find to the top of the grave so it wouldn't ever be plowed over. They buried Cain and Abel right beside him. I was the only one who knew about Ben, who he was and what he done, and wudn't anybody ever going to find out.

Everybody tried to help me but the going was slow. I missed Naomi a lot. She'd started nurse's training and they wouldn't let her come home. Debby was in California now and Bob only got home one day a week. I'd get really sad, and Mom and Dad would try to cheer me up, but they just couldn't pull me out of it.

After several weeks at home I went back to school. The kids treated me great. The sheriff come down a couple Sundays. The first time he showed up I was worried he was going to ask me a lot of questions about Ben, and while I wudn't sure, I figured knowing what I did was against the law. He never mentioned it though, just squeezed the back of my neck with his big hand and asked about the arm. It was a little strange, though. I saw him kind of look at me out of the corner of his eye once, like he was wondering what else I knew. Nobody asked anything about Ben. Not even Fred. LD didn't ask. His pa got more religious than ever, and Fred said Mr. Howard told the church that God had called him to move to Georgia and become a Holiness preacher and they'd be going after the crop year.

Lonnie come over one day. He looked happy and I told him that.

"I am happy, Samuel. I'd like t' go talk though. Someplace nobody can bother us."

That surprised me because Lonnie never said those kinds of things. "Let's go down to th' tobacco barn," I said.

When we got to the barn, we climbed up on the wagon and sat kind of catty-corner facing each other. He didn't say anything for a while, then he swallowed.

"Samuel, I know all what you done for me. I know you were afraid my daddy'd beat me t' pieces about hit someday if we told and that I was why you said not to tell. I acted like I didn't care, but I was scared. Hit should've been me what come forward but I didn't 'n' all this bad stuff happened. I wudn't a man and I come here t' tell you I was sorry."

Tears come up in Lonnie's eyes and I kind of looked away when I answered like I didn't know they were there. "Wudn't just you. None of us did right and what happened was all our faults. You're th' best man of all of us, Lonnie. I've thought that for a long time. And I'm always gonna be your friend."

Then we just kind of sat. He was the same boy I knew before, but somehow now he seemed different. Finally, he slid off the wagon, stuck his hand out, and we shook.

"I best be gettin' home. Pa and me are workin' up wood for winter," then he moved toward a ventilator, slipped out, and was gone.

I sat on the wagon for a while thinking about all that happened. I wondered if we went back to the start of things, would we have done different. Without knowing all that would happen if we didn't tell, I mean. I couldn't say and that really bothered me. Ben was dead, stock was killed, I went crazy, everybody around got scared out of their wits, and I still didn't know if I would have done things different. People thought high of me now and I was dumber'n owl shit. I went back to the house feeling good about Lonnie and bad about myself.

After Christmas, I started feeling a lot better and by the time the cast come off my arm for good, I was well enough in my head to visit Ben and Cain and Abel's graves. I lay on their graves and bawled, telling them what happened to me, and how I felt about them, and asked Ben to forgive me for letting him down and said that I was going to make it up to him someday.

41

It was about this time that things started going bad for the Mulligans. They hadn't been doing real great since Alfred got sick, but they still managed to get their work done. Also, they were moving to Red Bill Rogers' place a crop year away, and no matter what else happened, that kept them going.

Then Red Bill died. The Franklins got his farm because they had promised Red Bill, if anything happened to him, to take care of the magnolian idiot Red Bill lived with. The Franklins wanted to work the farm themselves, so that left Alfred out.

Alfred took losing the farm awful hard. He had been counting on cropping Red Bill's place and ever' penny he had was tied up in mules and equipment. Wouldn't have been so bad if there was anyplace else for him to rent, but times were changing and the new Ford tractors were really low to the ground and wouldn't turn over in steep places and everybody was quitting on horses and mules. If you wanted to get a good place to rent, you had to have a tractor. For a while Alfred just stopped talking, then he began going into wild spells where he'd tear up the house. He stayed that way until almost May and when he did start talking, it was to a wall. Fred said you could ask him a question and he'd set on that old no-back chair and turn to the wall and start telling it what you wanted to know. After a while, he talked to that wall even if you didn't ask him a question, sometimes gettin' flaming mad and hitting it with his fists, yelling he was being cheated by some guy named Cosmoton. One day Alfred grabbed Annie Lee by the throat and told her if he ever heard of her fooling around with that Rooshian Cosmoton sonamabitch again he'd beat her until she couldn't walk and did she understand that! Fred said it was the first time he'd ever seen Annie Lee scared.

Over the next few weeks, Alfred come around some. He still talked to the wall, but at least he didn't threaten to beat up on anybody. That was a tough summer, boy. With Alfred being like he was, Fred was left with all the Mulligans' work, and Dad and Mom and me with ours, but we finally got the crops out. I saw Fred every day because we swapped work. But that's what it was, work, with never a day off.

Alfred started doing a lot better about the end of tobacco setting time and helped quite a bit with getting in the hay. The crop looked good though, and we figured all the bad things had happened, then it set in raining and rained for two solid weeks. When it dried off enough we could walk through the tobacco again, we saw that half the plants were dying from wire worms. Dad talked about discing it up and doing a total reset, but we didn't have enough plants for that and had to reset by hand, which took two weeks of bending our backs.

The Mulligans' whole strawberry crop got mold from the wet and they lost it all, berries and plants. Fred and me got their tobacco reset and that seemed to help Alfred, who had almost gone plumb crazy.

Dad was feeling a little down and was tired, of course, but the price of hogs had gone to twenty-nine cents a pound. That really helped Alfred because he stood to make a lot more money from his hogs than he thought and said by God he didn't need Red Bill, he'd just rent someplace else. Dad felt good too because we had near a hundred head and they were going to be at two hundred pounds by late September. They looked great until one day Dad come in for dinner through the hog lot. He was quiet and Mom noticed it.

"Is something wrong, Morris?"

"I don't know yet."

"What do you mean?"

"I mean, I don't know yet," he answered gruff, and didn't look up from his food.

"Do you think something's wrong?"

Dad kept eating quiet, then said, "I think one of th' sows is sick."

"What makes you think that?" Mom asked.

"She just seems listless. She ate pretty well this mornin', but she's actin' strange." He pushed the rest of his food away and got up. "M'dom, I have t' change th' cattle this afternoon, then I'm gonna hoe corn. Can you watch that sow for th' rest of th' day?"

"Sure," Mom answered.

Dad left the house, then come back and stuck his head in the door. "If that sow looks any worse, have Samuel quit plowing and come get me, okay?"

"Okay," said Mom.

Dad looked at me, worried. "She looks any worse, you come get me . . . right?"

"Yes, sir," I answered, and he walked out the door and headed toward the fields.

I'd been plowing about an hour when Mom came and got me. It didn't take a vet to see which was the sick hog because she was coughing and stretched out on her side grunting as she breathed. I didn't know how sick she was until I tried to get her up. She wouldn't move even after I kicked her. Dad tried to rouse her too and when she didn't move, he called the vet.

About an hour later, the vet come and told Dad it was hog cholera. We dug a big pit and poured in slack lime and shot every hog and buried them. The next day, Alfred's hogs come down with cholera too. Dad looked like the world fell on him, and Mom was crying and saying why did these things always happened to us? Just when we were going good something always come along and knocked us down. Alfred just talked to the wall.

At night I could hear Mom and Dad talking, and Dad said if the tobacco didn't sell well we wouldn't be able to buy much of a place at all.

42

For about a week, Dad was sick as a mule over losing the hogs. I could hear him and Mom talking late at night after they went to bed. At first, they talked about not buying and staying on Berman's for another year, but Mom was against it because she said the show Nate was giving us just wudn't good enough and Dad should be on his own place.

By early August, everybody was surprised at how good the tobacco looked. After that, Dad bounced back. Alfred bounced back some too. The bad luck wudn't over though. One day come a really black cloud. First the wind hit, then the hail. When it quit, every stalk of corn and tobacco that wudn't twisted by the wind was tore to pieces by the hail. Alfred went plumb crazy and Dad couldn't eat or sleep.

Fred and me only went fishing once that whole summer. Lonnie was working every day and we never did see him. He didn't go to church anymore. His dad took on another three acres of tobacco on the Madison County side of the river and from what Mrs. Miller told Mamie, Lonnie's pa was going to let him keep half the money it made.

With everything that had happened I was almost as down as Dad. Then Bob come home from engineering camp and that made me feel better. One day he grabbed me around the waist, hoisted me over his head, and asked if I could go anywhere and do anything for one day, where would I go and what would I do?

"Go see th' Reds play and take Fred and Mr. Mulligan along."

"Done!" he yelled.

"Yippee," I shouted, and asked if it was all right to tell Fred.

"Sure," he said.

It was the first happy thing that happened in months and I took off, boy. I was at the barbwire gap before I remembered I didn't ask when we were going. I was turning around to go back when Fred saw me, and came running. "Hidey, hidey," he said, puffing as he come up.

"Hidey, Fred Cody," I said. "What you doin' nowadays?"

"Comin' t' see if you wanted t' go fishin'. We ain't been this whole year. I got an extry pole so you don't have to go back for yourn."

"That's a good idea," I said, and we walked back to the Mulligans' and began digging worms. While we were digging, I could hear Alfred's old radio blaring away with Waite Hoyt, the announcer, telling about the game between the Reds and Dodgers. Ewell Blackwell was pitching for the Reds and he was great so we went inside to listen a little.

Alfred was where he always was when he was home and a game was on, sitting on the no-back chair, his elbows on a little peeling table. In front of him was the old brown Delco-battery humpback radio. Alfred was yelling with every play and talking to the wall.

Carl Furillo come up for the Dodgers and Alfred said, "Ain't nobody got a hit off Blackwell yet. Come on, Whip . . . I always call him, Th' Whip," and Waite Hoyt said, "Blackie kicks and fires, and Furillo gets around on it and there's a drive out into deep right-center field, and that ball's up there, it's going . . . going . . . gone, over the right-field wall for a home run for Carl Furillo, his thirteenth of the season, and the score is tied one to—"

Alfred jumped up and screamed, "Shit-far! That dumb sonamabitch! He throwed hit right down th' center," and he leaped around the room, kicked over the no-back, kicked the bed, and screamed, "Shit-far" again and again, then Blackie got out of the inning.

The Reds scored a lot of runs the next inning and with Blackie pitching, it wudn't hard to know we were going to win, so Fred and me left. Alfred didn't though. He sat right there yelling and talking to the wall and was happy which was good because we only won about every fourth day, when Blackie pitched.

Heading down to the pond I kept trying to find the best way to tell Fred about the trip to see the Reds without showing how dumb I was about not finding out when. While we were unwinding our poles and baiting up I kind of matter-of-fact said, "Fred, how 'bout you 'n' me and Bob and your pa goin' t' Cincinnati t' see th' Reds play?"

Fred looked at me like I was an idiot. "Lordy, yes, hun'ney," he said, laughing.

"No, I mean it," I said. "Bob and me are goin' and he said it would be nice if you and your pa could come."

Fred cocked his head to the side and stared at me, then looked down at his hook as he baited up. He threw in and looked back at me again.

"When?" he said, and this time he wudn't smiling.

"Oh, sometime this month. We'll run up t' Cincinnati and see a game." The more I talked, the more Fred stared at me because he knew I had never seen a major league baseball game and I was talking like I went to Cincinnati every day.

"Shit," he said, finally, and moved his bobber closer to a fallen tree branch.

"I mean it," I said, with kind of a getting-mad voice as I put my own worm in the water. "You ain't makin' out I'm a liar, are you?"

Fred went blank-faced for a second, then his eyes got wide. "Hun'ney, you really mean hit! Bob's takin' us t' Cincinnati t' see th' Reds play?"

"Yep," I answered, and grinned.

"When?" he yelled.

"Don't know exactly yet, but Bob will tell me soon," which wudn't a lie.

Fred let out a "Yehoo! I can't wait t' tell Pa."

We didn't fish too long, because Fred was busting to tell Alfred, and the first time we didn't get a bite for a minute or two he said, "Come on, hun'ney, ain't no use us sittin' here if they ain't gonna bite," even though we'd caught about twenty big fat brim.

"Yeehoo! Hot dog! When?" Alfred yelled at the wall when we told him.

"Pretty quick here," I answered. "I'll tell y'all soon as I know."

"We goin' to a doubleheader and see Blackie pitch," Alfred said to the wall. "You just wait and see if we don't see Blackie pitch. Hot dog!"

The game was a doubleheader on a Sunday and sure enough Blackie was going to pitch. There were a lot of us going, boy. Alfred and Fred and Bob and me and one of Bob's buddies that Bob had to take because he owned the Jeep. It was a great Jeep. Bob's buddy got it army surplus. It was about six years old and didn't have sides, just a windshield, which was cracked near the bottom, with other cracks running out like a tree branch.

By eleven o'clock, we had crossed the Ohio River. I never saw such a river. It made the Kentucky look like a creek. I never saw anything like Cincinnati either. It seemed like we just went from one big road to another, with Bob and his buddy yelling and talking loud and drinking beer and whistling at girls. Alfred was laughing and talking with them and telling them all the things he done when he was their age, and Jack, that was Bob's friend, whipping the Jeep in and out of traffic, every now and then giving out with a rebel yell.

Pretty soon we come to the ballpark and it was something. Great tall rafters two decks deep and the green field looking like the lawns in the fancy parts of Lexington. Fred and me just stood there gawking, then some guy come around and showed us where to set.

The first game was great. Blackie pitched, and we won by about ten runs, but the second game was close, with Pittsburgh leading two to one in the sixth. It started to drizzle, and the clouds got heavier. In the eighth, Pittsburgh scored six runs and Alfred went wild, screaming about the "dumb sonamabitches" and about how bad they were playing. Bob and Jack kind of scooched down in their seats, then Bob said we ought to go since we had a long distance to travel.

We had just crossed the Ohio River when it started to rain. Man, did it come down, and we didn't have a top. Then it turned cold and Fred and me curled up together on the floor behind the seats with our teeth chattering. The further we drove the colder it got, then the windshield wipers went out and Jack had to drive with his head out the side. The lights were almost gone too, because something was wrong with the generator, so it was two in the morning when we pulled into Lexington. We stayed at Jack's folks' house for the night which was real nice.

The next morning, Dad picked us up. Alfred was coughing and said he had a cold.

That night, Fred come to the house. Dad answered the knock, and I heard him say, "What's wrong, Fred?" and I was there in a flash.

It was still raining and Fred was standing at the kitchen door dripping. You could see he was scared. "Pa's sick. He's coughin' like a fool, Mr. Zilski, and he's terrible hot."

Dad thought for a moment, then said, "He needs a doctor!"

"He said he don't," Fred said. "He didn't want me t' come here and I promised, but I'm afraid he's gonna die. I think Pa's gonna die," and he was snuffling tears.

Meanwhile, Dad was thinking. "Samuel, stay here with Fred. I'll be right back," and he went into the bedroom. In a couple minutes, he come back and said for Fred and me to get in the car. Fred didn't move and kind of made circles with his bare foot.

"We've got t' take care of him, Fred," said Dad. "Come on, let's go."

Fred shook his head. "We can't. He'll know I told you. I promised."

"I understand," said Dad. "I'll square you with him. Come on, let's go!"

When we saw Alfred, he was lying on the bed and talking to the wall. Dad spoke to him, but he just kept on talking about the ball game. At the first mention of a doctor, though, Alfred set up and said he didn't want no goddamn doctor and if he saw one he was gonna die. When Dad tried to talk to him he started babbling again, so Dad picked him up and put him in the car, then the four of us and Mamie drove to Doc Culbert's. When we got there, the doctor asked if he was going to get paid this time because Alfred's family hadn't paid any of their other bills.

"You'll get your goddamn money," said Dad, his eyes flashing. The doctor whirled around toward him. They stood like that for a few seconds with Alfred shouting stuff that didn't make any sense. Finally, the doctor began checking Alfred over. When he finished, he told us that Alfred had to go to the hospital, that he was pretty sick.

He must of been awful sick, because that evening, he died.

lfred's funeral was two days later. Things were supposed to start at ten and Dad and I drove over. We were both wearing our dark brown winter suits and dark ties which was a bad idea because the morning was already hot.

By the time we got there the Mulligans' yard was full of people. Cars and trucks, from pickups to Bert Raney's two-and-a-half-ton International were strung out on both sides of the Dry Branch Road. The cattle racks had been taken off Bert's International and it was backed up to the porch step with the driver's door open. Standing in front of the door was Mamie wearing a black dress with her arms around Thelma Jean, who had her face pressed up against her, crying. Annie Lee was standing on the porch in her new red dress and next to her was WK leaning up against the wall fooling with his car keys. Annie Lee's eyes stared straight ahead. I saw Lonnie and LD beside their dads and we all nodded. I kept looking for Fred but I couldn't see him anywhere.

Nothing happened for what felt like forever, then the preacher walked out of the house followed by Fred's uncle Charlie and three other men with the casket, which they put on the truck bed. The casket was beautiful. Charlie had worked all night shining it up with linseed oil.

The Mulligans had decided to bury Alfred on a bluff above the Miller place that Alfred had said was his favorite spot. Mr. Miller and a bunch of the men said they'd get a big rock and put it there for a headstone. Mr. Miller said that his family would keep the grave mowed.

Dad and me were walking toward our car when I looked back and noticed that all the Mulligans were in the yard except Fred. I guess they noticed it too, because Pers went in the house. Couple minutes later he come out and walked up to the flatbed and said something to Charlie and he jumped down and went into the house.

By this time everybody was at their car and you could hear engines fire up. Pretty soon, Charlie come out, and he walked up to the cab on Mamie's side and she and Charlie both went in and stayed for what seemed a long time. I guess it seemed a long time to a lot of people because they cut their engines. Finally, Mamie and Charlie both come out of the house shaking their heads. All of a sudden, Annie Lee got out of WK's Chevy and half walked, half run into the house. Couple minutes later she come out with Fred, who crawled up on the flatbed.

The International's engine started and there was a roar of motors everywhere. As the truck moved a path began to clear and in a few minutes we were all strung out and heading toward the Little Bend.

We drove to where Cuyper Creek ran close to the road, then we had to cross the creek to get to the grave spot. The truck would get stuck if we tried to drive across which meant everybody had to wade the stream, which was easy since it was real low.

"Okay," Pers said in a quiet voice, "which of y'all are pallbearers?"

Six people including Dad moved alongside the flatbed. One of them was Bess Clark.

Bess glanced down at the creek and then gazed out through the cornfield on the other side, which was turning yellow and had sharp stiff blades, then looked back at Pers, who was leaning with one elbow against the flatbed. "Pers, why don't we just bury Alfred on this side? Hit's gonna be a awful tussle gettin' him across, and hit's a long ways t' that bluff."

"No you ain't, neither!" Annie Lee screamed, standing with her hand on the coffin. "You ain't a-burying Pa where he don't wanta be. He's a-goin' t' that bluff!"

Bess nodded, then hopped up on the truck and grabbed one edge of the casket. "Let's get started," he grunted, then Dad and the other men grabbed hold of the bottom of the casket and put it on their shoulders and started wading.

The heat was worse now and the corn leaves cut everybody's hands and faces as we walked down the rows with the morning glories grabbing at our feet. Some of the pallbearers stumbled and cussed about the heat and the goddamn vines. Brother Taylor, the preacher, said for everybody to mind their tempers and show a little more respect, which they did.

At the bluff the men took turns digging. It was easy except for the heat because the dirt was sandy. Pretty soon, the grave was dug and the men dusted themselves off and stood back as Brother Taylor began preaching.

"Brothers and sisters, we gathered here t' say goodbye t' our good friend and father and husband, Alfred Mulligan. We all knowed him and his family for years and we all know he was good people. He's got a son t' carry on his name and he's a good one too," and he looked at Fred. Fred just stood there. Tears were running down his face and every now and then you could see him squeeze.

I felt awful and could see that Lonnie and even LD did too but they were just like me, they didn't know what to do. We knew better than to walk up and touch Fred because he would hunch our hands off. The only thing it seemed a body could do was stand beside him. I guess it come to all three of us at the same time because we started moving over to where Fred was almost like we planned it.

The women just stood around in their dark dresses like they were made out of oak, every now and then mopping their wrists or faces with white handkerchiefs because they were sweating hard while the sun, which never let up, melted them. They were all there except Mom and Lisa Shackelford and they had gone over the night before to pay their respects and make food. Everybody understood that somebody else from their families would go to the funeral.

The little breeze that had been blowing when we started down the corn rows stopped all of a sudden and there was dead quiet except for the preacher's voice. Not a cricket or grasshopper or bird made any noise. If you moved your foot, everybody heard the crunch in the red-hot sand so didn't anybody move.

" . . . come here out of Madison County almost twenty-five year ago. He was young then, young and strong as a bull, and he wudn't scared of nothin'. I remember hit well because we met and was young men together. We had a lot of good times. I remember that revival we was at when I declared for Christ. I started preaching after that and Alfred kept on workin' out for people and one day he met Mamie and it wudn't no time 'til he said he wanted t' get married and would I do th' job. Well, sir, I felt privileged and th' next week, I married them."

While Brother Taylor was talking, the flaming hot air was getting sticky wet from the steam that rose up from the river, which was just a little way off. People moved their heads around trying to pick up some air but it didn't work. No breeze at all. Just heat. The men were wearing ties and you could see the sweat trickle down to their collars and seep through into the front of their shirts which were sopping so you could see chest hair matted down underneath. It just kept getting hotter and hotter until the sun was one great ball of terrible fire. Brother Taylor went on and on in his big black suit which was soaked through with sweat and I knew he had to be dying inside it but it was Alfred's send-off and he was going to get what was coming to him. Folks kept shifting from side to side and every now and then one of the men would make a move toward his tie then stop because somehow Brother Taylor would be looking right at him. Most anybody got away with was Bess Clark running his finger around the inside of his collar. The ladies were fanning harder now, their hair sweating and sagging, and you could see straps through their wet clothes and hear a few gasping for air.

And still Brother Taylor went on and on. "Old Alfred wudn't

much of a churchgoer, and I have t' admit that ain't good, but he done a lot of things t' make up for hit. I remember back during that hard winter a few year ago he gave half his salt pork t' some folks that wudn't as well off as he was. And th' Lord looks kindly on them kind of doin's. He says so right here in this book," and he raised his Bible. "It says here a man's got t' have charity and if he don't have charity he ain't nothin'. That's what hit says here in this book. This book a God!" he yelled, and raised the Bible over his head.

Just then, thunder rumbled down the river and was the first sound except for Brother Taylor in quite a while and people kind of looked scared.

"And I am the resurrection and the light!" and the little thunder rolled again and the sky was getting darker through the haze in the Northwest. "And he that believeth in me though he were dead, yet shall he live . . ."

The heat seemed to close in and crush us. I almost couldn't touch my clothes they were so hot and the ground was burning my feet through my shoes and the sweat trickling into my eyes made everybody a blur, especially Brother Taylor, who was growing taller and straighter and stronger and louder and moving his arms slow upward, with his face all dark and hard and lips drawn back, his white teeth flashing as he spoke, and he kept going on and on and it kept getting hotter and hotter and the storm kept coming.

"Comes th' day of judgment th' graves are gonna open up. That's what the Lord tells us and he didn't say maybe they was, he said they was goin' to." The rumbles in the thunderhead grew a little louder and I could see the first jagged flashes of lightning and I knew the earth was waiting for the storm to cool and save it.

"And the seas . . . the seas will deliver up th' dead and God Almighty is gonna judge them, and he's gonna put th' sheep on his right hand and th' goats on his left and woe, woe to th' sinner 'cause they are gonna be condemned to everlastin' fire and damnation . . ." and both his arms was over his head now as he stood over the casket, his eyes glowing, his long, bony fingers sticking out like steel rods from his skinny wrists.

The lightning flashes were brighter now and beginning to be a little more jagged and longer and coming more often and Jennie Dee Wallace said a little soft amen that quivered some and then several of the ladies took it up, "Amen, amen," and Brother Taylor went on.

"And we know th' evil, the Lord tells us th' evil, tells us about Satan and his power, power of darkness . . ." and LD's daddy yelled, "Yes, Brother. Satan's always there temptin' th' righteous!" and the thunder rolled deeper and longer and people's eyes were wide and all the women were saying, "Amen" and some of the men too and Brother Taylor, who had put his arms down, shot them out stiff over his head and said:

"Lord, let righteousness come," and a cool breeze blew in, the first air that stirred in a long time, and the women felt it and said, "Oh Lordy Jesus, thank you, thank you," and the breeze picked up getting stronger and stronger, the thunderhead closing fast with the wind moving dust devils, swirling dirt into us, and some of the women went down on their knees, then the dust devils blew up and around Brother Taylor who was growing and talking upward and you knew who he was talking to and I was scared and I looked over at Dad and he was white and watching me. "And whosoever liveth and believeth in me shall never die," and a terrible crack of thunder come after a lightning bolt split the sky, and you could smell rain. "Amen . . . amen."

"And now my friends follow me in the Twenty-third Psalm. The Lord is my shepherd, I shall not want . . . He maketh me . . ." and the biggest dust devil I ever seen come boiling through, scouring sand into our faces and mouths. " . . . lie down in green pastures. He leadeth me . . ." and lightning flitted five or six times quick on all sides of us with thunder crashes at the same time. " . . . still waters . . ." and the wind come, come hard like it was blowed out of the mouth of God flapping the edge of the coffin where it wudn't tacked down good and Brother Taylor was a hunnert foot tall with his arms stretched commanding the storm. " . . . He restoreth . . ." and one of the women shrieked, "Oh Lord have mercy" that mixed into the thunder and flashes. " . . . in th' path of righteousness, for his . . ." BOOM! BOOM! BOOM! And the lightning was leaping and spitting and twisting and the clouds boiling, wild, wild, wild. " . . . Yea, though I walk through th' valley of th' shadow of death, I will fear . . ." CRASH, BOOM and the coffin lid began flapping and banging and Bess reached out to push it down but it wouldn't go so he started hammering the nail with his fist. Then the rain come, come in sheets and CRASH! CRASH! CRASH! and lightning split a tree above the river and fire flew everywhere and Bess leaped back wild-eyed and all the trees was crazy waving and Brother Taylor standing straight as an arrow with the wind and rain sweeping his black hair and his black coat fluttering out behind him. " . . . thy rod and thy staff, they comf . . ." and there was a terrible crash as three lightning bolts shot toward each other just over our heads, "Amen, amen, oh Lordy! Oh Lordy." " . . . cup runneth over. Surely goodness and . . ." CRASH, CRASH! " . . . all th' days of my life . . ." and the coffin lid started flapping harder and harder and Bess leaped up on top of it shouting, "Lower hit down . . . George . . . Pers . . . Morse . . . hep me lower hit down," and Mamie was wild-eyed on her knees, then flopped straight out on her face. "Hep us, Ed . . ." and they slid it down in the hole and started putting dirt in which was mud now, some shoveling, some pushing with their hands and feet. " . . . Ashes t' ashes and dust t' dust . . . th' Lord, giveth and th' Lord taketh . . ." CRASH! " . . . be th' name of th' Lord!"

44

I woke up with a god-awful hangover and called room service for a pot of coffee, some aspirin, and a glass of tomato juice. An hour later I felt better and decided to visit the University of Kentucky, my brother's alma mater.

The campus was beautiful, but not as beautiful as the UK I remembered Bob and I wandering through in 1948. Gone were the wide spaces between the ancient buildings, many of which had heard the whine of musket balls. In 1948, deep ivy had covered the double layers of redbrick walls that black people laid long before their sons and daughters had been allowed to attend the school. The dense foliage was eventually found to conceal so many defects that the Kentucky legislature had budgeted for new construction. Now, gleaming metal and concrete reared skyward. The Emerald City with a Southern drawl.

I didn't feel a connection to the new Oz. I walked across the parade ground, which was now much smaller than when my brother Bob and I had stood watching the ROTC march. The cadets had thrilled me. I had wanted to be one of them. I remembered how conflicted I felt during Vietnam and the hurt I caused Bob as I argued against the war. Those times tested both of us. I idolized him as a kid. He had fought in the war that saved civilization and survived. He was the fastest tobacco cutter in the neighborhood, a great boxer, loved the outdoors, and often took me with him on his outings. He gave me my first baseball glove, which I kept for thirty years. I lost it during a move and remain saddened by its absence. Then, of course, there was the bike, which I used all the way through college. We shared so many things, things to which no one else was privy. I felt a great sense of loss as I thought about Bob, my sisters, and Mom and Dad. Being the sole surviving member of a family is painful. Watching them fall one by one was like having pieces of my heart cut away. Fortunately, Nora was always there to give me the strength to endure. Somebody has to help you overcome loss or you never completely heal. I had learned this as a child because . . .

. . . After Alfred's funeral, Fred just stayed away from everybody. I went to the Mulligans' several times during September and nobody was around. I figured Mamie and Thelma Jean was at Bea and Pers'. Annie Lee was with WK and Fred was off wandering the hills. I quit going to the Mulligans', then, first Saturday in October, I tried again. This time, Mamie come to the door.

"Hidey, Samuel," she said soft.

"Hi," I said. "Fred home?"

"Naw, honey, he's out lookin' for timber t' cut for winter."

"Think he'll see me?"

Mamie thought for a few seconds. "Naw, don't think so. Hit's still too soon. Fred's just natural slow that way, you know how down he gets. Come in and set a spell."

I didn't want to but I did. It was strange in the living room. Everything was still there, the bed, stove, Mamie's chair, little peeling table with the humpback radio and the no-back. A breeze coming through the window kept fluttering a torn part of one drape and occasionally it would hang on the radio dial, which was still tuned to WLEX, the station where the Reds played. I must've been looking sad because Mamie said, "Lonesome, hain't it."

"Yeah," I said. "You still listen t' th' Reds?"

She shook her head slow. "Can't. Batt'ry's dead."

Then we just sat. It was like standing at a grave after everybody's left the funeral.

"What's going on down your way?" Mamie asked, motioning me to sit on the no-back.

"Nothin'," I answered, and kept standing.

Mamie nodded. "Go 'head 'n' sit on hit, honey. Alfred ain't gonna haint you. G'won, have a seat," and I did, but just barely on the edge. "How's your ma and pa?"

"Okay."

She smiled at me because she knew I was bothered. "How's th' rest of th' fambly?"

Her smile relaxed me and I slipped further onto the no-back. "Debby's in California."

"How's Naomi?"

"Naomi's gettin' capped around Christmas. She's gonna get through nurse's trainin'."

"That's great," said Mamie. "How's Bob?"

I really brightened up. "Bob's got a job for when he's graduated. Good one too!"

"Graduated!" and her voice rose. "Well, I swan! Seems like he just got back from th' war. Ain't been going t' college all that long, has he?"

I liked talking about my big brother. It made me feel good. "He had some college before th' war. That's how come he finished so quick."

Mamie shook her head again. "Seems like yesterday y'all were runnin' that trot line." The breeze flipped the drape until it covered the whole radio and Mamie walked over and unhooked it, then snapped the on dial. No sound come out, and she snapped it off, then turned back to me with tears in her eyes. The grooves in her face were deep and her stringy brown hair hung straight. "Hit wudn't fair things a-happenin' t' us this way. We had our show comin' t' us . . . t' Alfred." She let out a big sigh, and the breeze flipped the drape, making a pop.

Suddenly, I felt terrible. I had to get out of the Mulligan house. "How long you figure it'll be before Fred comes around?"

"Hard t' say," she sniffed. "Try back again next weekend. He's doin' some better 'n' seeing as how y'all are best friends, that might work."

I went out through the kitchen and climbed the gate. From its top, I could see Thelma Jean walking slow up the road from Pers'. I waved to her, but she just kept putting one bare foot in front of the other, heel to toe, like she never saw me.

The walk home was nice. Leaves were changing fast. Everywhere you looked was Life Everlasting. Squirrels were working hickory and walnut and oak trees harder than I'd ever seen. Flocks of ducks went south, one after another. The signs were talking about winter and they said it would be long and hard.

When I got back to the house, Dad was further down than ever. I didn't know why until late that night when talk from their bedroom woke me up. Their voices mumbled but I could hear them pretty good. They were talking about Mr. Berman.

"How can he say that?" said Mom. "Who else would take care of his shitting farm the way we do? He gives us every third lamb and he thinks he's being generous? Doesn't he realize that usually a third die, sometimes along with the ewes, and you save almost every one?"

Springs squeaked and I figured Dad turned over. "Nate's a city boy. I'm his first tenant."

"Well, why don't you tell him?"

"Tell him what? He's too damn ignorant to understand."

"What exactly did he say, anyway?"

There was a thump, and I knew Dad put his arm behind his neck and hit the headboard.

"He said he didn't like the arrangement and that it had to change. The most he would give us was every fourth lamb and none of the wool. He wants me to plant double the corn and put in a trench silo. He said he read about it in *Successful Farming* and that with it he can run double the number of cattle he has in the past."

"Trench silo? I didn't think trench silos worked around here."

"They don't. The water table is too high. We tried those years ago when I first came to Kentucky and worked for Mr. Farnsworth. The silage just molds and you lose it all."

"Did you tell him that?"

"Yeah."

"Well, what did he say?" Mom snapped, and her voice was tired.

Dad sighed real deep. "He said those were th' dark ages. That I ought to read *Successful Farming* and learn some of th' new stuff. He talked about corn pickers and combines."

"Why would we even want a corn picker or combine here?" asked Mom. "We only raise fifteen acres of corn. As rough as the ground is, we'd tear up the corn picker. And a combine? The only grain we raise is eight acres of oats, and we get that baled. Corn pickers! Combines! We don't even own a tractor!"

"Yeah." Dad giggled. It was the first time in months he had done that but I knew it wudn't a happy giggle.

"Did you tell him that?"

"I tried to. He said th' Wallace boy didn't think it was dumb."

"The Wallace boy?" and Mom's voice sounded like she couldn't believe him.

"Yeah, Rags' oldest wants th' place. Turns out, he's been putting a bug in Nate's ear. He's gettin' married and needs a farm to rent. He'd have his dad and brother right up the road for things like tobacco housing and stripping. Good deal for a kid. Big tobacco base."

Mom snorted. "Yes, and Nate would find out some things too. His cattle and sheep would quit making money when he didn't have you taking care of them. A shmozzle of Nate."

I turned my head into the pillow and stopped listening. Wow, what would we do if we left Berman's? Everything was changing.

I couldn't sleep so I thought about Joy West and what had just happened at school. Joy and I had always talked to each other, but this year we talked more than ever. It was weird how we'd keep meeting. We'd bump into each other seven or eight times a day. One day, Miz Callen asked for kids to help set up chairs in the auditorium before the Future Farmers meeting and sent Joy and me to the school storehouse to see how many chairs there were if we needed extra. The storehouse was a piece down the road from school and we skipped along laughing and talking, her telling me about their trip that summer to Lookout Mountain in Tennessee. On the way back we sat down under a big maple. It was a great day, real clear, and the fall breezes were blowing like they always do in Indian summer and fluttering Joy's blouse and making her long black hair stream away from her shoulders or wrap around her face. Somehow, and I really don't know how, we kissed each other. My heart pounded and my whole body seemed to shake a little as I looked into her eyes and she smiled. Then she said we had better be getting back. That was the first person I ever kissed outside of my family and I couldn't get it off my mind. Alone in the dark I started to tingle all over with an electric feeling and wanted to kiss her and hold her and see the wind blow her hair across her face.

45

Mr. Berman said we had to move and the next couple days were awful around the house. Most of the time it was dead quiet. Dad hardly talked, and when he did, it was about how he didn't know any way we could buy a place with what little we had for a down payment.

Mom wouldn't say anything for a time, then she'd yell at him and bawl. Then it would be silent again. It was really bad, boy.

I headed back to the Mulligans' the next Saturday. This time I decided, come whatever, I was seeing Fred. In just one week it had gotten deeper fall and we had our first killing frost. Trees that were only turning a few days before were yellow or even red, and the chill in the morning air was staying until almost noon. There was a little north wind starting too, and as I walked through the hickory and locust thicket it showered me with leaves. Everything that hadn't seeded was doing it in a hurry and a strange haze was starting. There was no mistaking the signs. Something bad was coming.

When I got to the barbwire gap, I could hear the sound of an ax biting wood in the direction of Cummings Hill. I went to the Mulligan house but it looked deserted, the only things moving around being a few old Dominicker hens. I climbed up on top of the hog lot gate and called. On my third call, Thelma Jean came out on the front porch. She had on a flowered feed sack dress. It was dirtier than usual and I guessed nobody was cleaning it for her.

"Whatchawant, Sam?"

"Fred around?" I asked, straddling the gate.

"Naw."

"Where is he?"

Thelma shrugged and looked away into the distance.

I threw my other leg over the gate and set on its top rail. "I'd like t' see Fred, Thelma Jean. We're best friends and it's a long time since we saw each other."

"Ain't none of your bidness where he is," she said, narrowing her eyes and looking at me. "Fred don't want nobody a-botherin' him. Whyn't you go way 'n' leave us alone."

I started to say something back hot when a voice from the upstairs window said, "He's cuttin' wood out on Cummings Hill, Samuel. I think he'll see you now."

It was Annie Lee. From the top of the gate I could see most of her and wudn't any doubt about one thing: Annie Lee was gonna have a baby. I remembered then that she had a pot belly at the funeral. She'd never had a pot belly before, and this was why.

"Thanks," I answered, and jumped down into the yard and began walking along the path through the weeds. I could feel her eyes following me. Before the path turned the corner of the house, I looked around. Annie Lee was sitting in the window smiling at me. I smiled back.

Any fool with ears could've found Fred. The thunk . . . thunk . . . thunk of his ax cut through the warming day like shotgun blasts. I circled where he was working, slipping from tree to tree. He looked different. His face had always been old, but now it kind of had lines. He was thinner too and moved slow. In his hands was an old single-bit ax and he was working on a fallen log about two foot thick. All around was worked-up limbs. You could look at the cut ends and tell it had been an awful job. The wood was mostly mashed apart. Fred's ax was dull as a rock. At the rate he was going, one cut through the log he was working on would be a half-day job. He didn't stop though. Thunk . . . thunk . . . thunk in a steady beat.

The first time he let up, I stepped into the open and called out. "Fred?"

For a few seconds I didn't know what he'd do, then he turned toward me with a little grin on his face. I went bounding down to him. "Hidey, Fred Cody."

"Hidey, Samuel," and he tried to sink his ax in the log for a rest but it just bounced off. He turned the blade up and looked at the edge. "Wouldn't cut hot butter."

"Looks like you could use a file."

Fred nodded, then sat down on the log and put one brogan on its top. He was wearing Alfred's old shoes, and for the first time since I'd known him, Fred had heels.

"How y' been?" he asked.

"Tolerable," and I straddled a log and faced him. "How 'bout you?"

"Doin' all right. Got a shit-pot full of work t' get done, though. Gonna have t' start strippin' tobacco soon. Not that there's much t' strip. Hit'll about pay our fertilizer bill and a little of th' grocery bill."

He stopped talking and looked around. "Ever see so much Life Everlastin'."

"Naw," I said, looking down the hillside where little puffy sprigs stuck out everywhere.

"Ducks left early. Squirrels goin' crazy. What they ain't a-storin' they're eatin' fast as they can. Saw a groundhog out here th' other day so fat he could hardly move. If I'd of had a stick, I coulda killed him he was so slow from fat."

"Gonna be a cold winter," I said, looking down when I spoke.

"Yeah," he half whispered. "Samuel, I got t' get lots of firewood and more grub. I been workin' like a dog for more'n a week cuttin' wood and what I've worked up won't last ten hard days. Boy, I wish we hadn't lost our hogs. We could've sold some and bought a chain saw and killed a couple and had plenty of wood and meat. We got t' have plenty of wood and meat."

I knew what he meant, and thought it was time to let him know. "Saw Annie Lee."

Fred kicked some dirt with his heel. "Figured y' did. Bea says hit's gonna come in January or February. Wouldn't you know hit, them's th' roughest months we have. I don't get up enough wood t' keep th' house warm, hit'll die."

"WK ought help get up wood too . . . don't you think?"

"Huh! Old WK run off somewheres soon's he found out he was gonna be a daddy. He's a egg-suckin' pup."

"Maybe he'll come back."

Fred shook his head slow and run his thumb along the ax edge. "He ain't a-coming back. He don't care about th' baby. Don't care about nobody but him."

"What you gonna do?"

Fred scraped his heel around in the dirt and sighed. "Keep at hit, I reckon."

This all just wudn't right. Then I thought of something. "Could you use a little help?"

He looked at me and his eyes widened. "I'd be appreciative. 'Specially if hit come with a cross-cut saw 'n' a twenty-minute shot on an emery wheel."

I got off the log and stood with my fists on my hips. "Pick out seven or eight trees that ain't too big and come over about four this afternoon and bring your ax. I'll get Dad t' let you use th' emery wheel and with a little luck, I'll meet you here tomorra mornin' with some hands," then I struck out cross-country to the Little Bend bottoms.

I had luck. Lonnie and his pa had just come in from fishing, and Mr. Miller was in a good mood. When I asked if Lonnie could help the next day even though it was Sunday, Mrs. Miller said it was okay because the ox was in the ditch. They even let Lonnie bring his own ax.

When I got home I got out our cross-cut saw, wedges, sledgehammer, and the rasp and put them aside for the next morning, then asked Dad if Fred could use our emery wheel. He said yes, and by the time Fred finished on the wheel, a body could shave with his ax. When Lonnie arrived the next morning, we grabbed everything and took off. By nightfall we had downed seven trees, cut them into two-foot sections, worked up most of the limbs, and left the wedges, sledgehammer, and rasp for Fred to split logs with. It was a tired Sunday, but I sure felt good.

Before Lonnie and I left, Fred asked me if I could come over the next Sunday and bring my slingshot and lunch box. I thought it was an odd thing to ask considering all he had to get done, but the next Sunday I came over with a lunch box full of sandwiches, a whole bunch of food from Mom for the Mulligans, and my slingshot. I told Fred not to eat much in the house because I had the lunch box stuffed for us. Boy, did Mamie, Annie Lee, and Thelma Jean eat. They didn't even notice when we left.

"Where we goin', Fred?" I asked when we got out of earshot of the kitchen.

Fred grinned at me and started through the backyard toward Cummings Hill, grabbing a gunnysack as we went. "Hun'ney, we gonna do somethin' best friends ought do but don't 'cause they don't think about hit. Bring your slingshot?"

He was sounding mysterious. "Yeah. Why'd you want me t' do that?"

"Because th' first thing we're gonna do is eat th' stuff in that lunch box."

That didn't make any sense as an answer. "Then what?"

Fred's grin got bigger. "Then I'm gonna tell y'."

We took off up Cummings Hill and I realized that we were on our way to where we felled the trees. A pretty good distance from the top we come to two shovels and a grubbing hoe. Fred sat down beside one of the shovels and said, "Let's eat."

The sandwiches didn't last long, even though there was a lot of them. When we finished eating I said, "Lunch box is empty."

Fred nodded. "Lunch box 'thout somethin' in hit ain't worth havin', is it?"

Boy, he sure wudn't making any sense. "Fred Cody, what you up to?"

Fred got up and pointed to the top of Cummings Hill. "See that big oak, and that littler oak down below hit?"

"So?"

"Line up th' handle of that shovel with those two."

I did, then said, "Now what?"

"Now look yonder," and he pointed around the side of the hill, where a big pine stood with a lot of little pines around it, and one small oak tree closer to us. "Take th' other shovel handle and line that big pine up with that oak this side of it and move everything t' where th' shovel handles cross."

I did, then waited for him to say something. He was fooling with me but it felt good to see him happy.

"Time t' start diggin'," he said, and picked up a shovel and I grabbed the grubbing hoe. We dug down about three foot and about that much square in the spot where the shovel handles crossed, then we hit a rock that covered the whole bottom. "Fred, we can't bust through that thing. It could go down forever."

Fred laughed. "Don't want to." Then he got a strange look on his face that gave me the willies. "Samuel, you 'n' me are best friends. We done a lotta stuff t'gether and we're still doin' hit. Th' things we done t'gether don't general happen t' folks. Things is changin', though. I got this feelin' we ain't gonna be makin' slingshots next year . . . probably won't until we're hepin' our kids make 'em. These here slingshots we got now are th' last we're prob'ly ever gonna make for ourselves together. Gimme yours."

I got my slingshot out of the back pocket of my Levi's and handed it to him. The way he was talking made me uneasy. He was dead-on earnest. "Whatcha gonna do?"

Fred took his slingshot out and kind of wrapped mine up with his, then he nodded toward my lunch box. "We gonna bury them in your lunch box and dig 'em up a long time from now. Hit'll be something we can remember about th' days when we didn't have no worries. Pa never had nothin' to remind him of a better time, and when things went bad, he just natural slid on down th' hill real sad. We had some good times together, me 'n' you, and this is gonna remind us of that someday. Long time from now, Samuel."

I wudn't hot on the idea at first because it didn't make a lot of sense, then I got to thinking about what was going on at home. Maybe it was a good idea after all. We put the slingshots in the box, wrapped the gunnysack around it, put the box in the hole, and shoveled in the dirt. I knew Mom was going to ask where the lunch box was and I sure couldn't tell her I buried it. I decided I'd think of something, though.

Over the next several Sundays, Fred and me did everything from cutting more wood to picking every apple in the neighborhood. We made ten deadfalls too, and stripped away on their tobacco crop. Every day, the weather got colder and the little north wind stirred harder.

46

It was a cold winter, boy. Snow on the ground from Thanksgiving on. The sky was overcast and there was this haze. Sometimes the haze turned into mist and drifted the valleys.

It was a terrible time for Dad. He brooded and worried about where we were going and ought we to buy a place or not. Mom was feeling bad too, and just fumbled around. I was the only kid at home now that Naomi was at nurse's training and I heard Mom say she wished Naomi was closer because she was about to go crazy alone. Most of the time the only sounds were the howling of the north wind. We finished stripping in early December because the crop was so short. When everything was totaled up, we lost almost three thousand dollars for the year.

I saw Fred a lot. I'd get home from school, do the milking and feeding, grab a bite and a flashlight and run to the Mulligans so we could set the deadfalls. We had saved two bushels of apples for bait. Anything that could be stored for winter, we stored. Hickory and walnuts, even acorns. Trouble was, the squirrels and groundhogs and had pretty much got everything.

Most of the time we were together, Fred would talk about Annie Lee's baby. It got so that was all he wanted to talk about. He and Annie Lee decided if it was a boy they were going to call him Alfred and if it was a girl, Alfreda. Alfreda didn't sound like much of a girl's name to me, but seeing as how things were, I let on I thought it was beautiful.

Through most of the late fall, things went okay for the Mulligans. There was plenty of firewood and rabbits, and Mom gave Fred my old clothes. She sewed some for the girls too, and a few church folks pitched in with salt butts.

In late December the hard cold hit, and the mist drove everybody into their houses. It was funny about that mist, how it hung over our valleys and hills and wouldn't go away. The sun couldn't burn it off and little swirls sometimes come all the way to the ground. Everybody talked about it at first, and then nobody did. Matter of fact, people kind of stopped talking. If folks met they'd mumble to one another, then stare out through the mist and shuffle back to their homes.

In mid-January the rabbits disappeared. We run the deadfalls day after day. Nothing! Wudn't even any tracks! When the salt butts from the church folks were used up the Mulligans didn't have anything to eat, other than some skim milk, flour, and chickens we gave them. One bushel of sweet apples was left from what we used to bait the deadfalls, and Fred and me decided the family might as well go ahead and eat them since there wudn't any rabbits.

About this time, it turned really cold. Night seemed to go on forever and folks got strange. The animals got even stranger, especially the dogs. They wouldn't stay around people if they could help it, and when you called them, they just slunk away. Pers's old coonhound near tore one of the Langley boy's arms off when he tried to pet him, and a Langley knows more about hounds than anybody. Pers went for his shotgun to kill the old devil and it run off and never come back. At home, our one-horn buck knocked Dad down and when he got up, the buck come again until Dad had to nigh beat it to death.

The worst come a couple weeks later when Uncle Lex went out to feed his hogs and didn't come back. Aunt Belle went to look for him and found an awful sight. Wudn't much left of Uncle Lex. Couple folks got together and buried what the hogs didn't eat.

With all the strange happenings, lack of food, mist, and terrible cold, Fred was happy. We'd be sitting around the Mulligan stove watching the fire flicker through its isinglass window and he'd break out singing "Old Dan Tucker" or "Filipino Baby" like he was Ernest Tubb or he'd grab Annie Lee around her middle and squeeze and she'd let out a yelp and yell, "Fred Cody, you're gonna hurt me and I'm gonna put a knot on your head," but she'd be grinning when she yelled it, and her face would just beam. Fred would laugh like a fool. The bigger Annie Lee got, the happier the family got. The Mulligans were the happiest folks around and everybody thought they were miserable something awful.

Late one afternoon I was getting ready to go to the Mulligans' when Mom said no.

"Morris, the radio says snow, high winds, and severe cold tonight. That's a long walk to the Mulligans' house. Suppose there's a blizzard?"

I could see Dad thinking but he knew I really wanted to go. "If there's a blizzard, he could probably stay there."

Mom looked at Dad like he was crazy. "At the Mulligans'?"

"Yeah," said Dad, shrugging his shoulders. "Why not?"

"What would he eat? They need every scrap of food they have for themselves."

"He's eaten supper."

"Supper? A supper like that wouldn't keep a bird alive. It's cold and dangerous in that old firetrap. Don't you give a damn what happens to him!"

Generally, that would have made Dad mad. Now, he kinda slumped in his chair. "M'dom, he's fine. He wants to help his friend. They've been through a lot together."

That seemed to bother Mom, and she got tears in her eyes and spoke soft. "Don't I help the Mulligans? Who cranks that cream separator every night and gives them milk? And clothes. How many clothes have I—"

"I know, M'dom. I know you have. You've done more than me. It's wrong that I haven't done more, but I've been feeling so bad that—"

"You always feel bad!" she yelled, and it went on and on like that until they forgot about me, so I got my mackinaw and slipped out.

God, it was cold. The snow and ice had frozen the barn door tight and I had to climb the hog lot gate. I thought about Uncle Lex and was glad we didn't have any hogs. When I climbed to the top of the gate behind the barn, I looked out at the mist which was layered above the little valley and hid most of the volcano hill. It didn't move. It just lay there like a spooky white blanket. I realized then that the wind had quit blowing. I jumped down and walked a ways, then stopped again. It was strange. Wudn't any sound of any kind. I dug my heel through the top of icy snow to make a little noise and an awful wail seemed to rise into the air. That scared me and I took off as hard as I could go, raced across the frozen creek, past the hickory and locust grove, and in no time I was at the gap. The wire loop fastener at the top of the gap was frozen to the post and when I touched it my fingers stuck giving that awful feeling and I jerked back.

Getting into the next field looked like it was going to be a problem since I didn't have any gloves and you got to use your hands to climb a fence. Then I remembered that the fence had a hole in it down by the pond. Soon I was in the field that led to the Mulligans' gate.

The wind began picking up making the cold worse. Then the wail come again and I tore out running. By the time I got to the house I was chilled to the bone and scared to death. I pounded on the door and yelled, "Fred . . . Fred!"

"Hello, Samuel," Fred said soft-like when he come to the door. His face was all lit up and his eyes was strange like they seen an angel. Then I realized what was happening. Annie Lee was having her baby.

47

Hit started 'bout four this mornin',” said Fred. “We called Bea and she come over and said hit was too early, but she come back 'round noon and been here ever since.”

“C . . . can I c . . . come in?” I asked.

“Old Bea's been upstairs with her most of th’ time. She says hits goin’ slow but that hits like that, though, th’ first time. I heard her tell mama hit was gonna be all right.”

“C . . . can . . . I come in?” I asked again, shuddering.

Fred just stood there, his eyes glowing like they had wind and fire in them, and his denim shirt moving in and out fast as he breathed. Then he realized what I asked. “Come on in, hun’ney. Hit's gonna be a great night,” and he threw his arm around my shoulder.

Mamie and Thelma Jean were in the living room, Mamie wearing one of Mom's sweaters and sitting in her rocker and Thelma Jean on the no-back in her Purina dress. Fred and me warmed ourselves, then Fred said, “Whyn’t you go up and see how she's a-doin’, Mama?”

“You just keep calm, Fred Cody,” Mamie answered with a little laugh. “Reckon I know more ’bout this sorta thing than you do. You just have a seat on th’ bed.”

Fred was fidgeting around the stove, his whole body moving. “You ain’t checked in a long while,” he said as the two of us went over and set on the bed.

“Fred, he don’t know nothin’ about babies and things,” said

Thelma Jean. "Him and Sam, they ought be run off. Hit's not right, old boys . . ."

"You shut your mouth!" snapped Mamie.

Thelma Jean kind of shriveled up, then she grabbed an old blanket and run to a corner and huddled under it until you couldn't see any of her.

Outside, the wind was getting loud and the snow was drifting. The temperature was dropping too, because when I went to the window to look out, the pane was so cold I could hardly put my fingers near it. Between gusts of blowing snow you could see more snow falling.

Inside, the coal oil lamps cast long shadows against the walls. Fred and I had flopped down on the bed and it was nice listening to the crackling of the fire, the squeak of Mamie's rocker, and the howling wind.

Pretty soon there were footfalls on the stairs. Fred was up like a shot but a quick look from Mamie froze him. She got out of her rocker real slow, then went into the next room where the stairs come down. From the bed, Fred and me could see Mamie and Bea through a crack in the curtain and hear fairly well, especially Bea, who talked loud. Alfred used to say you could hear Bea whisper five hundred yards off, which wudn't true, but it was close. Mamie's words faded in and out and sometimes you had to guess what she was saying from what Bea answered.

"What's . . . on Bea . . . heard . . . and she . . . nothing?"

"Lordy yes, them pains can't get no harder."

"She ain't . . . sound . . . not . . ."

"Never seen nothin' like hit. When they come she bites down on that old broom handle. She's chewed hit t' pieces. Plumb through in one spot."

"Hard . . . I mean . . . harder'n . . . other . . . been at?"

"Mamie, hit's th' hardest I ever seen. She didn't want me t' say, didn't want t' scare y'all, but I got t' thinkin' upstairs I had t' say somethin' 'cause hit wudn't right, you her mama 'n' all. Hit just wudn't right a-sayin' nothin'."

"What's wrong?" And this time we heard Mamie good.

Fred started to get up, and Mamie saw him through the crack in the curtains. "Fred Cody, you stay there!" she called, and he did, but just barely.

Mamie and Bea tried to talk lower after that, but their voices come through real clear. "I don't rightly know," Bea went on. "Maybe hit's butt first, or somethin'. We ought get a doc . . . now I know how y'all feel about doctors, but maybe one could help."

I saw Fred's eyes widen and I knew he wudn't staying on the bed much longer.

"Culbert couldn't make it even if she'd let him see her," Mamie said loud. "Th' road's drifted. I don't think he'd come even if he could. We owe him lots of money and can't pay a copper. You can bring hit up t' her, though. I'll walk there if she wants. I swear t' God, I'll . . ."

"That's not all why I come down, Mamie. They's something else. You ain't goin' t' like this, and I don't understand hit neither, but she wants t' see Fred."

Fred bounced off the bed and busted through the curtains. I saw him leap for the stair rail and Mamie's hand grab his arm and spin him around before the curtains fell back.

"Fred Cody, you ain't a-goin' up there! You get back inside!"

"I'm gonna see Annie Lee," he said.

All the time I had known Fred his voice never sounded like that. I knew that he was gonna see Annie Lee and wudn't nothing going to stop him.

"You get back on that bed, Fred! You hear me?"

"I'm gonna see Annie Lee," he said. "Let go my arm, Mama."

"Fred, there ain't nothin' for you t' do up there. You just a boy, son. You're a good boy, and you're gonna be a good man, but you just a boy now and there ain't nothin' you can do. Wouldn't be nothin' you could do if you was a growed man, less'n you was a doctor."

There wudn't any answer. I could hear a struggle and now and then see a flash of movement. Mamie was trying to stop Fred and he was wrestling her out of the way. From the sound I could tell things was about even, since Fred was giving it all he had while Mamie wudn't.

"No, Fred . . . baby, stop now . . . Freddie . . . Bea . . . hep me . . . Bea!"

"I can't, Mamie. I don't know what's right. She wants him up there. I just don't know what's right. I can't help. I got t' leave hit between you two . . . in God's hands."

The struggling got louder and something was knocked over. Mamie kept saying, "Naw, Fred! Naw, hit ain't right!" Then all of a sudden there was this shriek.

"*Fred!*"

It was Annie Lee. The struggle stopped and I heard Fred race up the steps with Bea and Mamie right behind him. I jumped up and ran to the curtains. All four voices were talking at once, but the one that came over clearest was Annie Lee's.

"All y'all get out 'cept Fred! I'll be, okay. I wanta talk t' Fred alone! G'won!"

Footsteps come down the stairs one at a time sounding like they would quit if Annie Lee didn't keep telling them to leave. They stopped at the bottom and I guess Annie Lee could tell.

"G'won back in th' livin' room," she yelled. "I got somethin' t' say t' Fred. I don't want nobody but Fred a-hearin' it. G'won." And suddenly her voice had a squeezing sound, and there was a high-pitched grunt.

Bea started back up the stairs, but Annie Lee yelled, "I'm okay! Y'all get back inside, I'm okay. Hit ain't a-comin'. I'll call y'all if hit starts comin'. G'won!"

I went back to the bed, and a moment later Mamie come in followed by Bea. Mamie sat down in her rocker, and Bea stood by the stove. Bea looked tired and she folded her arms and let her chin slump down near her chest, her eyes almost closed. Outside, the storm was going crazy with icy snow hitting the window. Nobody said anything for a while, then Bea saw me.

"Samuel Zilney! My Lord, how you've growed."

"Yes, ma'am," I said.

"He's growed sure enough," said Mamie. "Him and Fred make more'n a man. I can't tell you how much help Samuel's been since Alfred died. Wudn't for his help, we'd be out of wood and freezin' and wouldn't have stretched our foodstuffs near as far as we have. Been a big help."

Bea laughed kind of quiet, then said, "Never seen so many men at a birthin' in all my life. How old you, Samuel?"

"Twelve," I answered.

"Times is a-changin'," she said, raising her eyebrows and looking at Mamie.

"Ain't they," said Mamie, giving a big sigh.

It got quiet again except for the storm, and in a few minutes Bea walked over to the window, cupped her hands around her eyes, and looked out. "Hit's awful," she said. "Snowin' like a demon. Winds a-driftin' hit everywheres."

"Figured we were gonna have a bad one t'night," said Mamie.

There wudn't anything else to say. Time just hung. Finally, Bea said she better look in on Annie Lee whether she liked it or not, then went out through the curtains and up the stairs.

A few minutes later Fred come down and crawled onto the bed. He didn't say anything, just lay there staring straight up. Pretty soon, he started to shake, then rolled off the bed and ran for the door. Mamie started to yell for him not to go outside, but he was gone before she could.

I didn't know what to do. Outside, it was the wildest winter night ever. The door to the outhouse was banging, and stuff was slamming into the gate and fence. One time, I thought I heard the kitchen roof flop. I kept thinking of Fred. He might freeze to death. I got so worried, I went to the kitchen door and opened it.

It was terrible. You couldn't see anything for the blinding, swirling snow which had some kind of little ice chips in it. It was colder than I ever felt before and I knew dressed like he was Fred would die if he didn't come back inside soon. I was getting ready to go get him when there he was just a few feet in front of me, walking like a ghost, staring straight ahead. He brushed past me and I closed the door and followed. There was snow in his hair, and the light from the coal oil lamp made him look salt-and-pepper gray. In the living room, he stood by the stove with his hands behind him.

Mamie kept watching him, looking right at him, but he didn't look back. "What is it you know, Fred?" she asked. "I wanta know too. I'm Annie Lee's mama and I got a right."

Fred didn't answer straight out, or even look at Mamie. When he did speak, his words tumbled through the terrible sounds outside the house. "Little Alfred's dead."

Mamie's mouth fell open and she set forward in her rocker. "Fred, don't say a thing like that. You don't know that. Hit ain't even been born yet!"

"Little Alfred's dead," Fred repeated.

"But, Fred . . . you don't know that?"

Fred's head shook. "Annie Lee told me. She said he was dead and I know she's right. I'm sorry, Mama. It ain't right, him dyin'. I can't understand why God had t' do it. Little Alfred was all we had. We didn't ask for nothin' else. He was the onliest thing we asked for. I reckon he had t' die on account of th' sin, but I don't see why. WK could've died, or even Annie Lee. She said hit too. Don't see why it had t' be little Alfred. Just ain't right."

I heard Thelma Jean behind her blanket in the corner, then she come running over and flung herself on the bed beside me and started crying shoulder-shaking tears. For a couple seconds I didn't move, then she shook harder and harder and I put my hand on her back and patted her. She grabbed me around the waist and buried her face in my belly and I stroked her head and back and let her sob. She still stunk like she always did, but somehow now it was different. She couldn't help being who she was. She was Thelma Jean and she was feeling awful and wanted a friend. Somebody who could forget for a while how dumb she was and how much she stunk and right now I was him so I kept stroking her and stroking her and she kept squeezing and pushing her face into my belly until, finally, she quit.

The storm, which had kept getting wilder and I thought was going to lift the roof, began quieting down. I could hear footfalls on the stairs. The curtains opened and there stood Bea. Big like a mountain, her giant hands open toward us. Tears were streaming down her face. She tried to speak but a croak come out instead.

"We know, Bea," said Mamie.

"The cord was wrapped around hit's neck. She didn't make a sound. Just lay there through it all. Suffered harder'n anybody I ever seen. She knowed. I swear t' God she knowed. She didn't even ask."

When Bea stopped talking, she turned to Fred and looked at him for a few seconds like she was seeing a person she had never met before. "She wants to see you," she said, and he went through the curtains and into the dark.

The four of us just kind of set in the flickering lamplight. Outside it was dead quiet. I went to the window and rubbed a hole in the frost. The moon was out, and I could smell the cold through the windowpane.

Mamie got up, her skirt rustling. "I'm goin' upstairs," she said. "I'm gonna take Thelma Jean. I thank you for your help, Bea. You've done all a body could ask. You too, Samuel. Th'storm's over. Y'all can make hit home easy," and I knew she wanted us to go and so did Bea.

"Say goodbye t' Fred for me," I said, putting on my mackinaw. "Tell him I'm sorry about little Alfred. Tell Annie Lee that too."

I went out the kitchen door and when I climbed the gate I sat for a moment. A big moon was shining and everything was white. White the yard, white the trees, white the fields and the things beyond. Pure white. I jumped down on the other side of the gate and plowed through the snow toward home. When I come to the crest of the hill at the end of the hickory and locust grove, I stopped again and looked into the distance. The mist was gone. I could see the stock barn, and the gates in front of it all powdered white. Everything was beautiful in the light of the full moon. I took a deep breath, and it was clean and cold and went to the bottom of my chest. As I stood and looked I felt something was different. I didn't know what it was but somehow I knew it was always going to be different. It made me feel kind of sad. I trudged home through the drifts, said good night to the folks, who had been worried about me, and went to bed.

48

After that night, Fred did his usual thing and stayed away from everybody. I went back to the Mulligan house a couple weeks later. As I was climbing the hog lot gate I looked up to see Annie Lee in the upstairs window.

"Hi, Samuel."

I froze straddling the gate and turned toward her. I never saw anybody look so sad. "Hi, Annie Lee," and I couldn't think of nothing else to say. Then I said, "How y' doin'?"

"Tolerable," she said, and sighed. "Lookin' for Fred?"

"Yeah, I was."

"He won't talk t' you, Samuel. Won't talk t' nobody outside the fambly and don't say much t' us. You know how he is. I 'preciate your comin', but maybe hit's best t' give us a little more time."

I nodded and just straddled the gate for a while. Then I said, "Tell him I said hi."

"I will."

I jumped down to walk home, then heard Annie Lee say: "Samuel."

I turned and faced her. Her eyes were still sad but somehow they looked different.

"You're a good man, Samuel."

I thought that was a strange thing to say, but it made me feel good. "Thanks, Annie Lee. You're a good woman too."

Annie Lee just smiled at me. It was the sweetest smile.

I kept on being down in the dumps. Some because of Fred, but even more because we were going to leave Berman's. One day Dad got a phone call from a guy who had been looking for a farm for us. Dad sounded awful excited after the fellow told him about it and about how much it cost. The very next day the three of us took off for Indiana to see it. It sure was a long way. It seemed like we drove forever until we came to a town called Crawfordsville. That's where we met this guy who showed us the farm. It was ugly as a pig's ass, the buildings all run down, and only a couple trees on it. The fields looked like they had been cropped to death and the whole farm was real flat. I mean, wudn't enough slope to get a car rolling if its battery run down. Dead flat! The whole area was flat, every farm.

The house hadn't been lived in for a couple years and even though it had electricity and gas and a bathroom, everything was shabby. I felt better as soon as I saw the place because I knew we would never buy a farm that ugly.

We spent a couple of hours there looking, then driving around and ended up in the town of Crawfordsville. It was a pretty nice town and had a movie theater. It was thirteen miles from the farm we were looking at though, and that's a lot of pedaling on a bike. Mom and Dad sent me to the movies and said they would pick me up in a couple of hours. It was a good show. I was warm and happy until I walked out, and there was Mom and Dad waiting for me. They grabbed and hugged me and Dad said that I wudn't a sharecropper's kid anymore. We were proud owners of a fine farm!

"What farm?" I asked.

Dad laughed. "Why the one we just looked at, of course."

I nigh puked. How could they buy that old junk farm? Then Dad started talking about how we were going to fix it up and how it was going to take a lot of work because we couldn't hire it done and how he was going need me to have the same kind of backbone that he and Mom had. Then he said we were going to get a tractor and lots of equipment, that the guy knew where we could get all of that stuff and it was a lot for the money and for me to get in the car because they were going to go up and go through my new school right now.

The school was a big old thing, bigger than Middletown by a lot. It was ugly too, except for the basketball court, which was really nice. I stood and watched their team practice. They were good, boy. I never saw high school players that good before and I knew wudn't any way I was ever going to make that team. By the time we got back to Berman's, I was lower than a mole's ass and it's under the ground.

When the last day of March come around, we were ready to move. We had our furniture and everything packed into a great big truck which Dad had gotten use of as part of the deal for the farm. We had sold off most of our farm equipment since we were going to be farming with a tractor now, and what small amount of livestock we had was going to be hauled separate.

Things were set to leave early the next morning. I was real low. I figured we were leaving Berman's forever and I was going to miss it so much. Also, I wudn't going to get to see Fred before we left. It was toward evening when I decided to wander around the farm and take one last look. I went to the tobacco barn, and sheep barn, then down to the tenant house, which was empty now because Radar and his family had gone back to the mountains. I looked at the volcano hill and thought about not seeing it again. It hit me then that I didn't realize how much I liked that hill. I could see little patches of green and knew that by mid-April everything would be lush and the cows and sheep would just be eating themselves silly.

I walked back to the house, and instead of going through the yard, I went through the barnyard gate for a last look inside the barn. I pushed the door and flipped on the electric. Boy, did it look lonesome. I wandered on past the stalls until I come to the back doors, pushed one out, and stuck my head through. I couldn't believe what I saw. There was Fred, sitting on the top rail of the same gate where I first met him. He had heard the door squeak when I pushed it and turned his butt so he could face me. We just kind of stared at each other, then I came out of the barn and crawled up on the gate. He looked real old. His face was lined and leather tan from being out so much in the past few weeks. Just like the first time we met he was wearing a bunch of shirts and wore-out Levi's. He smiled kind of weak and when he did his eyes seemed to sink back in his head.

"How y' doin'?" he asked, holding on to the top slat and rolling his hands around on it.

"Okay, I reckon. We're leavin' tomorra mornin'.'"

Fred nodded. "What I heard. Where y'all goin'?"

"Dad and Mom bought a farm up in Indiana. We're gonna live up there."

"You seen hit yet?"

"Yeah. Saw it before they bought it."

"Is hit purty?"

I didn't want to lie, but I didn't want to tell him it was ugly either. It was my dad's farm, and he thought it was beautiful, and I didn't want Dad to feel bad if he ever heard what I said. "Not as pretty as it's gonna be when we get it all fixed up."

"What's hit like?"

"Flat as a stomped-on toad frog. Ain't more'n two, three trees on it. But they're pretty. No elm, though. Good thing I'm not makin' slingshots anymore. You doin' okay?"

Fred pursed his lips together and looked out at the pasture, which was pretty much still bare with little patches of green here and there and some rotting snow where the sun had a hard time getting to it. "I'm doin' okay . . . little better."

"That's good," I said.

There were so many things I wanted to say. Fred and his family had hard times coming and I was leaving and couldn't do anything about them. This deep, heavy feeling come up in my chest like somebody mashing my heart. "What y'all gonna do, Fred?"

Fred reached into an inside shirt pocket and come out with a sack of Life Everlasting and some brown paper sack and offered me a slip which I took. After we rolled our cigarettes and lit up, he took a deep puff and blew it out slow. "Don't know, Samuel. Mr. Berman come by th' other day and said we had t' move. He said he was sorry, but he hada have a tenant and I wudn't able t' do everything a man could yet . . . especially missin' my finger."

A lump come in my throat big as an apple and I had to wait to talk. After I fought back the lump I said, "Where y'all gonna go?"

"Ain't sure," he said, shaking his head slow. "Annie Lee said she knew a place in Spears behind some restaurant. Figure she and WK used hit some if y' know what I mean. She said if we fixed hit up ourselves and she took a job waitin' tables and me takin' dirty dishes to th' kitchen, th' restaurant people might let us live in hit free."

There was a little quiet spell, then Fred turned and looked into my eyes. "Samuel, I'm sorry I didn't come t' your door t' say good-bye, but somehow I just couldn't. You're my best friend, and I ain't never gonna have another one like you. After you and me and my fambly's straightened out, I want us t' get together. Hit might be a few years but we're gonna do hit."

Boy, did I have a lump in my throat now. I was gonna cry for dang sure and I hated it. I looked down at the ground until I thought I could at least say something without bawling. "You my best friend . . . too . . . Fred. We did a lot of things together, and I'll never . . . forget . . . you. It's a long way from here t' our farm, but I'm gonna get back. One of these times I'm gonna get back and we'll have a big time t'gether. You'll see. Whenever you want t' see me, just let me know and I promise I'll come runnin'."

Fred nodded. "I promise you too," then he eased off the gate. He put one hand on the gate's top and stuck his other between the slats and we shook. "G'bye old buddy. Tell your folks I said hi and thanks for bein' s' good t' us."

"G'bye Fred," I croaked. "Tell your folks I said g'bye too, and that I'll miss 'em."

I watched him walk until he topped the rise and went into the hickory and locust grove. I felt like crying, but then I thought, this wudn't the end. We were going to be seeing each other off and on all our lives. This was just the start of something different. That made me feel a lot better.

Early the next morning we drove out of the gate to our lane and headed for Indiana.

49

I had been driving aimlessly since leaving the university, consumed with memories. I was outside Lexington when I saw a fence row with a type of wild floribunda rose. The farmer on whose fence the roses were growing helped me pick an armload, then I took off, thanking him profusely. Now I knew exactly what I was going to do.

My journey to the Blue Hole took a slow, circuitous route as I checked mailbox after mailbox, still hunting for a name I recognized. No luck. I parked the car at the end of the blacktop and walked through the corn growing on the Little Bend's high bottoms. The blades were already tall and brushed my shoulders. The farmer had planted close to the edge of the cliff and I was careful not to step into a hundred feet of air.

Finally, the high bottom cliff flattened and I turned toward the river feeling certain I was now below the level of the sandbar. When I reached the water, all I could see, up or down the bank, was ordinary mud. The sandbar no longer existed, victim, I guessed, of a heavy flood.

I walked upstream toward the Blue Hole. As I got closer, I started feeling anxious. I had promised myself I wouldn't search for tracks, but to no avail. I would scold myself, then immediately start searching again. A lifetime later and my subconscious wouldn't let go. Sweat was pouring down my face and my T-shirt was soaked.

I glanced at my watch. One o'clock. It had to be a hundred degrees and the heat coming off the sand carried hot wet moisture that almost drowned me. No air was moving and the only sounds were the hum of insects.

Then I reached the little knoll. It rose small but proud above the brooding, pool-stage river. I climbed to the top and gazed at its fabled companion. The Blue Hole was absolutely still. Its water looked cool and inviting. I squinted toward the sun, a giant hazy ball of fire—Kentucky in July. Upriver, the brush-clad limestone cliffs and wide, green, mangrove-covered low bottoms shimmered through the heat waves. It reminded me of an impressionist painting.

I looked again at the Blue Hole. Its surface reflected the sky and cumulus clouds . . . cool, enchanted . . . waiting. *All right*, I thought, *enough procrastination, do what you came here to do*. I worked my way through the brush and when I reached the pool's edge, stared at my reflection. My immature cataracts made the image fuzzy so I eased onto my knees.

Hello, Cap'n Rhett, you gray-haired, half-bald, alta kocker!

Then I remembered the picture. I got my wallet out of the hip pocket of my jeans and began digging through credit cards, family pictures, and assorted junk. Yep, there was ten-year-old Samuel Zelinsky. Skinny, long-faced, big-nosed, and trumpet-eared, with shaggy hair and heavy eyebrows that shaded bright, laughing eyes and an impish smile. I held the picture next to my reflection. Little shit was better-looking than me.

I scanned the Blue Hole. It was amazingly beautiful, but in my mind a skeleton hand still lurked in its depths. I felt shaky. I knew what he would say—did say—and my life experiences confirmed he had been correct. It was time to conquer my fear and pay him honors.

I stripped naked. "This swim is for you, Ben," I whispered. Then, against every instinct, I plunged headfirst into the water.

I felt like I was immersed in an ice bath. Everything was dark and mysterious. The dark terrified me. Then I realized my eyes were closed. I opened them and looked about. The walls were straight up and down. I kicked hard and went deeper. I couldn't see the bottom even when the pressure hurt my ears. I could feel a cold upwelling; the pool was definitely spring-fed.

Air hunger forced me to ascend and by the time I reached the surface I was so in need of breath that my gasps hurt my lungs. I felt great! A conquering hero! "I'm here, Ben!" I shouted. "I'm swimming in it. I came back and I'm swimming in it. Samuel Zelinsky, Ben. You said I would someday and I have. I love you, Ben! God bless you wherever you are!"

The way back to the car was not easy, but incredibly enough, I didn't look for tracks. I walked downstream and, instead of returning as I came, turned inland as soon as the cliffs became low enough that I could labor my way to the high bottoms. I was immediately in a cornfield. This corn was taller than what I had walked through previously, the leaves up to my eyes and the tassels over my head. Then I made the mistake of taking what I thought was a short-cut. One cornfield led into another until I was lost and drenched in sweat from the awful heat. I decided the only logical way back to the car was to walk down the rows.

I had covered quite a distance when the corn row ended at a clearing about twenty feet across. A large stone stood in the center of the clearing with neatly clipped bluegrass surrounding it. I circled the marker and discovered a profusion of flowers growing on what I knew to be Alfred's grave. The Millers had promised to care for it and sixty years later somebody was making good their word. I found a pebble and put it on the stone.

I left the grave, walked into the next cornfield, and eventually came to Cuyper Creek. So much for dead reckoning. The stream was wider than I remembered. I stripped again and waded in. It turned out to be deeper too and I had to swim on my back to the other bank holding my wallet and clothes in the air, but I really enjoyed the cool water.

The drive down the Dry Branch Road was made on mental autopilot. My thoughts were of Ben. He had taught me so much. He rejected conventional thinking and demanded well-considered decisions as the path to action. You didn't stop if it became hard. And you ignored people's criticisms. Yet all I knew about Ben was what he presented to me. He took what he felt in his heart about his past to his grave. I wondered how often he thought about killing his wife and her lover and how much he had to have agonized about deserting his son. I remember the leaves he had arranged to look like a boy. And I could feel his arms around my body and hear his words, "I love you, Samuel." The anguish he felt during those twelve years after the murders must have been horrible.

The blacktop of the Dry Branch Road had been extended past where the school bus had turned around and now ended at the last tree of the oak grove. I parked and stood among the oak titans, mesmerized by the thin beams of undulating light that filtered through the canopy. At the foot of the oaks, a cornfield stretched to the river covering the area where the melon patch had grown. I got out my floribunda, circled the field until I came to the river, and from there downstream to distant trees. Then I saw it. The sycamore! Smaller than my oak friends, but proud and largely leafed. I ran my hands over the sycamore's trunk. It had grown mightier, but the river was undermining its roots. Eventually it would succumb to floodwaters. The thought made me sad. Then I noticed a chain around its trunk. Tethered to the other end of the chain was a skiff.

I found it difficult to breathe. When my emotions righted themselves, I took another bearing. I remembered the graves being about two hundred feet from the sycamore. With the floribunda under one arm, I used my free arm to move through the corn.

The clearing appeared as if by magic. I put the basket down and stared at the mighty stone that marked the grave, and flanking it the two flat rocks marking the graves of Cain and Abel. It was obvious that someone was meticulously caring for the graves.

I had visited this place innumerable times as a child, each visit one of tears and sorrow. Now I was returning like a surviving soldier, many years into his dotage, to the marker of a buddy who had fallen on a grenade and made that inexpressibly courageous exchange of his life for those of his comrades.

I spread most of the floribunda on Ben's grave, then divided the remainder between the dogs'. I felt terrible grief. My sorrow wasn't only for Ben; it was also for me. I had reached the end of my life dissatisfied. The visit to the world of my childhood had held up a devastating mirror that reflected my failures. I didn't fit in—anywhere! I never made even one real friend during four years at Harlan Jeffords High. I didn't fit in at Collingwirth either. NYU, the same. I had acquaintances on the Leland-May faculty, had helped many of them in their careers, but not one stood by me in my time of need. There was only my family.

Where were all my true friends? The ones I should have laughed and argued with, the ones who would mourn my death not for my accomplishments, but because my passing broke their hearts? I had made two close friends, Ben and Fred, and abandoned them both. Why? Because this part of my past was filled with pain and I didn't want to hurt anymore? Because I had delayed so long that I couldn't face Fred? I had fears, but I didn't think I was a coward. How had I let it happen?

Others were not totally blameless for my failures, I thought. Ben and Fred and this community had collectively fashioned me to live life among them, not in my new world. My rigid convictions of right and wrong, convictions ingrained in me by these very people and this strange land by the river, partly determined my path. I had lived in two different worlds and they had different rules. I had never been able to free myself from the philosophy drummed into me during my childhood. In my soul I had believed that philosophy to be true. I still did! Ben Begley, the man I now mourned, was a triple murderer, yet I loved him. He gave his life partly for a community to which he owed nothing. I understood why he sacrificed himself. God forgive me, I now thought he was right to end his life as he did because "society" would have executed my hero had they known his past. Then again, maybe not. My odd sense of justice might have been seconded by the people who raised his marker, seeing him as I did, a man lifted from disgrace by confronting the evil that had cowed the community. The world in which I chose to live my adult life just hung labels. He was a murderer! *The appearance of good was good and received accolades regardless of its verity; the fallen were damned forever so society needn't consider the whole of their humanity!* Somehow, I had lived a paradox, and the result was a less peaceful and possibly a less happy life than I could have attained had I not been so conflicted.

I placed a stone on the monolith and said a prayer over the graves, wondering if the God in whom I didn't believe accepted prayers from those like me who pondered the confused existence of the species he had made in his image.

A huge river fly landed on my face, and as I swatted it away, I became aware again of the heat. Sweat trickled from my forehead into the corners of my eyes. I took off my baseball cap and wiped my face, then gulped down half my bottle of water. I felt like a man straddling time, part of me in the 1940s, the other part in the twenty-first century. Something was missing between the halves, something that couldn't be filled by awards, money, or even Nora. I needed those things of my distant past—the human beings with whom I had shared this imperfect place. Canaan land, complete with heroes and Philistine metaphors. Without them, I wasn't whole.

I stared at Ben's grave. Six feet under that carefully groomed bluegrass lay the mostly cremated remains of a man I had loved as much as my father. If I could thrust my arms through the ground and bring him to the surface whole and in the quick, I knew what I would I say to him. Without willing myself, I began talking aloud, trying to control my voice.

"Ben, I've journeyed sixty years through a strange life, out of step with everybody except my wife. I've been successful but lonely, and now, in my old age, I'm disappointed. I've never known what was bothering me, but now I know part of the answer."

I pulled a weed from the edge of the grave. "I love you, Ben," I whispered. "I wish I hadn't stayed away so long. Perhaps you remember, I'm prone to that. Forgive me, and if there is a God, may he forgive us both."

The heat left me parched and I drank the remaining water. I felt better. This had to be what Nora hoped would happen. She wasn't sure of the answers I'd find but she understood that some of my angst lay between the two great bends of the river.

50

I turned to leave and was startled by the presence of a tall, thin, old man, standing in a corn row watching me. He was wearing Levi's, a blue, long-sleeved work shirt, and a straw hat. His face was angular, with big ears and a prominent nose. In his right hand was a hoe. He wasn't smiling, but he wasn't frowning either. I wondered if he had heard me speaking aloud. I approached him to explain why I was in what figured to be his cornfield. As I neared, his eyes remained fixed on the top of my baseball cap. I was struck with perfect clarity. "Hello, Melvin."

The thin man's eyes widened and he took a step back. "Afternoon," he said, raising his chin. "You know me. How come I don't know you?"

I walked up and extended my hand. "Melvin, I'm Samuel Zelinsky. The reason you don't know me is that we haven't seen each other in sixty years."

Melvin's arm rose slowly, then he grabbed my hand with a rush, his face blooming into a grin. "Recognized me 'cause I was lookin' at th' top of your cap, didn't you?"

I nodded and laughed. "Some things never change."

Melvin joined in the laughter. "Reckon they don't. Come here t' see old Ben?"

"Yeah," I answered, and glanced at the graves behind me. The heat waves rising off the sandy bottoms blurred the view. "This your cornfield?" I asked when I turned back toward him, aware that I was slipping back into the dialect of my youth.

"Daddy bought this bottom after y'all left. I was th' only one of th' kids stayed on th' farm. The others sold me their share after Mom and Daddy were gone." He motioned with his head toward the graves behind me. "I keep th' weeds off'."

Melvin sensed my fragile emotions and nothing was said for a few moments. "Sure somethin', ole Ben, wudn't he?"

I smiled weakly. "Yeah."

In the tradition of the hill people, Melvin just nodded, considering it a private affair. "Sure is hot," he said, removing his straw hat and running his hand over what remained of his gray hair. "Got my pickup yonder. That you at th' end of th' oaks?"

"Yep."

"How 'bout followin' me up th' house and gettin' some cold lemonade? This here corn's gonna make hit whether I hoe or not."

"How come I didn't see your name on th' mailbox?" I asked, certain I wouldn't have missed the name Langley.

"Truck hit th' old one. I put up that new one, but since th' mailman knows me, I ain't bothered t' put my name on hit. Wife keeps on me 'bout that," and we both laughed.

I followed the truck up the Dry Branch Road to the spot where the school bus had turned around, then we went up the Langleys' lane until we came to the house. It was two-story redbrick, with two porches, one leading to the kitchen and the other a large, screened-in affair that faced west and looked out over a valley. It was lovely.

Melvin's wife, Jenny, met us at the kitchen door. Melvin introduced me as Samuel Zelinker. I didn't want to embarrass him, so I didn't correct the mispronunciation. Jenny was a slim, pretty woman of about sixty-five. Her face was still smooth and her red curly hair had traces of gray. She was a little shorter than Melvin, and I got the impression she had been very beautiful when she was young.

It was my first time inside the old Langley home. The bottom floor had a large kitchen with a table and a beautiful dining and living room. Ice-cold lemonade appeared quickly, accompanied by

Jenny's offer of cherry pie. I couldn't resist. The slice was delicious, the cherries exploding with a sweet-sour taste. My mother's cherry pies had tasted almost exactly like Jenny's. When a second helping was proposed, I accepted along with a laugh from Melvin, who also had another slice. After we finished eating, I asked about his family.

"Everybody's someplace else . . . California, Ohio, Florida. Like I said, I'm th' only one stayed on th' farm. Hit's been a good life. Jenny and me have had a good life here. Don't know what I'm gonna do with th' old place. Gettin' too old t' run it and ain't got th' heart t' sell it."

Jenny's movements about the kitchen became quicker, and I could tell something was bothering her. "Mr. Zelinker, you tell that old man of mine t' sell this place before he gets hurt. Scares me t' death every time he gets out on these hillsides with that tractor. One of these times it's gonna turn over and squarsh him."

Melvin winked at me. "Aw, Jen, that Ford's steady as a rock."

I just smiled. I wanted to hear about everybody, but especially about my close friends. Somehow, I didn't want to start with Fred. "Ever see Lonnie?"

"Lonnie married Jeanette Dillard and they moved out West. Wyoming, I think. Remember that fight you and him had?"

I laughed. "Not much of a fight, I'm afraid."

Melvin put his elbows on the table and looked into my eyes instead of at the top of my head. "Hit was t' us boys. You done good. LD found that out too, I understand."

That shocked me. "You knew about the fight in the barn?"

"There was lots of talk after Ben was killed. You were in th' hospital then. Folks around here blamed LD's pa for what happened 'cause he was always blatherin' on about th' Devil so much nobody ever thought things through. That whole thing ended bad and could've been a lot worse if hit hadn't been for Ben and you. That's why th' Howards lit out for Georgia. Ain't heard from 'em since. All th' old peoples gone, Bess Clark, the MacWerters, the Dillards, the Shackelfords. You were sweet on Rosemary Shackelford, wudn't you?"

Another pitcher of lemonade materialized. "I wondered when you two were gonna get 'round t' girls," said Jenny, a big grin on her face.

I could not believe I blushed. All three of us laughed. "How did you know I was sweet on Rosemary Shackelford?"

Melvin grinned and leaned back in his chair. "Kind of hard t' miss when all a fella does for thirty minutes on a school bus is stare at one girl and only when she ain't lookin' at him."

Jenny sat down at the table, a big smile on her face. "I wanta hear about this."

I was still blushing. "I'm afraid it was a classic case of a young man falling in love with an older woman. She was sixteen, and I was . . . about ten, I guess. First thing I knew she was engaged. Broke my heart."

"Rosemary had four kids and has a whole passel of grandkids," said Melvin. "They all live somewheres down around Corbin. She sure was beautiful."

The statement was followed by an "Uh-huh" from Jenny, who was giving her husband that look every married man knows.

"I'm just sayin' what was," said Melvin, turning toward his wife, a sheepish grin on his face. "I was never sweet on her. I liked younger women with red hair." Jenny gave her husband a secret *That's probably BS but I still like it* smile.

During the next hour we covered a lot of people. Finally, there was no way to avoid the issue. Both of us felt uneasy and it was up to me to ask the question. "What happened to the Mulligans after we moved away, Melvin?"

Melvin shook his head. "Been dreadin' this. Reckon there's no easy way t' tell hit, so I just will. After y'all left, Thelma Jean got hit by a car while she was walkin' on th' highway and was killed. She was just moseyin' along, not payin' attention t' nothin', and it after dark. She wudn't right in the head. Y'all hadn't been gone but a few months."

My mind immediately resurrected Thelma Jean walking heel to toe up the Dry Branch Road so engrossed in her little world that she was oblivious to everything else. Poor Thelma Jean. That terrible winter night came back to me. I remembered how my hand felt as I stroked her back and hair, and the feel of her hot tears on my belly. "How did the family handle it?"

Melvin raised his brows. "Not too good."

"How so?"

"Fred's mama, Mamie . . . she just fell apart. For a few days, hit looked like she wudn't gonna make it, but then she come around. Short time after that th' family moved t' Spears, and Annie Lee got a job waitin' tables at a little restaurant. Fred got some work there too, but he wudn't old enough for a regular job. I went down there a time or two t' see him. Hit was tiny, th' place they was livin'. Two rooms and a kitchen attached t' th' restaurant, but they were makin' hit. Then a year later, Mamie died. Fred wouldn't talk t' nobody but Annie Lee for nigh a year. Annie Lee pulled him out of hit, though, and they started doin' pretty good again, Fred drivin' a truck and with what Annie Lee made waitin' tables, everything settled down."

Melvin stopped and I had the feeling only one shoe had fallen.

Jenny, who was at her gas range preparing supper, sought to rescue her husband. "Where do you live now, Mr. Zelinker?"

"New Hampshire." Then I turned quickly to Melvin before she could save him again. "More to th' story, right?"

Melvin sighed. "Well, yeah. Annie Lee met a fella. They got married and moved to Arizona. Got to doin' pretty well, I heard. Anyway, Annie Lee never come back."

Melvin fell quiet and stared down into his plate. There was a foreboding silence. The silence that comes just before a dawn artillery barrage.

"Where's Fred, Melvin?"

Melvin swallowed and his hands moved about the tabletop as though hunting for a place to exist. Finally he looked at me. "Fred killed hisself, Samuel."

I think my heart stopped. Finally, I was able to ask. "What happened?"

Melvin swallowed, then cleared his throat. "Saw him couple days before he done hit. He was pretty far down, but I'd seen him that far down before. Didn't have any idea . . . he shot hisself in th' head. Feel sorry tellin' you all this 'cause I know y'all were close."

I felt like I was smothering. "Folks, I need some air. I'll be back."

"Awful hot," said Melvin, as we rose from the table. "Maybe you ought not walk far."

Out of the corner of my eye I saw Jenny look at Melvin and barely shake her head.

"You goin' t' be all right, Mr. Zelinker?"

"Yes ma'am," I said, then left the house and began walking the fields, my mind in turmoil, my very being slathered in guilt. I had no destination. When I came to a fence I either climbed it or walked beside it. Finally, I stopped on top of a ridge. The view before me, hills, tall trees, and green valleys, was beautiful. Then I recognized where I was—this was the ridge we sat on during the fox hunts. I could almost see the dogs milling around, the men leading them toward a thicket, hear the yodel-like baying of Maude. Most of all, I remembered Fred's grin in the firelight as the evening rested his soul.

I also remembered the first time my father's Lexington friends had passed along the message that Fred would "like to see old Samuel again." I was in high school and we were at the supper table. I seemed to be perpetually unhappy, and I guess Dad was trying to cheer me up.

"Samuel, I heard from some folks who know Babe MacWerter. Babe told them Fred Mulligan said he'd like to see you. Want to go?"

"No."

"Why not?" said Dad. "You and Fred Cody were best friends."

I had shrugged and Dad hadn't followed up. What I had really wanted to tell him was that I never wanted to see hillbillies again. My youth and my desperate attempt to fit in with my peer group provided some semblance of an excuse.

The second invitation from Fred had come directly through

Babe MacWerter. I was middle-aged and Dad was an old man who would be dead in a year. We were wandering around the farm looking at the livestock. He seemed hesitant to bring it up, probably because I was having problems at Leland-May and he wanted me to have some peace.

"Samuel, I heard from Babe MacWerter that Fred Mulligan wants to see you. It's only a few hundred miles to Lexington. Why don't we go this weekend? You can spend some time with Fred Cody and I can see Ike and Mr. Gollar."

I didn't answer immediately, taking a moment to roll it around in my mind. Then I remembered the promise Fred and I had made each other. But I was tired and more than a little depressed. Nora and I had this brief moment away from my turmoil, and spending two days in Kentucky seemed unfair to us. "Dad, I just don't have it in me at the moment."

Dad had just nodded. The cold truth was that I had buried that part of my life. I abandoned Fred. I had abandoned my best friend and he had killed himself!

I stood in the boiling heat and tried defending my soul. Fred and I were men when this occurred. Our promises had been made during childhood. Somehow, my defense didn't wash with my unforgiving sense of justice.

I needed to know more about the life and death of Fred Cody Mulligan.

51

A half hour later I was sitting at the Langley kitchen table mopping my brow and drinking lemonade. I had said little since returning and my hosts were content to wait. Eventually, I decided I could discuss the issue. "Melvin . . . Jenny, I need to know about Fred's life. He was my best friend . . . risked his life for me, and after I left here, I never saw him again. I'd appreciate your being straightforward. Please don't worry about my feelings."

Melvin and Jenny glanced at each other, then Jenny looked away as if to say, *You decide. He's your friend.*

Melvin took a sip of his lemonade and began talking. As he spoke, he held the icy glass in one hand, put the other hand in his pocket, and stared at the center of the table. "While you were gone, Jen and me talked about what I ought say if you asked about Fred. I wudn't gonna tell th' whole story 'cause I knew you two were close and so many years have gone by. I thought maybe hit was best t' just let hit go. But since you've asked th' way you have, I'm gonna tell hit th' way it happened."

Melvin took another sip of lemonade, then turned toward me. "After Annie Lee got married and left, Fred had a hard time. Seemed like he was lost without Annie Lee and just stayed away from everybody. He still had a job drivin' a truck but he missed so much work th' company fired him. He started workin' odd jobs an' holed up in a little room he rented. I went over t' see him couple times but he hardly talked. It was really sad. One day I had t' go t' Berman's for somethin', and there he was, leanin' against th' tobacco barn. Well, I went over t' say hi and we talked. He was really down, said he'd lost everybody and would as soon die as live. Said he didn't wanta live th' way he was. I told him that wudn't any way t' talk 'cause we were young and had our whole lives. I got him t' go home with me, and Mom and Daddy told him t' stay with us 'til he felt better. While he was with us, he started doin' better. We went foxhuntin' a few times. Remember Mr. Rick and his hounds?"

I was so anguished by what Melvin was saying that it was several seconds before I realized he had asked me a question. "Y . . . yes. Did Fred ever ask about me?"

Melvin took a deep breath, and stared at his glass of lemonade. "Yeah, he did. He said he wished you was around, that you always helped him when he got down. I told him he ought go up t' Indiana and look you up. He never answered."

It was a response I knew could only be true. "What happened after that, Melvin?"

"He straightened up and got a job in the construction trade and before long he was makin' good money. He rented a nice place t' live after that, then he met a girl named Sue Ellen Biggs. Few months later they got married. Fred was real happy."

"Melvin and I went to the wedding. We'd just started dating," said Jenny.

"What was Sue Ellen like?" I asked her.

"She was a real nice girl," said Jenny, getting up to check the dinner she was preparing, speaking as she worked. "Sue Ellen was from South Carolina. A few months later, she and Fred moved there. They come for a visit some years later. They had a little daughter, cutest thing you ever looked at. We didn't see them again for . . . how long you figure, Melvin?"

Melvin cocked his head and thought. "Charles Edward had just started going to Middletown for junior high. That would of made hit about . . . thirteen years."

I was apprehensive about my next question. "How were they doin'?"

"Great," said Melvin. "Fred was makin' a fine livin' in th' building trades. They had their own home and Fred was driving a new Pontiac. Their daughter was just beautiful."

"And that was the last time you saw him? I mean before . . ." From the other side of the kitchen, I heard the oven open, and the smell of fresh-baked biscuits joined the odor of fried chicken. "How about us all going in the dining room and having supper?" said Jenny. "We can finish this discussion later with a little bourbon and branch water."

She's saving him again, I thought. "Okay. I've never had bourbon with branch water."

The fried chicken was from young fryers, the pieces small and sweet, but I couldn't eat and picked at my food.

When dinner was over, we sat quietly on the screened-in porch and sipped bourbon and branch water. I was comforted by the drink's soft sweet taste and musty fallen autumn leaves smell as we watched the late afternoon slip into dusk. It was a beautiful evening, and I was with beautiful people whose presence alone lifted my spirits. And drinking a lot of the bourbon and branch water, hoping it would blunt further pain that I knew was coming. Then a moment arrived when the conversation stopped.

Melvin cleared his throat. "You asked earlier if that was th' last time I saw Fred. He come back t' Lexington years later. He was havin' trouble. I went up t' see him. We talked for a while, then he told me what had happened. His daughter was a handful. When she got out of high school, she married somebody in the navy and they moved away from Charlotte. Fred and Sue Ellen almost never saw them. Then one day Sue Ellen had a heart attack and died and Fred just kinda fell apart. I asked him if he'd like t' come and stay with Jen and me for a while, but he said no, he'd be okay."

"Did he . . . ask to see me, Melvin?"

Melvin nodded. "I knew your daddy was still livin' 'cause him and Babe MacWerter kept in contact. I told Fred I'd ask Babe t' get hold of your dad. He said he'd appreciate it. Reckon you never got th' word."

Fortunately for me, I was full of bourbon. Then Jenny spoke:

"After Fred . . . died, Alfreda—that was his daughter's name— came t' th' funeral and looked after his affairs. She had a little girl of about two named Lisa June. She was real cute, and stayed with us a lot of weekends. Alfreda was divorced and got a job as a receptionist at Clay House. That's the fanciest restaurant in Kentucky, I think. She made good money. One day she met this rich fella from California and run off with him. I guess he didn't want Lisa June, because Alfreda left her with another couple who were her close friends. That couple split up when Lisa June was about eight. They both left th' state and Lisa June wound up in th' county home. We wanted to adopt her but th' county said we were too old. She spent some time in foster homes, then refused t' go anymore. She asked t' stay with us, but th' county refused us again."

"Alfreda never came to see her?" I asked.

Melvin shook his head. "What I hear, Alfreda's had a great life out in California. Had a couple more kids . . . didn't want anything t' do with Mulligans or Lisa June or Kentucky."

"It's a pity," said Jenny, gazing through the screen of the porch. "Lisa June's a lovely child. Smart too. She's goin' to UK part-time. She wants t' be a schoolteacher."

I felt as though the governor's call came through with a reprieve just as my executioner was about to push the button. I had to meet this girl. Surely there were things she needed and I could help her. At least I could make up a little for my miserable betrayal of her grandfather. "Jenny . . . would it be okay if I contacted her?"

A faint smile appeared on Jenny's face. "Want her phone number and address? Somethin' I forgot t' tell you—her last name's Winchester."

"If I see her, I'll have to tell her that I got her name from you. That's not goin' t' cause you any problems with her, is it?"

Melvin laughed. "Them two are close as peas in a pod. Ain't gonna cause problems."

Jenny asked, "Would you like me t' call her for you, Mr. Ze-linker?"

I was about to say yes, when I thought better of it. I had failed Ben and Fred, and I had failed myself. If I was to salvage any of my honor, I needed to meet Fred's granddaughter without anyone's help. "No ma'am. I'd rather do my own introduction."

Jenny nodded, then the smile left her face. "Mr. Zelinker, Lisa June is a sweet girl, but she's been hurt. Sometimes she comes off kinda hard. What I'm saying is, she might not take t' you right off. If I was you, I'd be gentle in my approach. It's going t' take a while t' get t' know her, and you're gonna have some bumps in th' road."

"Yes ma'am," I said, and got up from my chair. "Well, thank you all for the wonderful hospitality and the information. I have to get back to Lex—"

Melvin interrupted. "Don't think that's a good idea. You've had five a them things," and he pointed toward my bourbon glass. "State patrol loves throwin' people in the jug nowadays for less'n you've drunk. Stay here with us t'night and get a cold sober start in th' mornin'."

I decided Melvin was right. There was also something I wanted to do before meeting Lisa June. "Melvin, I'd like to visit Fred's grave tomorrow. Where's he buried?"

Melvin got up from his chair, stuffed his hands in his pockets, walked to the screen of the porch, and stared out. "He was cre-mated, Samuel. Alfreda scattered his ashes and wouldn't say where. That gal just wudn't much. I know this is botherin' you and I wish they was somethin' I could of done t' make hit easier but I knew you didn't want stuff gussied up."

When he turned back toward me the sadness in his face pierced my chest. "Hope I done right?"

"You did fine," I answered, hoping my voice wouldn't break. "Thank y'all for everything. Think I'll turn in."

Jenny nodded. "Good night, Samuel. I'll pray for Fred t'night."

"Thanks," I said, then my voice cracked. "If you're of a mind . . . me too, huh."

I didn't sleep much. Thoughts of Fred, broken and humiliated and dying by his own hand while a simple visit from me might have helped, haunted and shamed me. How many times had Fred come through for me, but when he needed me, I had let him down. And tomorrow, I was going to meet his granddaughter. What would I tell her? What in the world would I tell her?

52

The hours that followed were the worst since Nora died. I couldn't sleep and at 3:30 in the morning left the house and walked back to the ridge. The air was cool and laden with the smell of hay. Freshly mowed clover. In my mind, I could hear the clatter of Dad's old horse-drawn mowing machine, see the swath the blades made, hear him talking or singing to Daisy and Gabe as his team and his mowing machine served as backup.

I began to feel a little more peaceful as the early light filled the eastern sky and birds began to twitter. Thank God for nature. I returned to the Langleys' and bed.

It was nearly ten o'clock when I was awakened by Jenny, who said breakfast was waiting.

Melvin was already at the table when I arrived in the kitchen. He eyed me as he sipped his coffee. "Mornin'. Heard you get up and leave th' house little after three. Looks of your pants legs I'd say you hit some dew."

"It was like walking through fields after a rain," I answered.

Jenny set a plate of eggs, a small steak, and a giant mug of coffee in front of me. Melvin had been eating bacon. The steak meant Melvin had told her I was Jewish.

"How you doin' this mornin'?" she asked, standing beside me.

"Okay. I'm doin' okay," I answered.

Jenny smiled. "We're glad t' hear that. We were both pretty worried last night. Where you headin' this mornin'?"

"Back to my hotel for a little more rest, then I'm going t' call Lisa June. Jenny . . . Melvin, I thank y'all so much for your hospitality and honesty. You've been wonderful to me."

"Been great for us too, 'cept for th' hard part," said Melvin. "I never see anybody from our class. Those who ain't moved away have moved on, y' know. Hit's too bad what I had t' tell."

"You did everything right. Both of you."

I drove to my hotel about noon, showered and shaved, then went back to bed. I didn't rest. All I could think of was Lisa June. Fred was dead and Lisa June was as close to him as I could get. But what would meeting and helping Fred's granddaughter do to set my failures right? Lisa June never even knew her grandfather. Regardless, I was determined to meet her.

The address Jenny gave me was only a few blocks from UK. I drove through the maze of streets, the new and utilitarian merging with the narrow, beautiful, and in some parts, antebellum. Eventually I came to block after block of apartment buildings. Young men and women were everywhere, walking, bicycling, and jaywalking. Students.

I found the address, parked across the street, punched her home number into my cell phone, and got an answering machine. All I could do now was wait.

An hour later, an aging Chevrolet pulled into a parking space in front of the apartments. A tall, slim, dark-haired young woman got out. Her face was oval with high cheekbones, and framed by short hair arranged in an ear-hugging French cut. She wore a white, rose-covered blouse, open at the top button, white slacks that fit snug, but not overtly sexy, and black, low-heeled shoes. Her only jewelry was gold earrings and a simple gold necklace. She was lovely, maybe even beautiful. She didn't look anything like Fred. I decided not to approach her and watched as she ascended an outside staircase and entered the second floor.

A few minutes later, the young woman came out of the building and walked toward the car. She had changed clothes and was now wearing a simple white blouse, black hip-hugging skirt that extended just below her knees, and modest high heels. The jewelry was unchanged. Since she was the only person who had entered or left the building, I decided to ask if she was Lisa June. I got out of my car and walked toward her. "Excuse me, I'm looking for Miss Lisa June Winchester. She lives in this apartment building."

The girl cocked her head to the side and fixed me in her gaze. Her pose shook me. How many times had Fred looked at me the same way! "Who are you?" she asked suspiciously.

"My name is Samuel Zelinsky. If you're Lisa June Winchester, I was a friend of your grandfather."

The revelation brought a cold look. "I'm late for work," she said, then continued toward her car.

I played my only trump. "Jenny Langley gave me your address and telephone number."

By this time, the girl had gripped the door handle of the car. She let the hand slide free and turned toward me. Her face remained expressionless and she folded her arms. "I'm Lisa June Winchester. I've never heard Jenny Langley speak of you."

"I just met Mrs. Langley. Her husband, Melvin, and I went to school with your grandfather. His name was Fred Cody Mulligan. He had a sister named Annie Lee."

Still no smile. "What was th' name of the team you and Melvin Langley and my grandfather played basketball on in high school?"

"Fred didn't play high school basketball. He dropped out of school, and I moved away."

Perhaps ten seconds passed, then Lisa June turned, opened the door to her car, and spoke unemotionally with her back toward me. "I get off work at ten. There's a coffee shop on East High called Hot Java. Meet me there at 10:15."

Lisa June's response was in keeping with Jenny's comments. I hadn't been greeted like a returning prodigal; then again, I hadn't been turned away either. Besides, what should I expect?

I arrived at the Hot Java several minutes early, got a booth, ordered a cup of coffee, and sat sipping as I watched the door, ruminating on what to say when Lisa June arrived. I didn't want to push hard. Perhaps the most I could hope for was to connect her to her family and make them relevant to a woman who was essentially an orphan.

Then the door to the coffee shop opened and Lisa June appeared. She glanced about, her whole demeanor emanating mistrust. I went to meet her. "Good evening, Miss Winchester," I said, then smiled and extended a hand.

Lisa June barely shook it. She said nothing.

"I got us a booth. We're in the corner over there," and I motioned toward our table. "I appreciate the chance to talk. I know you must be tired."

She still didn't speak. Instead, she walked ahead of me, sat on the side of the booth with its back against the wall, put her purse beside her, and fixed me with a suspicious stare. "How was your coffee?"

"Awful," I said.

Lisa June smiled slightly. "Aunt Jen said you seemed like an honest sort. What do you want with me?"

This was to be a no-nonsense meeting. "Sixty years ago, I was your grandfather Fred Mulligan's best friend. My family sharecropped the farm where the Mulligan family lived. I knew your great-grandfather, your great-grandmother, and your great-aunts. Knew them well."

Lisa June blinked slowly. "Why should I care, Mr. Zelinsky?"

The question caught me off guard. "Th . . . they were good people. I think it would be worth your knowing about them. How much do you know about . . . ?"

"Not much. Why should you care?"

Again, her question was unnerving. I hedged. "Well, you're my childhood best friend's granddaughter. He's gone now, and you're the closest I can get to him. I guess that's it."

Lisa June's eyes moved about my face. The eyes weren't hard, more like . . . curious. She glanced at her watch. "I'm sure my grandfather was a good friend of yours, but I never knew him and really can't see the point of learning about someone who doesn't mean anything to me. But Aunt Jen asked me t' see you, so I will. I'm tired and have two classes to prepare for. I'd appreciate if you'd keep it short." Then she waved to the waitress, who took our orders. She requested separate checks. When the waitress left, Lisa June said, "Go ahead."

I tried to convey a coherent understanding of my relationship with the Mulligan family, but what came out was a haphazard tangle of disconnected memories. My frustration edged toward anger. This kid, whom I had never seen before, and was beginning not to like, was reducing me to a babbling idiot. Lisa June listened through a cup of bad coffee, then checked her watch.

"I have to go, Mr. Zelinsky. Thanks for telling me about my folks. Have a nice trip back to your home." With that she got out of the booth, shook my hand, put a dollar on the table for a tip, paid her check at the register, and left the coffee shop.

I struggled to my feet, stunned that she had simply walked away. I couldn't leave it like this. There had to be something more! I ran after her, putting a ten-dollar bill on the cash register as I passed it. By the time I got outside, she was opening her car door. "Lisa June," I called, "Wait up. Please wait!"

When I reached the car, Lisa June was in the driver's seat with the door ajar.

"Miss Winchester . . . Lisa June . . . I'd like to talk to you again."

The eyes that stared into mine showed frustration. "Why? Mr. Zelinsky, I don't care about my folks. They didn't give a damn about me. Something is on your mind and I get the feeling it's your problem and not mine."

Lisa June must have seen a look of desperation on my face because she looked away, then turned toward me again and sighed. "Look, it's a really busy time in my life right now."

I could feel my chances of saying what I needed to say slipping away. I felt I had to see her again or this issue would haunt me forever. "What you've said about something being on my mind is true, but it doesn't only concern me, it concerns you too. You're part of a decent family. You need a connection with them. I just touched on the people and did a very poor job of conveying their character. I haven't had a real chance to tell you about them, their lives, what they meant to each other. You're shortchanging them and shortchanging yourself!"

Not a flicker of emotion showed on her pretty face.

I pushed again. "You can't tell me you've never wondered about your family . . . wanted some kind of connection to them! No one wants to go through life alone!"

Lisa June sighed again, then took her phone out of her purse. "What's your number?"

I gave my cell phone number and she entered it. "I'll think about it," she said, then started the engine, backed out of the parking space, and drove away.

"Thanks," I said to the empty parking space.

53

Three days passed and no call. I was deeply disappointed. How could I go back to New Hampshire and leave my life dangling after everything I had so recently experienced? Fred ran through my mind in a continuous loop. Whole conversations burst into my consciousness, so real my senses experienced the moment. I could hear the inflections in his voice, like the first time we hunted frogs with slingshots and I had spooked my prey.

"Hun'ney, you got t' slow down. You ain't a-drivin' sheep." I could feel my frustration as I told him I wanted to watch and learn and I could hear his stubborn response. "You ain't ever gonna learn watchin'! You got t' get one or I don't shoot another frog." The deadfalls . . . the moments in the Mulligans' front bedroom when our mutual confessions strengthened the bonds between us . . . the pounding of my heart as we ran from Ben's melon patch with Fred holding his shirt tourniquet around my bleeding arm . . . that terrible winter and our final parting at the gate behind the barn.

Between the flashbacks, I tried to understand the situation. I wasn't sure what I wanted to happen in my relationship with Lisa June, but she was my last connection to Fred. I felt powerless. There was nothing to build on without her cooperation. Then, as I was wandering around a horse farm, my cell phone rang.

"Mr. Zelinsky, this is Lisa June Winchester. Tomorrow is Saturday and I'm off during the day. If you would still like to meet, we could have lunch together."

I almost yelled. Instead I said calmly, "I'd love to have lunch with you."

"Meet me in th' Keeneland Café at 1:30. It's near th' race-track."

I was excited about the meeting, but had no idea what to expect. I decided to tell her personal things I knew about the Mulligans, and about Fred and me. And, yes, about my failure to be there for Fred when he needed me. If she got up and left and never saw me again she would at least know that Fred was a good man, and that there were decent people in her family. That she didn't need to repudiate her relatives in order to change her life. This was a gift I could give and I considered it a gift worth having.

The Keeneland Café was Southern and horsey. Paintings of great thoroughbreds and jockeys covered the walls. Most of the male patrons wore coats and ties but I was dressed in a white shirt and dress pants. I looked about for Lisa June and found her in a corner table. She was wearing the same rose-patterned blouse and white pants she had on when I first saw her, but, as before, they looked fresh and neatly pressed. I was nervous as I slipped into my chair. "Good afternoon," I said. "Nice restaurant."

Lisa June ignored my salutation. "Have you enjoyed th' last few days?"

"Pretty much. I was at a horse farm when you called."

"Horses are treated better than people in Kentucky. What's it like where you live?"

"It's beautiful. Low mountains, lots of trees . . . small pictur-esque communities."

Lisa June scanned my face, then her eyes shifted back to mine. "You live in New Hampshire, right?"

"Yes. Did you learn that from Jenny and Melvin?"

She looked down at the table. "Google. You didn't tell me you were a famous professor. You didn't tell Jenny and Melvin either. Any reason why?"

The waiter appeared and handed us elegant menus, then recited the specials. "What's good here?" I asked after he left.

Lisa June glanced at the menu. "I used to work here as a waitress. The best thing they served then was the stuffed pork chops. You haven't answered my question."

Her tone wasn't harsh, but it didn't convey a lot of warmth. "When I met Melvin, I had been here several days and hadn't seen anyone I knew. Talking to him gave me a chance to find out what had happened to people I had known as a child . . . your grandfather, th' whole Mulligan family, as well as other people in the community. My professional life just didn't come up."

Lisa June fell silent. I got an uncomfortable feeling about the silence but decided to wait it out. Finally the waiter arrived and took our orders. "Like a drink, Lisa?" I asked.

Lisa June shook her head.

I turned to the waiter. "Do you have bourbon and branch water?"

"Sir, we have a creek running past the back door."

It was the first time I heard Lisa June laugh. It was so much like Fred's laugh. I ordered the bourbon and branch water. When the waiter left, I turned toward my lunch companion. "Jenny has told me a little about you. I'd like to know more."

Lisa June's smile slowly faded. "Why?"

My answer almost gushed out. "Because you're my best friend's grandchild!"

Lisa June thought for a moment. "How much did Aunt Jen tell you?"

"I know your mother got married again when you were very young and left you with some friends, that you spent at least ten years in an orphanage and foster homes, that you're an education major at UK, and that you spend time with the Langleys."

The waiter brought our salads and my bourbon and branch water.

"Not much else t' know," Lisa June answered after the waiter left.

I washed down some salad with a swallow of my drink. "I'm

sure there's a great deal more t' know about th' granddaughter of my best friend."

"The best friend of your childhood?"

"The best friend of my life."

Lisa June's chin pushed toward me and her eyes became cold. "If he was th' best friend of your life, how come you weren't concerned enough t' inquire about him for sixty years?"

The question hurt so much it took a few seconds before I could respond. "The story is long and involved. I would really like to tell it later."

Lisa June said nothing, she just continued to eat.

"What areas are you interested in teaching?" I asked.

No response.

The salad plates were removed and our entrées arrived. The stuffed pork chop was good, and I commented on it. I wasn't prepared for Lisa June's response.

"Dr. Zelinsky, I'm seeing you as a favor to two people who mean more t' me than anyone else in the world. I've had a hard time in the past, but I'm makin' progress. Then, out of nowhere, you show up with your fancy education and prizes and pry into my life. What do you want from me? Tell me what it is now or I'm walkin' out of here and I'll never see you again!"

The statement was delivered at a whisper but to me it was like a crash of thunder. I'm not sure whether I was angry at what she said or offended by the way she said it, but I reacted. "You know Lisa June, you're not th' only one who's had a hard time in life. My life hasn't been a bed of roses either. I've made mistakes and I regret them. I'm an old man and you're a young woman, but I hope when you're my age someone gives you th' benefit of the doubt when you're tryin' t' right your wrongs."

Lisa June appeared startled, then seemed to consider what I said. "All right. We can talk now or later. Which would you prefer?"

I was suddenly in the mood to talk. I filled in the areas that I had left out during our meeting in the coffee shop, giving it a recognizable timeline. I didn't embellish or soften my memories of the

Mulligans. The saga of the stolen rabbits and the hunger of the Mulligan family as Alfred starved them to buy his mules and equipment spared neither Alfred nor Fred nor me. I also told happy, funny things, and when I did, she smiled. During the story of the crazy man and the kindness and heroism of her grandfather, I saw a hint of tears in her eyes, tears that continued to accumulate as I spoke of Alfred's death, the stillbirth of Annie Lee's baby, and my efforts to help the Mulligan family. I ended with the parting conversation between Fred and me, and by admitting that I had no excuse for my sixty-year absence.

I breathed a deep sigh when I finished. "Well . . . that's what I remember. There are still a lot of stories, but I can't think of them right now. Ask whatever you want."

Lisa June looked vacantly at her plate. "What's there t' ask? You and my grandfather really were best friends. Y'all loved each other. Then you escaped from this Kentucky asylum, got an education, and didn't want anything more t' do with Mulligans. I understand that. I don't think you're awful. And I understand now that you're here lookin' for Fred's forgiveness for leaving him t' fend for himself when you promised otherwise."

Lisa June stopped speaking for a moment and this time she was the one who sighed. "But Fred Cody Mulligan is dead," she continued. "We're in th' same boat, Dr. Zelinsky. Neither of us can get what we want from Fred. But you're forgiven for whatever you think you might have done to him. As his granddaughter, I forgive you. From what you've said, I'm pretty sure that's what he would want me t' do."

She dabbed her mouth with the starched white napkin, then we both got up from our chairs, shook hands, and I watched as she went out the door of the Keeneland Café. That made me sad because I felt that I would never see her again, but I was also happy that she might have a new appreciation for at least some of the people in her family, especially Fred. I felt a bit easier. Freer.

There was really nothing I wanted to do now. I made reservations for my flight back to New Hampshire and decided to spend the remaining days with the Langleys. I hoed corn with Melvin. I had forgotten how morning glories tangled your feet in a cornfield. I tripped over them and fell on my face. That's an ignominious event for a farm boy. In the heat of the day, Melvin and I peeled to the buff, dove into the river, and swam under the broad leafy limbs of the old sycamore. I remembered Fred, Lonnie, LD, and myself swimming. Our bodies had been young and wiry and I commented to myself that Melvin and I looked wrinkled and old, the only way we could look. I wondered if Melvin was thinking the same thing. We went blackberry picking, filling several two-gallon buckets with big ripe wild berries. Jenny made blackberry cobbler, and it tasted just like Mom's. Mr. Rick's son brought his dogs over and we sat on the same ridge we had sat on sixty years before and listened to the hounds bay. And we passed around a pint of Old Grand-Dad. I was having fun. I was really having fun.

The Langleys never asked about the meeting between Lisa June and me, but one evening as we sat on the screened-in porch I spoke of the conversation. I told them I felt better about my life now than when I had first arrived. I had faced up to my failings to some degree and gained a little insight into why I had always felt like a foreigner after leaving Kentucky. "I've been thinking about Lisa June too. She's trying to get her education while working two jobs. What would you think about me setting up a college fund for her?"

"We tried that," said Jenny. "She won't take it."

That sounded like Fred. "Tell me what I can do then?"

"Well, she treasures being close with the people she cares about, but you live in New Hampshire. I suppose you could come see her from time t' time. She might like that. You're stayin' for dinner t'night, aren't you?"

Immediately, I knew what was happening. "Lisa June's gonna be here, right?"

Jenny smiled sheepishly. "She said your bein' here was all right with her."

The evening went well. Almost all of the conversation concerned my family and my career. Melvin had never met anyone from Brooklyn and I told my parents' favorite story. "That's what happened. She told Dad that it just wasn't right that the cow and the bull were forced to make love in front of everybody and that she thought he should put them in the barn so they could have privacy."

Melvin was doubled up laughing. "Did he do it?"

"Yeah, he did," I answered. "Nora never lived that down. Whenever we visited Indiana, Dad would bring it up. Nora would join in the fun. She was somethin' else."

"You and Nora had a really good marriage, didn't you?" said Lisa June.

"Yeah, we did," I answered. "Sure miss her."

Lisa got a faraway look in her eyes. "Miss your daughters and grandkids?"

The truth was, while I had called Candy a couple of times, I hadn't thought a lot about the family. Suddenly, I did miss them. "Yeah, I do. But I'll be seein' them soon enough."

When everyone said good night Lisa June gave me a little hug. It was a long way from a close friend hug, but I sensed a warming trend for the first time.

54

I decided to delay my departure for New Hampshire, knowing I was going to catch hell from Candy. While I had contacted her several times since my arrival, a lot of time had passed since we last talked. My response to Candy's "Hello" brought a "Thank God!" followed by a tongue-lashing. When she calmed down, she asked what I had been doing all these weeks.

"It's only been a few days since we last spoke, dear," I countered.

"Nonsense! Penny and I have been worried sick! What have you been doing?"

"Foolin'. I've decided to stay awhile before returning to New Hampshire."

"What does that mean?"

"Nothin' special. Y' know, there's some really beautiful women in Kentucky."

"You're kidding? You're running around with a hillbilly woman!"

"Bumped into some old friends. Candy, I'm happy and healthy and havin' a wonderful time. How are my grandkids doin' on their swim team?"

Candy laughed. "Eddie and Jack are coming in last, but they eventually finish."

"That's th' Zelinsky blood in them. We never quit! How's Penelope's family?"

"Heather has a boyfriend! Penny and Roger are beside themselves."

Heather with a boyfriend? How old was Heather now? Nora always knew these things. "Candy, how old is Heather now?"

"Sixteen. Stop finessing me. When are you coming home?"

It was a question I wasn't prepared to answer. "No idea. E-mail if y' need me. Tell everybody I love them and that I'm bringing back some typical Kentucky gifts. I'm workin' on a pickled ear from either a Hatfield or a McCoy. I already got a bear's head. Not t' fear, everything will already be mounted for your family room. Love y', honey." Then I hung up.

For the next week I spent time with the Langleys and some with Lisa June. Usually Lisa June and I met briefly for lunch or coffee in the evening. She began to warm up a little. Much of our conversation was about me. We talked about my favorite writers and why I liked them, the kind of music I enjoyed, my years teaching at Leland-May, and my research into the Cornish writers. Anything from politics to petunias was open for discussion as long as it didn't dig into the life of Lisa June Winchester. The instant we approached that subject, I could feel the battlements being manned. My willingness to reveal my life, however, was bringing us closer.

Other than seeing Lisa June and the Langleys, though, I was just passing the time. Then, on a whim, I decided to tour Kentucky. I changed out my Toyota for a BMW convertible, threw some underwear and two pair of jeans in my suitcase, put the top and windows down on the Beamer and just . . . took off. I drove the back roads which twisted and turned like black licorice sticks as I zipped under glorious canopies of oak, maple, and hickory. A couple of hours out of Lexington, I had an idea. I called Jenny, got Rosemary Shackelford's address (her name was Akins now), plugged it into the GPS system, then tooled along toward Corbin enjoying the Kentucky countryside and the wind in my few remaining hairs.

It was bittersweet, seeing the seventy-eight-year-old woman I had loved when she was a sixteen-year-old girl. She looked ancient, but she remembered me and gave me a big hug as I was leaving. I reflected as I drove away that sixty years in the past I would have given a year of my life for that hug.

I turned the BMW north and east and drove through the mountains of Eastern Kentucky. I had always wanted to see Natural Bridge, a huge stone ledge that had been undermined by wind and water. I was mesmerized by the sweeping beauty that Nature's genius had designed.

When I was driving away from the park, the BMW's fuel gauge turned red and I pulled into an Eastern Kentucky version of a quickie mart—a general store with one gas pump. An old man came out to fill my tank. While he worked, I wandered around the store.

The interior looked like something you would expect to see in 1890. It carried everything: clothes, hardware, groceries, fertilizer, kerosene lanterns, and probably buttons. Four old men in overalls were playing Rook using the top of a wooden barrel for a table. The proprietor entered, went behind the counter, then asked if that was going to be all.

"Not sure yet," I answered. "Any good place t' eat around here?"

One of the Rook players glanced in my direction. "Fair's goin' on, I'd eat there."

That sounded like an idea. "How do I get there?"

"Head west 'til y' come t' Texas, then foller th' signs."

Everyone laughed and I laughed with them.

"Aunt Tillie's Diner's ten mile up th' road," said one of the Rook players, concentrating on his cards. "Makes good catfish 'n' hush puppies."

"Best in these parts," another player added.

"Sounds good," I said. "Any candy bars around in case I miss Aunt Tillie's."

"Lucy Spencer just brought some fudge in for sale," said the proprietor. "Nobody makes fudge like Miss Lucy. I recommend hit."

That sounded good. "I'll take a quarter pound. Total me up."

I was walking out the door when I heard: "Run into any soldiers out there, wouldn't tarment 'em if I's you. Can't never tell what they'll do."

I turned and smiled back at my grinning nemesis. "Confederate, right?"

He bit down on his cigar. "Done met up with 'em, did ye?"

This time there was a roar of laughter. I pointed my finger at him and winked.

When I finished touring Eastern Kentucky, I turned west. Mountains became hills, which became rolling, bluegrass land. Green, wonderfully green, and sweet-smelling. I went all the way to the Mississippi River. I felt free. I didn't care that I was paying for a hotel room I wasn't using. I drank from Abraham Lincoln's childhood spring, explored Mammoth Cave, went fishing in Kentucky Lake, ate like a king, drank only the best bourbon, and lost all track of time. I didn't even know the day of the week.

Suddenly, I wanted to see Jenny and Melvin and Lisa June. My growing friendship with Lisa June was beginning to concern me. How would she respond if we became closer, then I left for New Hampshire? Would she feel I was yet another person deserting her? I needed some advice. When I got to Lexington, I called Jenny and wangled an invitation for dinner.

It turned out that my concerns were shared by the Langleys. We were on the porch after dinner, when Jenny said, "Y' know, Samuel, you're goin' back t' New Hampshire. I'm not sure how close you should get t' Lisa June if you don't plan t' spend a lot of time with her in th' future. She was out here while you were gone. You were all she talked about. If you get too much closer and just up 'n' leave, it might not go well for her."

"I think the same," said Melvin. "Hit's somethin' t' give thought."

I gave it a lot of thought. Anxious feelings, so recently vanquished, returned in waves. When I called her cell phone and she realized that it was me, her voice became happy.

"Where-have-you-been, Samuel Zelinsky? Aunt Jen says you've been gallivantin'."

"All over Kentucky. Let me buy you dinner and I'll fill you in."

There was a moment of hesitation. Then: "How do you feel about hamburgers, home fries, and cinnamon applesauce, with cherry pie and vanilla ice cream for dessert?"

"Sounds good. Where should I meet you?"

"Six o'clock at my apartment."

I was surprised by the invitation. "I . . . I'll be there. Is there anything I can bring?"

"Something for an upset stomach. I do make a good cherry pie, though. Why don't you bring vanilla ice cream?"

I spent the day browsing, reading the local paper and a day-old copy of the *Washington Post*. I couldn't remember what I read because thoughts of Lisa June dominated my consciousness. Sometime in mid-afternoon I was jolted by a dose of reality. I wanted to help Lisa June, but I didn't want to go beyond friendship, financial help, and being the occasional advisor. I was seventy-two. I didn't need any more commitments! I already had the commitments Nora and I brought into this world together! Fred had been my best friend, but . . .

By the time I reached Lisa June's apartment, butterflies were banging their way through my belt. Lisa June opened the door and gave me a beautiful smile. She was wearing jeans and a UK T-shirt. "Come on in, Samuel, and tell me how you like your hamburgers. I'm about t' put them in th' skillet."

I followed her inside, acutely aware that she had begun to call me Samuel. The butterflies in my stomach had turned into battering rams. This girl was moving our friendship along at a terrifying rate. I took a deep breath and told myself to calm down.

The apartment was a pretty little one-bedroom, with a living room, kitchen, and dinette. There was a long bookcase against one living room wall filled to capacity. On top of the bookcase was an eight-by-ten glossy of Jenny and Melvin Langley. The other furniture consisted of a TV and CD player that sat on a small table in one corner, a recliner chair with an end table and reading lamp, and a couch that was catty-corner against the wall facing the chair.

"Did you leave th' ice cream in th' car?"

My hand went to my forehead. "I forgot to buy the ice cream."

"Well, don't fret. We'll just double up on cherry pie."

For the next half hour, I sat in Lisa June's kitchen telling her about my trip as she made dinner. I began to relax. She seemed genuinely interested in my odyssey, laughing when I told her the story of the Rook players and looking sad at my descriptions of beautiful, mountainous, Eastern Kentucky where, unfortunately, poverty abounded.

Lisa June stopped her work after the comments about the mountain poverty and turned toward me, a hamburger flipper in her hand. "You know, I've met a lot of people from Eastern Kentucky since I started goin' to UK. It would be fun t' teach in th' mountains for a while."

"What are you interested in teaching?"

"I had thought th' early grades, but lately, more about high school," she answered, turning back to the hamburgers and shoveling them onto toasted buns.

"What courses?"

She turned toward me again, this time with a grin on her face. "Literature. The UK students that come out of Eastern Kentucky are all hot to get into somethin' that's goin' t' make them a living. I don't blame them. I'm in favor of using college for a better life. But they leave with an engineering degree and they've never even heard of Harriette Arnow or Jesse Stuart and they were great Kentucky writers. They'll never read them or any other great writer unless they get introduced to them before college."

"Where did you get your interest in literature?"

"At the orphanage," she answered, turning back to her work. "Not from th' people who ran it. The thanks go t' Aunt Jen. She went to college for two years. She reads all th' time, and even has Uncle Melvin readin' when there isn't a basketball game on TV. She checked out hundreds of books from th' library for me over th' years and delivered them during her visits. I used to lie in bed at night and read until lights out. I got straight A's in high school in my English and literature courses. I like t' write too, but I'm not very good."

"Jenny and Melvin have been very important to you, haven't they?"

Lisa June didn't answer, instead she seemed to pour energy into making the home fries.

The food was good, but our conversation had ended. I decided that my question about the Langleys had hit an unhealed wound. "Lisa, I'm sorry about touching a sensitive spot."

A weak smile returned to Lisa June's face. "You don't have to apologize, what you said was true. I just have a hard time accepting that th' only people who've ever given a damn about me are Jenny and Melvin Langley. Not one drop of their blood is in me. I have a mother out West who has never written me a postcard. I have a great-aunt th' same way. Do you know why I refused to go t' any more foster homes?"

I suspected what was coming and didn't want to hear it. I didn't want more guilt. It was Fred I had abandoned, dammit, not Lisa June! "No."

"Because the menfolk put their hands in my britches as soon as their wives weren't looking. I was going t' get pregnant and people were goin' t' say I was trash. I thought all my folks were trash until you told me your stories."

There it was, and to add to it, Lisa June's hands went to her face and she began to cry. "You know what it's like . . . t' think you come from trash? Cheap white trash!"

I felt horrible. I got out of my chair, walked around the table, and lightly placed my hands on her shoulders. I wanted to hug her, but I couldn't. This was too much, too much. I couldn't give any more. Suddenly, Lisa June rose from the chair, wrapped her arms around my chest, and cried. I stroked her hair and her back, and as I did, I thought about Thelma Jean. I had felt sorry for Thelma Jean, but I felt caring, compassion, hurt . . . I felt . . . I didn't know what . . . for Lisa June.

When she let go of me, she sat down again, then wiped her eyes.

"I don't generally do that," she said, sniffing back tears. "Don't feel sorry for me, I can't stand it."

I returned to my own chair, my mind in turmoil. I wanted to say things to comfort her, but nothing came out. Then words just began flooding from me. "Lisa June, you're not trash. You . . . you're a wonderful person. I am so proud of you. Your family wasn't trash either. I understand your pain concerning your mother and father, but there were many good people in your family. I'd like to tell you more about your family. Little things that I haven't covered."

When she nodded, I knew immediately that I had passed the point in our relationship of friendship, college funding, and advisor. This girl meant something special to me.

55

I spoke for two hours about things so small I couldn't believe I remembered them. Whenever I thought I had nothing left to say, Lisa June would ask a question, it would trigger something in my memory, and I was off on another story. Finally, she began clearing the table. "Aunt Jen and Uncle Melvin don't speak of th' things you tell me. I never thought I'd hear anything good about my great-aunt Annie Lee."

"Jenny and Melvin don't know most of th' things I've told you! I understand why you judge Annie Lee harshly, but she carries terrible wounds. She probably ran away from bein' a Mulligan because she wanted a second chance. Another life."

Lisa June scraped the dishes, then returned to her chair, put her elbows on the table, and took a sip of coffee. "Do you know where Grandpa Fred's buried?"

I thought the question odd. "Jenny and Melvin said your mom cremated him."

"That's what she told them, but it isn't true. Grandpa had a little piece of property that Mom knew about, but somehow th' county didn't. One day th' company I work for had me check records on somebody buried in potter's field and I came across the name Fred Cody Mulligan. Mom let him be buried there so she could sell th' property, keep th' money, and not have t' pay for a funeral. Potter's field is just outside Lexington. Would you like t' go?"

I felt weak. "Yes, please."

Two days later, Lisa June and I stood beside a numbered stone peg, one of hundreds that dotted a large open field. From a distance the pegs looked like rows of tiny soldiers. I placed the flowers I was carrying on the grave, and cried. When I stopped crying, Lisa June asked, "Would you like to be alone with him?"

I shook my head. "Not now. He was religious, though. I think he'd like it if we said th' Twenty-third Psalm."

Lisa June thought for a few seconds. "I remember a little. You start."

I choked up as I started. "The . . . Lord is . . . my shepherd . . ."

After we left the grave, I asked Lisa June why she had never told Jenny and Melvin where Fred was buried.

She didn't answer immediately. We were in the car when she said, "I thought about tellin' them, then I decided Grandpa's grave was all I had of my family. Th' only thing personal I would ever have of the Mulligans. I wanted it to be just mine."

"Why did you decide to tell me?"

"Because I think Grandpa would have wanted you to know," she said softly. "Samuel, I love Aunt Jen and Uncle Melvin and they might be hurt if they knew I told you and not them. I'd appreciate your not sayin' anything."

"I won't. Is it okay though if I visit th' grave ever' now and then?"

Lisa June smiled. "That's fine. Y'all have some catchin' up t' do."

We did, and over time that took place. "You don't own anything that belonged to your Grandpa, do you?"

"My DNA."

"Somethin' you can get your hands on?"

"Are you talkin' about somethin' Grandpa Fred gave you?"

"Actually, no. It's things that belonged to both Fred and me. Interested?"

Lisa June giggled. "You sly old fox, what have you got up your sleeve?"

"If you answer yes, you'll find out."

She laughed. "All right, yes!"

I turned at the next corner and pointed the BMW toward Old Cuyper Creek Pike.

Our first stop was a hardware store in Spears where I bought two shovels, a grubbing hoe, and two pairs of gloves. Lisa June kept asking me questions about what we were going to do and I would answer with a wink and a grin.

By the time we got to Cummings Hill, the shadows were lengthening. I looked at the top of the hill, which was probably three hundred yards from where we stood. About a third of the way to the top, trees began. At first, there were just a few trees, but at the top they became an oak forest. At first I didn't recognize any landmarks. Then I saw a giant oak near the top of the hill. Perhaps a hundred feet below the sentinel oak was a slightly smaller oak. Nothing else in that direction even approached the two in size. Those had to be the trees Fred had selected. I lined them up and lay my shovel handle as the third point for my first coordinate.

As I worked, I glimpsed Lisa June. She was sitting on the hillside holding her knees with a bemused look on her face, occasionally shaking her head and chuckling.

For the other coordinate Fred had chosen a big pine tree on the pond side of the hill. One large pine dwarfed the many smaller pines. I decided the large pine was the one Fred had chosen as a horizontal landmark, but there was nothing to line it up with because the oak was gone. Without it, I had no idea how to complete my triangulation. I wandered over to a limestone outcropping and sat, letting my legs dangle over the edge.

Lisa June joined me. "Problems?"

I sighed. "Lisa June, I'm afraid somethin' has destroyed one of th' landmarks your grandfather used for finding our treasure."

Lisa June, nudged me with her shoulder. "It's all right. I'd have liked to have somethin' that belonged t' him, but th' memories you gave me are more important than whatever you and he hid away. Let's go have dinner, I'm hungry."

I didn't feel like eating. I was no more than a few hundred feet from the only remaining relic from my best friend's life to which I had a true connection, and it was being denied me. Was this my final punishment for abandoning him, for letting him die alone in despair? God had eternity in which to punish me, why disgrace me in front of Fred's granddaughter? We walked toward the equipment that lay strung out like a dashed line. The moment I reached for one of the shovels, I had an epiphany. I returned to the rock ledge. When I reached it, I studied the angle it made with the line that ran down the hill. The ledge was thick. Bedrock, probably covered for millions of years until erosion uncovered it over the past sixty. Bedrock that Fred and I encountered when we buried the slingshots. I took a sighting down the ledge.

"Lisa June," I called, "get th' shovel that's farthest up th' hill and bring it down 'til I tell you t' stop."

Minutes later the shovel marked a spot and we began digging. We hit rock in less than two feet. I decided we should extend our dig uphill. An hour and a half later we were still digging, then my shovel point hit what sounded like metal. I put the shovel aside and scraped with the broad end of the grubbing hoe. Remnants of gunnysack appeared in the growing darkness. I freed the box and tore away the rotted cloth.

The lunch box was badly rusted and my shovel had crashed through one edge. My hands were shaking as I pried the box open.

There they were, the rubber and leather shriveled and barely recognizable, but the wooden handles were still intact. I recognized mine, picked it up and rolled it around in my hand. It felt good. I put it back in the box and picked up Fred's. It was all I had of my best friend. Then I remembered Lisa June and passed the handle to her. "Your grandfather made this over sixty years ago. When we buried them he said we would never make slingshots for ourselves again, only for our children. We had a pact that someday we'd come back and dig them up together."

My voice broke. "Fred's slingshot was his most prized possession. It's yours now."

The tears flowed from both of us as we held each other. A young woman and an old man had both found part of their past.

56

I canceled my reservations for New Hampshire. For the next few weeks, Lisa June and I spent a lot of time together. UK was between sessions and she was taking some vacation from her day job. We walked through the world of my childhood, Berman's, the Shackelford place, the graves of her family, and, of course, the Blue Hole, where we went swimming. I made elm poles and we fished where the four of us had caught the buffalo.

It was a wonderful time of year, the oaks and maples were slightly turning and the sky had a hint of October blue. It was a wonderful time for me too. One day Lisa June and I picnicked under the sweet apple tree. When we finished eating I was full and happy and stretched out on my back with my head propped up on a tree root. "Guess what I did yesterday?"

Lisa June was sitting against the tree's trunk, her jean-covered legs crossed. "I wouldn't be surprised at anything after watchin' you drive up in a new car. What?"

"Put a down payment on a little piece of property this side of Spears."

Lisa June's mouth fell open and her eyes lit up. "What's it like!"

"Beautiful land, not so good house. Kind of a cross between Walden and a moonshiner's paradise."

Lisa June's head went backward, and she laughed loudly. "That description could only come from a literature professor. I can't wait t' hear th' details."

I turned my head toward her. "Two weeks ago, I saw an ad for six and a half acres. It's heavily wooded. Th' only road in is a gravel lane. The house sets in a little clearing. There's a big pond surrounded by trees that I'm going to stock with bass. Wanta see it?"

Lisa June got to her feet so quickly she startled me. "Samuel Zelinsky, you take me there right now!"

The trees that bordered the lane to my house were tall and blocked a lot of light, making it difficult to see the gravel beneath the weeds. My new Ford must have thought it had died and gone to automotive hell as it plunged in and out of chuckholes.

"This is beautiful, just beautiful," Lisa June kept saying, clapping her hands and grabbing my shoulder and shoving me back and forth sideways.

"Wait'll you see my abode."

We rounded an oak and the lane ended. Lisa June began laughing. The house was a step up from present day Berman's, but it was a small step.

"Whadayathink?" I asked.

"The house is a wreck, but this forest is so beautiful. Where's th' pond? When are you gonna build a new house? It should be a cabin . . . th' furniture should be rustic, built like they did in th' early years in th' Kentucky Mountains. This place is just too beautiful for words. Just too beautiful," and she spun like a ballerina across the grass, holding her arms straight out.

"Come on, I'll show you th' pond," I called.

We walked past the house and into the trees. Shortly, we were beside a small lake nestled among the timber. A meadowlark trilled, then it became very quiet. "Like it?"

"Oh my God, yes!" Lisa June whispered and she stood as though transfixed.

"I like your idea for a cabin. Soon as escrow closes, I'll meet with an architect. I'd like to move in by next September. Spend the fall here."

Lisa June's face lost expression.

"What?" I asked.

When Lisa June answered, her voice reminded me of a little girl's. "Aren't you going to move to Kentucky permanently?"

I shook my head. "Spring and fall. Summer and winter with my kids and grandkids. New Hampshire is beautiful in winter and th' whole family skis. In summer, I can take th' grandkids trout fishin'. I'll spend spring and fall with you and th' Langleys and Kentucky. I'm th' man who has everything."

What happened next was an eruption Vesuvius could envy. "Oh sure! Everything's dandy for you. What about me? You go back to your kids and grandkids and see me in your spare time! Just what am I to you anyway! You come here and get tight with Aunt Jen and Uncle Melvin so you can spend time with th' little orphan girl? So you can feel less guilty about having let your best friend kill himself? That's what I am to you, isn't it, your highway out of th' guilt swamp. After that I'm nothin'! T' hell with you! Go back t' your damn family!"

With that, Lisa June Winchester ran out of the woods.

I felt . . . I'm not sure what adjective fits. Devastated? Destroyed? I just stood there as she disappeared. The worst fears of Jenny, Melvin, and me had come to pass. I walked into the trees in a daze, trying to understand how I had allowed this to happen. Then came a question: What was Lisa June to me? I stopped walking, leaned against a maple, and waited while my mind played with the issue.

I was probably there half an hour when I heard a twig snap. I looked up and there was Lisa June. Her eyes were red and a mask of anguish covered her face. She looked so much like Fred when he was hurt that it frightened me. She walked toward me with tentative steps until we were a couple of feet apart.

"I'm sorry," she said. "I'm such a bitch. You've been wonderful to me and th' last thing you deserved was th' crap I just laid on you.

I was just so jealous. I wanted you to myself. You to be my grandpa. I know you're not my grandpa, but I . . . I . . . Can you ever forgive me?"

I took one step forward and she lunged into my arms. I stroked her hair while she cried and squeezed my chest. I was still trying to understand what I felt. The only answer I was sure of was that somehow, I loved this child. Was it as much as I felt for my kids? I didn't know. Why the hell did I have to quantify everything anyway? I untangled us but held on to her arms. "Lisa June, I'm not good at expressing my emotions, but I'm gonna try in my own way. Promise me if I screw this up that you won't run away from me again. That you'll let me explain. Can you promise me that?"

Lisa June answered with a nod.

"I told you about th' death of Ben, th' time in his cabin when he was mortally wounded. I told him that I loved him before I ran out th' door for help. Earlier in our friendship he had said th' same thing t' me but I couldn't say it back to him. I'm sure that I did love him, but I just couldn't say it for some reason. It took his being minutes from death for me be able t' tell him that. I don't want that t' happen now. I love you, Lisa June. I don't know how much or anything else, just that I love you and I want to be as much grandfather as I can be to you until I die. That's all I know, Lisa. I hope that's enough."

Lisa June gave me a bear hug. "I love you too. Thanks for puttin' up with me . . . Grandpa."

Our arms went to our sides, then we stood looking at each other. Neither of us knew where things went from here. Then I heard myself say, "You ever been in New Hampshire?"

"No."

"Next year we'll go t' New Hampshire in June . . . after UK's spring semester ends. You can ride to New Hampshire with me, then fly back t' Kentucky whenever you want. Meet th' other people in my life."

Lisa June thought about my proposal. When she answered she was smiling. "I'd love to see New Hampshire."

I took a deep breath. "You know, I came here a couple months ago a dyin' man. I . . ."

Lisa June had started walking and stopped abruptly and turned to face me. Her eyes were wide and I saw her tremble. "What do you mean?"

I quickly remedied my error. "I'm perfectly healthy. What I meant was, I was dying a death of the spirit, not th' body. Society saw me as someone whose life had been successful, but I felt like a failure."

The look on Lisa June's face changed from fear to relief, then wonder. "I don't understand. How could someone who won th' most important prize in their field have considered himself a failure?"

This was not going to be easy to explain. "Lisa June, I was raised in these hills. Simple things in our little community took on special meanings, and you lived your life by those simple things. You told th' truth. You came through for your friends, no matter what, or you weren't a man. My childhood society was defined by simple rules and I believed them with all my heart."

The slight nod of Lisa June's head told me that she had gotten the big picture.

"Your life after leavin' Kentucky got a lot more complicated, didn't it?"

"Yeah," I said, "and I kept trying to live by th' old rules. I couldn't make the adjustments. The old rules didn't work in my new world and I paid a big price. Constant conflict with the rule makers and the rules that they made . . . and bent . . . without having problems of conscience."

Lisa June swallowed. "If I'd been there, I'd have used Grandpa Fred's slingshot on them!"

I laughed. "Slingshots are great for huntin' frogs and shootin' fence posts. I want you to remember something—if you wanta have a happy life, Lisa June, be willin' to bend little rules. Not the important ones, though. Important rules are best not bent."

I moved my head in the direction of the car, meaning that we should start back.

"Which rules do you think are the important ones?"

"Those covering truth," I answered. "Never disregard a vow made with all your heart without doing everything you can to keep it."

We walked to the car by way of a blackberry thicket, picking berries and shoveling them into our mouths until our hands and lips were stained red. It was getting late and Lisa June needed to get to her restaurant job. As we drove, I delicately brought up the subject of the Langleys' offer to help with her education.

Lisa June turned in her seat until she faced me. She wasn't angry, but she was obviously bothered. "Samuel, Jenny and Melvin have been great to me, but they aren't rich and they're getting old. When they're real old they might need that money and suppose I couldn't pay them back. What's good in this for Aunt Jen and Uncle Melvin? What do they get out of it?"

"Happiness. Jenny and Melvin would be helping someone they love dearly. Your education budget isn't going to destroy their estate. You'll undoubtedly pay it back. If you'll let me, I can add to th' kitty and that will cut back on the amount the Langleys have to contribute."

There was a brooding silence. I was so sure our friendship was on solid footing now that I hadn't considered what I said to be risky. Had I been wrong?

"This has to do with Fred, doesn't it," she said, turning to the front again.

Fine raindrops had started to fall. I turned on the Ford's wipers and watched them sweep as I thought about what she had asked. Then all fear of hurting her left me. "Some of it has to do with Fred, but mostly it has to do with his granddaughter who needs to learn from the life of her grandfather's best friend. If she doesn't, there are some kids in the Kentucky Mountains who will go through life without an appreciation of fine literature."

We drove quietly through the misty rain. When we were almost at her door she said, "I'll think about it." Then her demeanor became like that of a scolding daughter. "You know, you are somethin' else. You must've driven Nora crazy."

I parked next to the curb, and we stood together on the sidewalk. She hugged me and I kissed her forehead, then she ascended the stairs. At the door of her apartment she turned and called, "When are we gettin' together again? This time I wanta make some slingshots."

"I'll call when I find th' right elm tree, an old inner tube that ain't rotted, and some Bull Durham twine."

Lisa June laughed, then entered the apartment, and I was alone on the sidewalk. I was happy. I'd come a far piece, but I'd found my Canaan land.

Acknowledgments

A number of people have helped me bring this book to fruition. First, my writing group, the Monday Morning Club, which meets on Tuesdays every two weeks. Don't ask. These precious people, along with my wife, Joni, are greatly responsible for teaching me how to write. They are, in alphabetical order, Louise Goodman, Peggy Markham, Patricia Maxwell, Helen Ritchie, Elliott Schubert, Bess Tittle, Annette Winter, and Elsie Zala.

The following people read the rough manuscript and made comments with which I improved the original text. Again in alphabetical order, Naomi Alazaraki, Bob Arnold, Mary Barr, Bill Clark, Annie Gaunder, Joni Halpern, Justin Halpern, Jan Kunsa, Eileen Rendahl and Andrew Taylor.

A thank-you to David Watson, my editor at HarperCollins, and a special thank-you to Byrd Leavell, an agent with guts enough to take on a curmudgeon for a client.

DATE			